KU-323-926

FATE OF THE JEDI

ABYSS

BOOKS BY TROY DENNING GOLDEN

Waterdeep
Dragonwall
The Parched Sea
The Verdant Passage
The Crimson Legion
The Amber Enchantress
The Obsidian Oracle
The Cerulean Storm
The Ogre's Pact
The Giant Among Us
The Titan of Twilight
The Veiled Dragon
Pages of Pain
Crucible: The Trial of Cyric the Mad
The Oath of Stonekeep
Faces of Deception
Beyond the High Road
Death of the Dragon (with Ed Greenwood)
The Summoning
The Siege
The Sorcerer

Star Wars: The New Jedi Order: Star by Star
Star Wars: Tatooine Ghost
Star Wars: Dark Nest I: The Joiner King
Star Wars: Dark Nest II: The Unseen Queen
Star Wars: Dark Nest III: The Swarm War
Star Wars: Legacy of the Force: Tempest
Star Wars: Legacy of the Force: Inferno
Star Wars: Legacy of the Force: Invincible
Star Wars: Fate of the Jedi: Abyss

STAR WARS

FATE OF THE JEDI

ABYSS

TROY DENNING

arrow books

Published by Arrow 2010

2 4 6 8 10 9 7 5 3 1

This book contains an excerpt from the forthcoming book *Star Wars:
Fate of the Jedi: Backlash* by Troy Denning.

First published in Great Britain in 2009 by
Century
Random House, 20 Vauxhall Bridge Road,
London SW1V 2SA

www.starwars.com
www.fateofthejedi.com
www.randomhouse.co.uk

Addresses for companies within The Random House Group Limited
can be found at: www.randomhouse.co.uk

The Random House Group Limited Reg. No. 954009

A CIP catalogue record for this book is available from the British Library

ISBN 9780099542735

The Random House Group Limited supports The Forest
Stewardship Council (FSC), the leading international forest
certification organisation. All our titles that are printed on
Greenpeace approved FSC certified paper carry the FSC logo.
Our paper procurement policy can be found at
www.rbooks.co.uk/environment

Mixed Sources
Product group from well-managed
forests and other controlled sources
www.fsc.org Cert no. TT-COC-2139
© 1996 Forest Stewardship Council
FSC

Printed and bound in Great Britain by
CPI Bookmarque, Croydon, CR0 4TD

For my niece Jennifer Jane Denning
The smile behind Allana's

Acknowledgments

Many people contributed to this book in ways large and small. I would like to thank them all, especially the following: Andria Hayday for her support, critiques, and suggestions; James Luceno, Leland Chee, Pablo Hidalgo, Keith Clayton, Christine Cabello, Scott Shannon, Frank Parisi, and Carol Roeder for their fine contributions during our brainstorming sessions; Shelly Shapiro and Sue Rostoni for *everything,* from their remarkable patience to their insightful markups to their great ideas; to my fellow Fate of the Jedi writers, Aaron Allston and Christie Golden, for being such a blast to work with and for their myriad other contributions to this book and the series; to all of the people at Lucasfilm and Del Rey who make writing *Star Wars* so much fun; and, finally, to George Lucas for sharing his galaxy with us all.

THE STAR WARS NOVELS TIMELINE

OLD REPUBLIC
5000–33 YEARS BEFORE
STAR WARS: A New Hope

*Lost Tribe of the Sith**
Precipice
Skyborn
Paragon
Savior

3650 *YEARS BEFORE STAR WARS: A New Hope*

The Old Republic
Fatal Alliance

1020 *YEARS BEFORE STAR WARS: A New Hope*

Darth Bane: Path of Destruction
Darth Bane: Rule of Two
Darth Bane: Dynasty of Evil

RISE OF THE EMPIRE
33–0 YEARS BEFORE
STAR WARS: A New Hope

Darth Maul: Saboteur*
Cloak of Deception
Darth Maul: Shadow Hunter

32 *YEARS BEFORE STAR WARS: A New Hope*

STAR WARS: EPISODE I
THE PHANTOM MENACE

Rogue Planet
Outbound Flight
The Approaching Storm

22 *YEARS BEFORE STAR WARS: A New Hope*

STAR WARS: EPISODE II
ATTACK OF THE CLONES

22–19 *YEARS BEFORE STAR WARS: A New Hope*

The Clone Wars
The Clone Wars: Wild Space
The Clone Wars: No Prisoners

Clone Wars Gambit
Stealth
Siege

Republic Commando
Hard Contact
Triple Zero
True Colors
Order 66

Shatterpoint
The Cestus Deception
The Hive*
MedStar I: Battle Surgeons
MedStar II: Jedi Healer
Jedi Trial

Yoda: Dark Rendezvous
Labyrinth of Evil

19 *YEARS BEFORE STAR WARS: A New Hope*

STAR WARS: EPISODE III
REVENGE OF THE SITH

Dark Lord: The Rise of Darth
Vader

Coruscant Nights
Jedi Twilight
Street of Shadows
Patterns of Force

Imperial Commando
501*

The Han Solo Trilogy
The Paradise Snare
The Hutt Gambit
Rebel Dawn

The Adventures of Lando Calrissian
The Han Solo Adventures
The Force Unleashed
Death Troopers

REBELLION
0–5 YEARS AFTER
STAR WARS: A New Hope

Death Star

0

STAR WARS: EPISODE IV
A NEW HOPE

Tales from the Mos Eisley Cantina
Allegiance
Galaxies: The Ruins of Dantooine
Splinter of the Mind's Eye

3 *YEARS AFTER STAR WARS: A New Hope*

STAR WARS: EPISODE V
THE EMPIRE STRIKES BACK

Tales of the Bounty Hunters
Shadows of the Empire

4 *YEARS AFTER STAR WARS: A New Hope*

STAR WARS: EPISODE VI
RETURN OF THE JEDI

Tales from Jabba's Palace
Tales from the Empire
Tales from the New Republic

The Bounty Hunter Wars
The Mandalorian Armor
Slave Ship
Hard Merchandise

The Truce at Bakura
Luke Skywalker and the Shadows of
Mindor

NEW REPUBLIC
5–25 YEARS AFTER
STAR WARS: A New Hope

X-Wing
  Rogue Squadron
  Wedge's Gamble
  The Krytos Trap
  The Bacta War
  Wraith Squadron
  Iron Fist
  Solo Command

The Courtship of Princess Leia
A Forest Apart*
Tatooine Ghost

The Thrawn Trilogy
  Heir to the Empire
  Dark Force Rising
  The Last Command

X-Wing: Isard's Revenge

The Jedi Academy Trilogy
  Jedi Search
  Dark Apprentice
  Champions of the Force

I, Jedi
Children of the Jedi
Darksaber
Planet of Twilight
X-Wing: Starfighters of Adumar
The Crystal Star

The Black Fleet Crisis Trilogy
  Before the Storm
  Shield of Lies
  Tyrant's Test

The New Rebellion

The Corellian Trilogy
  Ambush at Corellia
  Assault at Selonia
  Showdown at Centerpoint

The Hand of Thrawn Duology
  Specter of the Past
  Vision of the Future

Fool's Bargain*
Survivor's Quest

NEW JEDI ORDER
25–40 YEARS AFTER
STAR WARS: A New Hope

Boba Fett: A Practical Man*

The New Jedi Order
  Vector Prime
  Dark Tide I: Onslaught
  Dark Tide II: Ruin
  Agents of Chaos I: Hero's Trial

Agents of Chaos II: Jedi Eclipse
Balance Point
Recovery*
Edge of Victory I: Conquest
Edge of Victory II: Rebirth
Star by Star
Dark Journey
Enemy Lines I: Rebel Dream
Enemy Lines II: Rebel Stand
Traitor
Destiny's Way
Ylesia*
Force Heretic I: Remnant
Force Heretic II: Refugee
Force Heretic III: Reunion
The Final Prophecy
The Unifying Force

| 35 | YEARS AFTER STAR WARS: A New Hope |

The Dark Nest Trilogy
  The Joiner King
  The Unseen Queen
  The Swarm War

LEGACY
40+ YEARS AFTER
STAR WARS: A New Hope

Legacy of the Force
  Betrayal
  Bloodlines
  Tempest
  Exile
  Sacrifice
  Inferno
  Fury
  Revelation
  Invincible

Crosscurrent
Millennium Falcon

| 43 | YEARS AFTER STAR WARS: A New Hope |

Fate of the Jedi
  Outcast
  Omen
  Abyss
  Backlash
  Allies

*An eBook novella

Dramatis Personae

Ahri Raas; Sith apprentice (Keshiri male)
Ben Skywalker; Jedi Knight (human male)
Han Solo; Captain, *Millennium Falcon* (human male)
Jagged Fel; Head of State, Galactic Empire (human male)
Jaina Solo; Jedi Knight (human female)
Leia Organa Solo; Jedi Knight (human female)
Luke Skywalker; Jedi Grand Master (human male)
Olaris Rhea; Sith Lord (human female)
Vestara Khai; Sith apprentice (human female)
Yuvar Xal; Sith Master (human male)

A long time ago in a galaxy far, far away. . . .

Chapter One

BURIED DEEP INSIDE THE JEDI TEMPLE ON CORUSCANT was the Asylum Block, a transparisteel cube standing in its own hidden atrium, bathed in artificial blue light and surrounded by tidy rows of potted olbio trees. Peering up through the leaves to a second-story wall, Leia Solo could see Seff Hellin kneeling in his cell. He was in the near corner, staring at his bloody knuckles as though surprised that hours of hammering at a fusion-welded seam might actually have damaged them. In the adjacent cell, Natua Wan was endlessly scratching at her door lock, trying to slip her splintered talons into a magnetic seal that a nanoscalpel could not have breached.

Seeing the pair in such a state made Leia's heart ache. It also terrified her, for both of Corran Horn's children had fallen victim to the same condition. Now, with Temple scientists no closer to identifying a cause, she was beginning to fear that this strange insanity might claim an entire generation of Jedi Knights. And that was something she would not allow—not when every new case reminded her of how confused and helpless she had felt losing Jacen to the madness of the Sith.

The golden outline of an access portal appeared in the invisible barrier field that enclosed the atrium. With Han and C-3PO following behind, Leia stepped into the leafy-smelling interior. She was not surprised to feel a subtle pang of loss and isolation. The olbio trees were filled with ysalamiri, small white reptiles that hid from predators by creating voids in the Force. The adaptation was an invaluable tool for anyone who wished to incarcerate rogue Force-users—and all too often lately, that included the Jedi themselves.

As the portal crackled shut behind them, Han leaned close and warmed Leia's ear with a whisper. "I don't think cutting them off from the Force is helping. They look crazier than ever."

"Seff and Natua are not crazy," Leia reprimanded. "They're ill, and they need our understanding."

"Hey, nobody understands crazy better than me." Han gave her arm a reassuring squeeze. "People are *always* calling me crazy."

"Captain Solo is quite right," C-3PO agreed. The golden protocol droid was standing close behind the Solos, his metallic breastplate pressing cold against Leia's left shoulder. "During our association, Captain Solo's sanity has been questioned an average of three times per month. By the psychiatric care standards of many conformist societies, that fact alone would qualify him for a cell in the Asylum Block."

Han shot a frown back at the droid, then turned to Leia with his best smirk of reassurance. "You see? I'm probably the only one in the whole Temple who receives on their channel."

"I wouldn't doubt that," Leia said. She gave him a wry smile, then patted the hand grasping her arm. "All joking aside, I just wish you really *did* know what's going on with them."

Now it was Han who grew serious. "Yeah. Seeing 'em slip away like this brings bad memories. *Really* bad memories."

"It does," Leia acknowledged. "But it's not the same

thing. By the time anyone realized what was going on with Jacen, he was *running* the Galactic Alliance."

"Yeah, and we were the enemy," Han agreed. "I just wish we could have stuck Jacen in a deten—"

"We *would* have, had there been some way to take him alive," Leia interrupted. They didn't turn down this lane often, but when they did, it devastated her, and she couldn't let herself be devastated now. "Let's just focus on the Jedi we *can* save."

Han nodded. "Count me in. I don't need anybody else's family getting caught in the kind of plasma blast we did."

Han was still speaking when Master Cilghal and her assistant Tekli appeared, walking between two rows of potted olbios. In their white medical robes, the pair made a somber impression: Cilghal a long-headed Mon Calamari with sad bulbous eyes, Tekli a diminutive Chadra-Fan with her flap-like ears pulled tight against her head fur.

Cilghal extended a web-fingered hand first to Leia, then to Han, and spoke in her rippling Mon Calamari voice. "Jedi Solo, Captain Solo, thank you for coming. I trust you were able to find someone to watch Amelia on such short notice?"

"No problem," Han said. "Barv's keeping an eye on her."

"Barv?" Tekli squeaked. "As in, Bazel Warv?"

"Yeah, Amelia just loves the big guy." Han smiled. "I'm beginning to think that girl's going to marry a Ramoan when she grows up."

The glance that Tekli shot up at Cilghal was almost imperceptible, as was the answering dip from the Mon Calamari's near eye—but not quick enough to escape the notice of a former diplomat.

"Is that a problem?" Leia asked. "Barv has always been very good with her."

"I truly doubt there's anything to worry about," Cilghal said. "It's just that the only link we've been able to establish among patients is one of association."

"What kind of association?" Han asked.

"Age and location," Tekli supplied. "All four victims were among the students hidden in Shelter."

Leia nodded. Shelter was the secret base where the Jedi had sequestered their young during the last part of the war with the Yuuzhan Vong. Located deep inside the Maw cluster of black holes and cobbled together from the remnants of an abandoned weapons lab, it had been a gloomy place to care for young Jedi—and now, it appeared, perhaps a dangerous one.

"Are you thinking environmental toxins?" Leia asked.

"We decontaminated the place pretty well," Han added. "But I suppose we could have missed something. The Imperials were making some strange stuff there."

Cilghal spread her hands. "It's impossible to say. At the moment, all we have is a simple observation." She lowered an admonishing eye toward her assistant. "The sample is too small to establish a statistical correlation."

"True, but it's the only firm link we have," Tekli countered. "And whether it's causative or not, Bazel *does* associate closely with both Valin and Jysella."

"Yeah, along with Yaqeel Saav'etu," Han said. "I've heard Barv call the four of them 'the Unit.'"

Leia raised a brow. "Did this Unit include Seff?" She glanced up and saw that Seff was still staring at his hands; in the adjacent cell, Natua continued to worry at her lock. "Or Natua?"

"Not that I ever heard," Han said.

Tekli confirmed this with a shake of her golden-furred head.

"You see?" Cilghal asked. "There are plenty of facts and connections, but which are significant? Are any?"

"If anyone can sort it out, it's you," Leia said. "In the meantime, there's nothing wrong with being careful."

"Of course not," Cilghal said. "So if you'd rather return to Amelia right away—"

"No, I don't think that will be necessary," Leia interrupted. "Artoo-Detoo is there, and he has standing orders to contact us if anything starts to look out of the ordinary. And we're very eager to help you."

"Yeah." Han glanced toward the cell block. "Judging by the looks of those two up there, you need it."

"Thank you." Cilghal turned and waved them toward the cell block. "But actually, the reason I asked you here is that Seff has begun to improve."

Han looked doubtful. "So he *didn't* tear up his hands punching walls?"

"He did," Cilghal admitted.

"But he *has* stopped," Leia noted. "Is that the improvement?"

Cilghal nodded. "A few days after we isolated them from the Force, both Seff and Natua began to exhibit symptoms of violent psychological withdrawal. Seff's present calmness suggests he may have entered a recovery phase."

"Wait a minute." Han cast an uneasy look toward Leia. "You mean they're *addicted* to the Force?"

"All we know is that there *appears* to be a connection," Cilghal said carefully.

"We're wondering if the Force acts as some sort of carrier for the madness," Tekli explained. "Or maybe a trigger."

Cilghal fixed a disapproving eye on her assistant. "That's all speculation at this stage, of course." The other eye swung toward Leia—a Mon Calamari ability that Leia still found a bit unsettling. "So far, we haven't been able to confirm either the withdrawal or the recovery."

"And that's why you need us?" Leia surmised.

Cilghal nodded. "We'd like to conduct a furtive encephaloscan to determine just how calm Seff truly is—"

"And you want us to distract him," Han finished.

"Would you mind?" Cilghal asked. "We can't establish a baseline stress pattern unless we keep his attention focused elsewhere. And you're the best con artists in the Temple."

"On *Coruscant*," Han corrected, a bit too proudly. He hitched a thumb toward C-3PO. "But Goldenrod here isn't going to be much help tricking anyone. Why'd you want *him* along?"

"Natua has been hissing as she works," Tekli explained. "I'm beginning to think she's talking to herself."

"That's entirely possible," C-3PO offered. "The phonetics of many reptilian languages have sibilant root patterns. I'd be happy to assist you in identifying the language, if you wish."

"A translation would be much more useful," Tekli said. "It might be helpful to know what she's saying."

"See-Threepio is entirely at your disposal," Leia said to Cilghal. "As are Han and I."

Cilghal thanked them and led the way to the Asylum Block. Tekli disappeared into the control room to retrieve a pair of stun sticks for the Solos and a tranquilizer pistol for Cilghal, then announced she would join them with the encephaloscanner once Seff was distracted. Leia and Han secured the stun sticks in the small of their backs, under their belts, then followed Cilghal to a turbolift and ascended to the second-story catwalk.

The cells arrayed along the catwalk were clearly designed to confine rather than punish, for they were furnished with flowform couches, holographic entertainment centers, and privacy-screened refreshers. Judging by the muffled screel of fingernails coming through the second door, the distinction of purpose was no comfort to Natua Wan.

The first door stood open. Inside the cell, a tall, powerful-looking human Jedi sat meditating, with an upturned palm resting on one knee and a wrist stump on the other. On the floor beside him rested an artificial hand, palm-up, with the thumb and middle finger touching. Dozens of surgeries and skin grafts had repaired his burn scars to the point where his face looked merely plastic instead of horrific, but his ears remained flat and misshapen, and the bristly texture of his short blond hair betrayed its synthetic origins.

As the group approached his door, the Jedi's blue eyes popped open, fixing first on Leia, then Han. "Princess Leia, Captain Solo," he said. "It's nice to see you again."

"You, too, Raynar," Han said. "You doing okay in here?"

"Very well," Raynar said. "Thank you."

A sad reminder of the price young Jedi too often paid for their service to the galaxy, Raynar Thul had gone missing on the same strike mission that had claimed the life of the Solos' youngest son, Anakin. Years later, Raynar had reappeared as UnuThul, the badly disfigured, insane Joiner who was leading the Killik Colony's expansion into the Chiss territories. Fortunately, Raynar had not proven too powerful to capture alive, and he had been residing in the Asylum Block for more than seven years while Cilghal helped him put his mind back together.

Had Natasi Daala been the Galactic Alliance Chief

of State at the time, Raynar would probably have been
frozen in carbonite and hung up in the nearest detention center—just as Valin and Jysella Horn had been
when they fell ill. And that thought made Leia about as
angry as a wampa in a sauna. Anyone whose mind
came undone because of what they had suffered for the
Alliance deserved to be nurtured back to health, not la-
beled a "danger to society" and treated like wall art.

Leia stopped at the entrance to Raynar's cell. "Hello,
Raynar. Cilghal has told us how much progress you've
made." Actually, the Mon Calamari had told the Solos
that all that remained was for *Raynar* to realize he was
recovered. "Is there anything you need?"

"No, I'm free to visit the commissary myself," Raynar said. He glanced toward the adjacent cell, where
Natua was still scratching at her door, then grinned a
bit mischievously. "Unless you care to do something
about all that racket? It's enough to drive a man crazy."

"No problem," Han said, reaching for the control
pad on the exterior of the cell. "It'll be quieter if we
close this—"

"On second thought," Raynar interrupted, "I may
be growing fond of the noise."

Han smirked. "I *thought* that might fix your problem."

"You should apply for therapist credentials, dear,"
Leia said drily. She turned to Raynar. "But seriously,
Raynar, if the noise bothers you, why don't you just
change your quarters?"

Raynar's eyes widened as much as his rigid brows
would allow. "Leave my cell?"

"The door has been open for quite some time," Cilghal said. "And if matters continue to deteriorate with
the younger Jedi, we may be needing your room."

"There are plenty of empty quarters up on the dormitory level," Han prompted.

Raynar retrieved his artificial hand, then rose and stepped toward the door. "Would I be welcome?"

"That depends," Han said with a smirk. "Are you going to do your own chores?"

"The days when I considered myself above doing chores are long past, Captain Solo." Raynar's tone was more distracted than indignant, as though he was so consumed in thought that he had failed to notice Han was joking. He stood at the door, considering his options, then shrugged and began to reattach his artificial hand. "I don't know if I'm ready. I don't know if *they're* ready."

Leia started to suggest there was only one way to find out, but before she could speak Raynar started toward the interior of his cell. Cilghal shook her head in disappointment, Han sighed, and Leia bit her lip in frustration.

"Relax," Raynar called over his shoulder. "I'm just going to pack. I *have* been here awhile, you know."

Leia's relief was bittersweet. As happy as she was to see Raynar leaving his cell, it made her wish that incarceration and rehabilitation had been possible for her son Jacen. But Jacen had been too powerful to capture and too destructive to leave free, and in the end there had been no choice except to hunt him down.

There had been no choice.

Leia reminded herself of that almost daily. Yet she knew that she and Han would go to their graves asking why they had not seen Jacen's peril in time to save him, why they had not realized until it was too late that their son was falling to the dark side.

Once Raynar had begun to pack his few possessions, Cilghal smiled and led the way down the catwalk again. As they passed the next cell, Natua stopped scratching at her door locks and pressed herself to the transparisteel, her narrow eyes fixed on Han. A ruddy flush began to creep up her delicate face scales, and she slid a hand along the wall, reaching out in his direction.

"Captain Solo." Even through the electronic speaker that relayed the words to the catwalk, Natua's voice was soft and cajoling. Leia was just glad that the Falleen's powerful attraction pheromones were safely trapped inside her own cell. "Please . . . get me out of here. They're hurting me."

"Not as much as you're hurting yourself," Han said, pointing to the crimson streaks that her bloody fingertips were leaving on the wall. "Sorry, Nat. You need to stay here and let them help you."

"*This* isn't help!" Natua slapped the wall so hard that the resulting *pung* caused C-3PO to stumble back into the safety rail. She began to curse in the strange hissing language Tekli had mentioned earlier. "*Sse-orhstki hsuzma sahaslatho Shi'ido hsesstivaph!*"

"Oh my!" exclaimed C-3PO. "Jedi Wan is promising to kill Captain Solo and his fellow impostors in a terribly unpleasant way. Fortunately, it appears that she hasn't thought through her plan very well. I don't even *have* intestines."

"Then you recognize the language?" Leia asked.

"Of course," C-3PO said. "Ancient Hsoosh is still the Language of Ceremony in the best houses of Falleen."

"Language of Ceremony?" Han echoed. "Like one they'd use to make formal vows?"

"Precisely," C-3PO said. "The elite classes have kept it alive for more than two thousand standard years to distinguish—"

"Threepio, that's not important at the moment," Leia interrupted. She could tell by the way Han was clenching his jaw that he was truly disturbed to have a mad Jedi making death vows against them. A lecture on the history of ancient Hsoosh just might be enough to make *him* yank out C-3PO's inner machinery. "Wait here and let us know what else Natua has to say."

C-3PO acknowledged the command, and Leia and Han followed Cilghal to the next cell. Seff had moved to the far corner, where he was kneeling, facing away from the door with his battered hands on his thighs. The barely perceptible rise and fall of his shoulders suggested that he was meditating, perhaps trying to calm his troubled mind and make sense of what had been happening to him.

Cilghal glanced back down the catwalk toward the turbolift, where Tekli was waiting with what looked like a meter-long recording rod that ended in a large parabolic antenna. When the Chadra-Fan nodded her readiness, Cilghal stepped closer to Seff's cell and rapped gently on the wall.

Seff, a sturdily built young man with square shoulders and light curly hair, answered without looking away from the corner. "Yes, Master Cilghal?"

His voice came from the small relay speaker near the door, and when Cilghal answered, she angled her mouth toward the tiny microphone beneath it.

"How did you know it was me?" she asked.

"It's . . ." Seff struggled for an explanation, then finally said, "It's *always* you . . . or Tekli. And Tekli wouldn't reach that high when she knocked." He shrugged. "So, to answer the question clearly on your mind: no, I have not yet developed the ability to touch the Force through an ysalamiri void-bubble."

"But you *do* seem to be feeling better," Cilghal said.

"I'll have to take your word for it." Seff remained facing the corner, but his tone softened. "I don't have a clear memory of how I was feeling before."

Cilghal rolled a hopeful eye in Leia's direction, then spoke to Seff again. "Do you remember why you're here?"

"That would depend on the meaning of *here*. I remember trying to rescue Valin Horn from a GA Security facility. And I remember being ambushed by someone who looked a *lot* like Jaina Solo." Seff stopped and shook his head. "I assume that I'm in the Jedi Temple detention center's Asylum Block, but none of it makes much sense."

"It probably *shouldn't* make sense," Cilghal said. She smiled with a relief that Leia did not quite share. "I'm afraid you've been suffering paranoid delusions lately."

Seff's head and shoulders slumped in a fairly convincing manner, and he continued to look into the corner without speaking.

"Seff, you're going to get better," Cilghal said. It was something any good mind-healer would say to a patient, whether or not it was true. "This is an encouraging sign."

Leia couldn't read Mon Calamari faces well enough to know whether Cilghal was sincere. But she *did* know that she herself wasn't convinced. Leia didn't like the way Seff continued to hide his face. And if he was having trouble remembering what had happened to him, how had he known earlier that it was always Cilghal or Tekli who visited?

Cilghal continued speaking into the relay microphone. "Seff, you have visitors. Would it be okay if we came inside?"

"Visitors?" Seff finally looked away from his corner, his pale eyes gleaming in curiosity. "Absolutely. Come inside."

Before Leia could express her concerns, Cilghal reached over and entered a code to deactivate the lock. As the door slid aside, Leia glanced toward Han and was relieved to see the same wariness in his eyes that she felt in her gut. If Cilghal was being too optimistic, at least there would be someone else ready to jump on Seff.

"Jedi Solo, Captain Solo . . ." Cilghal waved them into the cell. "After you."

"The *Solos*?"

Sounding more cynical than delighted, Seff rose and turned toward them. To Leia's surprise, there were no alarming glints in his eyes or twitches on his lips, nor anything obvious to suggest that Cilghal's relief was anything but warranted. But his brow rose just a little too slowly for his astonishment to be sincere.

"What are *you* two doing here?"

"We just wanted to check up on you," Han said. To prevent Seff from approaching the door, he held out his hand and crossed to the corner. "Good to see you're feeling better."

As Seff reached out in return, Leia readied herself to spring into action at the first hint of trouble. But Seff merely remained in the corner and looked slightly be-wildered as the two shook hands.

Leia moved her own hand away from the stun stick in the small of her back and went to stand with Han. "You *do* look much better than the last time we saw you."

Seff's eyes shifted in her direction. "From what I'm gathering, that wouldn't be difficult."

He flashed a self-deprecating smile, and Leia began to wonder if all the betrayals and disappointments she had suffered over the decades were beginning to make her too suspicious.

"Do you *remember* when you saw the Solos?" Cilghal asked. She remained just inside the door, as though her presence was an unpleasant requirement and she didn't want to intrude. "Aside from here on Coruscant, I mean."

Seff frowned for a moment, and Leia thought he was going to say that he couldn't recall.

But then he flashed that awkward smile again and said, "Wasn't it on Taris, at that pet show?"

"That's right," Han said. He clapped a hand on Seff's shoulder and slipped smoothly around into the corner, so the young Jedi would have to face away from the door as they spoke. "The one where the ornuk took the grand prize."

"Han, it wasn't the *ornuk*," Leia said in a reproachful tone. She slipped around to Seff's other side and stood opposite Han, so they had the young Jedi flanked on both sides and could quickly redirect his attention with a gentle touch. "It was the chitlik."

Han scowled. "What are you talking about? It was that big ornuk. I should know. It nearly bit off my ankle!"

Leia rolled her eyes and—seeing by Seff's slack jaw that their distraction was working—shook her head vehemently. "That was the cannus solix! You would've known that if you hadn't been off starting fights when the judges explained the difference."

"Hey, I didn't start that fight," Han countered, the edge in his voice so sharp that even Leia wasn't sure he was acting. "Is it my fault if—"

"How many times have I heard *that*?" Leia interrupted. Across the cell, she could see Tekli standing in the door, pointing the funnel-shaped antenna of the portable encephaloscanner at the back of Seff's head. "According to you, it's *never* your fault."

"That's right—it *never* is." Han turned to Seff. "You were at the show, kid. Who did they arrest?"

But Seff was no longer paying attention to Han. He was looking at the same corner he had been facing when they arrived, staring at a wavy blur in the transparisteel that Leia did not recognize as a reflection—until she realized why Seff had known it was Cilghal knocking earlier. Hoping to draw his attention back to her, Leia laid a hand on his shoulder.

"Seff, please forgive us," she said. When he continued to watch the reflection, she squeezed hard. "After you've lived together as long as Han and I have, you develop a few tender—"

Leia did not realize Seff was attacking until she felt his arm snaking over hers, trapping her elbow in a painful lock that she could not slip without snapping the joint. She whirled away, screaming in alarm, and barely managed to keep him from grabbing the stun stick secured in the back of her belt. In the next instant, Han was between them, bringing his own stun stick down across Seff's shoulder.

Seff pulled back, dragging Leia into the path of the strike. He still took most of the blow across his biceps, but she was jolted so hard that her knees locked and her teeth sank deep into her tongue.

Incredibly, Seff did not drop. He drove Han back with an elbow to the face, then sent him slamming into the wall with a side kick to the gut. Spinning toward the door, he finally released Leia's arm and launched himself at Tekli and Cilghal.

"No, you don't!" Seff yelled, landing two meters away. "I won't be copied!"

Both of Leia's legs and one arm had turned to noodles, but she still had one good hand with which to grab her stun stick.

By that time, Seff was only a pace from Tekli and Cilghal.

The *phoot-phoot* of a tranquilizer gun sounded from the doorway. Seff stumbled, one arm trying to slap the darts from his chest as he struggled to keep his balance. He took one more step, then Leia activated her stun stick and sent it spinning into the back of his legs. He crashed to the floor just centimeters from Cilghal's feet, then lay there twitching and drooling.

Cilghal turned to Tekli, then let out a gurgling sigh. "You may as well deactivate the scanner," she said. "I think we've learned what we need to know."

Chapter Two

IN THE *JADE SHADOW*'S FORWARD CANOPY HUNG TWIN black holes, their perfect darkness surrounded by fiery whorls of accretion gas. Because the *Shadow* was approaching at an angle, the two holes had the oblong appearance of a pair of fire-rimmed eyes—and Ben Skywalker was half tempted to believe that's what they were. He had begun to feel like he was being watched the instant he and his father had entered the Maw cluster, and the deeper they advanced, the stronger the sensation grew. Now, at the very heart of the concentration of black holes, the feeling was a constant chill at the base of his skull.

"I sense it, too," his father said. He was sitting behind Ben in the copilot's seat, up on the primary flight deck. "We're not alone in here."

No longer surprised that the Grand Master of the Jedi Order always seemed to know his thoughts, Ben glanced at an activation reticle in the front of the cockpit. A small section of canopy opaqued into a mirror, and he saw his father's reflection staring out the side of the canopy. Luke Skywalker looked more alone and pensive than Ben ever remembered seeing him—thoughtful, but not sad or frightened, as though he were merely trying to understand what had brought him to such a dark and isolated place, banished from an

Order he had founded, and exiled from a society he had spent his life fighting to defend.

Trying not to dwell on the injustice of the situation, Ben said, "So maybe we're closing in. Not that I'm all that eager to meet a bunch of beings called the Mind Drinkers."

His father thought for a moment, then said, "Well, I am."

He didn't elaborate, and he didn't need to. Ben and his father were on a mission to retrace Jacen Solo's five-year odyssey of Force exploration. At their last stop, they had learned from an Aing-Tii monk that Jacen had been bound for the Maw when he departed the Kathol Rift. Since one purpose of their journey was to determine whether Jacen had been nudged toward the dark side by something on his voyage, it only made sense that Luke would want to investigate a mysterious Maw-dwelling group known as the Mind Drinkers.

What impressed Ben, however, was how calm his father seemed about it all. Ben was privately terrified of falling victim to the same darkness that had claimed his cousin. Yet his father seemed eager to step into its depth and strike a flame. And why shouldn't he be? After everything that Luke Skywalker had suffered and achieved in his lifetime, there was no power in the galaxy that could draw him into darkness. It was a strength that both awed Ben and inspired him, one that he wondered if he would ever find himself.

Luke's eyes shifted toward the mirrored canopy section, and he caught Ben's gaze. "Is this what bothered you when you were at Shelter?" He was referring to a time that was ancient history to Ben—the last part of the war with the Yuuzhan Vong, when the Jedi had been forced to hide their young at a secret base deep inside the Maw. "Did you feel like someone was watching you?"

"How should I know?" Ben asked, suddenly uneasy—and unsure why. By all accounts, he had been an unruly, withdrawn toddler while he was at Shelter, and he recalled being afraid of the Force for years afterward. But he had no clear memories of Shelter itself, or what it had felt like to be there. "I was *two*."

"You *did* have feelings when you were two," his father said mildly. "You *did* have a mind."

Ben sighed, knowing what his father wanted, then said, "You'd better take the ship."

"I have the ship," Luke confirmed, reaching for the copilot's yoke. "Just close your eyes. Let the Force carry your thoughts back to Shelter."

"I know how to meditate." Almost instantly, Ben felt bad for grumbling and added, "But thanks for the advice."

"Don't mention it," Luke said in a good-natured way. "That's what fathers *do*—offer unwanted advice."

Ben closed his eyes and began to breathe slowly and deliberately. Each time he inhaled, he drew the Force into himself, and each time he exhaled, he sent it flowing throughout his body. He had no conscious memories of Shelter that were his own, so he envisioned a holograph of the facility that he had seen in the Jedi Archives. The image showed a handful of habitation modules clinging to the surface of an asteroid fragment, their domes clustered around the looming cylinder of a power core. In his mind's eye, Ben descended into the gaudy yellow docking bay at the edge of the facility . . . and then he was two years old again, a frightened little boy holding a stranger's hand as his parents departed in the *Jade Shadow*.

An unwarranted sense of relief welled up inside Ben as he grew lost in a time when life had seemed so much easier. The last fourteen years began to feel like a long, terrible nightmare. Jacen's fall to the dark side had never happened, Ben had not been molded into an adolescent assassin, and his mother had not died fighting Jacen. All those sad memories were still just bad dreams, the unhappy imaginings of a frightened young mind.

Then the *Shadow* slipped through the containment field and ignited her engines. In the blink of an eye she dwindled from a trio of blue ion circles into a pinpoint of light to nothing at all, and suddenly Ben was alone in the darkest place in the galaxy, one child among dozens entrusted to a small group of worried adults who—despite their cheerful voices and reassuring presences—had very clammy palms and scary anxious eyes.

Two-year-old Ben reached toward the *Shadow* with his free hand and his heart, and he sensed his mother and father reaching back. Though he was too young to know he was being touched through the Force, he stopped being afraid . . . until a dark tentacle of need began to slither up into the aching tear of his abandonment. He thought for an instant that he was just sad about being left behind, but the tentacle grew as real as his breath, and he began to sense in it an alien loneliness as desperate and profound as his own. It wanted to draw him close and keep him safe, to take the place of his parents and never let him be alone again.

Terrified and confused, young Ben pulled away, simultaneously drawing in on himself and yanking his hand from the grasp of the silver-haired lady who was holding it.

Then suddenly he was back in the cockpit of the *Jade Shadow*, staring into the fire-rimmed voids ahead. Scattered around their perimeter were the smaller whorls of half a dozen more distant rings, their fiery light burning bright and steady against the starless murk of the deep Maw.

"Well?" his father asked. "Anything feel familiar?"

Ben swallowed. He wasn't sure why, but he found himself wanting to withdraw from the Force all over again. "Are we sure we need to find these guys?"

Luke raised a brow. "So it *is* familiar."

"Maybe." Ben couldn't say whether the two feelings were related, and at the moment he didn't care. There was something hungry in the Maw, something that would still be there waiting for him. "I mean, the Aing-Tii call them Mind Drinkers. That can't be good."

"Ben, you're changing the subject." Luke's tone was more interested than disapproving, as though Ben's behavior were only one part of a much larger puzzle. "Is there something you don't want to talk about?"

"I wish." Ben told his father about the dark tentacle that had reached out to him after the *Shadow* departed Shelter so many years ago. "I guess what we're feeling now might be related. There was definitely some . . . *thing* keeping tabs on me at Shelter."

Luke considered this for a moment, then shook his head. "You were pretty attached to your mother. Maybe you were just feeling abandoned and made up a 'friend' to take her place."

"A *tentacle* friend?"

"You said it was a *dark* tentacle," Luke continued thoughtfully, "and guilt is a dark emotion. Maybe you were feeling guilty about replacing us with an imaginary friend."

"And maybe *you* don't want to believe the tentacle was real because it would mean you left your two-year-old son someplace really dangerous," Ben countered. He caught his father's eye in the mirrored section again. "I hope you're not going to try to psychoanalyze this away, because there's a big hole in your theory."

Luke frowned. "And that would be?"

"I was *two*," Ben reminded him. "And by all accounts, I didn't feel guilty about *anything* at that age."

Luke grinned. "Good point, but I still don't think we should worry too much about this tentacle monster of yours."

"It's not *my* tentacle monster," Ben retorted, miffed at having his concerns mocked. "You're the one who made me dredge it up."

Luke's expression hardened into admonishment. "But *you're* the one who's still afraid of it."

The observation struck home. Whether or not the dark presence he remembered was real, he had emerged from Shelter wary of abandonment and frightened of the Force. And it had been those fears that had allowed Jacen to lead him into darkness.

Ben sighed. "Right. Whatever this thing is, I've got to face it." After a moment, he asked, "So how do we find these Mind Drinkers?"

" 'The Path of True Enlightenment runs through the Chasm of Perfect Darkness.' " Luke was quoting Tadar'Ro, the Aing-Tii monk who had told them that Jacen had left the Kathol Rift to search out the Mind Drinkers. " 'The way is narrow and treacherous, but if you can follow it, you will find what you seek.' "

Ben swung his gaze back toward the black holes ahead. The brilliant whorls of their accretion disks were burning hottest and brightest along their inner rims, where a mixture of in-falling gas and dust was being compressed to unimaginable densities as it vanished into the sharp-edged darkness of twin event horizons.

"Wait. Tadar'Ro said *perfect* darkness, right?" Ben started to have a bad feeling about the monk's instructions. "Like, beyond an event horizon?"

"Actually, it's probably very bright on the way down a black hole," Luke pointed out. "Just because gravity is too strong for light to escape doesn't mean it can't exist, and there's all that gas compressing and glowing as it's sucked deeper and deeper."

"Yeah, but you're *dead*," Ben said, "and everything is dark when you're dead. Still, I see what you mean. I doubt Tadar'Ro expects us to fly down a black hole."

"No, not *down* one."

There was just enough anxiety in Luke's voice to make Ben glance into the mirrored section again. His father was frowning out at the two black holes, staring into the fiery cloud between them and looking just worried enough to twist Ben's stomach into a cold knot.

"*Between* them?" Ben could see what his father was thinking, and it didn't make him happy. In any system of two large bodies, there were five areas where the centrifugal and gravitational forces would neutralize each other and hold a smaller body—such as a satellite or asteroid—in perpetual equilibrium. Of those five locations, only one was directly *between* the two bodies. "You mean Stable Zone One?"

Luke nodded. "The Chasm of Perfect Darkness is an ancient Ashla parable referring to the twin perils of ego and ignorance," he explained. "The Tythonians spoke of it as a deep dark canyon flanked by high, ever-crumbling cliffs."

"So life is the chasm, darkness is falling all around," Ben said, taking an educated guess as to the parable's meaning, "and the only way to stay in the light is to go down the middle."

Luke smiled. "You've got a real feeling for mystic guidance." He lifted his hands away from the yoke. "You have the ship, son."

"*Me? Now?*" Ben considered pointing out that his father was by far the better pilot—but that wasn't the issue, of course. If Ben was going to face his fears, he needed to handle the flying himself. He swallowed hard, squared his shoulders, then confirmed, "I have the ship."

Ben deactivated the mirror panel and accelerated

toward the black holes. As the *Shadow* drew closer, their dark orbs rapidly began to swell and drift toward opposite sides of the cockpit, until all that could be seen of them were tall slivers of darkness hanging along the rear edges of the canopy. Ahead lay a fiery confluence of superheated gas, swirling in from two different directions and so bright it hurt Ben's eyes even through the *Shadow*'s blast-tinting.

He checked the primary display and found only bright static; the navigation sensors were awash in electromagnetic blast from compressing gas. The *Shadow*'s internal sensors were working just fine, however, and they showed the ship's hull temperature rising rapidly as they penetrated the cloud. It wouldn't take long for that to become dangerous, Ben knew. Soon the fierce heat inside the accretion disk would start fouling guidance systems and control relays. Eventually, it would compromise hull integrity.

"Dad, how about doing something with those sensor filters?" Ben asked. "My navigational readings are snow."

"Adjusting the filters won't change anything," Luke said calmly. "We're flying between a pair of black holes, remember?"

Ben exhaled in exasperation, then cursed under his breath and continued to stare out into the fiery ribbons ahead. At best, he could make out a confluence zone where the two accretion disks were brushing against each other, and the painful brilliance made it difficult to tell even that much.

"How am I supposed to navigate?" Ben complained. "I can't see anything."

Luke remained silent.

Ben felt the hint of disapproval in his father's Force aura and experienced a flash of rebellion. He let out a cleansing breath, allowing the feeling to run its course and depart on a cushion of stale air, then saw how he had been blinded by his anxiety over the navigation difficulties.

"Oh . . . right," Ben said, feeling more than a little foolish. "Trust the Force."

"No worries," Luke said, sounding amused. "The first time I tried something this crazy, I had to be reminded, too."

"Well, at least *I* have an excuse." Ben took the navigation sensors offline so the static wouldn't interfere with his concentration. "It's hard to focus with your dad looking over your shoulder."

Luke's crash webbing clicked open. "In that case, maybe I should get some—"

"Who are you kidding?" Ben shoved the yoke over, flipping the *Shadow* into a tight barrel roll. "You just want to bite your nails in private."

"The thought hadn't crossed my mind," Luke said, dropping back into his seat. "Until *now,* ungrateful offspring."

Ben laughed, then leveled out and checked the hull temperature. It was climbing even faster than he had feared. He closed his eyes and—hoping the gas was not so thick that friction would aggravate the problem— shoved the throttles forward.

It did not take long before Ben began to sense a calm place a little to port. He adjusted course and extended his Force awareness in that direction, then started to feel a strange, nebulous presence that reminded him of something he could not quite place—of something dark and diffuse, spread across a great distance.

Ben opened his eyes again. "Dad, do you feel—"

"Yes, like the Killiks," Luke said. "We might be dealing with a hive-mind."

A cold shudder was already racing down Ben's spine. His father had barely uttered the word *Killiks* before the memory of his stint as an unwilling Gorog Joiner came flooding back, and for the second time in less than an hour he found himself desperately wanting to withdraw from the Force. Gorog had been a dark side nest, secretly controlling the entire Killik civilization while it fed on captured Chiss, and Ben had fallen under its sway for a short time when he was only five. It had been the most terrifying and confusing time of his childhood, and had Jacen not recognized what was happening and helped Ben find his way back to the Force and his true family, he doubted very much that he would have been able to break free at all.

Thankfully, the presence ahead was not all that similar to Gorog's. There was certainly a darkness to it, and it was clearly composed of many different beings joined together across a vast distance—most of space ahead, really. But the distribution seemed more mottled than a Killik hive-mind, as though dozens of distinct individuals were joined together in something vaguely similar to a battle-meld.

Ben was about to clarify his impressions for his father when a familiar presence began to slither up inside him. It was cold and condemning, like a friend betrayed, and he could feel how angry it was about the intrusion into its lair. The Force grew stormy and foreboding, and an electric prickle of danger sense raced down Ben's spine. He could feel the darkness gathering against him, trying to push him away, and that only hardened his resolve to finally face the specter. He opened himself up, grabbed hold in the Force, and began to pull.

The presence jerked back, then tried to shrink away. It was too late. Ben already had a firm grasp, and he was determined to follow it back to its physical location. He checked the hull temperature and saw that it was hovering in the yellow danger zone. Then he focused his attention forward and saw—actually *saw*—a thumbnail-sized darkness tunneling through the swirling fires ahead. He pointed their nose toward the black oval, then shoved the throttles to the overload stops and watched the fiery ribbons of gas stream past the cockpit.

The ribbons grew brighter and more deeply colored as the ship penetrated the accretion disk, and soon the gas grew so dense that the *Shadow* began to buck and shudder in its turbulence. Ben held on tight to the yoke . . . *and* to the dark presence he was clasping in the Force.

His father's voice sounded behind him. "Uh, Ben?"

"It's okay, Dad," Ben said. "I've got an approach lane."

"A *what*?" Luke sounded genuinely surprised. "I hope you realize the hull temperature is almost into the red."

"*Dad!*" Ben snapped. "Will you please let me concentrate?"

Luke fell silent for a moment, then exhaled loudly. "Ben, the gas here is too dense for these velocities. We're practically flying through an atmo—"

"*Your* idea," Ben interrupted. The black oval swelled to the size of a fist. "Trust me!"

"Ben, *trust me* doesn't work for Jedi the way it does for your uncle Han. We don't have his luck."

"Maybe that would change if we trusted it more often," Ben retorted.

The black oval continued to expand until it was the size of a hatch. Ben fought the turbulence and somehow kept the *Shadow*'s nose pointed toward it, then the ship was inside the darkness, flying smooth and surrounded by a dim cone of orange radiance. Startled by the abrupt transition and struggling to adjust to the sudden change of light, Ben feared for an instant that the dark presence had led him off course—perhaps even out of the accretion disks altogether.

Then the cone of orange began to simultaneously compress and fade, becoming a dark tunnel, and a far worse possibility occurred to him.

"Say, Dad, would we know if we were flying down a black hole?"

"Probably not," Luke said. "The time–space distortion would make the journey last forever, at least relative to Coruscant-standard time. Why do you ask?"

"Oh, no reason," Ben said, deciding not to alarm his father any more than necessary. If he *had* flown them past an event horizon, it was too late to do anything about it now. "Just curious."

Luke laughed, then said, "Relax, Ben. We're not flying down a black hole—but will you *please* slow down? If you keep this up, you really *are* going to melt the hull."

Ben glanced at his display and frowned. The hull temperature had climbed into the critical zone, which made no sense at all. The surrounding darkness and the lack of turbulence meant they were no longer being blasted by heat from the accretion disk. The hull ought to be cooling rapidly, and if it wasn't . . .

Ben jerked the throttles back and was pitched against his crash webbing as friction instantly began to slow the *Shadow*. The area surrounding them wasn't dark because it was *empty*—it was dark because it was filled with cold matter. They had entered Stable Zone One, where gas, dust, and who-knew-what-else were floating in limbo between the two black holes. Worried that they weren't decelerating fast enough, he used the maneuvering thrusters to slow the ship down even further . . . then realized that during the excitement, he had lost contact with the dark presence he had been using as a reluctant guide.

"Blast," Ben said. He expanded his Force awareness again, but felt only the same meld-like presence he had sensed earlier—and it was too diffuse to be much of a navigation beacon. "We're back to flying blind. I can't feel anything useful now."

"That's not really a problem," Luke pointed out. "There's only one place in here where anything can have a permanent habitat."

Ben nodded. "Right."

Stable Zone One wasn't actually very stable. Even the slightest perturbation would start a mass on a long, slow fall into one of the adjacent gravity wells. Therefore, anything *permanently* located inside the zone could only be at the precise center, because that was the only place where the forces were in absolute equilibrium.

Ben brought the navigation sensors back up. This time, the screen showed nothing but a small fan of light at the bottom, rapidly fading to darkness as the signals were obscured by cold gas and dust. He activated the *Shadow*'s forward flood lamps and continued onward. The beams tunneled ahead for perhaps a kilometer before vanishing into the black fog of dust and gas. Ben decelerated even further, then adjusted headings until all external forces affecting the *Shadow*'s travel vector were exactly zero, and set a waypoint. Theoretically, at least, they were now on course for the heart of the stable zone.

When Ben shifted his attention forward again, he saw a blue fleck of debris floating in the light beam ahead. He instantly fired the maneuvering thrusters to decelerate more, but in space, even a relative creep was a velocity of hundreds of kilometers an hour, and they covered half the distance to the object before the *Shadow* responded.

Instead of the stony boulder or ice ball that Ben had

expected, the object turned out to be a young Duros. Ben could tell that he was a Duros because he wasn't wearing a pressure helmet, and his blue, noseless face and big red eyes were clearly visible above the collar of a standard Jedi-issue flight suit. Hanging on his shoulder was what, at that distance, appeared to be a portable missile launcher.

"Dad?" Ben asked. "Are you seeing this?"

"Duros, no helmet?"

"Right."

Luke nodded. "Then yes, I—"

The Duros was silhouetted by a white flash, and the silver halo of an oncoming missile began to swell in front of the *Shadow's* cockpit. Ben shoved the yoke forward and hit the thrusters, but even a Jedi's reflexes weren't that quick. A metallic bang echoed through the hull, and damage alarms began to shriek and blink. In almost the same instant, the Duros and the missile launcher floated past mere meters above the cockpit, and the muffled thud of an impact sounded from far back in the stern.

"Definitely no hallucination," Luke commented.

"Dad, that looked like—"

"Qwallo Mode, I know," Luke replied. Mode was a young Jedi Knight who had disappeared on a standard courier run about a year earlier. When an exhaustive search had failed to find any trace of him, the Masters had finally concluded that he had perished. "He's a long way from the Tapani sector."

"Assuming that *was* Qwallo." Ben extended his Force awareness behind them, but did not sense any hint of the Jedi's presence. "Should I make another sweep to see if we can recover him?"

Luke thought for a moment, then shook his head. "Even if he's still alive, let's not give him another shot at the *Shadow*. Before we start taking those kinds of chances, we need to figure out what's going on here."

"Yeah," Ben agreed. "Like how come he didn't need a helmet."

"And how he got here in the first place—and why he's shooting at us." Luke clicked out of his crash webbing, then added, "I'll handle the damage. If you see anyone else floating around with a missile launcher and no pressure suit, don't ask questions, just—"

"Open fire." Ben deployed the blaster cannons, then checked the damage display and saw that they were bleeding both air and hyperdrive coolant. To make matters worse, the yoke was sticking, and that could mean a lot of things—none of them good. "Got it. We've taken enough damage."

Ben switched his threat array to the primary display. At the top of the screen, the gray form of a mass shadow was clarifying out of the darkness. A yellow number-bar was adding tons to the mass estimate faster than the eye could follow, but he was alarmed to see that it was already into the high five digits and climbing toward six. There was no indication yet of the object's overall shape or energy output, but the tonnage alone suggested something *at least* as large as an assault carrier.

Unsure whether it was better to slow down to prevent a collision or accelerate to avoid being an easy target, Ben started to weave and bob. There was just a vague hint of danger tickling the base of his skull, but that only meant nothing had set its sights on the *Shadow* yet.

On the third bob downward, the yoke jammed forward and wouldn't come back. Ben cursed and tried to muscle it, but he was fighting the hydraulic system, and if he fought it too hard, he would break a control cable.

He hit the emergency pressure release, dumping the control system's entire reservoir into space, and then checked his threat array again.

The mass ahead was no longer a shadow. A silvery, elongated oval had taken shape in the middle of the display, the number-bar in its core now climbing past seven million tons. The oval was slowly drifting toward the bottom of the screen and shedding alphanumeric designators, indicating the presence of a debris field *and* the danger of an impending collision with the object itself. Ben hit the maneuvering thrusters *hard,* and the *Shadow* decelerated.

He heard a toolbox clang into the main cabin's rear bulkhead, and his father's alarmed voice came over the intercom speaker. "What did you hit?"

"Nothing yet." Ben pulled back on the yoke, using his own strength to force the vector plates down. "The control yoke's power assist is gone, and we've reached a debris field."

"What sort of debris?" his father demanded. "Ice? Rock? Iron-nickel?"

Ben thumbed the SELECT bubble active and slid it over to one of the designators: OBJECT B8. An instant later a density analysis offered a 71 percent probability that OBJECT B8 was a medium transport of unknown make and model.

But Ben did not immediately relay the information to his father. As the *Shadow*'s nose returned to its original plane, an enormous, gray-white dome was slowly coming into view. Dropping down from above and upside down relative to the ship, the dome hung at the base of a large, spinning cylinder ringed by a dozen small, attached tubes. Floating between the cylinder and the *Shadow* were nearly twenty dark flecks with the smooth lines and sharp corners suggestive of spacecraft, all drifting aimlessly and as cold as asteroids.

"Ben, you're worrying me," his father admonished. "How bad is it?"

"Uh, I don't really know yet." As Ben spoke, the *Shadow*'s lamp beams continued to slide up the spinning cylinder, to where it joined a gray metal sphere that looked to be about the size of one of Bespin's smaller floating cities. "But maybe you should come back to the flight deck as soon as things are secure back there."

"Yeah," Luke said. "I was just thinking the same thing."

As the lamp beams continued to reveal more of the station—at least that's what Ben *assumed* he was looking at—he began to grow even more confused and worried. With a second, dome-capped cylinder rising out of the sphere directly opposite the first, the thing reminded him of a station he had helped infiltrate during the recent civil war. It didn't seem possible that two such structures could exist in the galaxy by mere coincidence, or that he would have happened on this one by mere chance even if the two *were* related. He had the uneasy feeling that the Force was at play here—or, to be more precise, that the Force was putting *him* in play.

Now that they were actually in visual range of their target, Ben brought the full suite of sensors back online and began to investigate. To both his relief and puzzlement, all of the contacts appeared to be derelict vessels. They ranged widely in size, from small space yachts like the *Shadow* to an antiquated Tibanna tanker with a capacity in excess of a hundred million liters. Ben did a quick mental calculation of the total tonnage of the abandoned ships and shuddered. If these were captured spoils, there were some very impressive pirates hiding around here somewhere.

Starting to envision sensor masks and ambushes, Ben slid the *Shadow* into the cover of an old TGM Marauder. The ship looked as deserted as its sensor profile suggested, tumbling slowly with cold engines, open air locks, and no energy emanations whatsoever. But there was no apparent combat damage, or anything else, to suggest it had been taken by pirates.

Ben turned the sensors on the station itself and found it marginally less derelict. Its power core was active, but barely. A few warm areas suggested that at least some of its atmospheric seals remained intact. Approaching closer, he could see that three of the dark tubes attached to the upper cylinder had come loose at one end and were in danger of being launched away by centrifugal force. Whoever lived here—if anyone did—they were not much on maintenance.

The *clack-clack* of boots-in-a-hurry echoed through the open hatchway at the rear of the flight deck, then suddenly stopped. Ben activated the canopy's mirror panel and found his father standing behind the copilot's chair, jaw hanging slack as he stared at the slowly spinning station ahead.

"Remind you of anything?" Ben asked.

Luke's gaze remained fixed on the space station. "What do *you* think?" he asked. "It could be a miniature Centerpoint Station."

Centerpoint had been an ancient space station located in the stable zone between the Corellian worlds of Talus and Tralus. Its origins remained cloaked in mystery, but the station had once been the most powerful weapon in the galaxy, capable of destroying entire star systems from hundreds of light-years away. One of the few positive things to come of the recent civil war, in Ben's opinion, had been the facility's destruction. He was far from happy to discover another version hidden here, deep inside the Maw.

"I was afraid you'd say that," Ben said with a sigh. "What do we do now? Lob a baradium missile at it?"

Luke's voice grew disapproving. "Do we *have* a baradium missile?"

Ben dropped his gaze. "Sorry. Uncle Han said it was always smart to keep one—"

"Your uncle isn't a Jedi," Luke interrupted. "I wish you'd remember that."

"Sure," Ben said. "But maybe this one time we should think about the way he would handle this. If this place was built by the same beings that designed Centerpoint Station, the smartest thing we can do is get rid of it."

"And maybe we will—*after* we unjam our vector plates and replenish our hydraulics." Luke slipped into the copilot's seat behind Ben. "In the meantime, try to avoid hitting anything. I'll see if I can find a safe place to dock this bird."

Chapter Three

As hangar bays went, this one looked like a decades-old disaster zone. The main doors were jammed about halfway open, leaving the entire facility exposed to the dark vacuum of space. The decks were slowly revolving around the *Shadow* as the station rotated on its axis, and they were crammed with starcraft from a dozen different eras and classes, all facing the open exit for a quick departure. Hand tools lay scattered across hull tops, tank dollies were propped against landing struts, charging carts rested beneath retracted access panels. A film of pale dust covered everything, so thick on the older craft that it was sometimes difficult to determine the hull color. None of the vessels showed attack damage, but all those tools suggested they had needed some manner of repair, and many crews had not even bothered to raise the boarding ramp before abandoning their work.

As his son struggled to accommodate the station's rate of rotation, Luke extended his Force awareness toward the middle of the facility. On the journey in, he had sensed a concentration of life energy in the central sphere, a hazy cloud too large and diluted to be a single being, with no discernible focuses to suggest individual presences. It was still there, an area of heaviness and warmth in the faint fog of Force energy that permeated this part of the Maw. Luke could tell by the way it began to writhe up inside him that it had not only been monitoring their arrival, it had been *awaiting* them.

Ben swung the *Shadow* around to face the hangar exit, then put down—somewhat heavily—between an old TheedSpeed Galaxy Runner and a swoop-sized needle ship with a hatch about the size of a human hand. They completed the shutdown routine quickly, clicked out of their crash webbing, and went aft. Instead of following Luke to the suit locker, however, Ben stopped at the engineering station and began to call up system reports.

"Let's leave repairs for later," Luke said. He pulled a light, combat-rated vac suit from the locker and tossed it to Ben, then took another for himself. "I want to have a look around first."

Ben caught the suit with no outward sign of anxiety, but the sudden ripple in his Force aura was hard to miss. He was afraid of the strange presence monitoring them from the station center, and Luke wished he understood why. The snaky feel of its Force touch certainly suggested the "tentacle" that had touched his son at Shelter. But what, exactly, had the thing *done* that continued to haunt Ben more than a decade later?

"Ben, it'll be okay." Luke opened his vac suit and began to push his feet into the legs. "If you're remembering something else about your time at Shelter, it would be better to share—"

"Dad, I'm not trying to avoid anything out there," Ben said. "But we've already been attacked once, and the *Shadow* took some bad hits. It's just sound tactics to get things ready in case we need to leave in a hurry."

It was hard to know whether Ben was unaware of how his fear was controlling him, or just allowing it to interfere with his judgment, but it really didn't matter. The time was fast approaching when the young man had to face his demons or surrender to them, and—as

much as Luke wished it otherwise—the choice was one
that no father could make for his son.

Continuing to don his vac suit, Luke peered out the
viewport and scowled at the fleet of abandoned vessels.
"Take a look outside, then tell me again about sound
tactics."

Ben frowned and studied the equipment-strewn
hangar outside, then slowly flushed with embarrassment.

"Yeah . . . I see," he said, opening his vac suit. "We
aren't going to have time to finish our repairs."

"Probably not," Luke agreed. "A Jedi needs to be
observant, and being observant means—"

"Thinking about what you see," Ben finished, quoting one of Kam Solusar's favorite sayings. "I should
have asked myself why everyone was leaving their tools
lying around. It could be that something has been drawing—or taking—the ship crews away, and it doesn't
look like anyone makes it back here to finish their repairs."

"Which means?"

Ben peered out the viewport for a long time, obviously searching for some missed detail that would explain what was luring the crews away from their
vessels—and why no one was returning. Finally, he
turned back to Luke, shaking his head.

"I don't know," he admitted. "All that occurs to me
is that we shouldn't make the same mistake everyone
else did."

Luke smiled broadly. "Congratulations—that's *exactly* what it means."

Ben looked more puzzled than before.

"The trouble with *sound tactics* is that they make
you predictable," Luke explained. "Jedi shouldn't be
predictable."

Ben's eyes finally lit in understanding. "Got it," he
said. "From now on, we eat when *I'm* hungry."

Luke laughed, glad to see that Ben was relaxed enough to joke. "I don't think we have the supplies for that." He pulled their helmets from the suit locker. "Space yachts don't come with that much cargo capacity."

They sealed their suits and exited through the air lock into about a quarter standard gravity. Luke immediately began to feel a bit dizzy. Like Centerpoint Station, this habitat lacked true artificial gravity. Instead it created an imperfect imitation by rotating on its axis—a method that wreaked havoc on the delicate inner ear of many bipedal species.

Once the *Shadow*'s outer hatch had closed, Luke secured the hidden lock inside its framework by triggering a latch that could only be accessed with the Force. Meanwhile, Ben gathered some equipment from nearby ships, and they proceeded to camouflage the *Shadow* together. Ben tossed some hand tools onto an engine mount, and Luke leaned a torch kit against a landing strut. Finally, they used the Force to stir up a cloud of dust that would eventually drift back onto the *Shadow,* leaving it covered in the same gray blanket as the surrounding vessels.

They weaved their way through the tangled mass of ships and into the primary air lock at the back of the berthing deck. Like the hangar itself, the chamber was equipped with motion-sensitive lights that remained fully functional. So when Ben secured the hangar hatch behind them, the two Skywalkers patiently waited for an automatic valve to open and equalize pressure with the station interior.

They were still waiting two minutes later when the motion-sensitive lights switched off.

Ben's voice came over the helmet speakers. "Great— maybe we *should* have started on the repairs." His tone was joking, but with a nervous edge. "And waited until they sent someone to fetch us."

"Some*thing*," Luke corrected. He raised an arm, and the lights reactivated. In contrast with the hangar illumination, which had been tinted heavily toward the blue end of the spectrum, the light in the air lock had a distinctly green cast to it. "Or maybe we should just equalize pressure ourselves."

Luke reached over to the side of the chamber and pushed down on a lever, which he assumed to be the handle of a manual standby pump. A sharp *clunk* shook the entire air lock; then the ceiling slid aside and left them staring up into a cavernous darkness above.

Ben's hand dropped to the lightsaber hanging on his belt. "What's that?"

"The door, I think."

Luke extended his awareness through the opening. When he did not sense any danger, he Force-leapt up into the darkness and landed adjacent to the hole. Almost instantly dim green light began to pour from a nearby wall, illuminating a short length of squat, wide corridor. Ben arrived a moment later, still standing on the air lock floor as it rose into the hole through which Luke had just jumped.

"Do you get the feeling someone's making this easy for us?" Ben asked.

"Either that, or the equipment is just that reliable," Luke said. "I don't know which worries me more."

"The equipment, definitely," Ben said over the suit comm. "This place has the same external design as Centerpoint Station, remember? That *can't* be coincidence."

"Probably not," Luke admitted. "But this station can't be as dangerous. It's sitting between two black holes, and it would be pretty hard to target anything from in here. We can't even get navigation readings."

"Yeah, *we* can't," Ben agreed. "But *we're* not the ones who built it."

Luke frowned at the thought that another weapon similar to Centerpoint Station might exist in the galaxy. Fortunately, this one was much smaller, which meant it probably did not share the same function. At least, that was what he *hoped* it meant.

Luke checked his external readouts and was not surprised to discover he and Ben remained in a hard vacuum. He motioned Ben to the other side of the corridor. "And on that cheery note . . ."

They started toward the interior of the station, studying their environs as they walked. No more than two meters high but three times as wide, the corridor appeared to have been designed to move a lot of traffic quickly—an impression reinforced by two metal bands running along the floor, which might have been a guide ribbon for some sort of robotic hovercart. The walls and ceiling were made of a translucent composite that did not quite conceal the network of fibers, tubes, and ducts running behind them.

After the Skywalkers had traveled ten meters, the wall behind them fell dark, and a pale green glow began to pour from the next section. As Luke and Ben continued deeper into the station, they began to come across detritus of all kinds—vac suit helmets, an ammonia breather's air tank, blaster rifles, flechette launchers, and half a dozen single-wheeled carts with round bellies and gel-padded kneeling benches. Each time a new section of wall illuminated, the light grew more anemic, and soon the hue was more yellow than green.

"This place is starting to dark me out," Ben said, stopping beside a half-inflated vac suit. "Why can't they just pick a color?"

"Good question," Luke said. He was not happy to see Ben reacting to his feelings instead of focusing on the problem. "Maybe the colors are supposed to tell you where you are. You have a guess?"

"Yeah, maybe." Ben used his boot toe to flip the vac suit onto its back and shone his wristlamp into the helmet's faceplate, revealing a visage so shriveled and gray it might have been Ho'Din or human. "The lights could be a warning system, you know? Like blue means safe, green means danger, yellow means big trouble."

Luke felt only a faint tingle of danger himself, but that didn't mean Ben's theory was wrong—especially considering the body they had just found. He activated the status display inside his faceplate and found all radiation levels well within the normal range.

"Ben, are you sensing something that worries you?"

"You mean aside from that strange presence in the central sphere?" Ben asked.

"Right."

"And besides the fact that we're poking around a ghost station with no way to contact anyone?"

"Yes, aside from that."

"And that somebody really old, powerful, and mysterious obviously went to a lot of trouble to keep this place hidden from the likes of us?"

"And that, too."

Ben shrugged and shook his helmet. "Then no, I'm all systems ready." He stepped over the body and continued up the corridor. "Let's keep moving."

They continued up the corridor for another two hundred paces, passing a series of intersections and huge chambers filled with equipment so alien and mysterious that Luke could not even guess at its function. There were huge barrels made of the same material as the walls, surrounded by glowing coils of what appeared to be fiber-optic cable. In another chamber, they saw a silver sphere the size of the *Millennium Falcon* hovering over a disk of dark metal. The next cavernous room held a warren of containment-field cubes, each one holding a hammock, a couple of basins, and a large, wedge-skulled skeleton still draped in a thin yellow robe.

Reluctant to cross a still-shimmering barrier field that had probably sealed the entrance for centuries—if not millennia—father and son lingered outside the chamber for a time. They could not help debating whether the prisoners had belonged to the species that had created the station, were some enemy species the creators were fighting, or had been a crew from one of the vessels abandoned in the hangar, left here to die by a long-forgotten band of pirates. After discussing the likelihood of each possibility for several minutes, they finally realized they would never know and continued on their way.

Twenty meters later, they came to another detention center. The remains inside *these* cells were exoskeleton parts. Judging by the size of the thoraxes and abdomens, the inhabitants had been a little smaller than humans. Their chitinous skulls were large and heart-shaped, with openings for huge multifaceted eyes. Scattered around each cell were at least half a dozen small limb tubes and no more than four larger ones, suggesting insectoids with two powerful legs and four long arms.

Ben's voice came over Luke's helmet speaker. "Hey, those look like—"

"Killiks," Luke agreed. "Unu *did* claim they were involved in the building of the Maw and Centerpoint Station."

"As *slaves,* it looks like," Ben replied. "Dad, what *is* this place?"

"I don't know," Luke admitted. He shook his helmet and started up the corridor again. "But I intend to find out."

A few steps later, the next section of lighting activated and they found themselves facing the curved bulkhead of the station's central sphere. Their way forward was blocked by a translucent membrane bulging out toward them. Luke touched his gloved fingertips to it, then pressed lightly and felt it yield.

"That's air pressure," Ben observed. "It must be an emergency bulkhead seal."

"Probably," Luke agreed.

Luke activated his wristlamp and shone it through the center of the membrane. The view beyond was blurry, but he could see enough to find himself struggling to reorient his sense of direction. They seemed to be looking down into a dome-shaped chamber, with themselves and the membrane located near the top and a bit off to one side. A shoulder-high rail ran down the curving wall to the dome's circular floor, which had a ring of hatches running along its outer edge. Some of the hatches seemed to be open, but it was impossible to see more than that.

Luke reached out with the Force again and felt the Presence somewhere beyond the chamber. It was clear and strong and as large as a cloud, concentrated in the darkness ahead. But it was floating everywhere around them, too, above and below and behind. He felt it snaking up inside him, a growing hunger that longed only for his touch.

A shudder of danger sense raced up his back. Luke deactivated his wristlamp and stepped away from the membrane.

"You feel it, too?" Ben asked.

Luke nodded. "And it feels *us*."

"Yeah." Ben looked away, then activated his headlamp and shone it up an intersecting corridor. "So which way to an air lock?"

Luke was concentrating too hard to smile, but he was glad to hear his son sounding so determined. It didn't mean Ben was ready to face every demon from his past, but it did suggest he understood the necessity.

When Luke didn't respond right away, Ben swung his helmet lamp back around and said, "Right. Trust the Force."

"Always a good idea," Luke said, "but I had something else in mind."

He turned his hand vertical and began to push his fingertips against the membrane.

"You think it's a Killik pressure seal?" Ben asked.

"Something like that." Luke continued to push, stretching the membrane so far that it swallowed his arm to the elbow. "We know they were here, so it seems likely they would have adapted their own construction techniques from this technology."

By now Luke had pushed in his arm to the shoulder. He stepped forward, inserting his whole flank. The membrane continued to stretch. A lamp panel activated, flooding the room with white light, but his view of the chamber grew even blurrier. With nothing beneath him except a steep, curving wall, it felt like stepping off a cliff into a fog bank. He grabbed one of the rails he had seen earlier and brought his other foot across.

Luke started to slide down the wall, the membrane slowing his descent as it gathered behind him in a long, hollow tail. He was about halfway down when the tail closed, forming a new seal and bringing him to a sharp halt. He tried to pull free, but where the membrane had come together, it had grown rigid and unyielding. Releasing the rail, he unclipped his lightsaber and twisted around to cut himself free—then nearly fell when the tail of membrane suddenly snapped and sent him spinning.

He danced down the curving wall, fighting to keep his balance as changes in both the apparent gravity and his apparent attitude challenged even his Jedi reflexes. By the time he reached the bottom of the chamber, gravity had increased to about half normal, and he felt like he was standing on the wall he had just slid down.

Ben's voice came over the suit comm. "Dad, you okay down there?"

"Fine." Luke raised a hand to wipe his faceplate clear, only to discover that the membrane was dissolving before his eyes. When he did not see anything threatening, he said, "Come on through."

"Affirmative," Ben said. "Do I need to do that little dance at the end?"

Luke chuckled and looked up toward the membrane. "I guess that depends on how graceful you are, doesn't it?"

The membrane bulged inward as Ben began to push through. Luke returned his lightsaber to his belt and, now that the membrane was no longer obscuring his vision, took a moment to examine the chamber more closely. Clearly, it was a primary access point to the station's central sphere. It resembled a serving bowl that had been stood on its side. The wall to Luke's right was the interior of the bowl, a deep basin that curved up to the membrane through which he had entered. Three meters above this one was a second membrane, no doubt providing access from another part of the station.

Luke was standing on what would have been the inner rim of the bowl, a walkway that curved gently upward both in front of him and behind him. To his left, where the bowl's cover would be, rose a large, disk-shaped wall ringed by the hatches he had glimpsed earlier. About half of them were open, and through one of the doorways he could see the red strobe of a small alarm light.

Luke was just completing his survey when Ben arrived, nearly bowling him over as he came tumbling down the wall and crashed into a closed hatch. Ben cringed with embarrassment, and a long stream of static came over the helmet speaker as he hissed indiscernible curses into his microphone.

Luke glanced down at his son's membrane-clouded faceplate, then commented, "So much for that remarkable Jedi balance."

Ben cocked his helmet. "I thought you had to *pull* free."

"Me, too." Luke helped Ben to his feet and spun him in a quick circle, inspecting the vac suit for damage. "Everything looks fine. At least you know how to fall right."

"Lots of practice," Ben said. As the last of the membrane dissolved from his faceplate, his gaze dropped to the lightsaber Luke was still holding in his free hand. "Trouble?"

"Maybe." Luke pointed up toward the hatch with the flashing red glow. "Let's go have a look."

Luke returned the lightsaber to his belt, then led the way toward the hatch. As they ascended, the centrifugal force of the spinning station kept them firmly secured to the walkway, so that they always felt as if they were standing at the bottom of the room. The queasiness that had come over Luke when they left the *Shadow*'s artificial gravity grew a little stronger, and the station seemed even more alien and dangerous than before. This was not a place hospitable to humans.

On the way to their destination, they passed two other hatches, both open. One led to a larger version of the sloping wall by which they had entered their current chamber. The other provided access to a long corridor lined every couple of meters with simple sliding doors. Judging by the rumpled cloth and spare vac suit parts spilling out of many of the open doorways, the cabins beyond had served most recently as private quarters.

As they drew near the hatch with the flashing red glow, Luke began to hear a faint, rhythmic buzzing from inside. He checked his environmental status. The atmosphere in this part of the station appeared to be within survival tolerances, so he opened his helmet's faceplate—and immediately wished he hadn't.

The air wasn't just stale, it was fetid, reeking of a dozen different kinds of decay—a couple of which he had not smelled since the swamps of Dagobah. But there was also a more worrisome stench, an acrid odor that had filled the cockpit of his starfighter all too often: melting circuit boards. And the rhythmic buzzing was, of course, exactly what he had feared: the clamor of an alarm klaxon.

A surprised retch sounded behind Luke, then Ben gasped, "I think my sampler unit is feeding me static. This stuff *can't* be breathable."

"It sure isn't pleasant," Luke said. "Feel free to seal back up if you want to."

"Are *you*?"

Luke shook his head. "I have a feeling it's going to take *all* my senses to sort this out."

"Then it won't hurt to have an extra nose sniffing around," Ben said. "You can stop being so soft on me. Yoda wouldn't approve."

"Yoda would have made you do all the sniffing," Luke said, stepping through the hatchway. "And he would have had you convinced he was just trying to educate your nose."

Beyond the threshold, they found themselves standing on the observation platform of a large, trilevel room. Outside the front viewport shone a pulsing mass of purple light, lined by crackling veins of static discharge and haloed by tendrils of shooting flame. Luke's gaze was drawn to the strange radiance so powerfully that he found himself starting into the room without pausing to inspect the interior. He stopped three steps inside the hatch and corrected his mistake.

Each level was packed with tall white equipment cabinets, made of some carbon-metal composite that Luke did not recognize. Arranged in neat rows—one to each level—the cabinets stood about shoulder height, with slanted tops that were identifiable as control panels only because of the red lights blinking on their surfaces. Wisps of blue and yellow smoke were rising through the edge seams of several consoles and gathering up near the ceiling in a multilayered cloud.

Though the floors were littered with cast-off clothes, containers, and a generous layer of well-tracked grime, there was no sign of the corpses their noses had warned them to expect. Luke sent Ben to investigate the front of the room, then descended to the first row and stepped over to the nearest of the white cabinets.

Instantly a holographic representation of the entire station appeared a few centimeters beneath the cabinet's surface, then slowly began to spin. Messages began to appear around the perimeter of the schematic, written in a strange, flowing alphabet that Luke suspected even C-3PO would not recognize. When they began to blink and turn colors, he touched his hand to one. The hologram immediately enlarged to show the interior view of a stores hold, so overgrown with gray-green mold that the shelves looked like tall, rectangular trees.

Luke stepped over to another cabinet, this one leaking yellow smoke from a tiny melt-crevice flanked by blinking red lights. Again, a hologram of the station appeared. He touched his hand to one of the blinking lights. The schematic swung around, pointing the end of one of its long cylinders directly at him. A pair of circles, one green and one red, appeared over the cylinder. The green circle was fixed in the heart of the cylinder, while the red hovered a millimeter to the left, flashing and adding its own urgent voice to the clamor of buzzing that filled the room. It seemed clear that something important was out of alignment, but it would have been folly to attempt guessing what.

Luke moved to the next row, where the middlemost cabinet had a long row of lights blinking down one side. This time, the hologram showed nothing but gravity vectors surrounded by words and figures in the strange alphabet. Eventually, he began to recognize the image for what it was—an arrangement of black holes.

As Luke studied the holograph, he had an idea. To check his theory, he traced the route he and Ben had taken to this station, and his heart leapt so high into his throat he thought he might choke. There could be no doubt that he was looking at a chart of the entire Maw cluster.

He touched the binary system where the station was located. This time, the hologram did not zoom in to give him a more detailed view of the immediate area. Instead, the image rotated, swinging the binary system around to the back of an egg-shaped grouping of black holes so thick that he could no longer find it through the tangle of letters and gravity vectors. As Luke studied it, he noticed a crescent-shaped gap adjacent to the binary system where there were no letters or vectors at all. He touched a finger to the top of this area.

Half a dozen sets of gravity vectors began to blink red, outlining a long crack in the otherwise solid shell of black holes. One at a time, a copy of each readout appeared in a corner inset, surrounded by letters and figures he did not have the faintest hope of deciphering. Luke had no idea what *any* of this meant—and he was beginning to have the sinking feeling that he really didn't want to.

He was jarred from his thoughts when Ben's startled voice sounded from the front of the control room. "Ah, *kriff*—this is bad!"

"*What's* bad?" Luke snatched his lightsaber off his belt again, then Force-leapt over three rows of equipment and landed next to Ben in the front of the control room. "Be specific!"

Ben's gaze swung toward Luke, his face pale and his jaw hanging slack. He raised a hand and pointed out into the darkness between them and the writhing mass of purple light.

"Bodies," he said. "Lots and lots of bodies."

Chapter Four

WITH THE TEMPLE APEX PLAYING PEEKABOO BEHIND the fog and a cold mist swirling over Fellowship Plaza, Jedi Knight Bazel Warv felt as though he were walking on air. Maybe the wet weather touched a species-memory of the cloud forests that had once covered his native Ramoa. Or maybe he felt light-footed because he had spent two hours that morning watching his favorite little girl, Amelia Solo, and the rest of the day in the company of his friend Yaqeel Saav'etu. And any day spent with Yaqeel was a good one. She was smart and svelte, with silky Bothan fur that resembled spun gold on misty days like this, and she never seemed embarrassed to be seen with a beady-eyed, jade-skinned hulk like Bazel.

But today Yaqeel did not seem entirely at ease. There was a thorny side to her Force aura that usually came just before she growled-down someone for being rude, selfish, or otherwise irritating. Bazel could not imagine that *he* was the target of her ire—he never had been before. Yet he didn't think she could still be fuming over the way the lunch waiter had laughed when he tried to order a ten-kilogram basket of robal leaves.

Maybe Yaqeel was upset because they had not yet succeeded in their one assignment for the day: getting inside Tahiri Veila's residence to determine why she wasn't returning Jaina Solo's calls. Unfortunately, they had been under strict orders not to get caught doing anything illegal, and the building's Toydarian manager had not only resisted Yaqeel's Force-suggestion efforts, but had taken offense and made it clear he would be keeping a close eye on the apartment all day.

Still, Yaqeel hadn't seemed particularly disturbed at the time. She'd just shrugged and departed, then told Bazel they would return that night, after the Toydarian grew tired of keeping watch. So that left only one thing.

As they continued through Fellowship Plaza's famous Walking Garden toward the Temple, Bazel began to growl and grunt in the guttural language of his species. It wasn't *Yaqeel* that people had been avoiding all day, he assured her. She was too pretty for that. But between Chief Daala's press releases and Javis Tyrr's holoshow, Coruscant's citizenry had to believe the entire Jedi Order was going insane. When someone saw a pair of Jedi Knights coming down the pedway these days, it was only natural to duck around the nearest corner—especially when one of those Jedi was over a meter wide.

Yaqeel swung her long ears down, pressing them tight to her skull in what Bazel had learned to recognize as an expression of gratitude and affection.

"Thanks, Barv." She had started calling him Barv when they were hiding inside the Maw with the rest of the Jedi younglings, and the nickname had stuck. "But it's not the public."

She flicked an ear tip toward a row of neatly trimmed blartrees that lined the far edge of the broad pedway. "It's *them*."

Bazel didn't need to look to know who *them* was, and he ventured the opinion that it was nothing to grow angry about. The Solos were just keeping watch because they were worried that he and Yaqeel might fall ill, the way their friends had.

Yaqeel cocked her head in surprise. "When did *you* notice them?"

Bazel rubbed his long chin and, because his Ramoan throat didn't allow him to speak Basic, grunted his reply in his own language. It was difficult to recall whether he had smelled the Solos as he and Yaqeel were entering Tahiri's building, or as they were *leaving*. Probably as they were leaving.

Yaqeel punched him in the shoulder, hard. "And you didn't tell me?"

Bazel hadn't realized he needed to; wasn't her nose as large as his?

Yaqeel's ears shot forward. "Gee, *thanks*."

She picked up her pace. Bazel hastened after her, his heavy strides sounding like drumbeats as his big heels pounded the paving slabs. Beings ten meters ahead began to glance over their shoulders and look for convenient places in which to disappear.

Bazel paid them no attention. It wasn't like Yaqeel to be touchy, so he was afraid he had really hurt her feelings. As he lumbered after her, he kept up a steady refrain of grunts and groans, trying to explain that her nose was really as big as his only *in proportion* to the size of her face. But Yaqeel wasn't in any mood for explanations. She continued to move ever faster, until she was almost running.

They reached the end of the pedway, emerging from the Walking Garden into the open vastness of the Temple Court. Yaqeel continued to move at a brisk pace, angling for the south side of the huge pyramid, where there was a subsurface speeder gate that many Jedi employed as an entrance because of its inaccessibility to Javis Tyrr and his fellow holoslugs.

Finally, Bazel caught up to Yaqeel and spun around to block her way. Her eyes were wide and bulging, almost bloodshot, and the tips of her fangs were showing beneath her curled lips. Growing alarmed, he clamped a huge hand on her shoulder and demanded to know why she was suddenly so frightened of him.

Yaqeel's ears flattened to the sides. "It's not you, Bazel."

Yaqeel *never* called him by his proper name; clearly, something was terribly wrong. He snorted a question, demanding to know what it was.

Yaqeel glanced over her shoulder, back toward the Walking Garden. "*Them,* of course," she said. "Can't you sense the change?"

Now Yaqeel was really starting to frighten Bazel. When he asked her what change she meant, his voice broke into a shrill squeal that made passing beings circle around them even more widely.

"Oh, Barv, you're just so . . . *trusting.*" Yaqeel took Bazel by the wrist and started toward the speeder entrance again, this time at a more normal pace. "Don't let them know we're on to them. That's the mistake the others made."

Bazel began to have a sinking feeling. He inquired what others she was talking about.

Yaqeel stared up out of one narrowed eye. "The others like *us,* of course."

Bazel asked if she meant the rest of the Unit, Jysella and Valin.

Yaqeel nodded, adding, "And Seff and Natua, too."

They were just angling past the main entrance, where a full Galactic Alliance Security assault team—complete with armored hovercars—had been stationed as an assertion of Daala's authority. To either side of them sat a pair of newsvans, resting on their parking struts until the next opportunity came to embarrass the Jedi Order. Javis Tyrr was nowhere in sight at the moment, but Bazel recognized Tyrr's distinctive, half-winking "gotcha eye" logo on one of the vans, and he knew the bottom-feeding reporter would be somewhere close. He pulled Yaqeel to his other side, where she would be shielded from roving cams by his jade bulk.

His worst fears were confirmed when Yaqeel failed to notice what he was doing. "We'll free Seff and Natua first," she said. "Then maybe we can recover Jysella and Valin, find a safe place to thaw them out, and figure out what the kriff is going on."

It would certainly be good to figure things out, Bazel agreed. What he didn't say was that Yaqeel was breaking his heart. He hadn't grown as close to Seff and Natua at Shelter as he had to Yaqeel and the Horn siblings, but the quarters had been so tight that he had become friends with most of the other students, and he desperately wanted to see them leave the Asylum Block—*when they were ready*. Now Bazel's best friend was starting to act like she was on her way to joining them, which was certainly a better alternative to being frozen in carbonite like Valin and Jysella. *That,* Bazel would never allow.

As they approached the corner of the Temple, Bazel took one last look back toward the cam vans and found a single lens turned their way—no doubt capturing some stock footage of him so they would have something ready when they aired a report about the Jedi menace. He raised a hand as though to wave, at the same time shooting a Force flash toward the van that would wipe his image—and most of the day's other footage—from the cam's digital memory.

They rounded the corner and came to a hedge of tall rutolu bushes, the purple leaves as long and slender as daggers. A freshly worn path led through the hedge to a chest-high safety wall that protected the sunken entrance to the speeder gate, and it was here that Yaqeel reached for her lightsaber. Bazel was desperate to keep her from causing trouble outside the Temple, where she might injure a passerby and would certainly draw the attention of the GAS assault team. He grabbed her wrist and pulled her away.

Yaqeel spun on him with fire in her eyes, then sent a jolt of Force energy into his arm so powerful that Bazel squealed in surprise. He had never seen her do such a thing before; in fact, he had never seen *any* Jedi use the Force that way.

"*You,* Barv?" Yaqeel's hand dropped to her lightsaber. "They got you—"

Bazel gave a disgusted snort, pointing out they weren't going to free anyone from the Asylum Block by trying to fight their way *into* the Temple. The plan was to *fool* the Jedi, remember?

Yaqeel's hand remained on her lightsaber hilt, her long brow-fur rising at the ends as she studied Bazel. Finally, she said, "Barv, we *are* the Jedi."

Silently cursing the dim wits of his species and the sharp wits of the Bothans, Bazel took a deep breath and tried to accept that he would soon be in a huge amount of pain. Even under the best circumstances, Bazel wasn't a very good liar, and now Yaqeel would be using the Force to determine whether he was being truthful. That left him with only one option: to grab her and try to drag her inside the Temple before the GAS assault team arrived and the two Jedi got themselves killed.

And that was when Bazel realized he *could* lie to her. The key to defeating the Jedi truth-sense lay in believing the lie one told, and Bazel knew how to do that. He didn't know *how* he knew, or where he had learned it. But all he had to do was soak his words in a little Force energy, and then he himself would believe what he said. And everyone else would, too.

So Bazel simply shrugged and pulled his hand away from Yaqeel's lightsaber. He suggested that maybe rescuing Seff and Natua wasn't such a good idea, after all.

The . . . the *fakes* were bound to be watching them, and the instant he and Yaqeel started down toward the Asylum Block, they'd probably get jumped and end up in a cell themselves.

Yaqeel considered his words for a moment, then took her hand away from her lightsaber. "You're probably right, Barv. But we've got to *try*."

Bazel sighed in relief, using his newfound Force skill to make it seem like resignation. Then he asked Yaqeel if she was ready.

Yaqeel nodded. "As ready as I'll ever be." She grabbed the safety wall and pulled herself up, crouching on its mist-slickened top to glance back down at Bazel. "Remember to act normal, Barv. You can't let them shiver you out too much."

He assured her that he wouldn't give them away to *anyone* inside the Temple. It was another lie, of course, but he did not feel guilty about it. Once he had Yaqeel safe somewhere deep inside the Temple, he could try to reason with her, make her see that nothing sinister had happened to their fellow Jedi. And if he failed, at least there would be plenty of help to make certain she didn't fall into GAS's custody and end up like Valin and Jysella.

Bazel laid an elbow on top of the wall and swung a massive leg up so he was sitting astride it. He found himself looking down into a white duracrete trough, about five meters deep and just wide enough for two speeders to pass in opposite directions. At one end, the trough vanished into the tunnel that led down to the south-side speeder hangars. The durasteel gate to this entrance was wide open while a small, dome-shaped Lovolol cleaning droid polished the threshold.

Standing just outside that gate, next to an armored luxury speeder bearing the crest of the Imperial Remnant, were Jaina Solo and Jagged Fel. Head of State Fel wore a formal dress uniform with the tunic collar still fastened. Jaina was in a purple day dress styled just enough like a Jedi robe to make the lightsaber hanging from its belt look appropriate. They were wrapped in each other's arms, kissing and paying no attention to anyone else.

The fur on Yaqeel's neck stood on end, and her hand drifted toward her lightsaber again. Bazel knew his plan to get her safely inside the Temple had just run into a serious problem.

He leaned close to Yaqeel's ear and rumbled that Jaina and her friend were only interested in each other. Bazel and Yaqeel should just hop down, excuse themselves, and continue into the Temple.

Yaqeel shook her head. "What's that cleaning droid doing there?" she whispered. "Something's not right."

Bazel cursed under his breath, then explained that Jaina had probably been out with Head of State Fel having a late lunch—or early dinner—somewhere.

"Bazel, they're not *people*," Yaqeel hissed. "You *have* to remember that."

Bazel nodded and assured her that he would try.

Jaina must have sensed them watching, because she suddenly opened her eyes and peered up at them over Head of State Fel's shoulder. Instead of breaking off the kiss, she lifted a hand and fluttered her fingers at them. It was a casual wave, such as anyone might give in a similar position, but Bazel was beginning to see Yaqeel's point. With Han and Leia behind them and Jaina blocking their access to the Temple, the Solos had them in a perfect trap. Could it really be just coincidence?

Jaina must have sensed his confusion, because she pulled away from her companion and motioned them down.

"Sorry," she called. There was an uncharacteristic flush to her cheeks—subtle, but distinct enough for

Bazel to notice. "You're not interrupting anything, really."

Now Head of State Fel turned as well, his cheeks showing the same uncharacteristic flush, and Bazel's heart jumped into his throat. He couldn't imagine what had ever made him doubt Yaqeel's judgment; she was a Bothan, after all, and Bothans understood treachery a lot better than Ramoans.

"Please, don't let us hold you up," called the being who looked like Head of State Fel. "I was just leaving."

Yaqeel seemed frozen in indecision, so Bazel forced a smile and replied that it was no problem, they were in no hurry. He put a little Force energy into the words, but apparently the ability to tell a good lie could not get them out of everything. The being who was impersonating Jaina frowned and started to step around the car toward them, and Not-Fel leaned into the open door to say something to his driver.

Bazel hazarded the opinion that they might have walked into an ambush.

"*Might* have?" Yaqeel snapped her lightsaber off her belt and turned back toward the rutolu hedge. "Let's get out of . . ."

Yaqeel let the sentence trail off as a pair of beings who looked a lot like Han and Leia Solo came pushing through the hedge. They did not have the same flush Bazel had seen in the cheeks of Jaina and Head of State Fel, but he knew they couldn't be the real Solos because Han didn't have the ability to Force-jump, and that meant he could not enter the Temple by this entrance. Besides, Bazel's danger sense was going wild, and both Solos were holding something behind their backs, and he knew the *real* Han and Leia would never harm him or Yaqeel.

Not-Leia's eye went straight to the lightsaber in

Yaqeel's hand. "Yaqeel, what are you doing with your lightsaber out? Is there a problem?"

Not-Leia was still speaking when Yaqeel sprang, yelling, "*You* are—"

Not-Han's hand was already coming around. Bazel glimpsed the silver form of some kind of hand weapon, then heard the *phoot-phoot* of flying darts.

Yaqeel gave a startled cry, her knees buckling as she landed in front of Not-Leia. She activated her lightsaber and flicked her wrist around in a clumsy attack, but Not-Leia had already stepped out of range. The blade sputtered dead as the hilt spun from Yaqeel's twitching hand.

Bazel watched in horror as Yaqeel's eyes rolled back in her head and drool began to slide down the long red tongue lolling out of the side of her mouth. He bellowed her name and reached for his own lightsaber—then noticed the tranquilizer pistol Not-Leia was holding on him.

"Bazel, it's just a tranquilizer," Not-Leia said. "Yaqeel's going to be fine."

"Yeah," Not-Han agreed. "How about you?"

Bazel considered trying to use his mass to overpower them both and flee with Yaqeel. But he was still sitting astride the wall with his lightsaber hanging from his belt, and both Not-Solos were holding tranquilizer pistols in their hands. He simply wasn't quick enough, so he moved his hand away from his lightsaber and nodded, using his new skill to put a little Force behind the gesture.

The faces of both Not-Solos relaxed instantly, and Not-Han whistled in relief. "Good. I thought for a minute we'd lost you both."

Bazel shook his head to assure him they hadn't. He eyed a landing spot close to Yaqeel, then began to gather his legs under him. If he was quick enough, he might be able to snatch Yaqeel up and be through the hedge before—

"Stay up there, Bazel," Not-Leia ordered. "We'll pass her up."

"Yeah, we need to get out of here." Not-Han kicked Yaqeel's lightsaber aside, then holstered his tranquilizer pistol and stooped down to pick up her unconscious form. "That GAS team was already starting this way when we came through the hedge."

Bazel settled back astride the wall, then stretched a hand down to take Yaqeel's limp form. This lying skill was a handy thing, he reflected. If the impostors were just going to hand her up to him, maybe he could hang on to her until he saw an opportunity to—

His hopes of making an easy getaway came to an abrupt end when he heard a pair of small feet land atop the wall behind him. Both Not-Solos did a credible job of looking surprised. Not-Han even let his jaw drop.

"Jaina?" Not-Han gasped. "What are *you* doing here?"

"Long story," Not-Jaina said. By the sound of her voice, she was less than two meters behind Bazel—easily within reach of his gangling arms. "But maybe you'd better let *me* take Yaqeel."

Not-Han and Not-Leia both frowned and cast uneasy glances in Bazel's direction. It was then that Bazel saw the flaw in his plan. If the impostors were replacing real Jedi with their own copies, they would *know* whom they had already replaced—and whom they *hadn't*. They had been fooling *Bazel,* manipulating him into a vulnerable position so it would be easier to take him down. And his Ramoan mind had been too stupid to see it! Sometimes he hated being such a big spotted oaf, hated himself for being so easy to trick. And hated *them* for taking advantage of it.

Bazel let out an angry bellow, then spun around, flinging his long arm out toward Not-Jaina. He heard her yell in surprise, then felt a satisfying impact as he caught her across the torso and sent her flying.

The next thing Bazel heard was the *phoot-phoot* of flying darts. His face and arms erupted in fiery waves of stinging pain, and he instantly grew dizzy and sick. He felt himself falling and crashing into an oblivion of crumpling metal, and he hoped that all that throbbing meant there wasn't going to be enough of him left to copy.

Chapter Five

"SORRY ABOUT YOUR LIMO, JAG." HAN WAS STARING AT Jagged Fel's damaged speeder, now half hidden beneath Bazel Warv's green bulk. Through a side window, he could see that the impact had folded the roof a good sixty centimeters down into the passenger compartment. "Maybe you should find another dealer. You'd think an armored speeder would take a hit better than this."

"Crumple zones are part of the design. I assure you, it can take a volley of concussion grenades and still speed away." Jag turned toward Jaina, who was standing at the limousine's front fender with the driver's raincoat buttoned over her torn dress. "I'm just glad Jaina wasn't hurt."

Jaina glared at him. "I can take a hit, too, Jag."

Jag's steely eyes widened ever so slightly. "I'm sure you can," he began apologetically. "I just meant to say that you're more important to me than a million-credit limousine."

"I'd *better* be," Jaina shot back. "That doesn't mean I can't take care of myself."

Han had to bite his cheek to keep from bursting into laughter. He still found it hard to believe that Jaina was really going to marry this guy, and it was foul-ups like this that made him hope she'd come to her senses before it was too late. Jagged Fel was a decent enough fellow, and a fine pilot, to be sure. But he was also a stickler for rules and a slave to his honor, and Han had seen enough of *that* kind to know Head of State Fel would never, *ever* put Jaina ahead of his duty. And that just wasn't good enough for Han's only daughter—not by a long shot.

Jag finally withered under Jaina's glare and turned to Han, who laughed and slapped him on the shoulder.

"Son, you've got a lot to learn before you're ready to marry a strong woman," he said. "You might start by always remembering she can break your neck with just a glance."

"Han!" Leia scolded. She was sitting atop the safety wall, one hand reaching out over the speeder lane as she used the Force to lower Yaqeel Saav'etu's unconscious form down to the others. "You'll scare him off!"

"Hey, he should know what he's in for." Han winked at Jaina, and her scowl melted away, probably because she realized she was being too touchy about Jag's protective streak. "You've been threatening to break my neck for forty years," he reminded Leia.

"That has nothing to do with being a strong woman," Leia retorted. "Just one whose patience is too often tested."

Han turned to Jag. "And *that* reminds me—it pays to keep life interesting. These women can get bored just sitting around the apartment."

"That depends on who we're sitting around *with*," Leia said drily. She swung her hand toward the limousine, lowering Yaqeel onto its hood. "As interesting as it might be to explore my husband's nerf-headed theories on marriage, we'd better take care of our two patients. That GAS squad is right behind me."

"I'll get Bazel." Jaina turned to Han. "Dad, if you can take Yaqeel—"

"I'll help," Jag said, stepping toward the Bothan's

feet. At the same time, he glanced across the hood at the big-shouldered hump standing beside the driver's door with a T-21 repeating blaster at the ready. "Put that weapon away and stay quiet about this, Baxton."

"Yes, sir," Baxton confirmed, tucking the weapon back inside the driver's door. "As far as GAS is concerned, I didn't see anything."

"Lying to a GAS agent is a crime here," Jag said. "Just tell them you're not authorized to discuss my activities with anyone. That's well within your immunity rights, and you won't run the risk of arrest."

Baxton snapped to attention. "Thank you for considering my welfare, sir."

Han took Yaqeel's shoulders and helped Jag lift her, then started toward the tunnel. Bazel Warv's huge form floated off the limousine roof and followed them through the gate, where Han tripped over a cleaning droid with a faulty right-of-way routine. He fell to the floor with Yaqeel's shoulders slumped in his lap.

"Captain Solo?" Jag asked. "If she's too heavy, I can—"

"I just *tripped*," Han barked, clasping the Bothan to his chest with one arm and using his free hand to push off the tunnel floor. "The droid got in my way. I'm not *old*, you know."

"Of course not. I wasn't thinking that."

Han rose to his feet and glared at Jag across Yaqeel's unconscious form. "Kid, for a Head of State, you're a lousy liar."

The color drained from Jag's face. "Captain Solo, I have no doubts about your—"

"*Jag!*" Jaina's voice came from somewhere on the far side of the huge Ramoan bulk that was still out in the speeder lane waiting to float into the access tunnel. "Will you stop worrying about the old man's feelings and get *moving*? The last thing you need is a GAS squad seeing you actually help us hide a pair of crazy Jedi."

"Right." Jag stepped past Han and started down the tunnel backward. "*I'll* take the lead."

Knowing there was no time to protest, Han simply nodded, then shot a glower toward the little dome-shaped droid watching from just inside the gate. Its response modules must have detected his anger, because the droid expelled a cloud of steam cleanser and quickly spun its photoreceptor away.

Cursing under his breath, Han followed Jag around a tunnel bend into the hangar itself. Two apprentices stood at the entrance, looking worried and uncertain as to whether they should leave their duty stations. Han pushed Yaqeel's shoulders into the arms of the closest guard, a red-furred Jenet, then stepped out of the way as Bazel Warv's green bulk floated through the entrance behind him.

"Comm Master Cilghal and tell her we lost two more," Han ordered. He pulled the tranquilizer pistol from his waistband and slapped it into the hands of the Jenet's partner, a young Duros female whose dark eyes seemed about twice as bulging as normal. "And if either one twitches before someone gets here to take them off your hands, hit 'em *both* with a couple of tranquilizer darts."

The Duros accepted the pistol with an air of bewilderment and fear. "They went sick? *Both* of them?"

"You have your orders, apprentice," Jaina said, lowering Bazel into an empty speeder bay. "Just carry them out."

With that, she started back up the tunnel, Han and Jag following close behind.

By the time they rounded the bend, Han could see Leia just inside the tunnel entrance, standing toe-to-toe with a blue-uniformed captain who had managed to position himself on the threshold before she could lower the gate. A couple of paces behind him were ten troopers in black assault armor. And ten paces beyond *them,* four more GAS agents had Jag's driver, Baxton, at blasterpoint.

But what really bothered Han were the holocams. They were peering down from atop the adjacent safety wall, carefully recording every word and gesture that passed between Leia and the GAS captain.

"I have no idea what you're talking about, Captain Atar," Leia was saying. "Nothing has happened here that is any concern of yours."

"*I* decide what my concerns are, Jedi Solo," Atar spat back. He was a tall human with a dark mustache and shoulders as square as his chin, the kind of pushy officer who mistook his chest patch for a badge of entitlement. "And crazy Jedi are definitely at the top of my list."

Leia shrugged. "We don't have any of those here."

"Yeah?" Atar pulled his datapad off its belt clip and spun the screen around to face Leia. "What's *that*?"

Han, Jaina, and Jag were close enough now to see a green blob that could only be Bazel landing atop Jag's limousine. A moment later Jaina rose into view beyond the front end of the speeder, staggering slightly and holding her torn dress closed. The cam panned to the top of the safety wall and showed both Solos peering down into the speeder lane, looking horrified and still holding their tranquilizer pistols.

Han's gut began to tie itself in knots. Atar *had* them. And these weren't even shots from one of the holocams. Somehow, he had caught the whole thing on a . . . Han remembered the cleaning droid and spun around, intending to stomp it back to its circuits.

Fortunately, Jag had a better idea and seized the initiative by going to stand nose-to-ear with Atar. "What have you *done* to my speeder limousine, Captain?"

Atar did not quite snap to attention—Jag wasn't *his* Head of State, after all. But he reacted as any security officer would in such a situation, cringing almost visibly as he tried to weigh his assignment against the potential career recriminations of causing a diplomatic incident.

Finally, he said, "*We* didn't do anything, Head of State." He turned the datapad toward Jag. "If the Head of State cares to have a look—"

"I'm not interested in holodramas, Captain." Jag plucked the datapad from the captain's hands and tossed it down the access tunnel, where it could be heard shattering into a dozen parts. "I can see that you've done something—unless those *aren't* your men holding my driver at blasterpoint."

"No, sir, they, uh, I mean yes, they are, sir." Atar glanced back up the lane. "But we didn't realize the limousine belonged to you."

"You didn't query the transponder?" Jag demanded. He stepped forward, purposely bumping the captain back away from the threshold. "Or did you just *choose* to ignore the diplomatic code?"

"Neither, sir." Finally seeming to realize that he was being manipulated, Atar stood his ground when Jag tried to bump him back again, then said, "Sir, we are in hot pursuit of two criminally insane Jedi Knights, and diplomatic immunity does *not* give you the right to interfere. If you insist—"

"By all means, feel free to continue your pursuit," Jag said, "*after you release my driver and vehicle.*"

Jag continued to stand in front of Atar, who glared down at him for a moment before he finally turned and waved his men away from the limousine.

"Thank you," Jag said. "I'll be sure to mention your cooperation to Chief Daala when I meet with her in the morning."

"That won't be necessary, sir," Atar replied with ice

in his voice. "She'll have a full report this evening. Now, if you'll stand aside, I *do* have my duties to fulfill."

"Certainly."

Jag pivoted on one foot, taking pains to move aside without removing himself from the area. It wasn't what Han would have done, but he had to admit that Fel knew how to be a major pain in the rear without breaking rules. As long as he was standing in the area, the GAS captain did not dare risk starting a firefight and endangering the Imperial Head of State.

When Atar finally accepted that Jag would not be moving any farther, he let out a snort of exasperation and pushed forward again. By then, of course, Han had slipped over to the gate controls, and Jaina and her mother were standing just in front of the threshold, lightsabers in hand. The blades were not ignited, but the message was clear—GAS would not be coming inside without a fight.

"Jedi Solo, I *am* going to arrest Jedi Knights Bazel Warv and Yaqeel Saav'etu. Will you stand aside, or do I have to move you?"

Leia did not flinch. "I don't see anyone in imminent danger," she said, "and that means you would need a warrant to arrest them. We're not going *anywhere* unless I see one."

The hint of a smile flashed beneath Atar's thick mustache. "In that case . . ." He extended a hand behind him and called, "Karpette, front and center!"

A Rodian female stepped forward, her multifaceted eyes sparkling with far too much delight. "Yes, Captain?"

"The warrant."

She was passing him a freshly printed flimsiplast even as he spoke. Han saw the miniature printer hanging from her equipment belt and felt his stomach go hollow.

Atar examined the document briefly, then nodded and passed it to Leia. "The print is a bit smaller than usual, but I believe you'll find everything in order."

Leia accepted the document, her impassive face betraying none of the shock that Han knew she was feeling. She examined it briefly, then said, "Very clever, Captain."

"I really can't take the credit, Jedi Solo," Atar replied. "When it comes to the Jedi menace, Chief Daala has given the order to facilitate due process in every legal manner."

"So I see." Leia gestured Jaina to remain where she was, just outside the gate, then held the document out toward Han. "What do you think?"

Han took the warrant and squinted down at the tiny lines of legal text. It was a detention order rather than an actual arrest warrant, but that didn't negate its validity. The names were spelled correctly, their species were identified properly, the justifying incident was described accurately, and the chronostamp—less than five minutes old—was certainly valid.

"I'm no expert, but everything seems right." He looked over at Atar. "Who's Judge . . . *Lortle?*"

"Arabelle *Lorteli,*" Atar corrected. "Designated judge for all matters Jedi."

"*Daala's* appointee?" Leia asked. "A new one?"

"Yes, ma'am," Atar replied. "Now, since even *you* agree that everything's in order, we'll be taking custody of Jedi Knights Warv and Saav'etu."

He started to lead his squad across the threshold—until Leia raised a hand in his direction.

"Wait."

Atar stumbled back, and Leia turned to Han with

one of those defiant gleams that always came to her eye when she smelled something rotten in the halls of power. "I don't know, Han. How do we handle this?"

It was not a real question, of course, since Han was neither a Jedi nor a legal adviser. It was a signal. He watched as Jaina subtly checked to make sure she was clear of the gate's drop path, and he knew she understood it, too.

"It looks like we don't have any choice," Han said. He shrugged and passed the warrant back to Leia, then turned to Atar. "Wait here. We're gonna have to get Master Hamner involved in this."

Atar scowled. "We're not *waiting* anywhere," he said. "You'll bring those two Jedi out here at once."

Han sighed and turned to Leia. "I think we'd better do as he says, don't you?"

Leia nodded. "Yes, I think so."

She glanced over at the control panel, and the toggle button rocked to the CLOSED position. The gate started to descend so swiftly that she barely had time to look back and meet Atar's puzzled gaze.

"Okay, Captain—you win," she said. "We'll be right back."

"What? Wait!" he sputtered. "Why are you clos—"

The gate clanged shut, leaving Han and Leia alone together. Han hit the lockout switch to prevent it from being inadvertently opened by a returning Jedi Knight, and then turned to Leia.

"You know, sometimes I'm really glad I married you."

"Just sometimes?"

"Oh, I'm glad *all* the time—but at times like this, I'm *really* glad." He took her hand and started down the tunnel to check on the new patients. "How long do you suppose they'll wait?"

"It's going to take the good captain a few minutes to overcome his embarrassment and comm for new orders," Leia said. "So we've got a while."

"Good. Do you suppose Jaina's going to be okay out there?"

"Of course." Leia closed her eyes for a moment, and Han knew that she was reaching out to check on their daughter through the Force. "She's with Jag, isn't she?"

Chapter Six

EVEN WITH THE ROOF BUCKLED DOWN INTO THE PAS-
senger cabin, the Imperial limousine still had enough
headroom for Jaina to sit upright. Jag was another
story. Although he was not tall for a human male, he
carried much of his height in his torso, an unfortunate
trait that Jaina hoped would not be inflicted on any
children who also happened to inherit her short
legs . . . assuming, of course, they even *wanted* children.
Like a lot of things regarding their coming marriage,
starting a family wasn't something they had found time
to discuss yet, at least not in the way it needed to be discussed.

At the moment, Jag's long torso was forcing him to
do one of the few things that Jagged Fel did not do well:
slouch. He was hunched down next to Jaina, his head
against the roof liner and his shoulders pressed to the
back of the seat.

"Thanks for the getaway." Jaina glanced out the
back viewport at the still-confused GAS squad, several
of whom were pounding their weapon butts against the
closed gate and demanding that it be reopened. "Probably better for me not to be around when that gnakhead
Atar finally decides he's been had."

"Probably," Jag said. "But I *am* surprised your mother
manipulated him so easily. One would think Daala

would have more sense than to send a weak-minded commander to keep watch over the Jedi Temple."

"Jag, that wasn't a Force suggestion." As Jaina spoke, Atar turned to watch the departing limousine. "It was the Sligh Slipper."

"The *Sligh Slipper*?"

"A little trick my parents picked up before I was born," Jaina explained. She gave Atar a parting wave. The captain's face reddened, and he began to snap orders into his headset microphone. "Didn't you see how Dad noobed Atar?"

Jag fell silent for a moment, his brow slowly rising. Finally, he let out an incredulous snort.

"It's a good thing your father isn't a Jedi," he said. "Han Solo with Force powers would be a very frightening thing."

Jaina smiled and opened her mouth to agree—until she was nearly thrown from her seat as the limousine came to a sudden stop. She looked up to see a GAS assault speeder blocking the exit less than five meters ahead, its cannon turret pointing down the lane. Whether it was targeting Jag's limousine or the gate behind it was impossible to say.

"Those GAS guys are starting to get pushy," Baxton observed from the driver's seat. The privacy screen between them could not be raised because of the crumpled roof, so he didn't need the vehicle intercom. "I can just float over them, sir. Even if they open fire, our armor can take it."

Jag shook his head. "No, that would give them room to claim we intended them harm," he said. "Just step out and ask them to let us pass."

"And if they don't?" Baxton asked.

"Be insistent," Jag said. "Captain Atar is trying very hard to make us blink, but he's not going to cause an intergalactic incident by attempting to remove Jedi Solo from a diplomatic vehicle."

Baxton acknowledged the order, then stepped out and approached the assault speeder blocking their path. A young Duros officer popped out of the blaster turret, pointing at the limousine and making angry demands. Baxton stood his ground, shaking his head and pointing his own finger, insisting the speeder be removed. After a minute of shouting back and forth, the Duros suddenly jumped down to stand lip-to-nose with Baxton.

"Looks like Atar's orders were firm," Jaina observed. "Maybe I shouldn't have rubbed it in."

Jag turned to peer at her beneath the crumpled roof. "Rubbed it in *how*?"

"It was no big deal," Jaina said. "I just waved at him."

Jag closed his eyes in exasperation. "You *waved* at him?" he repeated. "As we were leaving?"

"Of course as we were leaving," Jaina retorted. "When do you think I'd wave at him?"

Jag let his chin drop. "You have *got* to stop antagonizing Daala's people." He looked away, and the dirty haze of a secret came to his Force aura. "This situation is getting out of hand."

Jaina spun to face him. "What situation is that?"

"The whole situation." Jag continued to look away. "Between the Jedi and Daala. It's not doing the Order any good."

"Tell me something I *don't* know," Jaina replied. "Like, whatever you're holding back."

Jag's nostrils flared, and he turned to meet her gaze with obvious effort. "I'm not sure I know what you mean."

"Jag . . ." Jaina opened her borrowed raincoat just enough to show the lightsaber hanging from the belt of her torn dress. "*Jedi*, remember? I know when you're lying."

Jag sighed. "I heard something that I shouldn't have—and that I definitely shouldn't be repeating to a Jedi."

"Jag, I'm your *fiancée*," Jaina said. "And I happen to be a Jedi. If that means you're going to try to keep secrets from me, maybe we need to reevaluate—"

"All right, I surrender," Jag said, raising his hands. "But if you get to play the fiancée chit, so do I. This has to stay between us."

Jaina nodded. "That's fair, I guess."

"No guessing," Jag replied. "This can't be like Qoribu."

Jaina winced. It was a low blow, but maybe one she deserved. During the Killik crisis, she had made a promise to Jag that she had later broken. Ultimately, her failure to honor her word had resulted in Jag's exile from the Chiss Ascendancy.

"Okay," she said. "This is locker stuff. I won't tell *anyone*."

"No matter what," Jag insisted.

Jaina's only reply was a stony silence. She had given him her word, and it was really starting to scorch her that he continued to question it. She looked forward and noticed the rim of something metallic lodged behind the beverage locker in front of her, between the two rear-facing seats. Maybe a glow rod or something had been knocked out of its storage slot when Bazel hit the roof.

As Jaina shifted forward to retrieve the object, Jag let out a sharp breath. "Shall I accept your silence as a yes?"

More irritated than ever, Jaina forgot about the glow rod and turned to scowl. "Accept it however you like."

"Fine." Jag took a breath, then said, "I overheard something alarming when I was in Daala's office yesterday. She's thinking of hiring a company of Mandalorians."

"*Mandalorians?*" Jaina repeated. "What the blazes *for?*"

Now it was Jag's turn to be silent, and Jaina quickly realized how ridiculous her question was. She had spent a couple of very sad months training with Mandalorians when she was preparing to hunt down her brother, Darth Caedus, and she could think of half a dozen reasons Daala might hire a company of Mandalorian commandos. But only one of them would make Jag nervous about telling her.

"For *us?*" Jaina gasped.

Jag nodded. "She's been inquiring as to how many supercommandos it might take to handle the Jedi," he confirmed. "Exactly what she's considering, I don't know. But it can't be good."

Jaina didn't know whether to be angrier at him or at Daala. "And you thought you were going to keep this from me?"

"Of course," Jag said. "I didn't want to put you in this position."

Jaina frowned. "*What* position?"

"Of having to keep my secret," Jag said. "It's a burden you shouldn't have to carry."

Jaina fell back in her seat, her anger changing to shock as she began to understand. "You expect me to keep this news to *myself?*"

Jag remained silent, studying her with his steely eyes, searching for a hint as to which duty she would honor—the promise she had just made to him, or the oath she had sworn to the Order, swearing to always put the Jedi first.

"Stang . . . this isn't fair, Jag."

"I'm sorry."

Jaina nodded. "Well, that's something."

"I'm trying to negotiate an autonomous membership in the Galactic Alliance," Jag explained. "So far, Daala keeps saying all or nothing. She thinks divided loyalties are what sparked the last civil war."

"She might have a point." Even as Jaina said this, she began to see a glimmer of hope that it might not be necessary to make this impossible choice. "Jag, could this be some kind of—"

"Test?" Jag finished for her. "We're not that lucky. I didn't hear it from Daala herself, just someone talking on a comlink when he didn't realize I was in the room."

"It could still be a test," Jaina said. "Chiefs of State *do* occasionally use proxies for that sort of thing, you know."

Jag shook his head. "Wynn Dorvan doesn't strike me as the kind who involves himself in those sort of games."

Jaina's stomach sank. Wynn Dorvan was Daala's top aide, a rare Coruscanti bureaucrat known as much for his integrity as his competence.

"Bloah," she said. "And you really need Daala to give in to you on this?"

"I'm afraid so," Jag said. "If I try to subordinate our government to the Galactic Alliance—especially one led by Natasi Daala—the Moffs will go into open rebellion. I barely have the support to bring us in as equals."

"And you're doing good to get that," Jaina said. "I doubt even Uncle Luke expected you to persuade the Moffs to consider unification at all."

"I have motivation. For the first time in recent memory, the entire galaxy is at peace." Jag took Jaina's hand, and a hopeful note came to his voice. "And if I can convince Daala to let the Empire come into the fold on its own terms, we just might keep it that way."

"But if the Jedi Order learns that she's sent for a company of Mandalorians, she'll take it as proof that divided loyalties can't work."

"Exactly." Jag squeezed her hand. "I'm sorry, but this is bigger than the Jedi Order. I think even Master Skywalker would want you to keep quiet."

"He'd want me to take it to the Council and trust the Masters to do the right thing," Jaina replied drily.

Jag's grasp started to slacken, but Jaina did not allow him to withdraw his hand. It hurt her to know he thought she might betray him a second time, but even she had to admit that his lack of faith was justified. He had risked everything when he trusted her word during the Killik crisis, and that had *cost* him everything. Who was to blame, really, if he found it difficult to trust her now?

Jaina turned to face him. "But Uncle Luke *isn't* leading the Council anymore," she said. "And the way Kenth Hamner has been caving in to Daala, a few Mandalorians just might be enough to make him turn us *all* over to be frozen in carbonite."

"So you won't tell the Masters?"

"Of course not," Jaina said. "Even if telling them were the right thing to do, didn't I just promise that I wouldn't?"

Jag gave her one of his rare smiles. "Thanks. That means a lot to me."

"It *better*." Jaina leaned toward him. "Because I wouldn't do it for anyone else."

Before she could kiss him, Jag's head snapped around toward the front of the limousine, and he scowled out the windscreen.

"Blast it," he said. "Look who's coming."

Jaina saw two humans slipping through the gap between the GAS assault speeder and the end of the safety wall. The first person was a stocky woman in headsets and a HoloNet news tunic, her attention focused on the joystick hand unit she was using to steer a heavy holo-cam floating ahead of her. The second human was a slender man in a yellow tabard, his tawny hair cut in a fashionable short-bang chop. Javis Tyrr.

"Why am I not surprised?" Jaina growled.

Tyrr's cam operator instantly turned to capture the still-raging argument between Baxton and the GAS officer. Meanwhile, Tyrr drew a recording rod from inside his tabard and continued down the lane toward Jag's limousine.

"Time to go," Jag said, opening his door. "I'll take the wheel. You grab Baxton on the way past."

Before Jaina could acknowledge the order, Tyrr pointed the recording rod in their direction, and a barely audible click sounded behind the beverage locker across from her. Recalling the metallic rim she had noticed earlier, Jaina hurled herself out Jag's still-open door.

"Down!"

She hit him square in the flank, driving him into the duracrete wall with enough force to draw a startled *oomph!* before they both dropped to the permacrete.

To Jaina's surprise, that was *not* the last thing she ever heard. Instead, she heard Jag yelling condition codes at Baxton and asking *her* what was wrong. She heard a shocked silence from Baxton and the GAS lieu-tenant, who had stopped arguing and spun around to look at her and Jag stacked on the permacrete. And from the interior of the limousine, she heard the barely audible hum of a tiny repulsorlift engine.

Jaina looked toward the vehicle and saw a small, dome-topped cleaning droid gliding out the door through which she had just dived. Its photoreceptor lin-gered on her face, and suddenly she knew how Javis Tyrr had been acquiring his images from inside the Jedi Temple. She started to rise, and the cleaning droid quickly banked around the limousine's open door and started up the lane.

"Oh no you don't!"

As Jaina rose, she thrust a hand at the cleaning droid and used the Force to summon it back toward her. Tyrr cried out in astonishment and scurried down the lane, angrily thumbing his recording rod, as though that might give the droid's repulsorlift engines enough power to break free of Jaina's Force grasp.

By the time the droid floated into her hands, Tyrr was only a couple of paces away, his full lips twisted into a self-righteous sneer.

"You can't *do* that," he said, still pointing the recording rod at the droid. "Trying to hide the—"

"Jedi Solo can't do *what*, exactly?" Jag interrupted, stepping to her side. "Recover a cleaning droid that's obviously malfunctioning?"

"That's no ordinary cleaning droid," Tyrr shot back. "And you know it."

"Are you saying that it belongs to you?" Jaina asked. The droid was still trying to pull free of her grasp, so she flipped it over and hit the primary circuit breaker. "Because if it *is* your droid, I'd be very interested to know how it found its way into the Jedi Temple."

"As would a lot of people," Jag said. He gave his head a quick tip toward the hangar gate, then gently pushed Jaina toward the limousine. "I'm quite certain that private espionage is as illegal in the Galactic Alliance as it is in the Galactic Empire."

Taking Jag's hint, Jaina extended her Force awareness toward the gate and sensed several GAS troopers rushing up the lane toward them. She slipped back into the limousine just an instant before Captain Atar's voice called out from behind the vehicle.

"What's the problem here?" he demanded. "I hope the Jedi aren't trying to intimidate you, Tyrr."

"Not at all," Jag said, turning to face the captain and his men as they approached the limousine. "I believe the esteemed journalist Tyrr was just preparing to admit that he had placed a private surveillance device inside the Jedi Temple."

Atar's scowl deepened. "I'm sure a reporter of Javis Tyrr's reputation would never resort to anything illegal." The captain shifted his attention to Tyrr. "Isn't that right, Tyrr?"

Tyrr's face reddened, but he nodded. "Of course."

Jag's lips tightened into a grim smile. "My mistake, then." He raised a hand and summoned Baxton, then slipped into the limousine next to Jaina. "I'd appreciate it if you ordered your men not to open fire as we pass over, Captain. I'm overdue for an important briefing."

Atar's eyes grew stormy, but he leaned down to peer inside. "Flying over won't be necessary, sir. I'll order the speeder to move aside as soon as Jedi Solo steps out of the vehicle." His gaze dropped to the droid in her hands. "And she should bring the cleaning droid—we may be needing it as evidence."

Jaina unsnapped her lightsaber and leaned across to glare at Atar. "Forget it, Captain." There was no way she was surrendering the spy droid—not when it had a recording of Jag telling her what he had overheard in Daala's office. "We're in an Imperial diplomat's vehicle, and that makes this droid Imperial property."

Atar stared at the lightsaber hilt in Jaina's hand for a moment, then finally nodded. "All right, Jedi Solo. You win this one." He looked away and motioned the GAS speeder aside, then turned back to her. "But you won't be able to hide behind your boyfriend forever. Sooner or later, the Remnant is going to come all the way into the Alliance. And when it does, GAS will still be here, waiting for the next time you screw up."

Chapter Seven

THE ONLY THING MORE DESTRUCTIVE THAN AN ANGRY Ramoan, Leia decided, was a Ramoan having convulsions. At present, Bazel lay pinned between two crushed airspeeders, shuddering, flailing, and—thankfully—trapped in one place. But half the vehicles in the hangar had already suffered crumpled hoods or smashed fenders, and the cargo lifter's doors had been too badly dented to open. Perhaps most troubling of all, the walls and support columns were spattered with a yellow froth so foul that every breath came with a gag.

"I shouldn't have hit him with a second dart," said Melari Ruxon, the Duros apprentice to whom Han had entrusted the dart pistol earlier. "But he kept trying to get up after the first one, and Captain Solo said—"

"You did nothing wrong, Apprentice Ruxon," Leia assured her. "Jedi Warv is a capable Knight. As long as he was even slightly awake, he would have been using the Force to counteract the tranquilizer."

"You didn't have a choice, kid," Han agreed. "I'd have done the same thing."

A note of relief came to Melari's face. "Really?"

"Absolutely," Leia said. "You know how this illness confuses the mind. How would you have felt if you *hadn't* fired the second dart, and he had recovered and fled back out into the plaza?"

"They're right, Mel, you did him a favor," said

Melari's Jenet partner, Reeqo. He laid a copper-furred hand on her shoulder. "If I go mookey, I don't want to end up iced and hanging in some GAS blockhouse for the rest of eternity. I'd rather be in a cage down below."

If I go.

Leia had not realized the situation had deteriorated far enough to make young Jedi worry about whether they would be among the next to lose their minds, but of course it had. Until the nature of the illness was understood, the only sure thing anyone knew was that being young and Force-sensitive put you at risk. No wonder they were frightened.

"Listen to me, both of you." Leia stepped around so that she could look each apprentice in the eye. "Things may look bad right now, but Master Cilghal *will* figure this out. And when she does, Barv will definitely thank you for keeping him out of carbonite."

The two apprentices exchanged glances, then Melari asked, "You're sure?"

"Trust me, she's sure," Han said. "I've been frozen in carbonite, and anything is better than that."

Reeqo nodded, seeming to take the Solos at their word. But Melari gazed back toward the mountain of mottled jade flesh still shuddering between the two airspeeders.

"So *anything* is better than carbonite?" she asked. "Even dying?"

Han shot Leia a questioning glance. When she nodded for him to tell them the truth, he laid a hand on the shoulder of each apprentice.

"If you're never gonna get out, then yeah, *anything* is better," he said. "Even dying. But Barv here isn't going to die—not today."

The feeling that came to their Force-auras was not exactly relief, but at least they seemed to understand. Leia confirmed their emotions through the Force and waved the two apprentices back toward the hangar entrance, where an unconscious Yaqeel Saav'etu remained slumped against the back of the guard booth. Her hands were affixed to the collision bar above her head by a pair of plastifiber wrist restraints.

"Let's have the patients ready to transport when Master Cilghal arrives," she said. "You two see to Jedi Saav'etu. Han and I will—"

Leia was interrupted by the *ding-swoosh* of an arriving turbolift. Expecting to see Cilghal and Tekli, she turned toward the station. Instead Kenth Hamner stepped into the hangar. His dignified features were taut with alarm, and as he marched through the carnage toward the Solos, his reaction steadily changed to outrage.

Leia grabbed Han's tunic sleeve and quickly led him toward Bazel Warv's still-shuddering form. Judging by Kenth's expression, this was not going to be a conversation they wanted apprentices to overhear.

Kenth intercepted them near the Ramoan's giant round feet, then demanded, "What happened?"

"Somatoll reaction," Han replied. Ready to spring away if Bazel lashed out, he squatted down and tried to find the pulse in the green guy's big ankle. "Seems it affects Ramoans a little differently than most other species. Who knew?"

"I'm not asking about Jedi *Warv*," Kenth snapped. "What happened with the GAS squad? They're threatening to blast open the outer gate if we don't surrender their prisoner. Don't tell me you two actually removed Bazel from GAS custody?"

" 'Course not," Han said, glancing up at Kenth. "GAS never even *had* custody."

Kenth barely spared Han a glance before turning to glare at Leia. "Why don't *you* fill me in, Jedi Solo?"

"I'd be happy to." Leia was careful to keep her voice warm and relaxed. It was hardly like Kenth to be sharp and uncivil, and she assumed that something must be very wrong to drive him to such behavior. "Han's right. Captain Atar never had custody of either patient. We were able to subdue both of them ourselves—"

"Hold on," Kenth said, raising a hand to stop her. "We're losing them two at a time now?"

"I'm afraid so," Leia said. She turned and pointed toward the guard booth, where Reeqo and Melari were carefully removing the restraints from Yaqeel's wrists. "Jedi Saav'etu went first, and Bazel followed her."

Kenth cursed loudly. "So it *is* contagious."

"We don't know that," Leia said. "If it's something dormant, it could have been triggered because they both encountered the same stimulus."

Kenth's glare returned. "I'm beginning to see where your daughter gets her stubborn streak, Jedi Solo," he said. "I'd appreciate it if you wouldn't try to play me."

"Hey, hold on a minute there," Han said, rising. "Everyone knows that Jaina gets her stubborn streak from *me*."

Kenth shot him a look that could have frozen a wampa. "You're not helping matters, Captain Solo. Quite the opposite."

Han's eyes grew hard, and Leia knew she was perilously close to having *two* angry men on her hands. She slipped over to Han's side and touched his arm, then nodded toward the control booth.

"Han, why don't you see if you can find a stool or something to stick between Bazel's teeth?" she asked. "With those tusks of his, he's got to be chewing the inside of his mouth to ribbons."

Han glanced at her briefly, then shifted his stare back to Kenth. "Okay," he said. "But if this guy keeps talking to you like you're some sort of—"

"Han!" Leia turned him toward the control booth. "Please go. I have this."

Han reluctantly allowed her to push him away, but continued to scowl back over his shoulder. Leia returned her attention to Kenth and waited in silence. She had learned a long time ago never to apologize for Han . . . especially when he wasn't the one at fault. Besides, maybe a few sharp words from a hothead smuggler were just what Kenth needed to help him regain control of his temper.

But it wasn't to be so. When Kenth finally spoke, his voice was as sharp as ever. "Jedi Solo, are you *trying* to get the Order disbanded?"

Leia cocked her brow, then calmly said, "I'm sure you know better than that, Master Hamner."

"Then why the *kriff* would you ignore a GAS arrest warrant, and do it on a live holocam?" He was nearly shouting. "Daala herself has been on the comm telling me that she can't allow this kind of public defiance, and I'm starting to agree with her. You know how bad our image is right now, and live feeds of you and Han ignoring a valid warrant only add to our problems."

Leia remained silent until she was certain he had finished, then allowed a little durasteel to come to her own voice. "And what would you have preferred we do? Serve Bazel and Yaqeel up to be frozen in carbonite?"

"Yes, if that's what the law demands," Kenth retorted. "The Jedi aren't going to survive, not if we keep trying to hold ourselves above the government—and above the *beings*—that we claim to serve."

Leia shook her head sadly, wondering how such a principled man could be so blind to what was right. "Kenth, I know you're in a tough spot, but think about what you're saying. Law *isn't* justice. We can't start turning young Jedi Knights over to Daala just because they've fallen ill—especially not when her solution is to freeze them in carbonite."

The flash of pain in Kenth's eyes suggested that Leia

had hit a nerve, but he was not ready to yield. "*That,* Jedi Solo, is not a Jedi Knight's decision to make." He pointed up the access tunnel, then said, "If we're lucky, Captain Atar and his squad are still—"

Leia was saved by the *ding-swoosh* of the arriving turbolift, and this time it *was* Master Cilghal and Tekli who stepped out. The Mon Calamari took one look at Bazel's shuddering form and gave a medication order to her assistant, then came over to stand with Leia and Kenth.

"I came as soon as I heard," she said to Leia. "*Both* of them?"

Leia took a calming breath, then nodded. "I'm afraid so."

Cilghal raised a finned hand. "No, don't be afraid," she said. "Now we have learned something."

"Learned *what*?" Han asked, returning with the stool Leia had requested. "You know what's wrong with them?"

"Not yet." Cilghal waved a hand vaguely toward Bazel, who already had Tekli's medication dart protruding from his throat. "But with Bazel and Yaqeel both ill, we can begin to draw some conclusions."

"Such as?" Kenth asked. While not sounding relieved, he at least sounded hopeful. "The Jedi could really use some good news about now."

"I said *begin,* Master Hamner." Cilghal turned to Han and Leia. "Captain Solo, if you'll assist Tekli with Yaqeel, Jedi Solo and I can handle Bazel."

Han looked to Kenth, indicating that the acting Grand Master had other ideas about how to handle the situation.

Cilghal rolled a huge eye toward Kenth. "Do you have an objection?"

"As a matter of fact, yes," Kenth said. "There's a GAS squad outside with a warrant for their arrest."

Cilghal dropped her gaze, and a sense of guilt began to fill the Force. "I see." She turned to Leia. "How many did they hurt?"

It was Han who answered. "*Hurt?* No one. We tranqed 'em right outside. GAS is only after them because the commotion got caught on holocam."

Cilghal's mouth fell open. "Then why would GAS want to arrest them?"

"Public endangerment," Leia supplied. "And even that is overstating it. We had them inside in two minutes."

Cilghal turned back to Kenth, her expression changing from guilty to confused to upset. "And you want to turn them over?"

"We were served a warrant, and we're required to submit to it," Kenth insisted. Judging by the color rising into his cheeks, Leia guessed that Daala had not bothered to tell him the charge when she commed to complain about the Solos' defiance. "But this might even work to our advantage. When the circumstances are reviewed in open court, I'm sure Nawara Ven can make the public see that the charges are completely unjustified."

"No," Cilghal said. "We will not allow Daala to freeze my patients in carbonite so you can try to score a public relations point."

Kenth's face grew stormy. "Master Cilghal, the decision isn't yours—"

"Nor is it yours alone. It is the Council's. And if you want to honor a frivolous warrant simply out of expediency, I will insist that you seek approval." Cilghal motioned the Solos toward the patients, then continued, "Until you have *that*, Master Hamner, I will be keeping the patients in the Asylum Block."

Not wanting to give Kenth a chance to countermand the order, Leia immediately pointed Han toward Yaqeel and turned to deal with Bazel herself. Tekli's medication dart had already put a stop to the convulsions, so she used the Force to lift the big Ramoan from between the wrecked speeders.

Leia had heard many times that "size matters not" when levitating an object, and perhaps that was true . . . for whoever had said it. But for her, it was all she could do to start Bazel floating toward the turbolift, and she was already beginning to tire when Han's voice cried out behind her.

"Hey, I think we just lost another two!"

Leia's concentration failed almost instantly, and Bazel hit the floor so hard it shook. Hoping a few more bruises would not make a difference to him, she spun toward the control booth and saw Han standing over Yaqeel's unconscious form.

The Bothan was still slumped against the control booth, but her hands had been resecured to the collision bar by a new pair of wrist restraints. To Leia's dismay, the only signs of Reeqo and Melari were a pair of gray apprentice robes lying on the floor next to Yaqeel, each neatly folded with a lightsaber on top.

"What happened?" Kenth asked, stepping over to the booth. To Leia's relief—and maybe her surprise—there was no accusation or anger in his voice, only weariness and sorrow. "Did you see?"

Han shook his head. "Sorry. I was busy watching the, uh, *discussion* over Barv." He gestured at the robes and lightsabers. "I didn't even notice Reeqo and Mel were gone until I saw this stuff."

"Well, they can't have made it far." Kenth pulled his comlink and started into the access tunnel. "Maybe we have time to stop them before they hurt someone."

"That isn't necessary, Master Hamner," Cilghal said. She extended a flipper-hand toward Kenth, using the Force to prevent him from breaking into a run. "Those two aren't a danger to anyone."

Kenth spun on her, frowning. "Cilghal, if you want to take the warrants to the full Council, fine. But we can't have any more crazy Jedi running loose on Coruscant."

"They're *not* crazy, even in the way you use the term, Master Hamner," Cilghal said. "At least, I'm ninety-eight percent sure they aren't."

Kenth's brow shot up. "Because?"

"Because they were never at Shelter," Tekli answered. "They're too young."

"And all the other patients *were*," Leia said, recalling their conversation when she and Han went to visit Seff Hellin. "Are you saying you've established a definite correlation?"

"A definite *statistical* correlation," Cilghal corrected. "Not cause-and-effect, but when we factor in Bazel and Yaqeel, the margin of error falls to less than two percent. Only Jedi who were hidden in the Maw during the war with the Yuuzhan Vong are in danger of falling ill."

Han's brow arched in alarm, and Leia knew what he was thinking even before he asked, "What if they weren't exactly *hiding*?"

Cilghal could only shrug. "I wish I could reassure you, Captain Solo, but the truth is we just don't know."

"Though, if it's something environmental, there's a good chance the risk would be related to length of exposure," Tekli added, glancing toward Leia. "And the fact that neither of the Masters Solusar has fallen ill may suggest that adults aren't as susceptible. You and Princess Leia are probably fine."

Han's expression remained anxious, and Leia knew he wasn't worrying about himself, or even about her. He was thinking about a certain red-haired little girl, wondering who would protect *her* if her grandparents suddenly set course for the nearest black hole.

"Han, relax," Leia said. "You'll be the first to know if I start feeling crazy."

An embarrassed smirk came to Han's face. "That's not much comfort, Princess," he said. "After hanging around with me all these years, you wouldn't feel the change."

"Oh, I'd feel it," Leia said, smiling. "Trust me."

"If you ask me, you've *both* been crazy for a long time," Kenth added, probably only half joking. "But I'm not sure I have faith in this new theory. If those apprentices didn't fall ill, why did they run off?"

Han glanced over at the folded robes and abandoned lightsabers, then frowned.

"If I had to guess," he said, "I'd say they quit."

Chapter Eight

IN SPACE AHEAD FLOATED A DISTANT CLUSTER OF FIERY whorls, each about the size of a finger ring and rapidly growing larger as the *Eternal Crusader* approached. With the edges of every whorl just touching the edges of those adjacent, the cluster was too uniformly dense to be natural. Yet with a diameter of more than a billion kilometers, it was too immense to be anything *but* natural. Around the middle of the strange formation, resembling a belt around a big belly, ran a line of larger, brighter whorls. In the middle of this belt, one pair hung close, connected by the distinctive curved accretion bars of a tight binary system.

The binary was the sole imperfection in the homogeneous formation. It had drifted out of place and seemed to be in danger of crashing into several of its neighbors. On the side opposite the impending collision, a small crescent of darkness had opened between it and the adjacent whorls, and through this crescent, burning deep inside a hollow shell of darkness, Vestara Khai could see the hot blue ember of a distant star.

Vestara's Master, Lady Olaris Rhea, pointed toward the dark crescent. "There."

A pale blond woman with pale blue eyes, Lady Rhea had a regal, lithe frame and an austere beauty as imposing as it was striking. Her manner tended to vacillate between self-assured and arrogant—not that she cared what Vestara or anyone else thought of her. She was a Sith Lord of Kesh, and it was others who needed to worry about what she thought of *them*.

"Do you see?" she demanded. "That must be where Ship went."

"Yes, Lady Rhea. I'll see if he's there now."

Vestara did not say she would *try* to locate Ship, nor did she ask if she should. Sith apprentices did not *try*, and they did not ask permission before acting. They were expected to know what their Masters required of them and then *do* it. If they failed in either regard, they suffered for it; if they failed too often, their suffering ended—permanently.

Vestara focused her attention on the dark crescent, then reached out in the Force and sensed a murky, tireless presence that she immediately recognized as Ship. He seemed surprised to feel her touch, yet this time he did not flinch or try to hide, as he had so many times before. He simply allowed her to maintain contact and feel his joy, as though he had passed beyond the Lost Tribe's reach and no longer feared being taken back to Kesh.

And perhaps that was so. Vestara felt another presence deep in the crevice beyond. Even more ancient and alien than Ship himself, this new presence was filled with the hunger and longing of the dark side, and powerful beyond comprehension. Though Ship had never actually *spoken* to her across such great distances, she could sense that he wanted her to understand his connection to this strange presence. Ship was a creature of service. When a being of strong will commanded him, obeying became his greatest joy, his *only* joy. Ship could no more disobey than Vestara could stop breathing.

Vestara understood. She had felt the ancient presence reach out to Kesh, the same as Ship had—the same as the entire Tribe had. But Ship should have waited for

Lord Vol to assign a pilot before leaving. The *Sith* had created Ship, and his duty was to the *Sith*. Therefore, Ship *would* return to the *Eternal Crusader* and accept Vestara as his pilot, and they would all proceed together.

Ship's amusement was unmistakable. He had a special relationship with Vestara. She had been the first Tyro he had found back on Kesh, and her presence had always burned more brightly for him than had others. But did she truly believe herself strong enough to command Ship *now*? Was she fool enough to think she could match wills with one as ancient and dark as the Maw itself?

Then Ship's presence was gone.

Vestara continued to stare out at the dark crescent, expelling her anger with a calming trick she had learned from her father: a condemning curse, followed by a promise to herself that she was not forgoing retribution, just giving it time to grow. By fleeing again, Ship was putting her in a delicate position with her Master, Lady Rhea—one dangerously close to failure.

Of course, part of Vestara's anger came from the knowledge that she had overreached her abilities. She had hoped to impress Lady Rhea and the other Sith by commanding Ship to return to the *Eternal Crusader*. But she had been mistaken to think she could match wills with the ancient presence that had reached out to them on Kesh—and Vestara did *not* allow herself to make mistakes. Mistakes got apprentices killed. Worse, they prevented Sith apprentices from advancing to Sith Sabers.

After a moment, Lady Rhea said, "Lost it again." It was a statement, not a question, and there was disappointment in her voice. "Ship continues to toy with you."

Vestara was quick to shake her head. She did not like

to disappoint her Master—especially when it was because she had made a mistake—and this time she saw no need.

"Ship is going . . . well, *inside*." She pointed toward the dark crescent. "Through there."

Lady Rhea raised a thin eyebrow. "You know this how?"

"I feel it," Vestara explained. "Whatever called Ship away from Kesh is hiding in there."

Lady Rhea narrowed her eyes and studied the crescent for a moment, then said, "Ship has been *allowing* you to find it."

"That's how it feels," Vestara confirmed. She would not have dared to contradict Lady Rhea even if it hadn't been so. "I see no other reason I'd be able to sense him when Lords and Masters cannot."

"As long as Vestara *is* sensing it."

The comment came from the opposite side of Lady Rhea, where Master Yuvar Xal was also standing at the command rail. With green, deep-set eyes and black hair hanging down to his collar, Xal's features were just a little bit too sharp to be considered truly handsome—a flaw that had no doubt contributed to his slow advancement on beauty-conscious Kesh.

"I find it, um, *interesting*," Xal continued, "that Ship chooses to reveal itself only through an apprentice."

Lady Rhea turned to glare at him. "Master Xal, are you suggesting that my apprentice has led us out here on a lark?"

"Not at all, Lady Rhea," Xal replied. "I'm concerned because she may have misconstrued what she's sensing in the Force."

Vestara glanced behind Lady Rhea and saw Xal's apprentice, Ahri Raas, looking in her direction. A Keshiri male, he was as gorgeous as most members of his species, with pale lavender skin, shoulder-length white hair, and large, expressive eyes—which he was now rolling to show his weary impatience.

Vestara shot him a half grin and nodded. Xal had been assigned to the *Eternal Crusader* as Lady Rhea's executive officer. In the way of the Tribe, that meant he had also become her primary rival for command of the vessel. Most likely, the conflict would be waged as it was now, on a level of constant innuendo and political maneuvering. But there was always the possibility it would come to violence, and that was something Vestara tried not to think about. If it did come to a ship-wide bloodletting, she and Ahri would be on opposite sides, and the last thing she wanted to contemplate was having to kill her best friend.

To Vestara's surprise, instead of continuing to engage Xal directly, Lady Rhea elected to do it through her. "What do *you* think, Vestara? Is it Ship we've been following, or some figment of your imagination?"

Taking her lead from Lady Rhea, Vestara leaned slightly forward and turned to lock gazes with Xal. It was a terrible affront for a mere apprentice to face a Master in such a manner. And that affront would suggest to the entire crew that Lady Rhea's power was so great that even her *charges* felt secure in challenging Xal.

"I know Ship's presence as well as anyone does," Vestara said. "And it *is* Ship I've been sensing."

Xal's eyes flashed emerald with rage, and the already quiet bridge fell absolutely still as shocked Sabers awaited his response. Had Lady Rhea not been standing there, Vestara was quite sure that response would have been a Force spike through her own heart. But Xal could not attack her in public without it being construed as an attack on Lady Rhea herself, and he could not yet have gathered the kind of support he would need for such a thing. The imperfections of his appearance simply did not permit him to work that fast.

The best response in such a situation would have been to demand that the apprentice's Master discipline her. But Xal was still trying to glare Vestara into an apology when Lady Rhea deprived him of the opportunity.

"I have every confidence in the acuity of your Force sense, Vestara," Lady Rhea said. "But I wonder if you've given any thought to *why* Ship keeps allowing us to find it?"

"I have," Vestara said, guessing what Lady Rhea was thinking by the way she had phrased the question. "But I don't believe Ship is leading us into a trap—at least not intentionally. I think he just wants us to understand why he left."

Lady Rhea paused and glanced over at Xal. "Master Xal, what is your opinion?"

"Who am I to question the word of *your* apprentice, Lady Rhea?" Xal's snide response was a not-so-subtle rejection of the graceful surrender Lady Rhea was offering him. "If the girl thinks she has a special link to Ship, and if *you're* willing to believe her, who am I to question your orders?"

"I see," Lady Rhea replied.

Xal had, in effect, told her that if she was wrong to trust Vestara, he intended to use her mistake to steal command of the *Eternal Crusader*. It was a terrible blunder. He was telegraphing his blow out of anger, and his poor judgment would count heavily against him in the crew's opinion. Now his only means to put himself back into a position to challenge Lady Rhea would be to kill Vestara in a way that couldn't be traced to him— and he was effectively declaring his intention to do exactly that.

Lady Rhea gave him a disappointed shake of her head, then said, "I'll tell you what *I* think." She was not even bothering to face Xal as she spoke, instead addressing herself directly to the bridge crew. "I think Ship is allowing only Vestara to find it because she is young. Someone older might have a stronger will—a will powerful enough to compel its return."

A murmur of agreement rustled over the bridge, and several crew members nodded openly. They were all Sith Sabers, mostly humans descended from the shipwrecked crew of the original *Omen*. But there was also a sizable number of lavender-skinned Keshiri who, like Vestara's friend Ahri, had risen from a disadvantaged social status to become full members of the Sith Tribe. Although there was no separate officers' caste aboard the *Crusader,* the three seats of authority on the bridge were all occupied by Keshiri Sabers, for—like all hierarchies in the Tribe—the ship's company was a strict meritocracy, with positions of responsibility awarded only according to ability.

"If Ship doesn't want to be forced to return," a melodious Keshiri voice asked, "why allow *anyone* to find it?"

Vestara's head snapped around.

"I mean, if it can hide from *you,*" Ahri continued, "it can hide from Vestara."

He shot her a frightened glance, and Vestara flashed him an apologetic smile. It wasn't Ahri challenging Lady Rhea, it was Xal, trying to use his apprentice to embarrass *her.* The difference was that Lady Rhea had the power to turn his ploy against him. If she decided to punish Ahri herself, Xal was not strong enough to protect his apprentice, and the rest of the crew would take that failure as a further sign of his weakness—which, of course, was the reason that Lady Rhea almost certainly *would* kill Ahri.

But Lady Rhea must have seen a trap that Vestara did not, because instead of punishing Ahri for daring to challenge her, she turned to smile at him.

"Very good, Apprentice Raas," she said.

Vestara winced for poor Ahri; now Xal would whip him for sure.

Lady Rhea continued, "I'm happy to see that *one* of you is thinking about something other than maneuvering me out of command."

"Uh, you are?" Ahri asked.

"Certainly. Tell me, why do *you* think Ship would go to such lengths to make sure we could follow it?" Lady Rhea shot a disparaging glance at Xal. "Why do you think it would have picked *that* place to let us find it again?"

Ahri swallowed, then said, "Because Vestara's wrong," he said. "It *is* leading us into a trap."

"Precisely," Lady Rhea replied. "And do you know *why*?"

Ahri fell into a thoughtful silence, obviously trying to puzzle out the same thing as Vestara. If Ship was what the records aboard the *Omen* indicated he was, he was a servant of the ancient Sith. Everything he had done since finding the Tribe—even the fact that he had researched the Battle of Kirrek and gone to the trouble of tracking them down—certainly supported that assertion. So why would Ship lead the *Eternal Crusader* into a trap? There simply *was* no good explanation.

Ahri reached the same conclusion a moment later. "I'm sorry, Lady Rhea." His voice quavered as though he expected to be beaten. "I have no idea."

"No?" An amused smile came to Lady Rhea's face. "Pity. I was hoping *someone* might."

A silence fell over the bridge as nervous Sith began to exchange glances, searching for someone who had the answer Lady Rhea sought.

Lady Rhea let the tension build a moment, then shook her head in despair. "*Laugh,* people," she ordered. "It's a *jest.*"

A burst of laughter, all the more powerful because of the tension it was releasing, rolled over the bridge. Lady Rhea waited for it to run its course, allowing it to purge all apprehension from the crew so it could function at optimum efficiency again, then finally raised her hand for silence.

"In all seriousness, I have no idea what Ship is doing here," she said. "But I *do* believe Vestara is right about it, and Lord Vol commanded us to return Ship to Kesh. So set battle stations and keep alert, everyone. We're going in."

The bridge bustled back to life, and the tiny crescent ahead quickly swelled to a giant, sickle-shaped abyss. As they drew closer, the blue ember inside brightened into a blue dot, and the dark presence that Vestara had sensed earlier grew steadily more distinct and more powerful. She wondered for a moment if that presence might be Ship toying with her, just pretending to be something else. Then she noticed the looks on the crew's faces and realized that if that were so, she was not the only one being toyed with. Some of her fellow Sith looked worried, some looked confused, and two Keshiri even looked enraptured. But no one showed any indication that they recognized the presence they were feeling.

Vestara glanced over and found Lady Rhea frowning in concentration. But her Master's gaze was not fixed on the dark crescent into which the *Crusader* was traveling. Instead Lady Rhea's eyes were focused on the two black holes revolving around each other in the binary system. Her expression was wary and alert, though not quite hostile, and Vestara could tell that her Master sensed something there—something she herself had not detected.

Vestara shifted her Force awareness toward the binary system and brushed a *third* presence. It was vast and cloudy, faintly dark and welcoming, but with a pair of bright seeds that felt almost threatening in their intensity. They seemed somehow more pure than the cloud in which they floated, knots of solidness adrift in an ocean of vapor.

Then the color drained from Lady Rhea's face, and she braced herself on the bridge rail, her knuckles whitening as she squeezed.

"Lady Rhea?" Vestara asked. "What is it?"

Lady Rhea continued to stare toward the binary system. "I'm not sure. It felt like . . ." She let her sentence trail off, then shook her head. "It's hard to say. I thought for a moment I recognized a presence."

"Recognized *what* presence, Lady Rhea?" Xal asked. "If Ahri is right about this being a trap—"

"It changes nothing," Lady Rhea interrupted. "We have our assignment."

"Only if we *know* Ship is in there," Xal reminded her. "Lord Vol said nothing about throwing our lives away in pursuit of phantoms."

The Force rippled with the crew's growing anxiety, and Vestara knew that Lady Rhea had made a rare mistake by admitting that Ship might be leading them into a trap. Everyone aboard could sense the strange presence waiting ahead, and she felt certain that a fair number of them had also sensed the smaller presence near the binary. A persuasive argument from Xal might be enough to make the crew doubt Lady Rhea's judgment. And when Sith began to doubt the judgment of a leader, it was seldom long before they took a new one.

Vestara knew Lady Rhea was strong enough to retain command until the *Crusader* was inside. But if they did not find Ship quickly, or ran into trouble before they did, Xal might well be in a strong position to challenge her authority. And if he won? There would be no doubts about Vestara's own fate.

She focused her attention on the growing abyss ahead. It was practically all she could see now, a vast smile hanging sideways in space, opening wide to swallow them down, with the tiny blue ball of a distant sun burning bright at the bottom of its belly. Vestara reached out to Ship, opening herself to the Force and begging him to answer her call, to reveal himself not just to her but to the rest of the crew as well.

Instead of Ship, Vestara felt a dark tentacle of need slithering into the void she had created, cold and lonely and hungry for her. It wanted to draw her close and keep her safe, to protect her from Xal and her jealous rivals back on Kesh, from the crewmembers she fought on pirate raids, and from the Jedi with whom the Tribe was preparing to do battle. It wanted her to come to it inside the abyss, to join it in its ancient hiding place, where it could keep her safe . . . forever.

Terrified and confused, Vestara tried to pull away, drawing in on herself and trying to return her focus to the bridge of the *Crusader*. It was like trying to pull away from her own intestines. The thing was rooted inside her now, pulling her toward it almost physically— no, not *almost*. She could feel it actually drawing her into the railing, using the Force to drag her deeper into the abyss.

Then a collective gasp went up from the rest of the crew, and Vestara knew they felt it, too.

Chapter Nine

"WHEN YOU SAID *BODIES, LOTS AND LOTS OF BODIES*,"
Luke complained through his helmet microphone, "I
sort of expected them to be *dead* bodies."

"Who knew?" Ben asked. "Do they look alive to
you? Do they *feel* alive?"

Luke had to admit they did not. He and Ben were
standing just inside the chamber they had seen from the
control room, held to the floor by the station's centrifugal force. But they were shining their helmet lamps
"up" into the chamber's weightless interior, where a
gently undulating sea of limbs and torsos was slowly
drifting past their heads.

The writhing light they had observed through the
control room viewport was still visible, though only as
an inconstant purple glow silhouetting the bodies above
their heads. Every few seconds, a hand or foot would
twitch, or a puff of breath vapor would rise from someone's mouth, providing subtle evidence of life. And that
was the *only* evidence. Even their Force presences
seemed almost nonexistent, so faint and dispersed that
they could not be separated from the diffuse aura that
permeated this whole part of the Maw.

"They don't feel like *anything*," Luke admitted. "At
least not anything I've felt in the Force before."

He hit a chin toggle inside his helmet, activating a
faceplate display that showed the environmental read-

ings in the chamber. Seeing nothing more troubling than a slightly elevated CO_2 reading and a chilly room temperature, he put his life support on standby and reopened his faceplate.

As the seal broke, the ammonia reek of unwashed bodies filled his nostrils. Because human noses were so poor at discerning distinct odors, he struggled to identify individual smells. The strongest was simply the result of too many unwashed bodies in a confined space. But there was also an undertone of decomposition, and—barely detectable—of desiccated flesh. Not everyone in the chamber was still alive.

Then the odors all combined into a single eye-watering stench, and Luke had to call on the Force to prevent his stomach from rebelling. After a few shallow breaths, he conquered his revulsion and began to feel the bite of cold air on his nose and cheeks. The temperature wasn't quite freezing, but it was cold enough to make him wonder whether someone—or something—was trying to limit the rate of decay in the chamber.

Ben's helmet hissed open, then Ben gasped, "Bloah! And I thought before that smells couldn't *get* any worse."

"Then you haven't spent enough time with Hutts," Luke observed. "We'll have to correct that."

Ben half suppressed a gag, then asked, "You'd do that to your own son?"

"Consider it continuing education," Luke said. "A Jedi Knight should be comfortable in any environment."

"I'll bet Yoda wasn't this cruel."

"Yoda lived in a swamp," Luke reminded his son. "He made me *eat* stuff that smelled worse than this."

"No way."

"Absolutely." Luke did his best Yoda imitation.

"Hmmm . . . slaur roe fresh from the swamp. Tickles the throat, it does, and the belly it fills."

A croaking noise came from inside Ben's helmet.

Luke chuckled. "Just breathe through your teeth," he said. "You'll get used to it."

Luke began to shine his headlamp on the beings floating nearby. They were dressed in light overalls or two-piece utilities, both of the type worn beneath vac suits, and their feet were either bare or covered in boots. Many were humans, but there were beings from most spacefaring species: Falleen, Twi'lek, Bothan, and dozens of others. They were universally gaunt and un-kempt, and those in older fashions appeared noticeably thinner and more slovenly than those wearing modern clothes.

When a headlamp illuminated their faces, they would usually shift their gazes or even move a hand to shield their eyes. But once in a while, especially when the individual was particularly emaciated or dressed in especially old fashions, the pupils would fail to con-tract, and there would be no reaction at all. Ben was shining his lamp on one such body, a half-mummified Bith male in a sleeveless Old Republic–era jumpsuit, when he finally let out a nervous groan.

"This is really starting to shiver me out."

"Me too." Luke reached in front of a young Wook-iee female and shone his headlamp on his hand, then watched in growing confusion as her eyes focused on it only briefly before turning inward again. "I think they're *meditating* to death."

"Yeah, that's pretty murk, all right," Ben said. "But take a look at *this*."

Luke turned to see a line of liquid beads floating in the beam of his son's headlamp, curving down out of the mass of bodies above. He had seen too many similar beads in too many space battles *not* to know what they were, and their bright crimson color suggested they had been shed fairly recently.

"Who's bleeding?" Luke asked.

Ben activated his wristlamp and turned to shine it behind them, following the crimson trail up into the tangle of floating bodies. Several beings had strings of red ovals on their clothes, but there were no rips or wounds visible, and all of the stains appeared too small to be the source of the heavy blood trail.

"Only one way to find out, I guess." Ben hitched a thumb toward the interior of the chamber. "Shall we?"

Ben's tone was casual, but there was an edge to his voice that suggested he did not relish approaching any closer to the purple mystery above. And Luke didn't blame him. The writhing radiance might be no more than a manifestation of harnessed gravitic energy, similar to the Glowpoint in the much larger Centerpoint Station. Or it might be a tangible embodiment of the Force, the source of the alien longing that had terrified Ben so much as a toddler. Whatever it was, Ben was ready to face it and stare down his old fears, and Luke had never been prouder of him.

"Yeah, I think we'd better," Luke said. "Somebody up there must be hurt. Why don't you take the lead?"

Ben nodded, then sprang away. Although there was no artificial gravity to draw him back down, he had to use the Force to counter his angular momentum and avoid hitting anyone. Almost immediately, he let out a startled cry, and a frightened chill came to his Force aura.

"Ben?" Luke called. "What's wrong?"

"Um, nothing," Ben assured him. "Just surprised. I think my old friend found me."

Luke frowned. "*That* old friend?"

"Well, it sure isn't Tahiri," Ben replied. "But don't worry. I can handle it."

"You're sure?"

"We'll see." Ben paused between a pair of floating bodies, now about three meters above and three meters behind Luke. "You coming?"

"Right behind you."

Luke sprang off the floor, then reached out in the Force to counter his angular momentum. As soon as he began to pull himself toward the far side of the chamber, a cold tentacle of longing rose up inside him, urging him to come closer, to surrender to . . . *what*? Luke had no idea, only that its presence felt ancient and powerful and somehow familiar, that it seemed to recognize him and care for him and yearn for his eternal companionship.

"*Oh,*" Luke said. He bounced off a warm body, then used the Force to pull himself after his son. "That's kind of . . . unsettling."

"I guess you could call it that," Ben said. "I'd just say scary."

"Yeah," Luke agreed. "That, too."

He reached Ben's side, and together they continued to follow the blood trail deeper into the chamber. As they drew nearer to the center, they began to see tendrils of purple light sliding down between the floating figures. Sometimes it was actually shining *through* the bodies. But the alien presence did not seem to be pulling them closer to the glow. Rather, it appeared to be all around them, enfolding them and holding them within itself.

Finally, they entered an area where there was no clear blood trail, just a lot of beings flecked head-to-toe with crimson stains. One of them was a Duros with a steady trickle of blood bubbling out of a nasty compound fracture of the thigh. Judging by the color of the bone end and the surrounding flesh, the injury was fairly recent. The Duros had lost so much blood that his noseless face had paled from blue to almost white, and his large red eyes had gone pink with shock. But if any other beings in the vicinity had noticed their companion's trouble, they had not bothered to rouse themselves from their meditations. Even more shocking, at least to Luke's mind, was the standard-issue Jedi flight suit in which the victim was dressed, and a faint flatness of the cheeks that Luke thought he recognized from the reports on a certain missing Jedi.

"Ben, does that look like Qwallo Mode?"

"Yeah," Ben said. "Besides, a Duros in a Jedi flight suit can't be anyone else. My only question is what's he doing here?"

"Good question. Maybe *he* can answer." Luke opened one of the thigh pockets on his pressure suit and removed his medpac. "If we can save him, that is."

He pulled out a pair of laser scissors and cut away the jumpsuit leg. Ben strapped a pressure kit around the injured thigh, but he had barely begun to inflate the cuff before the patient snapped his head around to look at them. Luke laid a gentle hand on the Duros's shoulder.

"It's okay, Qwallo. You'll be fine as soon as we stop the bleeding." Luke wasn't actually sure of that, because Mode—assuming this *was* Qwallo Mode—had already lost a lot of blood. But one of the first things a person learned in emergency medical training was to keep the patient calm. "Do you recognize me?"

Mode's eyes swung toward Luke, then grew wide and panicked. He began to flail his arms and kick with his good leg, battering both Skywalkers.

"Blast!" Ben said, struggling to inflate the pressure cuff. "Do you think he's got it?"

"Maybe." Luke did not need to ask what *it* was. Before entering the Maw, they had received a message from Cilghal describing what had happened to Natua Wan at the pet expo, and both Skywalkers realized that her illness meant that the Jedi had no idea how wide-spread the psychosis might be. "I guess that's as likely an explanation for his disappearance as any."

Luke slipped around and began to restrain Mode's arms, then started to project soothing feelings through the Force. Immediately the tentacle inside him began to grow stronger and more distinct, filling him with a cold yearning that—alien as it was—reminded him all too much of the lonely ache that he had been living with since Mara's death.

Mode twisted at the hip, bringing up a knee that Ben barely caught on a forearm.

"Stang!" Ben said. "Sedatives?"

"Rather not," Luke replied. "With as much blood as he's lost, we might kill him."

"Then perhaps you should let him alone," said a deep voice behind them. "You seem to be doing more harm than good, yes?"

Luke glanced back to find the flat-nosed face of an ancient Gotal hanging upside down in the purple light. With large patches of skin flaking off the tall sensory horns atop his head and broad features so emaciated they seemed all brow and teeth, he was obviously not far from death himself. He was also wearing the thread-bare remnants of a sleeveless, tabard-style Jedi robe dating from nearly a decade before Palpatine.

Behind the Gotal floated several more beings in various stages of starvation. There was an age-yellowed Givin who, with his exterior shell of bones, looked like the walking skeleton he was. There was a skinny Or-tolan with an atrophied trunk and a body so thin it seemed nothing more than a leathery bag of wrinkles. There were even a pair of yellow-haired humans, a gaunt male and cadaverous female in green-striped jumpsuits that had been all the rage before the recent civil war.

Luke saw nothing to suggest that they—or anyone else in the immediate vicinity—were affiliated with the Jedi Order, and he decided the presence of two Jedi from two different eras was probably little more than coincidence. He signaled Ben to keep working, then continued to hold Mode's arms as he looked back to the Gotal.

"The greatest harm lies in doing nothing, Jedi . . ." Luke let the sentence trail off, reaching for the Gotal's name. When none came—and the Gotal didn't volunteer one—he shrugged and finished, "We're trying to save this Duros's life."

"There is no life," said the Gotal. "There is only the Force."

"That's not right," Luke said, frowning. The Gotal was misquoting one of the most important tenets of the Jedi Code—one that lay at the heart of the Jedi's willingness to sacrifice themselves for the good of others: *There is no death, there is the Force.* "If you're a Jedi, you know that."

"I once believed I was a Jedi." The Gotal's gaze slid away from Luke's. Whether he was embarrassed or simply recalling another time was impossible to say. "I called myself Seek Ryontarr."

"I've seen that name in the Jedi Holocron," Luke said, using the Force to bolster his memory. "You vanished on a mission to rescue the Nath Goordian heirs."

Ryontarr's gaze swung back to Luke. "Not *vanished.* I found them in a habitat near here," he said. "I disabled their abductors and rescued the heirs."

"There's no record of their return to Nath Goordi," Luke pointed out. "And if they *had* been returned, I doubt there would have been a war of succession."

An enigmatic smile came to Ryontarr's emaciated face. "There are many kinds of rescue."

A raspy *pop* sounded behind Luke, and Mode began to wail in pain. Luke looked back to see Ben straddling the patient's injured leg, still holding it by a bent knee and pulling as he worked to set the broken femur. Although Ben was clearly using the Force to hold the hips and upper body still, Mode's free leg was flailing about wildly as he tried to kick away his caregiver.

Luke reached out with the Force to immobilize the thrashing leg. He half expected Ryontarr or one of the other spectators to attack while his attention was diverted, but the group seemed content to wait and watch. Ben quickly finished setting the leg—at least as well as was possible under the circumstances—and Mode's wail faded to a moan.

After a moment, Mode gasped, "Please . . . stop. I was only trying . . . trying to help you, Master Skywalker."

Luke raised his brow. "You recognize us, Qwallo?"

"Of course . . . I know you," Mode said. "I'm *seeing* you."

The emphasis on the word *seeing* suggested that Mode meant something more by it, but Luke was more interested in what the Duros *hadn't* said. "You don't think we're impostors?"

Qwallo shook his head. "Not possible," he said. "I know that now."

"Then why did you fire on the *Shadow*?" Ben demanded. "You *are* the one who did that, aren't you?"

"Of course he is," Ryontarr said, peering at Ben over Luke's shoulder. "Don't you recognize him?"

"Yeah . . . but *how*?" Ben asked. "I mean, he wasn't even wearing a vac suit. And how'd he get *here*?"

"You'll understand soon enough, young Jedi Knight," Ryontarr said. He looked back to Luke. "You'll understand *everything*, if you'll just leave poor Qwallo be. Whether you realize it or not, you're doing him nothing but harm."

"He's lost a lot of blood," Luke said. "And we're *not* going to leave him to die."

"No?" Ryontarr shook his head. "I wish you would reconsider. You have no idea—"

The screech of a discharging blaster sounded somewhere above, and the smell of scorched flesh began to waft down through the tangle of floating bodies.

Ryontarr sighed, expelling a breath so stale it might have been in his lungs for a decade, then asked, "Do you think you can stop us all from dying?"

Another blaster screeched, this time close enough that Luke glimpsed a brief flash as its bolt streaked from the weapon's barrel into the head of the person firing it. There was a brief grunt of pain, and the acrid odor of scorched flesh grew stronger.

"Uh, Dad." Ben glanced over his shoulder, toward where the second blaster had discharged. "Maybe we should hear Jedi Ryontarr out on this."

"Don't call him a *Jedi*." Luke exhaled through clenched teeth, then glared at the Gotal in disgust. "I can't believe you were *ever* a Jedi."

Ryontarr shrugged. "Once, I was also young and a slave to the beliefs of others."

"But these deaths aren't *Seek's* doing," said one of Ryontarr's companions, the emaciated Ortolan. His nasal voice was raspy and hard to understand, for his trunk was so weak from disuse that it could not uncoil, merely loosen. "They're *yours*."

Still holding Qwallo by the shoulders, Luke continued to glare at Ryontarr. "I'm not the one ordering them to blast themselves."

"You assume I am in charge because of what I once was." Ryontarr spread his arms, as though inviting Luke to examine him in the Force. "But *you* are the one who is acting without understanding."

"You see, it is nothing to die beyond shadows." This time, it was the yellow-haired woman who spoke. Her voice was warm and patient, as though she were a mother correcting a child. "But to live trapped in a body, that is . . . *anguish*."

"Wait a minute." Ben was still floating in front of Mode, holding the injured leg. "You're saying people are killing themselves because they don't want us to interrupt their *meditations*?"

"Mind Walking is not meditation, but yes," said the yellow-haired man. His voice was close enough to the woman's to suggest they were siblings. "Life is only a dream, our bodies mere phantasms of a long and restless sleep. When you keep us bound to our bodies, you interfere with our awakening."

"It's not our intent to interfere with your . . . awakening," Luke said. He wasn't sure he understood—or *believed*—everything Ryontarr and the others were telling him. But at least Qwallo's wish to be left alone was starting to make sense. "There's no reason for anyone else to blast themselves."

"Then you'll leave Qwallo to return beyond shadows?" asked Ryontarr. "If his body dies with him in it, his return will be very difficult."

Luke looked down at Mode. The last thing he wanted was to leave the Duros to die, but Mode had already made it clear that he did not want their help. Besides, Ryontarr was right about one thing—unless he wanted the place filled with dead bodies, Luke had no choice except to agree.

"If that's what Qwallo wishes, then yes." Luke turned toward Mode. "We'll let you return beyond shadows. But first, I would like to ask you something."

Mode nodded. ". . . Hurry."

"What happened when you disappeared?" Luke asked. "Why didn't you complete your mission?"

"I became . . ." Mode shook his head sadly. "*Confused*."

Luke and Ben exchanged glances, and then Luke

asked, "You believed you were surrounded by impostors, didn't you?"

Mode's eyes grew wide. "How did you know?"

"It's been happening to some other Jedi Knights," Luke said.

"Then you have come to . . . the right place," Mode said. "All will grow clear here."

"I'm glad to hear that, Qwallo." Luke hazarded a glance around, half expecting Ryontarr to try to hush the Duros before he revealed some mysterious secret. When the Gotal and his companions seemed content to let the conversation continue, Luke asked, "And you no longer think we're impostors?"

Mode shook his head. "No, I know better now."

"How?" Ben asked, not bothering to hide his excitement. If they could figure out what had cured Mode, then they might have something helpful to tell Cilghal when they left the Maw. "What happened?"

Mode curled himself into the weightless equivalent of a seated position, so that he was facing Ben. "I went beyond shadows, and I saw the truth. You can't be impostors . . . because you're not real." He took Ben's hands. "Only the Force is real . . . and it's beautiful, Ben. So, so beautiful."

To his credit, Ben managed to avoid jerking his hands away in horror. But his jaw dropped and his brows arched, and even a half-dead Duros could read the dismay in his eyes.

Mode pulled his hands free of Ben's, and his tone grew harsh. "You'll see, Ben," he said. "Now that you're here, you will *have* to see."

Mode reached out in the Force and tried to pull himself away, but Luke was still holding his shoulders.

"One more question," Luke said, refusing to release the still-pulling Duros. "Why did you fire on us?"

Mode frowned over his shoulder at Luke. "I told you . . . to help you."

"With a *missile*?" Ben demanded. "Some help."

"It is," Ryontarr insisted. He floated down and gently began to pry Luke's hands off Mode's shoulders. "We know how many attachments you have to the physical world, Master Skywalker. Qwallo was just trying to cut them, so they can't pull you back."

Luke looked down at Mode in astonishment. "You were trying to maroon us?"

"He was trying to free you," Ryontarr corrected. "It is those attachments that bind you to your life of dreams."

He motioned Luke and Ben to release Mode. When they complied, he turned and began to float away. Luke frowned and started to go after him, but the yellow-haired woman slipped over to block his path.

"It is your dreams that lead you astray, Master Skywalker," she said.

"Just as it was your nephew's dreams that led *him* astray," added her brother. "It was one of Jacen's dreams that convinced him he had to return to the unreal galaxy."

"Then Jacen *was* here?" Ben asked.

His excitement was sizzling through the Force like an electric current, and Luke could tell by the smug glimmer in the siblings' eyes that they had felt Ben's reaction—and that it was exactly the result they had hoped to achieve.

"We were told that Jacen came here," Luke said, nibbling at the bait. "That's one of the reasons we did, too."

"Even though you were warned away," said the Ortolan, "and told we drink minds."

"Something like that," Luke admitted. He sensed that the discussion had entered a new and more dangerous phase with Ryontarr's departure, but he could not figure out why—what it was the Mind Drinkers wanted from him and Ben. "But I'm curious. How do you know what we were told about you?"

The woman smiled. "Because the Aing-Tii fear the truth as much as they fear Those Who Dwell Beyond The Veil," she said. "And they told Jacen the same thing when *he* came to find the cold thing."

Luke and Ben exchanged puzzled glances, then Luke asked, "The *cold thing*?"

"That's what Jacen called it—the cold thing in the Force," the Ortolan said. "He said he sensed it when he was with the Aing-Tii."

Luke nodded. The term fit the disturbance in the Force that he and Ben had felt just before departing the Aing-Tii, and Tadar'Ro had told them that Jacen had left the Kathol Rift after sensing something in the Maw that wasn't right.

"Did he find it?" Ben pressed.

The woman smiled at him. "He found *us*, Ben."

"That doesn't answer my question."

"Only because you are afraid to see the answer." She turned away and began to drift through the bodies, her brother following close behind. "When you are no longer afraid, you will have your answer."

Ben scowled and started after her, but Luke put out a hand. He wasn't ready to take the Mind Drinkers' bait yet—not until he knew why they were dangling it.

"My nephew *didn't* find the cold thing," Luke surmised. "Or it wouldn't have let him leave."

The woman stopped and smiled back over her shoulder. "Very good, Master Skywalker. He saw something else—something dark coming that he believed only *he* could stop."

Recalling the visions he had experienced in the opening days of the last civil war, Luke started to feel sick and sour inside. In his dreams, he had seen a mysterious dark man with a shrouded face—a face that had remained shrouded until Jacen killed Mara and *became* the dark man, the Sith Lord Darth Caedus.

And *this* was where it had begun, where Jacen had taken that first tentative step into the shadows.

Luke shook his head, silently raging at the tragedy, wondering how he had missed the hubris that had led Jacen to such a mistake—how he could have allowed a young man, a victim of Yuuzhan Vong torture and Sith brainwashing, to feel that the weight of the galaxy rested on his shoulders alone.

"I should never have let him go." Luke was speaking more to himself than the Mind Drinkers or Ben, wishing he had been wise enough to insist that Jacen stay with his family and friends after the war—to understand that no one who had suffered as his nephew had should be allowed to wander the galaxy alone. "He became the darkness he feared."

"*Jacen,* Master Skywalker?" The woman and her brother floated back toward him, their faces looking genuinely distressed—and disbelieving. "You think *Jacen* became the darkness?"

Luke nodded, confused at their confusion. "This happened before Qwallo arrived, so I assumed you would know: Jacen became Darth Caedus."

The two siblings looked at each other and nodded, then the brother said, "We've *heard* that—but it is not so. It's just part of the dream you mistake for truth."

"Jacen couldn't have *become* the darkness," the woman added. "His motives were pure. He could no more slip into darkness than a star could."

Luke shook his head sadly. "I wish that were so," he said. "But—"

"It *is* so," the Ortolan insisted. "If you won't take our word for it, come see for yourself."

"How?" Ben asked. It was clear by his scowl that Ben knew as well as Luke did what the Mind Drinkers were suggesting—and that he found it equally suspicious. "Jacen's been dead for two years."

"There is no death." It was the Givin who said this, speaking for the first time in a dry, gravelly voice. The living skeleton drifted around to face them, positioning his bony frame at Luke's shoulder. "There is no life; there is only the Force."

Luke turned to meet the Givin's gaze. Looking into the dark recesses of his exoskull was like gazing into the empty sockets of a human skull.

"You're saying I can *meet* Jacen beyond shadows?"

"We are saying we can help you see what Jacen saw," the Givin rasped. "Then you will be able to look into his heart. Whether it will speak to you is not for us to decide."

"Of course," Luke said. "I understand."

He knew better than to think he might actually be able to talk to Jacen, and Luke wasn't sure he would want to if that *were* possible. But the Givin *was* promising to help him understand what had happened to Jacen—and wasn't that the whole purpose of the journey?

When Luke did not instantly refuse the offer, Ben's eyes grew wide. "Dad, you know they're leading you on. Jacen's dead, and nothing is going to change that."

"I know." As Luke spoke, the cold tentacle inside began to grow larger, sliding up a little higher, scratching at the lining of his stomach and esophagus as it sought to root. "But this may help me understand what happened to him."

"Then you'll be returning beyond shadows with us?" The woman smiled. "I'm sure you'll find it very . . . enlightening."

"*If* I decide to come along," Luke corrected. "First, I need to know what you want from me and Ben."

"*Want* from you, Master Skywalker?" asked the brother. "What makes you think we *want* anything?"

"How hard you're working to get it," Ben answered frankly. "You haven't exactly been subtle, the way you're dangling Jacen out there like bait."

"Is that how you see it?" The woman's smile vanished, and she turned to float away. "Then I suppose there's only one question remaining: can you resist?"

Her brother winked at Ben, then nodded to the Ortolan and turned to follow. The Givin remained where he was, floating beside the Skywalkers, patiently awaiting their decision.

"Well, whatever's going on here, it's happening beyond shadows." Luke met his son's eye. "I don't think we've got a choice, Ben."

Ben swallowed hard, but nodded. "Yeah—I just wish we knew what *beyond shadows* is." He eyed the emaciated bodies floating around them, then said, "Maybe we should eat something first."

"I appreciate that, Ben. But you know it's not *we*."

Ben lowered his brow. "Dad, I've got to face this, too. You can't protect me from it."

"I'm not protecting you, Ben—I'm giving you an order." Luke smiled, then added, "*Someone's* got to repair the *Shadow*."

Now Ben looked truly frightened. "*Alone?* That could take a week!"

"Let's hope not." Luke looked around the chamber and wrinkled his nose. "I don't think I want to be in here that long."

"That's for sure," Ben said. "We'll probably *never* get this stink out."

Luke chuckled. "I can see you've never been stuck in a Star Destroyer trash compactor." He floated closer to his son, then clapped both hands on Ben's shoulders. "Now listen—*don't* come after me. If something goes wrong, you get back to Coruscant and tell the Masters what we found here. Okay?"

Ben scowled. "What's going to go wrong?"

"Probably nothing." Luke glanced at the Givin, who was a little too quick to nod his reassurance. "But if something *does,* we don't want both of us wasting away here, and nobody knowing what we found. So that's an order."

"Okay." Ben nodded, but his gaze slid away. "I've got it."

"You *promise*?" Luke pressed.

"Dad, I've *got* it." Ben's eyes came back to Luke's. "There's no sense both of us getting stuck here. I'm not an idiot. I can see that."

Luke held Ben's gaze for a moment, then finally nodded. "Good." He gave Ben a hug, then said, "I'll try to keep this short."

"You better," Ben said. "Just one question before you go."

"Sure."

Ben turned to the Givin. "How long do we have?"

The Givin tipped his head. *"Have?"*

"Before this place blows." Ben gestured vaguely toward the control room, where the alarms could still be faintly heard. "You *have* noticed what's going on in there, right?"

"Oh, the alarms," the Givin said. "I forget about them. They've been going off for a little more than two years now."

Ben shot Luke a worried look, then asked, "A little *more* than two years? Like twenty-seven months, maybe?"

"Yes, precisely." The Givin nodded. "Since shortly after Centerpoint Station was destroyed, if the dates we were given are correct."

Ben's face fell—almost as far as Luke's stomach sank.

"But you haven't noticed any problems?" Ben pressed. "You're not worried about anything?"

"What is there to worry about?" The Givin spread his bony hands. *"There is no life, there is no death . . ."*

"Yeah, I get it," Ben grumbled. *"There is only the Force."*

Chapter Ten

THE SECRET TO BEING A GREAT LEADER, DRIKL LECERSEN reflected, lay in the ability to recognize intelligence and ambition totally unencumbered by morality. And in the newsfop currently seated on the couch of his rented Coruscanti apartment, he had found *all* of those things in great quantity.

Javis Tyrr's giant bright smile was a trap waiting to snap, his silky warm voice a lie in the making, his polished good looks bait on a hook. Tyrr would sell his sister for a scoop, or vibroknife his best friend for an exclusive, and a private researcher had provided evidence of both. The man was, in short, the perfect tool for a cornered predator such as Lecersen, a wounded bloodfin reduced to attacking from the safety of the shadows.

Lecersen's reflections came to an abrupt end as the scene on the hotel suite vidwall drew to a close, with a durasteel gate dropping down to hide the departing forms of Han and Leia Solo. He watched the pair escape unscathed—as they always seemed to do, from nearly any mess they created—and a familiar burning began to build in his stomach.

How the Solos could unabashedly ignore the same law that they insisted everyone else obey was beyond him. The sheer gall of such behavior was enough to justify destroying them, as was the memory of Han Solo holding a blaster on him aboard the *Anakin Solo*. But that wasn't why Lecersen was doing this. This was about survival, about making certain that neither the Solos nor the Jedi were ever in a position to threaten him or the Moff Council again.

Because Jagged Fel wasn't going to be the Head of State of the Galactic Empire forever. He wasn't smart enough, mean enough, or ruthless enough. Sooner or later, he was going to make a mistake, and Lecersen was only one in a long line of Moffs who would be standing behind him when he did, holding a vibrodagger and ready to plunge it in.

The scene on the vidwall switched to Jaina Solo as she ducked into the crumpled Imperial limousine, ignoring the GAS captain's repeated orders to open the gate. Lecersen paused the video, then turned to his guest, who was sprawled on the couch sipping a glass of Ryborean gax that would have cost him a month's wages.

"Javis, my good man, I saw that live three hours ago," he said. "You did very well making the Solos and the Jedi look bad, without mentioning the fact that there were no grounds for an arrest. But I see no reason to watch it again. You can rest assured that I consider our relationship a valuable one."

"It's about to get a lot more valuable." Tyrr took a long sip of gax. "Keep going. I haven't put everything on the air yet."

Lecersen cocked a gray brow. "I wish you would've just said so. I really don't enjoy having my time wasted."

"*This* isn't a waste, I promise you." Tyrr tipped his glass up, gulping down a swallow of gax that was probably worth three hundred credits, then reached for the decanter on the serving cart. "You mind?"

"Not at all," Lecersen said, speaking between clenched teeth. "I'll break out the braboli next time."

Lecersen turned back to the vidwall and thumbed the remote, fast-forwarding through the confrontation between Fel's driver and the GAS lieutenant, then through Tyrr's own arrival. Finally, the scene switched to a view of Jaina Solo's face and not much else. After a moment of confusion, it grew apparent that the dark bands framing her image were a nerf-hide speeder seat on one side and a beverage cabinet on the other.

"Very impressive," Lecersen said. "You slipped a spy droid inside Head of State Fel's limousine."

"*Your* spy droid," Tyrr corrected. "This came from that little cleaning unit you set up for me."

Jaina's voice sounded from the vidwall speakers. Lecersen listened with only moderate interest as she thanked Fel for sheltering her and revealed that it had been her own con-artist father who had tricked the GAS commander into letting the Solos close the gate in his face. Then Fel mentioned Daala, and after a rather protracted negotiation over terms, the conversation grew very interesting very fast.

"I overheard something alarming when I was in Daala's office yesterday," Fel said. "She's thinking of hiring a company of Mandalorians."

Jaina's exclamation of *"Mandalorians?"* was only slightly more astonished than Lecersen's own. He turned to face a smirking Tyrr, listening in ever-growing disbelief as Jaina rattled off questions.

Then Jag confirmed, "She's been inquiring as to how many supercommandos it might take to handle the Jedi. Exactly what she's considering, I don't know. But it can't be good."

Lecersen paused the video, then asked, "Did I really just hear Fel reveal a Galactic Alliance secret to a *Jedi?*"

Tyrr nodded. "He makes her promise not to tell any-one," he said. "It's kind of touching, if you're into that doomed-love stuff."

"Doomed leaders are more my style," Lecersen replied.

He thumbed the remote again, then watched in growing delight as Fel reminded Jaina of her promise and made her swear not to reveal what she knew to the Jedi Council. The conversation ended an instant later, when Fel cursed and said, "Look who's coming."

The vidwall went dark, and Tyrr volunteered, "That's all from the spy droid, but there's another shot at the end of the chip that you need to see."

Lecersen left the chip running, but asked, "Why does the limousine shot end there? Who did they see com-ing?"

"Me," Tyrr said. "The situation was getting tricky, and I needed to get in and download from the spy droid."

"How tricky?" Lecersen asked, suddenly growing worried. It wouldn't be a *disaster* if the spy droid fell into Jedi hands—as long as the Jedi didn't realize Tyrr was the one who had slipped it into their Temple. "I warned you not to get caught with it. If the Jedi realize you have Imperial help, your usefulness to me will come to an abrupt end."

"Relax . . ." Tyrr took a long swallow from his gax, then said, "The spy droid never left the Temple—I took the download via comm wave. Now look at this. The beginning is exclusive—everyone else was busy filing their report when I caught this little gem."

The hangar-access tunnel appeared on the vidwall again. The GAS squad was still standing outside it, the troopers looking bored, and the captain shaking his head in frustration as someone yelled at him over his headset. Then, almost so fast that Lecersen did not see it, the gate suddenly rose about a meter and dropped back down again.

The startled troopers spun around and pointed their weapons at the ground, and the GAS captain snapped something into his headset microphone. A moment later two young Jedi, a Duros female and a Jenet male, rose into view and tried to walk through the middle of the squad. At least Lecersen *assumed* they were Jedi. They were dressed only in tunics and trousers, with no lightsabers hanging from their belts, so it was difficult to be certain.

"They were Jedi apprentices," Tyrr explained.

"Were?" Lecersen gasped. "You mean GAS—"

"No, they're okay," Tyrr said. "They resigned from the Order."

"Resigned?" Lecersen echoed. "Jedi can *do* that?"

Tyrr shrugged. "Who's going to stop them?"

Lecersen turned back to the vidwall, watching with interest as the GAS captain questioned the young pair. Although it was not possible to hear the conversation, it seemed apparent that the former Jedi were completely unintimidated. After a moment, the figures began to grow larger as Tyrr and his cam operator descended the lane.

"He ended up letting them go after we got there," Tyrr explained.

"Nothing to hold them on?" Lecersen hazarded.

"Better," Tyrr replied. "They claimed they resigned because they didn't want to be party to breaking the law."

Lecersen turned to face him. "Please tell me you got that."

"Sorry," Tyrr said. "But it was all efflux anyway. They just said that so GAS would be forced to let them go."

"And you know this *how*?"

Tyrr flashed a truly self-satisfied smirk. "It's in my interview," he said. "I've got them on full holo admitting they don't want to be Jedi anymore because they don't like the way Daala is taking charge of the Order."

Lecersen broke into a huge, spontaneous smile. "*Did you now?*" He stepped over to the serving tray and retrieved a glass for himself, then picked up the gax decanter and poured for them both. "Why don't we watch that interview, and then I'll tell you how I'm going to make you a very wealthy man."

Chapter Eleven

IN HER EIGHT-YEAR-OLD GRANDDAUGHTER'S LAP LAY A pale ball of fur named Anji, the last of the nexu cubs Leia had been forced to orphan at the pet expo three weeks earlier. The cub's four eyes gleamed in the flickering light of the vidwall as she kept watch over the Solos' modest apartment, but she held her spine quills flat against her fur and her toe claws retracted into her paws. Clearly the little creature felt content in her new home—even with dulled quills, clipped claws, and a dental implant that prevented her from biting hard enough to draw blood. The sight of the creature with Allana brought a lump to Leia's throat, for Jacen had been just as loving and gifted with animals, and it made her happy to know that some of the good in her son had survived in his daughter.

Anji raised her head and began to scent the air, prompting Allana to frown and turn toward Leia's end of the couch.

"Grandma, you can't be sad. It makes Anji think something's wrong."

A tear welled in Leia's eye, but she smiled and reached out to stroke the nexu's fur. "I'm not really sad, Allana." She opened her heart to the Force and let flow the joy that raising Allana brought her. "Sometimes I remember sad times, but having you here makes your grandfather and me very, very happy . . . and nothing will ever change that."

Allana considered this, her brow furrowing in the same two places Jacen's had at that age. Leia thought for a moment her granddaughter was going to ask whether Anji made her happy, too.

Instead, a cloud of fear came to Allana's gray eyes, and she asked, "Even if I get sick and go crazy like Barv did?"

Leia's heart suddenly felt like it was skipping. "Sweetheart, you're never going to get sick—not like Barv and Yaqeel. You've never even *seen* the Maw."

"But I'm in hiding, just like they were." As Allana spoke, she shook her head, her long black-dyed hair swinging back and forth. Anji's quills came up, and the cub began to look around for trouble. "And I *don't* want to live in carbonite. Not ever."

"Oh, Allana, you don't need to worry about that." *Now* Leia understood. She and Han had been on edge all afternoon because the Jedi Council was still trying to decide how to respond to the arrest warrants for Bazel and Yaqeel. "That's *not* going to happen to you."

"How do you know?" Allana demanded.

"Because you've got Anji." It was Han who said this, returning to the room with a tray of hot chocolates. "Kid, do you really think *she* would let anyone put you in carbonite?"

Allana's eyes brightened, and Leia immediately felt the girl's fear dissipating into the Force.

" 'Course not," Allana replied. She began to stroke Anji's head, and the little nexu settled back into her lap and began to growl in contentment. "She'd knock 'em flat if they even thought about it."

"I have no doubt." Leia flashed Han a smile that said *nice save.* As a grandfather, he seemed to have a Force-like sense of what Allana needed to hear to feel safe and loved, and—not surprisingly for Han Solo—it had nothing to do with logic. "That must be why your grandpa asked your mother to let you keep Anji."

Allana's eyes widened, and she turned to Han. "Forever?"

Han smiled and said, "Nothing's forever, kid. But for as long as Anji's happy and doesn't start eating our friends, yeah."

To Leia's surprise, Allana did not seem troubled by Han's blunt truthfulness. She merely hugged the little cub, then smiled up at Han.

"Thanks for convincing her, Grandpa."

"You're welcome, sweetie." Han put the tray on the beverage table in front of the couch, then sat down on Allana's opposite side. "Your mother used to ride rancors when she was a girl. It wasn't that hard to convince her you could handle a little thing like a two-hundred-kilo forest predator."

Allana's eyes got even bigger. "My mom rides *rancors*?"

"*Used* to ride rancors. That was a long time ago." Leia took a pair of mugs off the tray and passed one to Allana, then shot Han a warning scowl behind their granddaughter's back. "And the rancor was tame."

Allana's head swung around toward Leia. "They have *tame* rancors?" she gasped. "Can *I* ride one?"

"Sure thing, kid," Han said, smirking at how Leia's strategy had backfired. "The next time we're on Dathomir, we'll find you a nice big one."

"Really?" Allana continued to look at Leia. "You won't say no?"

Leia narrowed her eyes at Han. "Of course not, sweetheart. I promise." It was a pretty safe promise to make; Dathomir was one of the last places she expected to visit anytime soon. She picked up the vidwall remote and passed it to Allana. "In the meantime, grandpa's program has already started. Do you want to change the feed for him?"

"Yeah." Allana pointed the remote at the signal receiver. "*The Perre Needmo Newshour* is coming up!"

"Thanks, kid."

Han took his hot chocolate, then leaned back and wrapped his free arm around Allana's shoulders. The ritual had started one day when a bad dream interrupted her nap, and she had come and curled up beside Han. The next day she had appeared as soon as the program started. The day after that she had been waiting on the couch when the Solos entered the room. After that, Han had started to bring in three hot chocolates instead of one Gizer ale, and a tradition had been born. Leia sometimes worried about such a young mind being subjected to so much news, but one of the reasons she and Han liked *The Perre Needmo Newshour* was that at least a third of the items were *good* news. Besides—as Allana herself had pointed out—the Chume'da of the Hapan Consortium needed to know how the galaxy worked.

Allana thumbed the remote, and the cartoon spiders on the vidwall were replaced by the much-wrinkled image of Perre Needmo, an elderly news anchor. His Chevin face seemed to be all snout, save for his beady eyes, gray lips, and square yellow teeth. He had two tufts of unruly silver hair, one covering the crown of his narrow skull, the other hanging from his barely discernible chin.

As expected, the top story concerned the events in which the Solos had been involved that day. A small inset of the Jedi Temple hung in the bottom corner of the vidwall as Needmo's baritone voice rumbled from the ceiling speakers.

". . . legal crisis continued today when Jedi Knights

Saav'etu and Warv fell victim to paranoid delusions."
File images of Yaqeel and Bazel appeared in the corners
of the vidwall. "According to witnesses at the scene, the
pair began to behave oddly outside the Jedi Temple and
were quickly whisked inside by Han and Leia Solo. The
matter escalated shortly afterward, when a GAS special
tactics squad attempted to execute an arrest warrant for
the two Jedi Knights. The squad was left standing outside a hangar door. The Jedi Council is said to be considering at this hour whether the Order is obligated to
honor the warrant. An in-depth analysis of the precedents and constitutional implications follows this report."

The images on the vidwall were replaced by a close-
up of Jag's crumpled limousine speeding across Fellowship Plaza.

"No one was injured in the incident," Needmo continued, "but a diplomatic airspeeder was badly damaged when Jedi Warv was sedated and fell on the roof."

Leia glanced over and saw her granddaughter frowning in concern. "Allana, you know that Barv and Yaqeel
wouldn't want you to be worried about them, don't
you?"

Allana nodded. " 'Course I do. They're my friends."

When her frown did not disappear, Han asked,
"Why do I hear a big *but* coming?"

Allana rewarded him with a big smile. " 'Cause
you're pretty smart, Grandpa," she said. "Maybe Barv
doesn't *want* me to worry, but I can't help it. He and
Yaqeel are my friends."

"I worry, too, sweetie," Leia said. "But we have to
try not to. Master Cilghal is working very hard to help
Barv and all of the other sick Jedi Knights, and there's
no one more capable. She'll figure it out."

The reassurance did little to lift the cloud of doubt

from Allana's brow. "Not if the Jedi Council gives them to Chief Daala."

Leia started to say that the Masters would never do that, then stopped herself. Obviously, that wasn't true. The Council wouldn't still be in session if the Masters weren't at least *considering* turning Bazel and Yaqeel over to Daala, and Allana was smart enough to realize that.

Leia looked to Han and found no help there. Earlier, he had wanted to storm into the meeting so they could argue the case themselves. But Leia had insisted that their presence would only be an unwelcome distraction, that they had to trust Kenth and the other Masters to reach the correct decision on their own. Now, after five hours of suspense, she was beginning to wonder whether she had made the right call.

Leia would not have blamed Han if he had just left her hanging, watching with an amused smirk as she tried to come up with a reassuring answer for Allana. And maybe with something less important than their granddaughter, he would have. But there were a handful of things that Han Solo never gambled with, and Allana was one of them.

After a brief silence, he just squeezed Allana's shoulder and said, "Hey, even if the Jedi Council *does* give Barv to Chief Daala, it won't be forever. We'll do everything we can to get him back. Okay?"

"You promise?" Allana asked. "We'll work just as hard as Master Horn and his wife, right? Everyone knows they're not giving up until they get Valin and Jysella back."

"Yes, just as hard," Leia said. "We won't give up, either."

"And that's a promise, kid," Han added.

For Leia, any doubts about letting Allana see the

news vanished. She and Han were raising more than their granddaughter. They were raising the heir apparent to the Hapan throne, and Leia could imagine no better way to prepare Allana than to show her how Han and Leia Solo responded to adversity and uncertainty.

"And when your grandfather decides to do something," Leia added, "it's pretty hard to stop him."

"Yeah," Allana said, nodding. "He's as stubborn as a ronto in rut."

Han snorted, and Leia's brow shot up. "*Where* did you hear that?" she asked.

"I overheard Master Durron say it," Allana said, looking worried. "Why? What's a rut?"

"It's when you keep doing the same thing over and over just because you've gotten used to doing it that way," Han said. When Leia let her breath out in relief, he looked up and winked. "You thought Kyp meant something else?"

"Not at all," Leia said. "What else *could* he have meant?"

Allana frowned first at her, then at Han. "I'm not a baby, you guys. Mom taught me how to tell when someone's fibbing. You could have just said you'll tell me later."

Leia smiled. "And so we will."

"When you turn fifty," Han said.

Allana rolled her eyes and looked back to the vidwall, where the screen now showed an image of Melari Ruxon and Reeqo Swen walking away from the Temple without their robes or lightsabers.

"The crisis appears to be having an effect on Jedi morale as well," Needmo reported. "Shortly after the incident, two apprentices were seen departing the Temple. In a subsequent interview with journalist Javis Tyrr, the two admitted they had resigned from the Order.

Tonight we'll examine whether those resignations are meant as a warning to Chief Daala, and how a mass resignation of Jedi Knights might affect the stability of the government. We'll also discuss the Chief of State's surprising assertion that, like high-ranking military officers, Jedi remain subject to government authority even after they resign."

Melari and Reeqo were replaced by an image of Tahiri Veila in shock shackles and manacles, heavily guarded and being led into the Galactic Justice Center. Han came off the couch sputtering and spewing hot chocolate; Leia simply dropped hers.

"What the blazes?" Han shouted at the vidwall. "Now they've gone too far!"

"The former aide-de-camp to rogue-Jedi-turned-Sith-Lord Jacen Solo has been arrested on charges of atrocities against the galaxy," Needmo reported. "A former Jedi Knight herself, Tahiri Veila has been accused of several crimes during the recent civil war, including the assassination of the Imperial Remnant's popular head of state, Grand Admiral Gilad Pellaeon. We'll have a rundown of the complete list of the accusations against her in the analysis segment of our program."

"I can't take it." Han pointed at the remote in Allana's hands. "Turn it off, sweetheart."

Allana pointed the remote at the control receptor, and the vidwall paled back into a transparisteel viewport looking out over Fellowship Plaza toward the Galactic Justice Center. Han stood fuming for a moment, then turned to face Leia.

Before he could speak, Allana said, "I don't understand. Did someone *else* kill Admiral Pellaeon?"

"No, dear," Leia said. "There were a lot of witnesses, and they all say it was Tahiri."

"Then *shouldn't* she stand trial for it?"

Leia looked to Han for help, but he was still gnashing his teeth and shaking his head. She looked back to Allana.

"That's a complicated question," Leia said. "Unfortunately, lots of people are killed during wars. You know that."

Allana nodded. "By *soldiers*," she said. "On the other side. But I thought Tahiri was on my father's side."

"For much of the war, yes," Leia said. "But not at the end."

"But when Tahiri killed Admiral Pellaeon, she was on my father's side, wasn't she? And so was Admiral Pellaeon."

"Not exactly," Leia said. "Admiral Pellaeon wasn't really on anyone's side at that point."

"So he *wasn't* in the war?"

"Not officially," Leia said. "From what we've been able to learn, he was still thinking about which side he wanted to be on."

"Then Tahiri wasn't supposed to kill him," Allana insisted. "You're not supposed to hurt people who aren't part of the war."

Leia smiled and shook her head at her granddaughter's unrelenting logic. Allana was beginning to convince *her* that Tahiri should stand trial. Leia retrieved her dropped mug from the floor, then stalled for time by calling for C-3PO.

Finally, she said, "You're going to make a great Queen Mother someday, Allana. Those are very astute questions."

Allana beamed with pride, but said, "I recognize a Solo Slide when I see one, Grandma. Don't try to put me off with flattery."

This actually jolted Han out of his tantrum. "She's got you there, Grandma."

He looked around at the hot chocolate he had

sprayed all over the room's white décor, then shrugged, quaffed down what remained in his mug, and turned back to Allana.

"It's like this, kid. You know what spies are, right?"

Allana's eyes grew wary and frightened, and Anji rose in her lap and arched her back. Allana carefully set her hot chocolate on the table, then nodded.

"I know."

A pained look came to Han's face, but he pressed on. "I thought you probably did. Well, Tahiri was sort of spying for Jacen. And when she found out that Admiral Pellaeon didn't want to bring the Imperial Remnant into the war on his side, Jacen gave her an order."

"To assassinate Admiral Pellaeon?"

"That's right," Leia said, once again amazed—and grateful—for how well attuned Han seemed to be to their granddaughter. "Tahiri was following orders, just like any soldier."

Allana's frown remained. "Do soldiers *always* follow orders?"

"*Almost* always," Han said. "When they don't, they need a really good reason."

Allana considered this for a moment, then cocked her head up at him. "Then you must have had a *lot* of really good reasons when you were a soldier."

A laugh—a *guffaw,* actually—exploded from Leia's belly. She reached down and mussed her granddaughter's black-dyed hair.

"You don't know the half of it, sweetheart."

"Yeah, but I always got the job done," Han said. He winked at Allana. "Besides, nobody loves a yes-man."

Allana nodded seriously. "Mom says the same thing," she agreed. "I think that's why she's still so lonely. Hapan men are *all* yes-men."

Leia had a sudden, sad glimpse of her granddaughter's future: a smiling, redheaded woman standing beside a white throne, surrounded by beings of all species—Bothans and Hutts, Ishi Tib and Mon Calamari, even humans and Squibs—but somehow still alone. There was no man standing *with* her, no one like Han to whom she could turn for comfort or support. Allana Solo was going to live in a time of unprecedented peace and harmony, a time of prosperity for all the species of the Galactic Alliance. But *she* would be the one who kept it, the one to whom the rest of the galaxy turned when that peace was threatened.

That was the destiny for which the Solos were preparing her. Leia knew from their brief visits to Tenel Ka how lonely such an existence could be, how wearying and frightening it was every day. What Leia did *not* know was whether she had the courage to condemn Allana to that destiny, to doom her to a life in which her word steered the fates of worlds.

". . . that right, *Leia*?"

Startled from her reverie, Leia forced a smile and nodded to Han. "Umm . . . if you say so, dear."

Han frowned, puzzled and irritated. "I sure do," he said. "We're talking about her grandfather, after all."

"Right. Prince Isolder was a good man," Leia said. "*And* independent."

Han shook his head in exasperation and started to chastise Leia for not paying attention, but Allana cut him off.

"It's okay, Grandpa. You're not always listening to Grandma, either."

Han's expression changed from irritation to guilt, and Leia patted Allana's back.

"You're quite the peacemaker, aren't you?" she asked. "Don't ever lose that, okay?"

"I won't, Grandma," Allana said. "But what were you thinking about just then? You felt so sad."

Leia hesitated, dreading the prospect of trying to

keep her vision hidden from Allana. Fortunately she was spared the necessity by C-3PO's timely arrival.

"Please excuse the interruption, but—" C-3PO stopped three steps into the room and ran his photoreceptors over the hot chocolate sprayed over the couch, the beverage table, and the floor. "Oh, dear. I see Mistress Allana spilled her hot chocolate again."

"Hey, it wasn't me!" Allana thrust her cup toward him, sloshing more hot chocolate onto the couch. "Look."

"I'm afraid Han and I are the culprits this time," Leia said. "Where have you been? I must have called for you five minutes ago."

"I'm terribly sorry, Princess Leia. I was answering the secure holocomm." C-3PO turned to point down the hall toward the den. "Wynn Dorvan is asking to speak to you or Captain Solo. I tried to explain that you don't take calls during *The Perre Needmo Newshour,* but he was most insistent. He seems to think you have been ignoring a message he sent."

"*The* Wynn Dorvan?" Han asked.

Leia added, "As in Chief Daala's personal assistant?"

"Yes, that would be the correct Wynn Dorvan," C-3PO said. "Though I certainly understand your confusion. There are more than one hundred and seventy thousand Wynn Dorvans listed in the Coruscant directory."

The Solos traded puzzled glances. They knew Wynn Dorvan from the days of the New Republic. As the underdeputy of tenolodium reserves, he had uncovered a lucrative skimming operation run by his own supervisor. Rather than ask for a cut—as many bureaucrats in his position would have done—he had risked his life to bring the matter to the attention of the New Republic Chief of State—who happened to be Leia at the time. After that, he had risen steadily through the ranks on the strength of his reputation. And now he was Chief Daala's personal aide.

"Shall I tell Master Dorvan that you'll be happy to return his call after *The Perre Needmo Newshour*?"

"No, we'll take it now," Leia said, starting toward the den. "Stay with Allana."

"And call the Ess-Nine," Han added, waving a hand at the hot chocolate. "That stuff stains if you don't get it up right away."

Leia led the way down the hall to the extra bedroom that served as their den, then stepped over to the small holocomm unit in the corner. Floating above the holo-projection pad was the fist-sized head of a nondescript man, his only remarkable feature being the fact that not a strand of his brown hair was out of place.

"Hello, Wynn," Leia said, folding her arms across her chest. "Isn't the HoloNet a rather expensive way to comm across town?"

"That's why nobody will think to monitor it," Dor-van replied. "Is your end secure?"

"Scrambled and secure," Han assured him. "What's all this about? If Daala is trying to backchannel some-thing on those arrest warrants—"

"Actually, Chief Daala doesn't know anything about this matter," Dorvan interrupted. "And I hope she never finds out. That's why I'm using a scrambled holo-comm unit."

"We're listening," Leia said. "According to Three-pio, you think we've ignored a message from you?"

"Regarding the Mandalorians," Dorvan replied. "Are the Jedi *trying* to convince Chief Daala she has no other choice? As soon as those apprentices left the Tem-ple, she instructed me to secure funding for a full com-pany. I'll be able to delay things for a week or so because she wants it kept off the ledgers, but beyond that—"

"Wait a minute," Han said. "A *company*? Are you telling me Daala is about to send for an entire *company* of Mandalorians?"

"Of course," Dorvan answered. "Haven't you seen Head of State Fel in the last few days?"

Han and Leia exchanged glances, and Leia began to have a sinking feeling. Jag had some fairly rigid ideas about duty and honor, and he might have felt that carrying messages for Dorvan would create a conflict of interest for him.

After a second, Han said, "Oh yeah, *that* company."

Dorvan's head dropped. "He didn't tell you."

"Head of State Fel seems like a strange choice for a courier," Leia said. "Especially when you're obviously willing to risk direct contact with us."

Dorvan looked up again. "He wasn't actually a courier," he explained. "I just made sure he overheard what Chief Daala was considering, so that I wouldn't have to risk my job—and my freedom—by contacting you directly. Given Fel's relationship with your daughter—"

"You assumed he'd do the right thing," Han finished, his tone growing hard. "Me too."

But Leia wasn't so easily convinced. "Nice try, Wynn, but you can tell Chief Daala we didn't fall for it."

Dorvan's brows came together. "Fall for what?"

"Her bluff." Leia leaned closer to the hololens, so that her face would be appearing to grow larger at the other end of the connection. "You're as honest as bureaucrats come, Wynn. You'd never betray Daala like this."

"And surely not for free." Han leaned down beside Leia, then flashed one of his smirky half smiles. "Like Leia said, nice try. You had me going there for a minute."

Dorvan's face reddened. "I am *not* bluffing!" he said. "And I would *never* do this for money."

"No?" Leia asked. "Then why would you do it?"

"For the good of the Alliance, obviously!" Dorvan spat back. "Or am *I* the only one who thinks it would be a travesty for Chief Daala to drive the Jedi into disbanding?"

"Is that what she's trying to do?" Leia asked.

"It's certainly an outcome she's willing to accept, if necessary. But I do think she sincerely believes the Order should be brought under government control." Dorvan licked his thin lips, then added, "And frankly, considering recent events, I have to wonder if she might be right."

"Then why talk to *us*?" Han demanded.

"Because even if Daala is right about that much, she's wrong about everything else," Dorvan said. "She thinks the Sith are no more than Jedi in dark robes, and that the only way to keep them from returning is to keep the Jedi under the government's thumb."

"And you don't share that belief?" Leia asked.

"Would I be taking this kind of risk if I did?" Dorvan replied. "There are dark things out there in the galaxy, Princess Leia. I understand that. And I also understand that it's a terrible mistake to confuse those dark things with the Jedi Knights who are trying to protect us from them."

Leia considered this for a moment. "Let's say I believe you for now—Daala is going to send for the Mandalorians. What is it that you want me to *do* with this information?"

"Use it, Princess Leia." Dorvan's face grew smaller as he leaned away from his own holocam. "Pass it along and use it."

Chapter Twelve

TEN MINUTES AFTER SIGNING OFF WITH DORVAN, HAN and Leia were in the apex of the Jedi Temple, stepping out of the turbolift into a white larmalstone foyer. To one side, a heavy blast door guarded the Situation Room, a state-of-the-art command center filled with tactical displays, HoloNet feeds, and enough comm stations to put the flagship of most GA fleets to shame. To the other side, a sealed security door protected the Grand Master's offices, which Kenth Hamner had only recently occupied.

Rumor had it that Kenth had claimed the offices reluctantly—and only because it was too difficult to oversee the Order's affairs from his old Master's office on the floor below. But Han didn't buy that. Kenth's move was a pretty transparent attempt to assert his authority as Luke's replacement. And the attempt was bound to fail, because Luke *couldn't* be replaced. There was only one Luke Skywalker, and a Jedi Order without Luke at the helm just wasn't likely to stay an Order very long.

Directly opposite the turbolift stood the ornate double doors to the Council Chamber. Two apprentices were always assigned to guard the entrance, but today they were being overseen by a tall, brown-haired Jedi Knight with a slender face and dark, piercing eyes. The mere presence of any Jedi Knight indicated the Masters didn't want to be disturbed; that the Jedi Knight was

Jaden Korr told Han that someone—no doubt Kenth Hamner—didn't want to be disturbed by the *Solos* in particular.

Han leaned close to Leia's ear and whispered, "We should've brought Allana."

"She'll be fine with Threepio and Artoo," Leia said. "Threepio's practically a nanny-droid himself, and we're not going to be more than a few minutes."

Han shook his head. "If they've been arguing this long, it might not be that easy to swing them our way."

"Han, we *agreed*," Leia said. "We didn't come here to discuss the arrest warrants."

"Yeah, I know," Han replied. "But as long as we're here anyway, we might as well bring it up."

Leia exhaled in exasperation, but Han had timed it just right: before she could warn him against trying to undermine Kenth's authority, Jaden Korr stepped out to block their way.

"Jedi Solo," Korr said. His eyes slid toward Han. "Captain Solo. I'm sorry, but the Council has left strict instructions to prevent all interruptions."

"And I'll bet they mentioned us by name," Han said.

Korr smiled. "As a matter of fact, Captain Solo, yes, they did."

"And since we know that," Leia said, "*you* know that we wouldn't be here unless the matter was vitally important."

"Nevertheless, I have my orders," Korr said. "And I was specifically reminded how persuasive you two can be."

"Yeah, but you're also a Jedi Knight," Han said, "and that means you're trained to follow your own initiative."

"Of course."

"Now is the time to do so, Jedi Korr," Leia said. "We've come into possession of some information the

Masters need to hear—*before* they make their final decision about Barv and Yaqeel."

The resolve in Korr's face began to crack, but his piercing gaze remained fixed on Han—no doubt because he knew that it would be easier to read the truth of the assertion in Han's Force aura.

After a second, Korr sighed and looked away. "Okay, I'll take a message inside—and I shouldn't even do that much. Grand Master Hamner said—"

"*Grand Master* Hamner?" Han erupted. "Don't tell me the *Masters* are actually calling him that now?"

"Since about two hours ago, when Master Katarn came out during a break," Korr said. "He said it was time for the Masters to set a proper example for the rest of the Order."

"I'll bet I know whose idea *that* was," Leia said, letting the acid drip into her voice. "And he's being presumptuous."

Korr nodded, but said, "Did I mention it's just temporary? Apparently, the Council feels Master Hamner might command a little more authority from . . . well, *you*, if the Masters show their support."

"The *Council* feels that way?" Han shot Leia a worried glance. If Kenth could persuade the Masters to call him *Grand* anything, he probably had the votes to turn the sick Jedi over to Daala. "Or *Kenth* does?"

Korr shrugged uneasily. "Does it matter?" He looked to Leia. "You said you had some important information?"

Leia looked to Han, as though suggesting that *he* relay the information, and Han knew that she had reached the same conclusion he had. The Solos really had to get inside that Chamber and set the Council straight.

Han cast a meaningful glance at the two apprentices standing behind Korr, then nodded him toward one side of the foyer. Korr cocked his brow, but followed. Han put an arm around the Jedi Knight's shoulder, then, being careful to keep him facing away from the door, leaned close.

"I can't tell you how, but we have this on good authority." Han kept his voice nearly inaudible, so that Korr would have to concentrate on him instead of what was happening behind him. "Chief Daala is getting ready to call in the Mandos."

Korr's eyes widened. "Mandalorians?" he gasped. "Supercommandos?"

Han made a disparaging face. "Come on," he said. "Those guys can't even agree on a color for their armor. There isn't anything *super* about them."

That actually drew a smile from the usually staid Jedi. "Except maybe their ability to overheat Jedi jets." He shook his head in disbelief. "Is Daala *trying* to provoke us?"

"I don't think so," Han said. "That old dame is just space-crazy enough to think a few hundred tin suits might actually scare the Jedi."

Korr snorted his opinion of that possibility—then heard the soft click of a latch opening. He spun toward the Council Chamber just in time to see Leia pushing a door open, while the two apprentices—a human male and a Mon Calamari female—stood behind her, protesting that they weren't supposed to let her through the doors. Korr's mouth fell open in surprise, closed in anger, then finally broadened into an embarrassed grimace. He turned to Han, only half scowling.

"I *knew* she was going to do that."

Han slapped him on the shoulder. "If you say so, Jaden."

"Well . . . I would have let you in anyway." Korr started back toward the door. "The Council needs to hear about this."

"Yeah," Han said, accompanying him. "If nothing else, they can probably use a good laugh."

Korr did not even crack a smile. "What's so funny about killing Mandalorians, Captain Solo?"

Korr paused at the door to reassure the two apprentices that no one had expected them to physically restrain Leia Solo, then he and Han followed her into the Council Chamber proper. It was a bright, moderately sized room elegant in its simplicity, with a circle of high-backed chairs sitting in a transparisteel viewport bay designed to give visitors the subliminal impression that Masters were floating above the city. Every seat was equipped with a holocomm unit to allow the participation of Masters who happened to be away from the Temple when a meeting was called, but today all of the Masters—except Luke himself, of course—were present in person.

And by the look of it, they were all hopping mad. Saba Sebatyne was sitting motionless in her chair, her slit-pupiled gaze sliding from one Master to another while her forked tongue flicked between her lips. Cilghal was perched on the edge of her seat, her Mon Calamari skin flushed crimson with rage. Kenth Hamner and Kyle Katarn were glaring at each other across the circle, while Kyp Durron was on his feet, actually pounding his fist in the air, his graying hair trimmed short and neat, but his rumpled brown robe still looking like something he had slept in.

And Corran Horn . . . Corran was the scariest of all, just sitting slumped in his chair, glaring at the floor as though trying to focus all the Force energy he could draw into that one spot. Han could only imagine how the current debate must be playing to him, sitting in a room with a dozen of the most powerful Jedi in the galaxy, listening to them arguing *not* about how they were going to get his two sick kids out of carbonite,

but about whether they should turn two more young
Jedi Knights over to the same people who had frozen
Valin and Jysella.

In Corran's place, Han wouldn't have been anywhere
near a council chamber. He would have been holed up
in a warehouse somewhere, planning how he was going
to break into the GAS blockhouse where his kids were
being held and get them back. But Corran had always
been a law-and-order kind of guy. Even now, when the
government that he had always served so loyally had
turned against his own children, here he was, still trying
to work within the law to set matters right. It wasn't
something Han could have done, not even something he
could truly understand, but he *did* admire it. Corran
was a man of principle, and he stuck to those principles
even when they became a dagger in his own gut.

When Leia reached the edge of the seating alcove,
she stopped and folded her hands in front of her, waiting in silence for someone in the circle to acknowledge
her. Han and Korr did the same thing. Interrupting a
Jedi Master in the middle of an argument with another
Jedi Master was a good way to end up with a Force-
clamped mouth. It might look like the Council hadn't
noticed them, but Han had been to enough of these
things to know that every Master in the room had realized the Solos were coming even before Leia had
brushed past the apprentices.

To Han's dismay, however, the Masters were no longer
arguing about whether to honor the arrest warrants.
They were arguing about something he would have
thought was a given: whether to intercede on Tahiri's
behalf.

". . . we demand her release," Kyp was saying.
"Tahiri was vital to winning the battle at Shedu Maad.
If she hadn't come back to us, we'd have lost our entire
hangar complex."

"I'm not sure that excuses some of the things she did during the war," Kenth said. His voice and manner were restrained, but Han didn't need the Force to know by the way he kept his stare fixed on Kyle Katarn that something bad must have passed between them shortly before. "She *assassinated* Gilad Pellaeon."

"A lot of people killed a lot of people," Kyle replied. His voice was just as restrained, but his stare did not leave Kenth's. "What about Cha Niathal? She played an equal part in Jacen's coup, and I don't see any charges being filed against *her*. Daala is only going after Tahiri to make a statement—a statement directed at *us*."

"I agree with Master Katarn," Cilghal said. "Chief Daala is taking the resignations of Melari and Reeqo as a bolt across her bow."

"How so?" asked Kyp.

"The only thing more frightening to Chief Daala than an independent Jedi Order is no Order at all," Cilghal explained. "So she reads the resignations as a warning: if she continues to push, the Jedi will disband and spread across the galaxy as independent agents. Then it will be impossible for *anyone* to control us."

Kyp smiled. "Not a bad idea, when you think about it."

"It's a *very* bad idea," Kenth grumbled, finally looking away from Kyle. "How do you think we would accomplish anything?"

"And we still have the dozens of Jedi Knights who were hidden at Shelter as young ones," Cilghal pointed out. "If we disband—"

"Hold on," Kyp said, waving both palms. "*Joke*, okay?"

Cilghal's eyes narrowed ever so slightly, but she simply inclined her head. "Of course, forgive me." She turned to the other Masters. "Perhaps if we sent Leia to explain—"

"No. We explain *nothing* to Daala." It was Corran who said this, though his gaze remained fixed on the floor. "That would imply the Order *answers* to her—and the day that happens, you're going to have a lot more than apprentices resigning."

A heavy silence fell over the circle as the Masters considered his words. Then Saba Sebatyne hissed, "Massster Horn is correct. The Jedi Order is no thedyklae herd. We are shartuukz."

Kyp turned to her in obvious confusion. "Uh, sure," he said. "What's a shartuuk?"

"A guard beast," Saba explained. "It protectz the lair from zo'oxi and tarnoggz."

"Oh, *that* explains it." Kyp rolled his eyes, then asked, "And zo'oxi and tarnoggs are what, exactly?"

"Alwayz hungry." Saba leaned forward and jabbed a talon toward the viewport, where the silver cylinder of the Galactic Justice Center was just visible on the far side of Fellowship Plaza. "Like any tyrant."

Kyp nodded. "Ah—of course." He turned back to Cilghal. "We can't explain to Daala. We're the shartuuks, and *she's* the zo'oxi."

"Tarnogg," Saba corrected. "Zo'oxi are skin parasitez. The shartuuk eatz them off."

"I don't know," Kyp said. "Zo'oxi sounds like a pretty good description of most of the politicians I've—"

"In any case," Cilghal interrupted, "we're the shartuuks, and shartuuks don't explain. Where does that leave us with Tahiri?"

"Well, she's not a Jedi anymore," Kenth said. "And that means we can't demand anything on her behalf."

"Not that Daala would listen if we tried," Kyle replied. "But we *can* and *should* support her. I insist on that much."

"As does this one," Saba agreed. "The Order will send Nawara Ven to represent her."

"And plant the idea in a few media heads that there's a disparity of treatment between her and Cha Niathal," Kyle said. "Maybe even provide some background on Niathal and Daala's partnership after the Battle of Fondor."

"Good," Corran said. "That should put some pressure on Daala to give Tahiri an easy out."

When no one objected, Kenth let out a long sigh. "Agreed."

For the first time since the Solos had entered the room, Corran raised his gaze—and turned it on Jaden Korr.

"Now, Jedi Korr, perhaps you'd be good enough to tell us why you ignored orders and allowed the Solos to interrupt us?"

Korr's face reddened, but he met Corran's gaze and said, "I'm sorry, Master Horn. I didn't have a choice."

"*Of course* not." It was Korr's former Master, Kyle Katarn, who said this. He turned to Kenth and said, "I *told* you we should have done this somewhere else, *Grand* Master Hamner."

There was just enough sarcasm in Kyle's voice to make Kenth clench his teeth visibly. "Next time, we will," he said. "But since they're here now, perhaps *you* would care to inform them of our decision regarding the arrest warrant."

Han's heart jumped into his throat. "*What?*" He started forward without thinking—until Leia caught him by the arm and physically held him back. "You've already decided?"

"Afraid so," Kyp said. He started across the circle toward Han. "And it was a tough one—"

"But you haven't done it yet, right?" Han asked,

growing desperate. If Kyle Katarn was addressing Kenth as *Grand* Master even in the privacy of the Council Chamber, then Bazel and Yaqeel were as good as hanging on Daala's wall. "There's something you *really* need to know first."

"I doubt that very much," Kenth said. He took a deep breath, then rose and started across the circle. "Han, Leia, I know how much you care about all of our troubled Jedi Knights, and I think I even understand why. But Luke isn't here at the moment, so you need to respect the chain of command now. Your behavior is starting to be disruptive, and it's *not* going to change any of our decisions."

"*This* might," Leia said. There was so much suppressed anger in her voice that when she released Han and started to step forward, he grabbed *her* arm. "We just learned that Daala is hiring a company of Mandalorians."

Kenth stopped three steps short. "When?"

"Don't know that yet," Han said. Angry as he was at Kenth, he had to admire the man's discipline and focus. He didn't waste time doubting them, and he didn't ask stupid questions like *For us?* He just got down to the important details. "She's still getting the money together. But she's serious about it."

"I see. Is there anything else you can tell us?"

"I'm afraid not," Leia answered. "But our source has promised to keep us informed. We'll pass along whatever we hear as soon as we hear it."

"Thank you," Kenth said, not bothering to ask for the identity of their source—or to question the source's reliability. He started to turn back toward the circle of Masters. "Obviously, we have something *else* to—"

"Hey, hold on a minute," Han said. "What about Barv and Yaqeel? This *has* to change their situation."

Kenth stopped and stared at the ceiling for a moment, then shook his head. "No, I don't believe it does." He looked around at the rest of the Masters. "Does anyone else feel a need to revisit the arrest warrant decision?"

The Masters all shook their heads—even Corran Horn.

"You can't be serious!" Han protested. "You can't just hand them over!"

Han's first hint that he had badly misread the situation was a loud sissing sound from the vicinity of Saba Sebatyne's chair.

"Oh, Captain Solo!" She slapped her knee with a huge, scaly hand, then rasped, "You are so easy to play!"

Han scowled and turned to Leia, who merely spread her hands and looked even more confused than he was.

After a moment, Kenth said, "The Council has come to an . . . *arrangement* that we all hope will be best for the Jedi Order *and* the patients." He turned to Saba. "Master Sebatyne, perhaps you would be good enough to explain what the Order needs the Solos to do."

Saba inclined her armored head. "Of course, *Grand Master Hamner*." She looked up, then turned to Leia. "Jedi Solo, the Council needz you to contact Queen Mother Tenel Ka. We have a very great favor to ask of her."

Chapter Thirteen

UNTIL SHE HAD ACTUALLY DISASSEMBLED ONE, JAINA had never appreciated the magnificent complexity of a cleaning droid. Scattered across the long lab table were soapy-smelling sprayers, misters, brushes, polishing heads, vacuum nozzles, disintegrators, infradryers, logic boards, and a dozen other pieces of semi-miniaturized equipment that seemed entirely pertinent to the droid's function. What had *not* proved pertinent—once she had identified its true nature—was the tiny parasite droid that she had found spliced into its control systems.

Disguised as a stain analyzer-dissolver module, the parasite was a marvel of espionage engineering, so cleverly designed that Temple security could not be faulted for having missed it. Instead of requiring its own lens and microphone, the parasite had hijacked the cleaning droid's photo- and audioreceptors. It didn't even need its own data storage unit. Instead it had overwritten the host's entire stain-recognition bank, then partitioned off that part of the datachip for its own use. To transmit, the parasite simply waited until it was near an open door, then inserted a burst of compressed data—coded to sound like normal interference static—into the cleaning droid's communications stream. That much, Jaina had figured out.

What she *hadn't* figured out was how Javis Tyrr could have come by such a sophisticated device. The parasite droid was clearly state-of-the-art surveillance equipment, the kind that cost millions of credits—probably *tens* of millions—to produce. Journalists simply did not have access to those kinds of resources—especially third-rate hacks like Tyrr.

Jaina took a much-needed sip of caf. She allowed her gaze to run over the table at random, asking herself who *would* have the resources to acquire secret-police-grade surveillance equipment, as well as the desire to put it into Tyrr's hands. Daala was an obvious possibility. But she and Tyrr seemed an unlikely team, given that Tyrr's reports had been nearly as hard on *her* as they had been on the Jedi.

A soft chime sounded behind Jaina. She spun her stool around to see what the computer had turned up for her this time . . . and she had her answer.

On the display was a visual comparison between two miniaturized logic chips. The one on the left had come from the parasite droid. The chip on the right had come from a supply of eavesdropping equipment captured near the end of the last civil war, when the Jedi had boarded the *Anakin Solo*. According to the caption below the image, the equipment had been recovered from the temporary quarters of one of the Imperials who had been aboard at the time, a certain Moff Lecersen.

Jaina suddenly felt like she had a bellyful of snakes. She found her comlink in hand without recalling that she had reached for it. She thumbed Jag's quick-code, then waited in a growing fury during the five seconds it took him to answer.

"Nice to hear from you," he said, leaving no doubt that his aide had checked to make sure it was her before passing him the comlink. "This will have to be fast. We're on our way to—"

"Cancel it," Jaina said. "We need to talk."

"Jaina, I *can't*. Chief Daala is expecting me."

"I don't care if the Emperor himself has been resurrected to meet you," Jaina said. "You need to hear this, and you need to hear it *now*."

Jag fell silent for a moment, then said, "What's wrong?"

"When you get here." Jaina did not even consider giving him a hint; if Lecersen could help Javis Tyrr slip a bug into the Jedi Temple, then he could also plant one in Jag's limousine. "I'll have an apprentice meet you in the east hangar."

Jaina clicked off without awaiting a reply, then commed the apprentices' dormitory to arrange for Jag's escort. She was trying to keep a clear head, despite the cold rage building inside her. At the end of the last civil war, Lecersen and the other Moffs had been happy enough to accept a Jedi-appointed Head of State, rather than face execution for the war crimes they had committed in deploying their nanovirus. But they had never quite gotten over the indignity of having those terms dictated by Luke Skywalker. And now they were absolutely *chafing* under their new Head of State's steadfast refusal to tolerate the usual corruption in the Imperial Remnant. So Jaina saw no reason to doubt that Lecersen was behind the eavesdropping. Her only questions were how much he had heard, and how much damage it would cause Jag and the Jedi.

Jaina turned back to the lab table and picked up the tiny circuit module that was the cause of her anger. It would be a tremendous help to know how much of their conversation the parasite droid had been able to pass along to Javis Tyrr. Now that she knew something about its design and origin, that might even be possible—but not without help. While Jaina had always been capable with machines, slicing a piece of espionage equipment this sophisticated required someone more than just "capable." If she messed up, the module would almost certainly self-destruct.

What Jaina needed was Lowbacca's help. She knew he would be happy to give it, but then he would hear the conversation about Daala and the Mandalorians. And how could Jaina ask *him* to keep a secret that she herself wasn't even certain she should be keeping?

A soft *whoosh* sounded from the front of the lab as the door slid open. Jaina checked her chrono and saw that only five minutes had passed since she had commed Jag.

"Wow, that was fast," Jaina called, still studying the parasite droid. "You must have been right on top of the . . ."

She let the sentence trail off as she sensed who was actually coming through the door. The Force auras belonged not to Jag, but to her parents, and both were very sad—and very angry. Jaina quickly set the parasite droid back on the table and turned, just in time to see her mother leading the way into the cluttered laboratory.

Of course her mother's gaze was drawn straight to the tangle of circuits and feedwires in front of Jaina. "What's that?" She ran her eyes over the cleaning droid parts. "This looks like your room when you were twelve."

"Was it really *this* tidy?" When the joke failed to lighten the dark mood, Jaina explained, "I think I found out how Javis Tyrr has been getting his images from inside the Temple."

Jaina knew better than to lie about the droid. Attempting to lie to a Jedi mother would be more than futile—it would set off alarm bells. Instead, her only hope of keeping her secret about the Mandalorians was to appear relaxed and just avoid the subject.

"You remember the cleaning unit that was working near the hangar door when Barv and Yaqeel went around the bend?" When her father nodded, Jaina picked up the parasite droid and twirled it between her thumb and forefinger. "I found this little guy hidden inside it."

When neither of her parents showed any interest in how Jaina had found the bug—one that had been missed by Temple security at least a dozen times—she knew something was terribly wrong. She returned the parasite to the table, then watched in growing concern as her parents came closer.

"What is it?"

Her father came to her side. "Sweetheart, there's just no easy way to tell you this."

He took both her hands, and Jaina sighed with relief. At least no one else in the family was dead. If someone *had* died, her father would have crushed her in a bear hug—and anyway, she would have felt it in the Force first. There weren't that many Solo-Skywalkers left.

When her father did not seem able to say any more, Jaina turned to her mother. "Did Ben go?" she asked. "I know Cilghal thinks it's the students who were at Shelter that are at risk."

"Ben's fine, as far as we know," Leia said. "This is about Jag."

"No, I just talked to Jag. Unless there's been an assassination attempt in the last . . ." Jaina checked her chrono and was alarmed to see that Jag could be arriving any minute now. ". . . ten minutes, he's perfectly well."

"He won't be after you hear this," her father said. "Brace yourself, kid."

Jaina frowned. "For what?"

"Sweetheart, there's something Jag has been keeping from you." Her mother glanced at her father, then continued, "Your father and I thought you should hear it from us first."

"What?" Jaina pulled her hands free of her father's grasp, then cocked her brow. "You're going to tell me Jag's been seeing someone else?"

To Jaina's dismay, her parents did not even crack a smile.

"Worse," her father said. "He's been holding out on you."

"I seriously doubt that, Dad." Jaina plucked at her robe. "*Jedi,* remember?"

"So's your mother," he countered. "And she only knows *half* my secrets."

Her mother shot him a quick *so you think* glare, then turned back to Jaina. "Jaina, you can't know about this—"

"Because if you did, *we* wouldn't have had to hear about it from a spy." Her father took her hands again. "Jaina, sweetheart, Chief Daala is sending for Mandalorians."

Jaina's stomach sank. She finally understood what her parents had come to tell her about Jag, and she knew how betrayed they must feel by his decision to keep the information secret. But she also felt immensely relieved, because *she* no longer had to struggle with her own divided loyalties by keeping the secret herself. In truth, she'd been wondering how long she could hold out.

"This is good information," her mother said, apparently misinterpreting the reason for Jaina's thoughtfulness. "It comes right from the top."

"So?" Realizing that she had to react as though this *wasn't* old news to her, Jaina pulled her hands free again and raised a thumb. "First, who *cares?* Unless Boba Fett is coming himself, we can handle a company of Mandos without getting our robes dirty."

"But there will still be a battle," her mother reminded her. "And in that kind of fight, *everyone* loses something."

"Yeah," her father agreed. "And right now the last thing the Jedi need showing up on the holonews is a bunch of dead Mandalorians on the Temple doorsteps."

"Point taken," Jaina said.

She really didn't want to ask this next question. Clearly, her parents already knew—*somehow*—that Jag had been keeping his knowledge to himself. Her only chance to redeem him in their eyes would be to make them see that Jag had been honor-bound to keep the secret. Well, to make her *mother* see it—her father would never understand. But if Jaina could convince her mother, then her *mother* would eventually make her father forgive Jag.

"But I don't see what all this has to do with Jag," Jaina continued. "Unless those Mandalorian companies are arriving on Imperial transport?"

"It wouldn't surprise me," her father snorted.

"Well, it would *me*," Jaina shot back. "The Moffs made it death for Boba Fett to return to Mandalore *forever*. I don't see the Mandalorians asking *anyone* in the Empire for a ride."

"True," her mother said. "But you're a smart girl, Jaina. You *know* what we mean."

Jaina sighed. Letting her chin drop like a ten-year-old caught in a fib, she surreptitiously checked her chrono once more. It had been nearly a quarter hour since she had commed Jag. Assuming he had been on his way to meet Daala, he couldn't have been very far from the Temple at the time. He'd be here any minute, and the last thing she needed was for him to come striding into the lab before she made her parents understand *why* he had kept the secret—at least if she wanted them to come to the wedding.

"Okay," Jaina said. "Let's say Jag *did* know the Mandalorians were coming. So what? That doesn't mean he should tell *us*."

"What are you, going bugbent again?" her father exploded. "We're the closest thing he's got to family right now! And Luke's the one who *gave* him that gig."

"And that *gig* comes with a long list of duties and obligations," Jaina replied, just as hotly. "None of which includes being a Jedi! He's having enough trouble keeping the Moffs in line without getting into the middle of our problems with Daala."

Jaina knew by the long silence that followed that she had just let the rancor jump out of the pit. She hadn't been shocked enough—*angry* enough—to be hearing this for the first time. Her father winced like a sabacc player who had just realized he was betting into a perfect hand, and she turned to find her mother studying her with a slack jaw and narrowed eyes.

"You *knew*," her mother said. "And you didn't tell anyone."

Jaina let out a long breath. "Mom, there's a lot at stake—"

"Wait a minute," her father interrupted. He looked to her mother, then pointed at Jaina. "*She* knew about the bucketheads?"

Her mother closed her eyes and nodded. "Yes, Han. Jaina knew about the Mandos, and she knew Jag wasn't telling us. That's why she's defending him."

"I'm defending him because he was keeping the oath he swore to always act in the Empire's best interests," Jaina replied. "The oath that he swore because *Uncle Luke* pushed him into becoming their Head of State."

Her father's gaze turned cold and angry, rocking her back on her heels. "What about the oaths *you* swore?" he demanded. "Don't they count, now that you're about to become High Lady Fel?"

He shook his head in disgust, then spun on his heel and stormed off toward the door, leaving Jaina too stunned to reply—and on the brink of falling back into the dark well of solitude and remorse that had nearly swallowed her after she had killed Jacen. She turned, and found her mother's gaze only marginally less condemning than her father's, though the expression on her face was one of disappointment rather than anger.

"Mom, you need to understand," Jaina said.

Before she could explain how Jag was trying to bring the Remnant fully into the Galactic Alliance, her mother raised a hand to silence her.

"Jaina, we'll talk about this later," she said, starting after Han. "Right now, I'd better make sure Han doesn't hurt someone."

Jaina nodded, thinking that her mother was just speaking in exaggerated terms—but then she, too, felt a familiar presence approaching the lab doorway.

"Oh, *kriff*!" Jaina started toward the front of the lab—until her mother pointed a finger at the stool.

"*Sit,*" she ordered. "*I'll* handle your father."

The door *whoosh*ed open even before she finished speaking, then Jagged Fel came striding around the corner in full ceremonial collar and tabard—and ran headlong into Han Solo coming through the other way.

"Oh, Captain Solo—my apologies," Jag said, reaching out to steady him. "Jaina didn't say you would—"

"Out of my way, sleemo!" Han's palms caught Jag near the armpits and sent him stumbling back into his astonished Rodian escort. "Don't think I won't blast you just because it might start a war."

With that, he bulled past and vanished from sight, leaving Jag standing slack-jawed as Jaina's mother stepped into the doorway.

"Uh, Princess Leia," Jag said tentatively, "I'm not sure what *that* was about—"

"Sure you are," Leia interrupted. She stepped closer to Jag, not stopping until she was nose-to-chest, then glared up into his eyes. "My daughter seems to think you had a good reason for keeping quiet, and maybe you *did*. But this should probably be the last time we see you inside the Jedi Temple for a while."

Jag's face fell. He looked angry, guilty, and embarrassed all at once, but he didn't try to argue or explain. He simply nodded.

"Of course—I understand." He looked toward Jaina, then asked, "Would it be acceptable for me to have a few words with Jaina before I go?"

Leia scowled into the lab. "I think you'd better," she said. "You two definitely have some things to discuss."

With that, she turned and vanished down the hall after Han.

Jaina dropped onto the stool and sat staring at the floor as she listened to Jag's heels click across the floor toward her.

"I know better than to think you told them."

There was just enough of a question in Jag's tone to hurt Jaina, and make her feel even more alone. She reminded herself that once, long ago, she *had* given him a reason to doubt her promise. It helped her bite back the sharp reply that had risen almost automatically inside her.

"I don't know how they found out," she said evenly. "They mentioned a spy, but they weren't in a mood to talk about it."

Jag stopped in front of her and nodded. "I don't suppose it matters, at least not at this stage." There was more confidence in his voice now, and relief. "But it *is* going to complicate things."

Jaina looked up and snorted, so shell-shocked by the implications of what had just happened—for her, the Jedi, and the future of the Galactic Alliance—that she felt on the verge of hysterical laughter.

"You don't know the half of it."

"I'm sure I don't," Jag said, reaching for her hands. "But we'll get through it, I promise. When your parents realize how important this secret was to the unification talks, they'll understand the impossible position I put you in."

"Yeah, well, don't expect them to forgive you for *that*." Jaina managed a weak smile, then pulled her hands free. "But that's not what I meant. Do you recognize *this*?"

She retrieved the parasite droid from the lab table and held it in front of him.

Jag's eyes went wide. "I'm afraid I do." He glanced at the parts scattered in front of Jaina. "From inside the cleaning droid?"

Jaina nodded. "Afraid so," she said. "Lecersen?"

"Probably. I'll know for sure once I access its memory."

"How do you know I haven't done that already?" Jaina asked.

"Because it's still in one piece, and you still have all your fingers."

Jag reached for the parasite droid, but Jaina quickly pulled it away.

"Not so fast," she said. "The Jedi need to get *something* out of this mess."

Jag let out a long breath, then nodded. "Okay," he said. "You can have it back when we've removed the self-destruct charge and copied its memory."

"Deal." Jaina stretched up to kiss him, then said, "But I think there's one other thing you're going to need it for."

Jag frowned in bewilderment.

"Show it to Daala." Jaina put the droid in his hand and folded his fingers around it. "It might do us *all* some good."

Chapter Fourteen

SHIP WAS OUT THERE IN THE FERN-AND-FUNGUS JUNGLE.
Vestara could feel his dark presence somewhere across
the crimson river, up on the shoulder of a fume-belching
volcano that dominated the horizon ahead. He was
pushing at her in the Force almost physically, battering
her with fear and alarm and anger in his efforts to make
her turn back. He did not want her and the rest of her
companions to remain here with him. Ship had taught
them everything they needed to restore the Sith Empire
to the galaxy, and now he wanted them to abandon him
to his fate and fulfill their own destiny.

Vestara understood all this. But Grand Lord Vol had
sent the *Eternal Crusader* and her crew to return Ship
to Kesh, and return Ship they would. Vestara concentrated on Ship's presence for a moment, then raised her
hand and pointed to a dark outcropping of basalt,
about a quarter of the way up the volcano.

"Ship is somewhere near there," she said. "I don't
know where exactly, but he must have a view of us.
He's pushing very hard to turn me back."

Lady Rhea studied the outcropping from the barren
bank where the recovery party was standing, out in the
full light of the blue sun. Normally they would have
tried to shelter themselves by crouching beneath the
fern-trees along the river, but they had learned the hard

way that the foliage on this strange planet was to be feared more than the oppressive heat.

After a moment, Rhea nodded and brought a comlink to her mouth. "*Crusader.* You have our position?"

"Affirmative."

The reply came in the melodious voice of Baad Walusari, the Keshiri Saber she had left in command while she led the recovery party. In most navies, it would have been the executive officer who assumed control of the vessel while the commander was away. But a Sith who made such a foolish mistake was unlikely to find herself in command of *anything* when she tried to return to the vessel. Master Xal was right there with the search party, where Lady Rhea could keep an eye on him.

"Very good," Lady Rhea commed. "Ship is hiding on that volcano to our west. Be ready with the tractor beam if it attempts to move."

Walusari acknowledged the command, and Lady Rhea began to issue orders to the recovery party, assigning search pairs and calling for a careful approach on a wide front. Vestara and Lady Rhea would make straight for the outcropping, of course, with everyone else fanning out to either side of them.

"Ship is too smart to show itself where the *Crusader* can get a sensor lock," Lady Rhea finished, walking in front of the long line of Sabers she had brought down for the recovery operation. "So it will be someone in this party who finds it. If that happens to be you, report its location, then wait for me to arrive and take control of the situation personally. Is that clear?"

Most of the Sabers assured her it was, but a ginger-skinned woman named Axela Zin asked, "What if Ship attempts to flee?"

"Don't let it," Lady Rhea replied. "Ship obeys any

Sith with a strong will. You all have that, or you wouldn't be here. Simply order it to remain where it is, then wait until I arrive."

Axela dropped her chin in submission. "Thank you for your counsel, Lady Rhea. I'm most grateful."

Rhea dismissed the gift with a flick of her hand. "Think nothing of it, Saber Zin. I'm certain others were also in need of guidance." She stopped at the opposite end of the line from where Vestara was standing, then turned and said, "I'm sure I don't need to remind you to watch yourselves in this jungle. But if something *does* get you, die quietly. Your family will be rewarded if you do—and punished if you don't."

Lady Rhea was correct: the reminder wasn't necessary. Already, four members of the recovery party had been taken by the carnivorous plants that seemed to be more the rule than the exception on this strange world. But the exhortation to die quietly was received with the shudder that Vestara was certain Lady Rhea had intended, being as it was a none-too-subtle reminder that the reach of a Sith Lord extended even beyond a subordinate's grave.

After giving the warning a moment to sink in, Lady Rhea signaled Master Xal and Ahri to wait, then waved the rest of the party across the river. Most of the Sabers elected to simply Force-jump to the far bank, and, as they landed, Vestara was sorry to see a trio of long-thorned boughs swing down from a tall, funnel-shaped tree to impale ginger-skinned Axela Zin. Already holding her lightsaber in hand, Zin quickly cut the boughs free of their woody stems, but more were already swinging down from other directions. Her search partner and another Saber quickly drew the glass parangs from their belt sheaths and hurled them into the melee. By the time the blades arrived, Zin was already swaddled in vines and being drawn up into the tree's crown. Vestara hoped the fact that she wasn't struggling also meant she was already dead.

"Not a whimper," Xal noted, stepping over to join Lady Rhea. "I believe her son is a Tyro."

"Make a note, Vestara."

Although Vestara had every confidence in her ability to remember even a long list of names correctly, her own survival was far from assured. So she dutifully removed a small leather writing case from her pocket, then pricked her finger with a blood stylus and wrote Zin's name on a leaf of loub-paper.

"Her name is noted," Vestara reported. "Did you wish to add something about the son?"

Lady Rhea nodded. "The boy shall find his Master when we return."

As Vestara made the note, Xal smiled his approval.

"Very generous." He looked across the river to where the rest of the Sith were already vanishing into the jungle. "You had some special counsel for me?"

"I did," Lady Rhea said. "Recovering Ship is more important to Grand Lord Vol than who claims credit for it. If you or Ahri find it, he'll hear no other names."

Xal's brow rose. "Most thoughtful," he said. "And yet Ahri and I are only two among many. It is just as likely that someone else will find Ship . . . especially since you have given them such a significant lead over us."

"And if they do, your name will be mentioned alongside my own," Lady Rhea promised. "I want *nothing* to interfere with recovering Ship. Is that clear?"

Xal dipped his slender head in a gesture of acceptance. "In that case, may I suggest we proceed? If we fall too far behind, there will be a gap in the search line."

Lady Rhea studied him for a moment, no doubt wondering—as Vestara was—how long it would take

Xal to decide that there was more to be gained by betraying the agreement than honoring it. Finally, she dismissed him with a wave.

Vestara returned her writing packet to her robe, then watched as Xal and Ahri crossed the river, dancing across the surface and using the Force to keep their feet from sinking. They had to pass near an island covered in dozens of green lizards, but the creatures seemed completely uninterested in them. They merely continued to lie with their wings spread, basking in the harsh light of the blue giant sun, and barely raised their long necks as Xal and Ahri raced past. But the island was surrounded by dozens of strandy yellow water plants that, despite the river's current, all seemed to be growing toward the lizards. As Ahri and Xal approached, several of these strands swam across their path, then suddenly struck like snakes, coming at them from all sides.

Ahri and Xal ignited their lightsabers and twirled into a spinning flurry of slashing and splashing that left them hidden behind a rising veil of steam. A couple of withered and smoking stalks came tumbling out of the cloud, and soon the pair were dancing onto the far shore. They scrambled up the bank in a series of short leaps, using the Force to push aside—and sometimes even uproot—every bush in their path, then clambered over the rim of a red sandstone outcropping and vanished into the jungle beyond.

Lady Rhea pointed at the outcropping. "You see where they came out of the river?"

Vestara nodded. "Yes."

"Good. Draw your weapons." Lady Rhea unhooked her own lightsaber and pulled the parang from its belt sheath, then said, "That's where we'll go. Once we're across, we'll traverse to our own corridor and go find Ship."

It was so classically Sith that Vestara could almost have predicted it: force a subordinate to take the initial risk, then come in behind and claim the kill. Vestara stepped to the edge of the bank where Lady Rhea would have a good view of her as she drew her weapons, then unhooked her lightsaber and unsheathed her parang. An instant later she felt a nudge in the Force and knew she had permission to proceed.

Vestara opened herself to the Force and felt it rush into her, so dark and cold it was almost overwhelming. She had never before been to a place so strong in the Force, where it actually raised tiny bumps on her skin and made her spine crawl with excitement. None of them had, and she could tell by the precision with which even Lady Rhea drew on the Force here that they were all just a bit frightened of its strength. Of course, that did not stop anyone from actually *using* it. No true Sith would ever allow fear to stand between her and power.

Vestara sprang into the air, using the Force to boost herself higher and pull herself to the outcropping Lady Rhea had indicated. Back on Kesh, or on any other planet with near-standard gravity, she would have been able to Force-leap only about halfway across the crimson river. But on this strange world, she crossed the distance easily and came down lightly, ready to defend herself both with her weapons and with the Force.

When no branches swung down toward her head and no vines lashed out to snare her ankles, Vestara raised the hand holding her lightsaber and signaled that it was safe. Lady Rhea arrived on the outcropping an instant later, and together they traversed downstream along the riverbank. After fifty paces, they reached their search corridor and turned into the jungle, Vestara taking the lead and traveling about five paces ahead. Although her danger sense was far less adept than that of her Master, there was no question of Lady Rhea assuming the hazardous point position. An apprentice was first and foremost her Master's servant, and that meant taking the initial brunt of any attack that came their way.

The foliage in the jungle was mostly fern-trees and giant pillar fungi, which—so far, at least—had not proven to have an appetite for animal flesh. Still, Vestara worked with both lightsaber and parang, cutting away any frond, tendril, or lobe that lay within a meter of their path. The plants, they had discovered, usually preferred to attack by surprise, taking their prey from the rear whenever possible.

As they walked, Ship continued to push against Vestara in the Force, urging her to turn back and leave. It was Ship's destiny to serve, and he had no choice but to obey the powerful Will that commanded him to serve here. But it was the Tribe's destiny to rule, and they could not do that from here. Vestara paid the entreaties no attention, save to note that Ship could probably still see them if he could articulate his concerns to her mind so clearly.

They had traveled about a kilometer up the shoulder of the volcano when Lady Rhea issued a sharp command, catching Vestara in mid-step.

"Stop—*now.*"

Vestara obeyed instantly, using the Force to catch her weight as it shifted toward her front foot. She stood there using the Force to balance on one leg as Lady Rhea closed the five paces between them. At Vestara's side, the Sith Lord paused, using the Force to peel away a thin mat of cellulose so perfectly camouflaged that it was impossible to tell it from the humus-covered ground.

Beneath the mat lay a bushy green rodent about the size of a human hand. Half rotted, the creature was impaled on a carpet of finger-length barbs protruding up from a mesh of half-buried roots. Vestara carefully lowered the foot that had almost stepped into the trap, then made note of the yellow, fan-shaped leaves of the bush from which the roots seemed to emanate.

"Thank you, Lady Rhea," Vestara said. "That would have been most painful."

"Probably fatal," Lady Rhea corrected. "Those barbs are poisoned."

Vestara let her gaze drop back to the barbs, trying to study them without being too obvious about it. She saw no hint that the rodent had died of anything other than being impaled, but she knew better than to question her Master's pronouncement.

Instead, Vestara said, "This is a backward sort of world, don't you think, where the plants eat the animals?"

Lady Rhea nodded. "There's *nothing* natural about this world, from where it's hidden to the life-forms that inhabit it." She looked up into the jungle, her eyes narrowing in thought. "That's why Ship led us to it, I think. By virtue of its very existence, this unnatural world is a place of great power."

"I beg your indulgence, Lady Rhea." Inside, Vestara was cringing at the punishment she would no doubt receive for disagreeing with her Master, but she had to be sure that Lady Rhea was fully apprised of Ship's attitude—the mission might depend on it later. "But I don't think that Ship actually wants us here. He keeps trying to push me away."

To Vestara's surprise, Lady Rhea actually smiled. "Of course it does. It wants to make certain we're worthy."

Vestara saw at once what her Master was thinking. "You believe our presence here has something to do with the Return?"

"Exactly." Lady Rhea's eyes shone with approval. "Ship has been preparing us all along."

Vestara had to agree: it seemed very possible. According to Keshiri myth, a species of mysterious Destructors returned to the galaxy every few eons to wipe out civilization and return all beings to their natural, primitive states. Through a combination of historical accident and fate, the Lost Tribe's Sith ancestors had crash-landed on Kesh more than five millennia earlier, and the Keshiri natives had greeted the survivors as the legendary Protectors destined to defend their world when the Destructors returned.

At first, the Sith had viewed the myth as nothing more than a convenient way of holding dominion over a much larger native population. But as the centuries passed, their descendants had started to uncover archaeological evidence suggesting that the myth was actually historical fact. Eventually, the Lost Tribe had come to accept that their act of deception was, after all, their destiny.

And now, here they were, led to a place of darkness by a Ship as old as the Sith themselves—a place that had obviously been constructed by beings who possessed power and knowledge beyond imagining. Was it a leap of logic to believe that Ship had led them here for a purpose?

Vestara inclined her head to her Master. "Your wisdom outshines the sun above, Lady Rhea. I see no reason Ship would have led us to such a world, if not to bestow on us the might that we need . . ."

She let the sentence drop off as she suddenly *did* see another reason Ship might have brought them to such a place.

"Vestara?" Lady Rhea used the Force to shake her arm. "Is something wrong?"

"I . . . I don't know," Vestara confessed. She turned

to look Lady Rhea directly in the eye. "I just had a thought—one that must be wrong."

Lady Rhea frowned, for this phrasing was the only acceptable way for an apprentice to disagree with one's Master. "Why must that be?"

"Because I'm sure you have already thought of this possibility and dismissed it," Vestara said. "But what if Ship brought us here because *this* is the home of the Destructors?"

Vestara knew by the way that Lady Rhea's eyes hardened that she *hadn't* thought of that possibility, but she was disturbed enough by the idea that she didn't even bother to pretend otherwise.

"You have an alarming imagination, Vestara." Lady Rhea remained lost in thought for a moment, then said, "Very well, *why* would Ship lead us to the home of the Destructors?"

"What if Ship has been their servant all along?" Vestara asked. "If the Destructors were aware of the Tribe's destiny, what better way to preempt it than to send an agent to lead us into their grasp?"

"A sound tactic." Lady Rhea gestured for them to begin climbing again, then followed close behind as Vestara circled around the bed of barbed roots. "But *we* are not the Tribe. What would the Destructors gain by destroying one frigateful of warriors?"

Vestara furrowed her brow. That *was* a problem. "You're correct, of course. A spy is worth nothing to an enemy if he is not in their house."

"And why would Ship have come to us in the first place?" Lady Rhea pressed. "The Tribe was trapped on Kesh, but now we roam the galaxy at will. Ship has done nothing but make us stronger."

"True," Vestara said. "But *now* our focus is on the Jedi, not the Destructors. The goal may be to keep us looking in one direction when we should be looking in the other."

"Then what are we doing *here*?" Lady Rhea asked. "If this *is* the home of the Destructors, Ship has done nothing but draw our attention to it."

"And reveal its location," Vestara added, seeing the weakness of her own argument. "I apologize, Lady Rhea. I have done nothing but fill your head with foolish notions."

"Our *enemies* sometimes have foolish notions, Vestara, and it is good to understand them." As Lady Rhea spoke, they crested the shoulder of the volcano and saw ahead the dark outcropping that was their destination. "Do continue thinking on this—and fill my head with any other foolish notions you may have."

"As you wish," Vestara promised. "Thank you for not thinking poorly of me for suggesting such nonsense."

"There's no need for gratitude," Lady Rhea said. "Just be careful not to voice your foolish suggestions where *others* can overhear. We *do* have our reputations to consider."

Vestara smiled, then realized that she had not felt Ship trying to push her away for several minutes now. She used her lightsaber to hack through an umbrella-sized leaf that came dropping down from a tangle of foul-smelling vines, then extended her Force awareness up toward the outcropping—and instead of Ship, she felt her friend Ahri.

Even before Vestara could curse under her breath, Lady Rhea asked, "What is it?"

"Apprentice Raas," Vestara said. "I think Master Xal abandoned the search corridor you assigned to him and went straight to the outcropping."

"And that surprises you because . . . ?"

Vestara exhaled in exasperation. "Because I thought you made a deal with him."

"I *offered* him a deal," Lady Rhea corrected. "Which he didn't decline."

"Isn't that the same as accepting?"

"Close enough," Lady Rhea said, snorting in amusement. "Obviously, he had no intention of honoring our agreement in either case."

"So why offer it?" Vestara asked.

"You tell me," Lady Rhea countered. "What did I accomplish?"

Vestara thought for a moment, then saw what she had done. "You got him playing *your* game," she said. "He thought he was already deceiving you, so he didn't try something else."

"We'll make a Saber out of you yet." Lady Rhea put a hand on Vestara's shoulder and stopped her, then spoke more softly. "Now tell me about you and Apprentice Raas. You're close enough that you can recognize his Force aura?"

Vestara immediately felt guilty. "There's no disloyalty to you, Lady Rhea. Ahri and I have been best friends since we were Tyros."

"I thought as much," Lady Rhea said. "That's why Xal picked him."

Vestara's brow shot up. "I thought it was because Ahri is . . . well, Keshiri."

"And Xal is . . . *not*?" Lady Rhea smiled. "That's part of the reason, I'm sure. It never hurts to draw the eye away from one's weaknesses—as you well know."

Lady Rhea ran a finger along the carefully applied eye swirls that Vestara painted on every morning to draw attention away from the small scar at the corner of her mouth.

"But the truth is, Master Xal was hoping that Ahri's relationship with you might be of benefit."

"*Me?*" Vestara gasped. "Because of Ship?"

"Because you are *my* apprentice," Lady Rhea said. "I'm sure Xal was hoping that your friendship with Ahri might give him some *insight* into my thinking on occasion."

Vestara's heart rose into her throat. "Lady Rhea, I *never*—"

"I know, Vestara," she said. "And I'm sure that's why Xal is so disappointed with your friend."

Vestara's heart sank. The last thing she wanted was to make Ahri's life difficult, but she wasn't going to betray her own Master to make him look good.

But that was exactly what Lady Rhea seemed to have in mind. "I don't know how close you two are," she said. "But it wouldn't hurt to let Ahri make some progress."

Vestara's eyes went wide. "You mean . . ." She knew what Lady Rhea meant, but she couldn't quite bring herself to say it aloud—not when it meant betraying her best friend. "You mean you want me to use Ahri?"

"I *mean* Xal will be coming for you," Lady Rhea replied, growing exasperated. "It might be nice if you had a friend who would give you a little warning."

"Oh." Vestara paused, realizing that Lady Rhea was suggesting exactly what she had thought . . . and that her only real choice was to take the advice or die. "When you put it like that . . ."

Lady Rhea nodded. "Exactly." She released Vestara's shoulder and pointed up the slope. "Now let's go get Ship."

Expecting Xal's parang to come flying out of the jungle at any moment, Vestara led the way up the cliff to where she sensed Ahri waiting. To her delight, when she found him, he was not lurking in ambush, nor was he standing out in the open acting as bait. He was crouching at the base of the outcropping, hiding between two boulders and watching the entrance of a volcanic cave that seemed barely large enough for Ship to enter.

Although Vestara and Lady Rhea were using the Force to approach in complete silence, his head swung toward them when they were still twenty paces away, and the look of relief on his gorgeous face was enough to eliminate all thoughts of ambush from Vestara's mind. She used the Force to spring across the last dozen meters to his side, then crouched beside the boulders where he was hiding.

"What is it?" she whispered.

Ahri shrugged. "Master Xal wanted to bring Ship out alone," he said. "He told me to stay out here and let him know when I saw you."

Vestara frowned. "*Did* you?"

Ahri shook his head. "I can't even feel him," he said. "*You* try."

Vestara frowned, but reached out in the Force and was immediately overwhelmed by the same dark longing she had experienced as they approached the system. There was *something* inside the cave, hungry and lonely and powerful, but it wasn't Xal. Nor was it Ship.

She turned to Ahri. "That's . . . not good."

"Tell me about it," he said. "What do you want to do?"

"I don't know." Vestara looked down the hill, then reached out to Lady Rhea and poured confident feelings into the Force. "Follow orders?"

Ahri nodded. "When in doubt . . ."

A moment later, Lady Rhea came striding up the slope, looking far less concerned about the situation than Vestara suspected she truly was. She stopped in front of the cave mouth and peered into the darkness, then spoke without turning to look at Ahri or Vestara.

"I suppose Master Xal is in there?"

"As far as I know," Ahri answered. "He went in about five minutes ago."

"Ship?"

Ahri shrugged. "We heard something, but . . ."

"Never assume," Lady Rhea finished. She extended a hand toward Ahri, using the Force to float the glow rod out of its loop on his equipment belt. "Don't you know it's bad form to lose your Master, Apprentice Raas?"

Ahri shot Vestara a nervous glance, then, when she gave him a reassuring smile, said, "I was only following his instructions, Lady Rhea."

She gave him a sly smile. "I'm sure you were."

Lady Rhea activated Ahri's glow rod, then tossed it into the cave. Vestara caught a brief glimpse of something large and gray dangling from the ceiling—or perhaps it was a lot of somethings, all of them long and writhing, with suction cups on the undersides and yellow barbed hooks at the ends.

The glow rod bounced across the floor and rolled in a slow circle, casting a disk of pale blue light across the porous walls. A writhing, man-sized mummy was briefly illuminated, wrapped in purple silk and hanging on the back wall; then the light slid past and came to rest on the dark gullet of a long black tunnel descending into the heart of the mountain.

Lady Rhea pointed a finger at the glow rod, calmly using the Force to roll it back across the floor until the disk of light came to rest on the purple cocoon hanging from the back wall. Vestara was not at all surprised to see the outline of Master Xal's sharp-featured face in the silk, a small bubble over his mouth popping in and out as he struggled to breathe.

"Well," Lady Rhea said, "I don't think Ship did *that*."

She motioned Vestara and Ahri toward the cave mouth.

Vestara swallowed hard, then turned to Ahri. "He's *your* Master," she said.

Ahri nodded. "Lucky me," he replied. "If this doesn't go well—"

"Yeah," Vestara promised. "I'll just kill you."

Ahri slipped out of his hiding place, then ignited his lightsaber and dived into the cave. When the gray tentacle-things hanging from the roof did not immediately drop down to ensnare him, he came up slashing at Master Xal's cocoon.

Vestara did not see what happened next, exactly, because she was diving into the cave after Ahri. She rolled across the lumpy floor, then came up on Xal's other side, bringing her red, Lignan-powered blade down along his flank.

Freed from the wall if not his cocoon, Xal pitched forward and would have slammed into the floor had he not used the Force to break his fall. Paying him no more attention, Vestara pivoted around to face the gray tentacles she had seen earlier.

They were no longer dangling from the ceiling. In fact, they were nowhere to be seen at all, though there was a definite slurping sound coming from the direction of the dark tunnel the glow rod had revealed earlier. Vestara quickly used the Force to swing the beam around toward the passage . . . and found herself looking at an attractive, svelte woman. Her eyes were gray, and her shoulder-length hair was the color of honey.

Vestara was still struggling to comprehend what she was seeing when Ahri sprang up in front of her, his lightsaber flashing at the woman's shoulder. There came the distinctive sizzle of a superheated blade slashing through flesh and bone, then the acrid tang of scorched flesh.

Suddenly Ahri was slamming into the cavern wall behind Vestara, his lightsaber no longer burning. His head struck with a sickening thud. Vestara watched in horror as he dropped twitching to the floor, then ignited her own blade and leapt to the attack.

In the next instant she found herself hanging in the darkness, holding a deactivated lightsaber and staring into a pair of large gray eyes as cold and lifeless as pearls. Suddenly Vestara had another foolish notion as to the reason Ship might have led them here—one that frightened her far more than all the others. Perhaps Ship had brought them here not to destroy the Tribe, but to *free* the Destructors.

The woman lowered her hand, sending Vestara crashing to the floor of the cavern.

"My apologies," she said. "I wasn't sure you were real."

Chapter Fifteen

IF TIME HAD AN EXISTENCE BEYOND THE BODY, LUKE could not find it. Now that he was rising out of his physical being, he saw that moments and years were the same. A heartbeat lasted a week, a lifetime flashed by in an instant. But *Luke Skywalker* remained, a manifestation of Force energy that embodied his essence in both mind and form. And that essence was now more real and tangible than the flesh-and-blood husk he had left floating among the purple-tinged bodies in the makeshift meditation chamber.

"*Five . . . ,*" The skull-faced Givin's raspy voice came to Luke from somewhere behind and below. "*There is no life, there is only the Force.*"

It was a perversion of the Jedi Code, but Luke dutifully repeated the phrase as he exhaled, allowing himself to accept it—even to believe it. He did not think that the "Mind Walkers," which was how the station inhabitants referred to themselves, meant the phrase as a mockery or an insult. They were simply expressing the truth of the universe as they saw it, and he knew enough about meditation to realize that the precise phrasing of a mantra was the code that unlocked the door to a particular realm of the mind.

Another year went by. Or maybe it was only a second. Luke inhaled slowly, picturing a big yellow 5 in his mind, focusing on nothing but that image.

"You are rising higher," said the aged voice of Seek Ryontarr. The horn-headed Gotal was floating in front of Luke—or perhaps it was above him—speaking to him in the soft voice of a meditation coach, guiding him to a higher consciousness. "You are barely connected to your body. You feel contact only at your heels now, now your shoulders, now the back of your skull."

And it was true. Luke only felt attached in those places. Everywhere else, he was floating free, at one with the Force.

"Six . . . ," the Givin rasped.

Luke changed the image in his mind to a big yellow 6. He began to let his breath out, feeling himself growing lighter and more . . . apart. Each time he exhaled, it seemed to take longer, and this time it felt as though a week passed while he was emptying his lungs.

"There is no life," the Givin said. "There is only the Force."

Luke repeated the phrase. He felt his shoulders lift free of his body, leaving him attached at only the heels and the head.

"You are almost free now," Ryontarr told him. "When Feryl says seven, the last bonds will dissolve. You will no longer be attached to your body. You will rise from the shadows into the pure radiance of the Force."

Ryontarr paused, as though waiting for Luke to change his mind. And perhaps he would have, had there been another way to learn what had happened to Jacen here—to look into his nephew's heart, as the Mind Walkers had promised, and see why they believed Jacen could not have gone dark.

The skull-faced Givin, Feryl, rasped, "Seven."

Luke felt his body fall away, and then he was floating in a cloud of violet radiance, staring up into the purple glow at the heart of the chamber and tingling with cool pleasure. He raised his real hand and saw that it looked the same as it always had, then raised the artificial one and saw only a shadow in its place. He tried to touch it. His fingers vanished into the darkness, just as they would into any shadow.

"You cannot touch what is not real. Your cybernetic hand is just illusion, as much a shadow as flesh and bone." Ryontarr reached out to tap Luke's chest. "*That* is real."

"What, exactly, is real?" Luke asked. "My spirit?"

"Your Force presence. It's your true self, a swirl in the living Force that animates your physical body." Ryontarr tapped Luke's chest again. "*This* is what truly exists." He pointed over Luke's shoulder. "It gives form to *that*."

"*That* being my body," Luke clarified.

When Ryontarr dipped his tall horns in the affirmative, Luke slowly spun around and saw his body floating among a dozen others. Although it did not appear nearly as haggard and hollow-cheeked as some of those around it, the eyes were sunken, and his face looked dry and pale. To his surprise, his vac suit appeared to be mere shadow, as did all the clothes he saw. Even the walls of the meditation chamber—what little he could glimpse of them through the mass of floating Mind Walkers—appeared to be nothing but shadow.

"Our bodies appear more substantial than the inanimate material," Luke observed. "Is that because our bodies are imbued with the living Force?"

Ryontarr shook his head. "We Mind Walkers come from a great many traditions: the Disciples of Ragnos, the Fallanassi, the *Jensaarai,* the Potentium Heretics, the Reborn, the Far Seekers, the Inner Seers, and ten dozen more. We have *all* brought our own understandings of the Force—that the Force is a rainbow, that it has a dark side and light side; that it has the three aspects or four, that it has two sides *and* two aspects . . ."

Ryontarr let the sentence trail off, his voice having risen to such a level of disgust that Luke thought he might actually shout. Instead the Gotal sighed and shook his head.

"It's nonsense, all of it," he continued. "There is *one* Force, *the* Force . . . and many ways to see it."

Luke looked back to his body. "Then my body is more substantial than my clothes because . . . ?"

"It's *not.*" Ryontarr pointed at it. "Touch it."

Luke obeyed—or tried to. When he pressed his hand to the body's face, it simply sank through the cheek. The body's eyes widened in momentary alarm, but immediately grew vacant and glassy again.

"You haven't *abandoned* your shadow body yet," Ryontarr said. "There's still a tiny part of you inside, because you aren't ready to give it up entirely."

"And that part is giving it form," Luke surmised. He did not accept everything Ryontarr claimed, but he was here to learn why Jacen had fallen to the dark side—not argue Force theory. He pulled his hand out of his body's face, then frowned at its sunken eyes and dry skin. "Will that vestige of me also keep my body hydrated and fed?"

"In the sense you mean . . . yes," Ryontarr said, holding Luke's gaze a little too steadily. "The Force will sustain your body for as long as you remain attached to it."

Luke cocked a brow and glanced around the chamber. "There are a lot of starving bodies in here."

"What can I say? Many of us have lost our attachment to the shadow world." Ryontarr looked to Luke's body. "You have just arrived, and your attachment is still strong."

"So, my body is safe."

It was the Givin, Feryl, who answered. "If you are afraid, you can always return to your body just by seeing yourself inside." He drifted around in front of Luke, his deep-set eyes gleaming orange in the depths of his skull-like face. "It is only *leaving* that is hard."

It did not escape Luke that Feryl had not actually *said* that his body would be safe, and he felt fairly certain that Ryontarr had been trying a little *too* hard to appear truthful when he had claimed the Force would sustain his body.

"If you don't believe me, just try," Feryl urged. "What do you have to lose?"

"Nothing at all," agreed Ryontarr. "Now that we've shown you how, you can return beyond shadows anytime you wish."

"But you won't be here to guide me," Luke surmised. "I'll have to retrace Jacen's steps without your help."

Ryontarr shook his head. "You have only to call us before you start."

"We'll be here waiting." Feryl turned and began to rise into the ball of purple light. "Think on it all you like, Master Skywalker."

"There is no hurry," Ryontarr agreed, following. "Time is an illusion."

Luke frowned and glanced down at his body's sunken eyes. He could sense that the Mind Walkers weren't telling him the whole truth, but it didn't feel as though they wished him harm. And they were clearly willing to let him be certain of his body's safety before proceeding. But time *did* still matter to Valin and all the other young Jedi who were losing their minds, and if he could discover whether Jacen's visit here had something to do with their delusions, the sooner he did so the better. Too, there were those mysterious alarms flashing and blaring in the control room. When *any* alarm went active, he could not help feeling that time mattered very much.

"Wait." Luke used the Force to pull his vac suit's water tube free of its mounting clip so he could position the suck-nozzle between his body's lips, then went to join the Mind Walkers. "Where are we heading?"

Ryontarr pivoted around, half facing him, then pointed toward the purple radiance crackling in the center of the chamber. "We are going into the light, Master Skywalker."

Luke smiled. "Into the light?" he repeated. "That has an ominous ring to it."

"Not at all," Ryontarr said, also stopping to wait. "You have *already* gone into the light—just as you are still inside your body, about to begin the releasing meditation."

"All is permanent," Feryl added. "All things that *will* happen have *already* happened. All things that have *already* happened are *about* to happen."

"Time passes inside *us,* Master Skywalker," explained Ryontarr. "It is only *our* finite nature that parses the galaxy into seconds and eons."

"So I've heard," Luke said, recognizing some of the philosophical underpinnings of the assertion. There was a definite Aing-Tii influence, with a bit of the Potentium unity doctrine and perhaps even a hint of Heresiarchian determinism thrown in. He found himself wondering just how the Mind Walkers had melded together so many different Force traditions. "A finite mind cannot comprehend the infinite galaxy."

"You *will*." Feryl motioned Luke after him, then started toward the purple glow again. "Come into the light with us."

As Luke followed the pair toward the crackling radiance above, he began to understand the origins of the

term *Mind Walking*. Every time he started to swing a
foot forward, he simply found himself a pace ahead of
where he had been the moment before, as though he
were teleporting ahead one step at a time. Eventually,
he realized that he merely had to *think* about moving to
discover that he had already done it.

The trio was still three meters away from the purple
glow when a tentacle of light crackled down to touch
Luke's chest. His entire presence immediately turned as
purple as the ball of light itself, and he was filled with a
bone-shivering joy a thousand times more intense than
anything he had ever before experienced. He felt as
though he had become the Force and the Force had become him, and he was flooded with a calming bliss that
seemed as deep as space. Pain, fear, anguish—even the
memory of such suffering—vanished. He knew only the
pure, eternal joy of existence, a song as vast and ageless
as the universe itself.

Luke remained in the song more than a year, and less
than a second. He did not remember because the past
was yet to come; he did not desire because the future
was already gone. He saw the galaxy, the universe, the
Force itself in its beautiful infinite entirety, a thing both
within and without, limitless and sublime and wholly
beyond comprehension.

A raspy voice said, *"Walk."*

Then Luke was standing in a shadowy arcade, looking out on an ancient courtyard overgrown with tree
ferns, club mosses, and pillars of scaled fungi. In the
center of the courtyard sat the curving basin of a formal
fountain, the water jet gurgling somewhere inside a pall
of steam so filled with sulfur that it was more brown
than yellow.

"The Font of Power," said the raspy voice.

Luke turned his head toward the speaker. He saw a
skull-faced Givin—*Feryl,* he recalled—next to him, and

he began to remember where he was . . . or rather, to remember the quest that had led him here, since he had no idea where *here* actually was. Luke was on a mission. He needed to find out why Jacen had fallen prey to the dark side. He needed to determine whether his nephew's sojourn had anything to do with the psychoses troubling so many young Jedi Knights.

Luke was still reorienting himself when a second voice—this one deep and refined—said, "If you have the courage to drink of it, you will have the power to achieve anything."

"*Anything?*" Luke glanced over to find the flat-faced Gotal, Ryontarr, standing to his other side. "That's a big promise."

"There is no limit to the strength that can be drawn from the Font of Power," Ryontarr replied. "You can drink as deeply as you wish."

"*Can* I?"

Luke turned back toward the courtyard. The tree ferns pushing up through its disarrayed cobblestones seemed as substantial and normal as his own form, as did the rest of the plant life, the mosses hanging from the arcade pillars and the line of fungi ringing the fountain's basin. But like the walls back in the station's meditation chamber, the ornate stonework was shadowy and incorporeal, with edges just distinct enough to suggest sculpted decoration that was both sinuous and grotesque.

"Seek, before we left the station, you told me that my body still appeared substantial not because it was filled with the living Force, but only because I remained attached to it." Luke pointed at a hairy yellow club moss as tall as he was. "But the plant life here appears substantial, too—and I'm not attached to *it* at all."

"But another presence *is*," agreed Ryontarr. "Go on. You will see."

Luke stepped out of the arcade into the light of a harsh blue sun. As he grew accustomed to its glare, he saw that the courtyard sat in the bottom of a deep jungle valley, with steep walls blanketed in alien plant life rising to all sides. The highest wall, located at the far end of the courtyard, ascended more than a kilometer to the dipping rim of a volcano crater.

Luke continued forward and slowly came to realize that the whole courtyard was filled with the acrid stench of sulfur. The fumes weren't burning his throat or nose, since he did not actually seem to be breathing them. But they *were* making him queasy, and as he drew closer to the fountain, something inside him protested so violently that he felt as though he might retch.

When he reached the basin, Luke could finally see through the curtain of steam to the font itself. It was a jet of water about as thick as his leg, so filled with sulfur and iron that it was as brown as a tree trunk—and so permeated with Force energy that it literally sent him stumbling back, his head spinning and his stomach churning. The fountain was not just *tainted* with dark side power, it was *imbued* with it—as if it were rising up from some deep-buried reservoir of dark-side energy that had been building, preparing to blow for not just millennia, but since the beginning of time itself.

Luke resisted the temptation to start hurling accusations. The Font of Power was clearly a dark-side nexus, and Ryontarr, at least, would understand what that meant. Such nexuses arose as a result of any number of events—all of them bad. Perhaps a powerful user of the dark side had once lived in the valley—or merely been killed there. The Valley of Dark Lords on Korriban had become a dark-side nexus because it had been inhabited by Sith Lords for so long, and a nexus had formed in orbit over Endor after Palpatine died there.

Whatever the case, as a former Jedi Knight, Ryontarr would have known better than to think Luke would actually drink from the fountain without noticing the nexus. The Gotal had to have brought him here for another reason—some less obvious form of corruption, or perhaps just to test him.

When Luke finally felt calm enough, he turned to Ryontarr and asked, "What happened here?"

Ryontarr spread his hands to indicate that he didn't know. "It's as much a mystery as the Maw itself," he said. "But does it matter? If you drink of the fountain, you will have the power to save the Jedi Order from extinction."

"From *extinction*?" Luke felt like he had been hit in the stomach with a Stokhli spray stick. Was *that* how their problems with Daala were going to end? Or were the delusions going to wipe them out? "Have you seen that?"

Ryontarr nodded. "I'm sorry."

Luke turned toward the fountain, wondering if drinking of its waters truly *was* the only way to save the Jedi Order—if *that* had been enough to convince Jacen.

"How does it happen?" Luke asked. "The extinction, I mean."

"It has *already* happened," Feryl said. He pointed a bony finger past Luke, toward the fountain. "Drink. It is the only way to save your Order."

Luke frowned in confusion—until he recalled that time did not exist beyond shadows. Of course, that didn't mean that the Jedi were safe. Far from it, with young Jedi going mad and Daala determined to bring the Order itself to heel. Given all that, extinction seemed like a real possibility sooner rather than later.

Luke turned to study the fountain. He could feel its dark power swirling around him, inviting him to use *it* to save what he had spent a lifetime building, what he loved more than life itself. And he was tempted, just as every man was when he saw an easy way out of a desperate situation. All he need do was return to the basin, stick his head into the dark geyser, and drink of those poison waters.

But even if Luke were willing to corrupt himself, he wouldn't be saving the Order. He would only be making it dependent on his own strength, and that was no more a formula for building a strong organization than it was for raising a healthy child. If he wanted the Order to survive him, he had to let it strengthen itself by going through this struggle without him—just as he had to let Ben make his own mistakes, if Ben was going to develop the wisdom to lead the Order after Luke was gone.

When Luke did not return to the fountain, Ryontarr asked, "What are you waiting for, Master Skywalker? Surely you want to save the Jedi Order?"

"Of course I do," Luke said, spinning on the Gotal. "But you and I both know I *won't* do that by drinking from this fountain."

"Then how will you save it?" Feryl pressed.

"*I* won't," Luke said. "The Order is strong enough to save itself."

Ryontarr and Feryl exchanged glances, obviously disappointed in Luke's decision.

"Stop playing with me," Luke ordered. He fixed his glare on Ryontarr. "You *knew* I'd never drink from that fountain. So why bring me here?"

"Why indeed?" A thin smile came to Ryontarr's lips, then his gaze shifted away from Luke back toward the fountain's yellow smoke. "Because you asked us to."

"There is no need to be angry with us, Master Skywalker," added Feryl. "If you are afraid to see what you came seeking, it's no fault of ours."

Luke frowned. "*Afraid?*"

He turned back toward the Font of Power—and felt a chill of danger sense race down his back.

Staring out of the yellow fog were a dozen sets of eyes, some too narrow and spaced too wide to be those of any species Luke recognized, others more round and human-like, all burning with the golden anger of the dark side. They were set in puffs of black vapor shaped like heads, more than half resembling the large, wedge-shaped skulls that Luke and Ben had seen still locked in the detention cells aboard the space station.

The other heads seemed more familiar in shape. One was lumpy and large-browed, with the long head-tails of a Twi'lek. Another was more triangular, with the long snout and triple eyestalks of a Gran. The rest were human, but so badly distorted with sunken cheeks and bony jawlines that they were difficult to recognize.

Recalling what Feryl had promised back in the meditation chamber—that Luke would be able to look into Jacen's heart—Luke began to understand why the Mind Walkers had brought him here: perhaps *Jacen* had drunk from the fountain. He started back toward the basin, searching for the head that most closely resembled his nephew's.

As Luke drew closer, a new patch of dark vapor began to coalesce in the steam. He went straight toward it, wondering whether he would be able to speak with it—and unsure what he should ask it first: *Why did you turn to the dark side? How could you murder my wife? What did I do wrong?*

By the time Luke had reached the edge of the basin, the dark cloud had grown to the size of a human head. But it had a long cascade of golden hair that fell into the bubbling waters of the fountain pool and vanished, and its eyes were tiny, silver, and deep-sunken, like two stars shining out of a pair of black wells. A tentacle of cold, wet *nothingness* reached out to Luke, wrapping itself around his leg, then sank into his flesh and began to squirm up inside him.

Luke gasped and tried to back away, only to discover that he was pulling the vaporous thing along with him. To his astonishment, it appeared to be female, with a large, full-lipped mouth so broad that it reached from ear to ear. Her stubby arms protruded no more than ten centimeters from her shoulders, and in place of fingers, her hands had writhing tentacles so long that they hung down past the rim of the basin.

Luke.

The voice sounded cold and familiar and half-remembered inside Luke's mind, a dream-lover's whisper. The cloud smiled, revealing a mouthful of curved teeth as sharp as needles, then extended a dark tentacle in his direction.

Come.

That was the last thing Luke intended to do. Whatever else this thing was, it was female—and that meant it wasn't *Jacen*. Luke took a step backward, then suddenly he was in the arcade again, standing between Ryontarr and Feryl. When he looked down at his hand, he was surprised to see that it was neither shaking nor sweating—but somewhere, he felt pretty certain, his entire body was trembling in fear.

Luke turned and glared into the depths of Feryl's bottomless eye sockets.

"*That* . . . was . . . not . . . Jacen."

"Of course not," the Givin answered. "Jacen wasn't even tempted."

Ryontarr clasped a hand over Luke's shoulder. "But don't feel bad, Master Skywalker. In the end, you did the right thing, too. That's all that matters."

Chapter Sixteen

WITH PUCKERED BROWS HANGING LOW AND HEAVY OVER
hollow eyes and bony cheeks, Rolund and Rhondi
Tremaine reminded Ben of Ugnaughts more than humans. The two Mind Walkers were seated in the
Shadow's galley, sucking down sip-packs of hydrade
from the medbay and squeezing raw nutripaste straight
from a ten-kilogram storage bladder. Their yellow hair
lay helmet-pressed to their heads, their nostrils were in-
flamed and flaky, and their lips were so chapped and
split, it was a wonder the hydrade wasn't dribbling out
through the cracks.

Having just checked the supplies in medbay, Ben
knew that the hydrade had come from the last case,
while the nutripaste was the third bladder that he had
lost to hungry Mind Walkers in a week. If the drain on
their stores continued at this rate much longer, the first
thing the *Shadow* would need to do upon leaving the
Maw was reprovision. Still, he did not chase the pair
off, or even object to their foraging. What little he had
managed to piece together about Sinkhole Station—as
the inhabitants called it—had come from talking with
hungry Mind Walkers, and on their last visit the
Tremaines had proven more informative than most.

Ben stopped in the galley hatch and studied the
wretched pair for a moment, then shook his head in disgust. "I could get you a couple of glasses of hyperdrive

coolant," he said. "Your deaths would be long and painful, but it has to be better than what you're putting yourselves through."

Rhondi shook her own head and pulled the sip-pack away. "Too hard to go beyond shadows when you're barfing blood," she explained. "But thanks for the suggestion."

Rolund licked a gob of nutripaste off his fingers, then nodded at the equipment satchel in Ben's hand. "What's with the tool bag?" he asked. "The last time we were here, you said you were just *finishing* the repairs."

Ben nodded. "I did."

He stepped into the galley and started to join the Tremaines at the table, then thought better of it and put the bag on the staging counter opposite. Mind Walkers were ravenous for fluids and food when they returned from beyond shadows, and he didn't want to share the contents of the satchel. He covered the maneuver by drawing a glass of hubba juice from the conservator, then left the satchel on the counter and turned back toward his guests.

"We've been spaceworthy for two days," Ben said, joining them at the table. "Now I'm just bored waiting around."

"If you say so," Rhondi said. Her gaze slid across the aisle. "So what don't you want us to see in that satchel?"

Ben smiled. "Sorry—I guess that wasn't as subtle as I thought," he said. "It's just an intravenous kit, and I don't want you guys draining the drip bag on me."

"An IV?" Rolund asked, his frown mirroring Rhondi's so precisely that it unsettled Ben. He still hadn't established whether they were twins or just regular siblings, but sometimes they seemed as close as Killiks. "What for?"

"My dad's suck-nozzle keeps coming out of his mouth," Ben explained. "He's starting to get pretty dehydrated."

The Tremaines managed to avoid looking at each other, but the glimmer of alarm that flashed through their hazel eyes was unmistakable. For an instant, Ben thought that the problem suggested something was going wrong beyond shadows, and he waited with clenched teeth for one of them to break the news to him. Instead Rhondi deliberately looked away from the IV kit, as if it suddenly held no interest, and Rolund reached out a little too casually to squeeze some more nutripaste from the storage bladder. Then Ben figured it out: the suck-nozzle wasn't *falling* out of his father's mouth.

Someone was *removing* it.

Ben grabbed his hubba juice and took a long drink, quieting his anger and considering what to do. He would learn nothing through furious accusations or violent threats, and would probably only be placing his father in greater danger. So far, the Mind Walkers did not seem interested in killing Luke Skywalker, because if that was their intention, there had been plenty of opportunities to make an attempt over the last week. But they did seem eager to let him die. The difference was subtle yet significant, and *that*, Ben knew, was what made it the key to puzzling out what the Mind Walkers were really doing here.

Ben returned his hubba juice to the table, then fixed his gaze on Rhondi and sat waiting with an attitude of silent expectation. She responded by smiling politely, then looking away and squeezing some nutripaste from the storage bladder onto her fingers. Ben continued to hold his gaze on her, keeping his expression thoughtful and attentive, letting her know that he was studying her every move and contemplating what it meant.

The last time the Tremaines had come to raid the *Shadow*'s stores, Ben had used the technique and quickly had them spilling their life histories. Like most of the younger Mind Walkers at Sinkhole Station, the pair had actually been born inside the Maw, at a secret colony that Admiral Daala had established toward the end of the warlord era. And like all Force-sensitives born there, Rolund and Rhondi had been deemed unsuitable for military service. Instead they had been groomed from childhood to become intelligence operatives.

Upon reaching adulthood, they were sent out to spy for the Maw Colony. Their assignments had varied widely, from gathering information to subverting security on vessels targeted for appropriation. For the next decade, they served in an espionage organization so efficient that Daala was able to keep the colony well supplied and growing while she managed to assemble and equip the entire Maw Irregular Fleet—all in utter secrecy.

Then came the Second Galactic Civil War and the destruction of Centerpoint Station. The Tremaines and the Maw Colony's other Force-sensitive agents began to experience terrible longings to return home. When Daala denied their requests, the longings became paranoia, and the operatives universally began to believe that the whole war had been orchestrated just to expose *them*. Eventually, the paranoia became obsession, and the agents deserted en masse. Stealing any vessel they could find, they began to return to the Maw, following a mysterious urge to seek refuge in its heart—a compulsion that invariably led them to Sinkhole Station.

The other Mind Walkers—those who had not actually been born in the Maw—had simpler stories. Universally Force-sensitive, they had all experienced a strong emotional connection to the Maw the first time they visited it. That bond grew stronger over time, compelling them to journey ever deeper into the cluster of black holes. Eventually, they arrived at Sinkhole Station and began a lonely, ascetic existence in which they spent all their time communing with the mysterious Force presence that had drawn them here.

Then, a couple of years ago, the ascetics' meditations had started to take them to new heights. They began to see the ineffable truth that all life was illusion, that the only existence lay beyond their bodily shadows in the divine glow of the Force itself. Their presences actually began to leave their bodies as they meditated, traveling to a beautiful paradise dimension where there was no pain or suffering, no anger or fear, only the pure eternal joy of *being*.

Ben had no idea what to make of this "paradise dimension," but it was clear that the destruction of Centerpoint Station had changed something fundamental in the Maw. Whatever that change was, it had rippled across the galaxy like a Force nova, turning hundreds of Force-sensitive beings who had once lived inside the Maw into delusional paranoids. And the thing that frightened Ben, that had had him gnawing at his insides like a hungry cancer for the last two days, was that *he* had lived in the Maw for two years early in his life.

After a long two minutes, Rhondi finally grew uncomfortable with Ben's silent scrutiny. Still licking nutripaste from her fingertips, she met his gaze and said, "That's not necessary, you know."

Ben continued to watch her. "What?"

"The quiet stare," Rolund answered. "We probably know more about interrogation than you do. If you have a question, just ask. We have nothing to hide, I promise."

"Okay." Ben kept his gaze fixed on Rhondi. "Why don't you want me to put my father on an IV?"

This time, the Tremaines did not betray their alarm even in their eyes. But Daala's trainers had not taught them how to conceal their emotions in the Force, and Ben could feel their surprise in their auras as clearly as he had seen it earlier.

After a barely discernible pause, Rolund asked, "What makes you think we care about that, Ben?"

Ben sighed. "Answering a question with a question is kind of artless, don't you think?" He placed both palms on the table and leaned forward. "If you think that's going to work on a Jedi, you *definitely* don't know more about interrogation than I do."

Rhondi slumped back in her seat, unconsciously signaling her fear by leaning away from Ben.

"Rolund said you have nothing to hide," Ben pressed. "I *hate* it when people lie to me."

"We're not lying," Rhondi insisted. "It's just that your father doesn't need an IV."

"The *Force* will sustain him," Rolund added.

Ben cast a meaningful glance at the storage bladder resting between them. "Like it sustains *you*?"

Rhondi nodded eagerly. "Exactly."

A cold fury began to worm its way up Ben's belly. These people were lying to him. Determined to remain calm, he took a deep breath—then a second, and third. He was in danger of losing his temper, which meant he was also in danger of losing control of the interrogation. And perhaps *that* was why they were deceiving him—because they knew he would be easier to control if he grew angry.

They were subtle, these Mind Walkers, more dangerous than Ben had realized. He took yet another deep breath, and once he felt relatively calm again he sat upright, casually propping his hand on his thigh . . . close to his lightsaber.

"So the Force is *all* you need to sustain your bodies?" he asked.

"Absolutely," Rhondi assured him. "What *is* a body, but the Force given form?"

"Good question," Ben acknowledged. "But I've got another one. If you don't need anything but the Force to sustain yourselves, why are you tearing through the *Shadow*'s stores?"

To Ben's surprise, Rhondi turned to Rolund and smiled. "I *told* you he'd notice that."

Rolund shrugged and kept his attention fixed on her. "It was better than the *Food is just the Force in the form of matter* nonsense *you* wanted to try."

"And you're *both* dodging my question." Ben stood and stepped back from the table. He was starting to get the feeling that the Tremaines—and *all* the Mind Walkers who had come to the *Shadow* for handouts—had been setting him up for a betrayal. "I want an answer, or I want you gone."

Rhondi began to look worried—and just a little ashamed. She turned to Rolund, who was glaring at Ben in open resentment, and said, "I think we'd better tell him the truth, Rolund. He seems to be upset."

"And I'm growing angrier by the second," Ben warned. They had been lying to him all along, he realized, and that could only mean they intended him harm. "I don't like feeding enemies."

"We're not your enemies," Rolund said, arching his brows. He actually looked hurt—but in a practiced, well-rehearsed way that suggested his long years of espionage training. "We've just been trying to help you."

"*All* of us have," Rhondi added. "The sooner the *Shadow* runs out of supplies, the sooner you'll see that the only *real* sustenance you need is the Force."

The cold rage began to snake its way higher, working

itself into Ben's heart and mind. Something inside was urging him to ignore the Tremaines, to kill them before their lies killed *him*.

Ben shook the urge off. He could feel the deception in Rhondi's words, but he was a Jedi, and Jedi did not murder people for lying to them.

After a moment, Ben said, "There are other ways to prove your point—ways that might actually convince me."

Rolund smiled warmly. "Perhaps you would care to enlighten us?"

"Sure. It's pretty simple, actually." Ben pulled the nutripaste bladder to his side of the table, then used the Force to pluck the hydrade sip-packs out of their grasps. "Just return to beyond shadows and stay there without drinking or eating anything. If you last more than a week, I'll believe what you tell me."

If the suggestion struck any fear or outrage in the hearts of the Tremaines, Ben did not feel it in their Force auras. Instead Rolund pretended to consider the idea for a moment, then turned to his sister.

"I don't know, Rhondi," he said. "What do you think?"

"I think a week is a long time for Ben to wait for his proof," Rhondi said.

She reached for the sip-pack Ben had taken, but something made him jerk it away. The cold rage inside was slithering up higher, reminding him how the Mind Walkers had used Luke's memory of Jacen to lure his father beyond shadows. And now they were at it again, trying to prevent Ben from keeping him alive—and to trick him into going beyond shadows himself. Maybe the Tremaines *did* need to die . . . if he wanted to keep his father alive, maybe *all* the Mind Walkers needed to die.

That last thought was what finally shocked Ben out of his rage. He could not believe the idea of mass murder had actually crossed his mind. That seemed just crazy . . . which, of course, it *was*. Ben had spent two years in the Maw, and now he was beginning to have paranoid thoughts about the inhabitants of the station.

The conclusion seemed . . . *alarming*.

Ben passed the sip-packs to the Tremaines. "You'd better go," he said. "And if I were you, I wouldn't come back."

Chapter Seventeen

WITH A GALLERY OF OLD REPUBLIC ARCHITECTURAL studies on the walls and a seating area dominated by two chic LevitaRest couches, the room had obviously been decorated with an eye toward style rather than function. It also appeared far too tidy to be the office of a working judge. Atop the fashionable Freefloater desk, there was not a single document folder, nor even a reading lamp or datapad. In fact, the only indication that someone actually *used* the chamber on a regular basis was the lingering trace of a sweet, fruity perfume that Jagged Fel felt quite sure the room's current occupant would not be caught comatose wearing.

Tall and regal, with long copper hair going to gray, the woman was standing with her back to him. Dressed in her usual uniform of slacks and a white faux-military tunic, she was gazing out a long panel of one-way transparisteel into a gray-walled courtroom that was as austere as the office was fashionable. The room was packed with Jedi, reporters, and other spectators, but the woman's attention was fixed on the general area of the defense table, where a blond, stoic-looking Jedi-turned-"finder" sat next to her lumpy-faced attorney, a male Twi'lek named Nawara Ven.

Without looking away from the courtroom, the copper-haired woman motioned to a vacant spot beside her. "Head of State Fel, won't you join me? This won't take long, and I suspect you're as interested in Jedi Veila's arraignment as I am."

"I have no doubt the proceeding will be quick, Chief Daala," Jagged said. Because he had requested this meeting at the last minute, Daala had asked him to join her in the chambers of Judge Arabelle Lorteli. "But Tahiri Veila hasn't been a Jedi for nearly three years."

"So I've heard." Daala continued to look into the courtroom, but Jag thought he glimpsed the hint of a smile at the corner of her mouth. "Then this *should* be interesting."

As Jag drew closer to the viewing panel, he saw the Solos sitting in spectator seats behind the defense table. Han and Leia were at the far end of the row, while Jaina was at the other end, with six unoccupied chairs between them. Jag felt a stab of guilt, because he knew *he* was the cause of the rift in the Solo family. What he didn't know was what else he could have done; it simply would not have been honorable to ignore his duty to the Galactic Empire by telling the Jedi what he had overheard about Daala and the Mandalorians.

As sad as Jag was to see the Solos so obviously at odds, he was not surprised to find them at Tahiri's arraignment. They had been protective of her for the last couple of years, perhaps because her change of heart at the end of the civil war had saved a great many Jedi lives. Or maybe they felt bad about how Caedus had played on her emotions to lead her down a dark path. Or maybe they just felt close to her because of what she had meant to their son Anakin. Probably, it was all of those things.

Whatever the Solos' reasons, Jag just wanted to convince Daala to drop the charges against Veila. First, it was the right thing to do. Second, helping Tahiri just might redeem him in the eyes of his future in-laws.

He stopped a pace from Daala's side, then gently

touched a knuckle to the one-way transparisteel. Although it was impossible to see through the panel from the other side, both Jaina and Leia instantly looked in his direction.

"No secrets from the Jedi," Daala commented. "What do you imagine they will make of your presence here . . . with me?"

"I'm sure they'll know exactly why I'm here." Jag hoped that he sounded more confident than he felt. "To help you see the mistake you're making."

Daala looked at him and cocked a brow. "You don't approve of my methods?"

"I don't approve of using the judicial system as a political weapon," Jag replied. "It smacks of tyranny."

Daala appeared to consider this for a moment. Then her expression grew unreadable and she said, "We are all products of our past, Head of State Fel . . . but I see your point."

A door in the back of the courtroom opened, and the sergeant of the guard called attendees to their feet. Once everyone had obeyed, a slender, blue-haired woman entered the chamber. With high, arching brows and a wide, full-lipped mouth, she looked like an attractive human woman of no more than seventy—save for a thin, too-long nose that identified her as a member of the Zoolli species.

As she ascended the stairs to the judge's bench, Daala turned back to the courtroom. "We can talk about judicial independence after the arraignment," she said. "Trust me, you won't want to miss *this*."

The obvious eagerness in Daala's voice made Jag's stomach sink, but if she *was* willing to talk about the abuse of power, he might actually have a chance of changing her mind about what she was doing here—as long as he didn't anger her first by denying her a moment of vengeance.

"Very well," he said. "You *were* kind to see me here, and on such short notice."

"Without an agenda," Daala reminded him. "That alone gives me a pretty good idea of what we're going to be talking about."

Jag nodded, but before he could answer, the sergeant's gravelly voice came over the intercom's courtroom feed.

"The Court of Jedi Affairs stands now in session, the honorable Arabelle Lorteli presiding. Be seated and be quiet."

Even before the court complied, Judge Lorteli began to speak in a pinched, nasal voice that sent shivers down Jag's spine. "I must say, I hadn't realized my reputation was growing quite so fast."

The remark was greeted by a round of good-natured chuckling, which immediately drew a surprised scowl from the judge. She glared down her long nose at the attendees, then shot an angry glance toward her court sergeant.

"Quiet!" the sergeant bellowed.

A stunned silence fell over the courtroom, and Judge Lorteli tried to hide the flush that had come to her cheeks by pretending to examine a data screen hidden behind the bench. Jag immediately had doubts about the woman's worthiness for the bench, and the smirk that came to Daala's face was all the confirmation he needed. The Chief of State had known exactly what she was doing when she appointed this particular Zoolli to the Jedi bench.

Once the color had drained from Lorteli's cheeks, she looked up again and peered over the bench. "What I *meant* to say, of course, was that I'm a bit surprised to find this much interest in a simple arraignment."

Without waiting for the judge to give him permission, Nawara Ven rose and began to speak. "That unusual interest is due to the public outrage at this blatant abuse of the judicial, Your Honor. The arrest of Tahiri Veila is nothing more than a cynical political ploy—"

"That's enough for now, Counselor," Lorteli interrupted, raising her hand to the Twi'lek. "And you are . . . ?"

Nawara's head-tails twitched so violently that they slapped against his back. "You know perfectly well who I am, Your Honor. I've appeared before you a dozen times this week alone."

"On behalf of various Jedi," Lorteli clarified. "Would that be correct, Counselor Ven?"

To Jag's surprise, the judge did not seem irritated in the least by Ven's retort, and Jagged began to have a bad feeling about what was going to happen in that courtroom.

Apparently, Ven had the same feeling, because his reply was uncharacteristically short. "Of course."

"And the Jedi are paying you to represent Tahiri Veila?" Lorteli continued.

Ven drew himself up tall and still. "We haven't discussed payment yet, Your Honor," he said. "But for the past two years, Tahiri Veila has been consulting as a corporate . . . *finder*, I guess one would say. I understand she's been very successful, so it was my impression that she would be paying her own expenses."

"Not kriffing likely," Daala muttered under her breath. "She doesn't have twenty thousand credits to her name."

Tahiri was far too well trained—by the Jedi *and* Darth Caedus—to show any surprise she may have felt at Ven's assertion. But Judge Lorteli seemed momentarily stunned, as though Ven had deviated from a carefully rehearsed script. She let her gaze drop for a moment, obviously consulting her data screen again, then pursed her lips in resolve and looked to Tahiri.

"Defendant Veila, are you a Jedi?"

"No." Tahiri answered without rising, a gesture of disrespect that suggested she knew as well as Ven did where the judge was heading with this argument. "Not at present."

"But there was a time when you *were* a Jedi, correct?"

"Correct."

"And that was prior to the recent Galactic Civil War?" Lorteli asked.

Before Tahiri could answer, Ven was leaning forward, bracing his bulk on the defense table. "Your Honor, I really must protest this line of questioning. My client's employment prior to the war has no bearing on the plea she's here to enter."

Lorteli did not even look at him. "Your objection is overruled, Counselor Ven."

"On what grounds?" he demanded.

"On the grounds that I haven't accepted you as this defendant's representative . . . and I am unlikely to do so."

A murmur of surprise rustled through the courtroom, and Han Solo rose, his mouth open to shout—until his wife pulled him back into his seat and used the Force to pin him there. Jaina simply slipped forward to the edge of her seat, her angry glare fixed on Lorteli. Even Tahiri finally seemed to be taking a keener interest, leaning forward and propping her elbows on the table.

Once the sergeant of the court had issued the obligatory demand for quiet, Lorteli fixed her gaze on Tahiri again.

"Answer the question, Defendant Veila. Were you a Jedi prior to the recent Galactic Civil War?"

"Yes." Tahiri shot a spiteful glance toward the bewildered Bith at the prosecutor's table. "*Before* I committed the acts for which they want to put me on trial."

"I understand that," Lorteli said. "But in your capacity as a Jedi Knight, you were privy to a great many secrets that the Jedi Order might not want revealed in open court, were you not?"

"Oh, we *all* know where the Emperor buried his treasure, if that's what you're asking," Tahiri said, slumping back in her chair. "I'll be glad to draw you a map, if it will get these charges—"

The rest of her offer was lost to the din of guffaws and chuckles that rolled through the courtroom, and even Daala snorted in amusement.

"That one has guts," she said. "I have to give her that."

"What does she have to lose?" Jag asked. "A blind Gungan could see that you've had this court rigged from the start."

Daala smirked. "*Now* who's prejudging, Fel? Judge Lorteli is merely trying to ensure that the defendant has adequate counsel."

Once the sergeant had restored quiet again, Lorteli glared down at Tahiri. "Shall I take that as a yes?"

"Take it however you like." Tahiri glanced back at Han and Leia, then added, "But even if I *do* know any secrets, I won't be sharing them with anyone in this room."

Lorteli actually smiled at her. "That choice, of course, is entirely yours," she said. "But since any such information you care to provide might very well have an impact on the disposition of your own case, I cannot allow Nawara Ven—or any other counsel with such a clear conflict of interests—to participate in your defense."

The courtroom burst into cries of outrage, and this time Leia Solo did not bother pulling Han back down. Jag looked away, shaking his head in disgust.

"At least you had enough sense not to gloat in open

court," he said to Daala. "Please tell me you really don't believe the Jedi—or their allies in the Senate—will respect what you did in there?"

"Of course not." Daala deactivated the intercom speaker, then also turned away from the viewing panel. "But I had to send a message of my own. If the Masters believe they can intimidate me by threatening to dissolve the Order—"

"I wasn't aware they *had*," Jag interrupted. "Everything I hear suggests those apprentices resigned on their own."

Daala rolled her eyes. "*Please,* Head of State, if you were really that naïve, the Moffs would have killed you two years ago." She started across the room toward the beverage center. "May I offer you something to drink? Polar water or fizzee, perhaps?"

"Nothing, thank you," Jag said. Daala had stopped offering him intoxicants after their second meeting, a grudging acknowledgment of respect, since he had made it clear that he felt state business deserved clear heads. "But I wish you would reconsider what you're doing here. It's not the law that you're enforcing."

Daala opened the cabinet and, without turning around, asked, "Then what is it?"

"*Your* will," he said. "And it's obvious to more than just the Jedi. When you put Tahiri Veila on trial, and at the same time leave one of the *architects* of the coup free to retire in peace, it smacks of corruption."

Daala paused for a moment, then asked, "You're talking about Cha Niathal?"

"Of course," Jag replied. "Tahiri and Admiral Niathal *both* changed sides. Do you really think you can put one on trial and let the other live in peace? The public will think you're repaying Niathal for helping you become Chief of State. I hear the Senate *already* thinks so."

"And it won't matter that they're wrong." Daala nodded, then pulled a glass out of the cabinet and filled it with fizzee. "Perception is everything."

Jag nodded. "That's the nature of democracy." To his surprise, Daala seemed genuinely concerned. Perhaps there was hope of dismissing the charges against Tahiri after all. "When you accepted the post, you promised to make the Galactic Alliance a just society for *all* beings. You can't do that by using the courts as a political weapon."

Daala turned, then sipped her fizzee and asked, "So what do you recommend?"

"Dismiss the charges against Tahiri and abolish the Jedi court," Jagged said. "If a Jedi *deserves* to be charged, do it through the normal court system. If you truly want the Jedi to obey the same laws that everyone obeys, it's the only way to make that work."

Daala considered this for a moment, then said, "That's certainly one way to approach the problem. I'll give it some thought." She took another drink of her fizzee, then looked at her chrono. "If we're done here, I have to be back in my office for a staff meeting in ten minutes."

Jag bit back the urge to press the matter by revealing what he knew about the Mandalorians. He was tempted to tell her that she was a fool if she believed that hiring Mandalorians was going to accomplish anything other than getting a bunch of people killed. But Daala had at least promised to reconsider her approach to dealing with the Jedi—and that was more than he had actually expected to achieve.

Instead he said, "There *is* one other thing we need to discuss." He reached into his tunic pocket and withdrew the parasite droid Jaina had given him, then went to the beverage cabinet and laid it on the serving counter in front of Daala. "Do you know what this is?"

Daala picked up the droid and raised it to the light, then said, "It isn't ours, if that's what you're thinking. Not that I wouldn't *love* to eavesdrop on you and the Moffs, but, frankly, your sweeps have been too thorough."

"I'll send my security officer your compliments," Jagged said. "But this is *ours*."

Daala raised a puzzled brow. "And you're showing it to me so I know what to look for?"

Jag smiled. "We're not bugging you," he said. "*This* is how Javis Tyrr has been getting his stories from inside the Jedi Temple."

Daala scowled. "I know you don't expect me to believe that *you've* been helping him."

"Hardly." Jag slipped the parasite droid back into his tunic pocket. "*Lecersen* has."

Daala's eyes lit with instant understanding. "The filthy Hutt slime! I should have realized."

"You're not the only one," Jag said. "But the past is the past. The question is, what do we do about it now?"

Daala's expression went blank. "*We*, Head of State? He's *your* Moff."

"A Moff who's been playing you and the Jedi against each other," Jag pointed out. "And I'm pretty sure it's not just Lecersen. There are a lot of Moffs who have reason to strike at you, me, and the Jedi."

Daala's green eyes grew so cold they almost went blue. "Then I suggest you handle them, Fel." She banged her glass down on the cabinet so hard that the fizzee splashed onto the CrystaClear surface. "If you like, I can put you in touch with a *very* good bounty hunter who would just love the job."

Now it was Jag's turn to frown in confusion. "You're

going to continue this vendetta against the Jedi?" he asked. "Even knowing that it's the Moffs who have been stirring up trouble?"

Daala's face turned stormy. "Let me assure you that bringing the Jedi to heel is my own idea, Head of State, and it's *anything* but a vendetta. It's high time that someone brings these vigilantes under government control and puts a stop to their incessant power struggles."

"*Power* struggles?" Jagged gasped. "Is that who you think the Jedi are fighting? *Themselves?*"

"Head of State, a Sith is just a Jedi who's gone off his meds," Daala declared. "Why do you think Dark Lords keep popping up?"

Jag shook his head. "Chief Daala, you are so tragically wrong," he said. "The Sith are real, they're out there, and the Jedi are the only ones who can turn them back."

"At least we agree on those first two points. The Sith are real, and they're definitely out there." Daala checked her chrono again, then started for the door. "But if we really want to protect ourselves from the Sith, it's the Jedi we need to watch. History has *proven* that."

Chapter Eighteen

SHE CALLED HERSELF ABELOTH, AND SHE LIVED IN A CAVE on the side of a volcano because she said the plants there were not so voracious. But Abeloth loved the water. Every morning, she would take the search party down to the crimson river, and the entire group would swim and splash for hours. Then, once they were exhausted, they would crawl out of the water and bask on the beach, alongside the huge drendek lizards that had come down to take the sun on their green, outstretched wings. And while the party was resting, no one needed to worry about eel vines snaking out of the river to snare unmoving ankles, or a hedge of smogbrush filling the air with a cloud of poison pollen, or even a swarm of thirsty fangballs tumbling up from behind. When Abeloth was near, the plants *never* attacked.

Vestara knew she should have been alarmed by that, but she wasn't. The truth was, she was too grateful for any respite to be suspicious of it. The search party's Sith discipline remained strong enough that they felt compelled to split up and spend at least a few hours a day trying to find Ship, and the sheer terror of those patrols was so wearying that no one cared *why* they were safe when they were with Abeloth. When you saw a mat of dead leaves suddenly chomp off the foot that had just stepped on it, or heard a companion scream because a beautiful white flower had just squirted acid into her eyes, all you really wanted was to be back in the cave with Abeloth.

It was still before high sun when Vestara felt Lady Rhea's Force summons. She glanced over to find Ahri still lying on his back with closed eyes. The azure tint that had come to his lavender skin beneath the blue sun only made him all the more gorgeous, and Vestara was grateful to Lady Rhea for suggesting that she spend more time with him. In addition to being easy to look at, he was her best friend, and his Master was so pleased by their obvious closeness that he had finally stopped beating poor Ahri. It did not even bother Vestara that Xal clearly hoped their friendship would prove useful in spying on Lady Rhea; as long as he believed something valuable might come of the relationship, he was unlikely to seek revenge for the embarrassment Vestara had caused him on the approach to this strange planet.

Without opening his eyes, Ahri said, "She's early today. Are we going farther out?"

"Not that I know of," Vestara answered. Lady Rhea had warned her to start expecting such innocent-sounding questions; Xal would want to determine how willing Vestara was to discuss her Master's plans with Ahri. "Lady Rhea still thinks Ship is hiding on the other side of the cave ridge."

Ahri opened his eyes and propped himself on an elbow. "What do *you* think?"

"*I* think we'd better hurry." Vestara knew he was asking if she could still feel Ship, but Lady Rhea had instructed her to keep secret the unhappy truth—that she had not felt a hint of Ship in the Force since the day he had led them to Abeloth's cave. She snatched Ahri's tunic out of the sand and threw it at him. "If we're the last ones there again, we'll end up out on a flank."

Ahri was instantly on his feet, using the Force to

catch the shirt and lower it over his upraised arms. Vestara also dressed with the aid of the Force, and in less than a minute they were joining the rest of the search party. Lady Rhea was already standing on the large boulder she used as a speaking dais. Fortunately, a lot of people had been caught off-guard by the early summons and were still straggling in, so she barely seemed to notice as Ahri and Vestara took their places.

But Master Xal, standing on the riverbank behind the boulder, studied the pair with a narrow-eyed smirk that suggested he believed their relationship had advanced further than was the case. Happy to buy Ahri another beating-free week by letting Xal believe what he wished, Vestara forced a blush and let her gaze slide down toward the foot of the boulder, where Abeloth stood looking out on the gathering Sith as though *she* were the one in charge of the search party.

Abeloth looked lovely and more or less human, but today her hair was brown and long instead of honey-colored and shoulder-length, as it had been when Vestara and Ahri had found her in her cave. Her nose was also a bit longer and straighter than usual, and her eyes were a bit more silver than gray, with a definite upward slant at the outer corners. Abeloth's face changed like that, seeming to take hints from the appearance of anyone with whom she spent time. And somehow it only served to make her more enchanting, as though each new detail deepened the luster of her beauty.

So enraptured by her radiance was Vestara that she did not realize Lady Rhea had begun speaking until Ahri nudged her.

"Why's she so flamed?" he whispered. "It's not like we haven't been *looking*."

Vestara covered her distraction by patting the air to quiet him. "Shhh."

Ahri frowned in confusion, then seemed to notice her

gaze sliding away from Abeloth and rolled his eyes in mock exasperation. *"Focus,"* he hissed. "You're about to get yourself put on point."

Given her consistent failure to locate Ship in the Force, Vestara knew that was all too likely already. She nodded and returned her attention to the top of the boulder.

". . . have failed," Lady Rhea was saying. Although her angry gaze was hardly focused on Vestara alone, it did not exclude her, either. "Gather your things. We meet the shuttle in two hours."

The news hit Vestara like a body blow. She was the one who had guided the mission after Ship, and if they returned to Kesh without the wayward vessel, the failure would reflect as badly on her as Lady Rhea. But it was Abeloth's voice, not Vestara's, that cracked the stunned silence that followed.

"Without Ship?"

Lady Rhea's tone softened—as did everyone's when they spoke to Abeloth. "The *Crusader* is running low on fuel and stores. If we stay much longer, we won't be leaving at all."

The explanation only seemed to alarm Abeloth all the more. "But you *can't* leave without Ship." She turned to face the body of the search party, as though a handful of mere Sabers could overrule a Sith Lord. "Lord Vol will be disappointed in you."

Lady Rhea seemed as surprised by the reaction as Vestara. Her eyes grew confused for a moment, then her expression hardened as she finally seemed to gather her thoughts. "Didn't you tell us you had been marooned here for thirty years, Abeloth?"

Abeloth nodded. "That's right."

"Then I would think you'd be dying to get back to civilization."

"And I *am*." Abeloth continued to look at the rest of

the search party. "But I'm only thinking of you, my friends. Your Circle of Lords will not look kindly on this failure."

"I'll handle them." Lady Rhea glared down on Abeloth with a look of quiet appraisal, then asked, "You haven't changed your mind about wanting to return to Kesh with us, have you?"

"Not at all," Abeloth said. Lady Rhea's expression grew noticeably softer as the castaway turned to face her again. "I'm as eager as you are to leave this place."

"I'm glad to hear it."

Lady Rhea's smile managed to retain some of its predatory edge, and Vestara could almost read the thoughts flashing through her Master's mind: Abeloth would make up for Ship's loss.

Enthralled as they were, every Sith in the search party knew that Abeloth was no ordinary woman—if she was a woman at all. Sometimes it seemed to Vestara that Abeloth was no more than a swirling halo of Force energy that presented itself as a woman because its true form could not be comprehended by their mortal minds. But other times, Abeloth seemed exactly what she claimed to be: a lonely castaway so desperate for companionship that she refused to be alone, a woman driven so near to madness by her long isolation that she had assumed she was hallucinating when Vestara and Ahri entered her cave to rescue Xal.

Of course, there were a lot of things that didn't make sense about either possibility. First, Abeloth had never explained exactly *how* she had imprisoned Xal—a Sith Master—in a cocoon. She claimed to have no idea why Vestara had sensed Ship on the ridge near her home, yet accepted as perfectly logical the fact that it had been Ship that had led them to her in the first place. And when Vestara had inquired about the tentacle-thing she had glimpsed on the cave ceiling, Abeloth's only reply had been that they had nothing to fear from any animal on this planet.

As Vestara was considering all this—and waiting for the strange contest of wills between Abeloth and Lady Rhea to be resolved—she felt the touch of a familiar presence.

You should never have come, Ship said inside her mind. *Now you can never leave.*

Vestara swung her gaze down the river, then gasped aloud when she saw a familiar winged-ball silhouette hovering in the distance, just above the water.

"Vestara?" Ahri asked, turning toward her. "What is it?"

"It's—" Vestara started to point, then saw Abeloth watching and realized that the castaway was eavesdropping. Besides, Lady Rhea would not appreciate being drawn into another futile Ship-chase when she had already given the order to leave. Vestara dropped her gaze. "Nothing."

"*What* was nothing?" Abeloth's voice was a cold blade cutting through Vestara's lie. "You saw something downriver?"

"I thought so." Vestara sneaked a glance down the river and, much to her relief, saw that the tiny silhouette had already vanished. "But I was—"

Vestara was interrupted by the chime of Lady Rhea's comlink. She turned and saw her Master pulling the wand from her belt, at the same time raising her free hand for silence. Lady Rhea had barely thumbed the activation switch before Baad Walusari's excited voice began to sound from the tiny speaker.

"A thousand meters at bearing one sixty from you," the Keshiri said. "Ship just crossed the river and seems to be headed for the shuttle clearing."

Lady Rhea's eyes widened in shock. "Ship is letting you track it?"

"When it's above the canopy, we have a heat signature," Walusari explained. "When it's in the jungle, we have a damage path. As long as Ship is moving, we can track it."

"Good. Keep me updated." Lady Rhea clicked off her comlink and turned to Vestara. "See if you can force it to return to us."

Without awaiting Vestara's acknowledgment, Lady Rhea drew her weapons and began to issue orders. By the time Vestara had located Ship in the Force again, the search party was deployed across a thousand-meter front and Force-running across the river. Abeloth fell in behind Lady Rhea, crossing the water as easily as the Sith Lord herself, and Vestara took advantage of her presence to concentrate on Ship instead of plants.

Vestara pressed down on Ship's presence with all the willpower she could summon, commanding him to return to the river and await her order. Ship *wanted* to obey—she could feel that much, even with her attention divided between trying to track the wayward vessel and using the Force to keep her feet bouncing across the water.

But there was something defeated and lost in Ship's spirit, like an uvak with severed wing tendons. He was . . . *afraid*, crushed beneath a will strong beyond Vestara's ability to imagine. To obey her was to defy *it*, a power that had reached across space and time to summon Ship for no other reason than it was *lonely*.

Vestara could see how hopeless it was to think she had the strength of will to break the grasp of such a being. Still, she continued to cling to Ship's presence, if only because that would help her locate the meditation sphere if Walusari and the *Crusader* lost his trail. Once they caught up, Lady Rhea would be the one demanding Ship's obedience.

And *that* thought was what nearly got Vestara killed.

She was almost across the river when a whirlpool opened ahead and swallowed Lady Rhea whole. With her attention focused on Ship instead of the dangers of the situation, Vestara was taken completely by surprise, and she found herself stepping into the same swirling pit before Abeloth caught her arm.

"Siphon reed," she said, pushing Vestara away from the whirlpool. "Keep going or it will get you, too."

Most apprentices in Vestara's situation would probably have done exactly as Abeloth instructed, reasoning that it was a lot easier to get a new Master than a new life. Ahri would certainly have been happy to leave *his* Master to be digested by almost any plant on the planet. But if Lady Rhea were gone, Xal would become the mission's new commander, and *that* meant a death just as certain as being swallowed by the siphon reed— though probably far slower and more humiliating.

So Vestara jerked her arm from Abeloth's grasp, then ignited her lightsaber and let herself sink beneath the river's surface. The water was so full of crimson silt that she was blinded almost instantly. Filmy ribbons of wet cellulose wrapped themselves around her legs, squeezing her calves so tightly that her feet and ankles began to swell. She bent her knees and, unsure whether she was pulling the weeds up to her or herself down to them, drew her parang and began to slash at the plants.

At the same time, Vestara reached out in the Force and felt Lady Rhea to the right and a little bit below her. She lashed out with her lightsaber, water hissing and bubbling as the heat of her crimson blade turned it to steam. She felt the weapon slice through something the size of her own waist. She brought the blade back in the other direction and found another of the giant stalks, then quickly began to whirl, cutting away half a dozen more before the area seemed clear.

But there was no glow in the water beneath her, and

Lady Rhea's Force aura only seemed to be growing more frightened and confused as the siphon reed retracted, pulling her deeper into the river. Vestara could feel by the ache in her own chest—and by her growing compulsion to breathe—that her own air was running out, too.

It hardly mattered. Better to drown here than to suffer the degradations Xal would heap on her if *he* became the mission leader. Vestara grabbed her Master in the Force and pulled, hard.

Lady Rhea failed to come popping out of the severed stalk. All that happened was that Vestara's ears and sinuses began to ache as she pulled herself deeper, and the water began to darken as the sun's light vanished into the suspended silt. Lady Rhea's presence began to calm, though it was impossible to say whether this was because she felt Vestara coming, or because she was losing consciousness.

Then Vestara bumped into the stump of a severed stalk and knew that she had caught up to the retreating reed. She could feel Lady Rhea in the swirling darkness below, less than a meter away, but it was impossible to know whether they were at the bottom of the river or still descending.

Vestara didn't care which. She reached out with her lightsaber, bringing it around as though to tap Lady Rhea along the flank. She caught a glimpse of brown as the blade split the stem open, then immediately thumbed the switch off.

An instant later, a human body slammed into her chest, and the last of her air left her lungs in a stream of ascending bubbles. Uncertain whether Lady Rhea would be conscious, she wrapped her arms around the body—then felt herself shooting upward as her Master used the Force to pull them to the surface.

As the water turned from black to crimson, Vestara

had to fight the urge to exhale in relief. Lady Rhea had obviously survived and was still conscious—unless *Abeloth* was the one pulling them to the surface. Although the castaway had dodged most of the search party's questions about her training, she was obviously both strong in the Force and capable of . . .

The blue disk of the sun began to ripple down through the crimson water, but Vestara was too preoccupied—too *frightened*—to notice even when they broke the surface.

Abeloth had been *with* them. The meaning of that finally sank in.

The siphon reed had attacked Lady Rhea, and Abeloth had done nothing to stop it. In fact, no plant had ever attacked someone while they were in Abeloth's presence.

Vestara heard a loud, croaking gasp and felt a flood of bodily relief as her lungs filled with fresh air. Lady Rhea made a similar sound as she also began to breathe, then squirmed free of Vestara's grasp and turned to kiss her.

"I owe . . . you . . . my life," she coughed. "Whatever you desire, Vestara, it will be yours."

"First, to leave this river alive," Vestara said. Seeing that both of her Master's hands were free of weapons, she shoved her parang into Lady Rhea's grasp. "Abeloth is trying to—"

Vestara's explanation was interrupted by a loud outcry from shore, then she felt herself and Lady Rhea rising out of the water.

"Don't worry," Lady Rhea said. "We're safe."

Vestara shook her head. "No. She betrayed—"

"Of course we're safe," Lady Rhea interrupted, not seeming to understand. She pointed upstream. "Your friend Ahri has us."

Vestara turned in the direction Lady Rhea was pointing. Ahri was standing on the shore about fifty meters away, his weapons at his feet and both hands extended toward them. Most of the search party was rushing down the shore to protect Lady Rhea if she was attacked again. Master Xal remained at Ahri's side, his jaw clenched and his dark eyes burning as though he were contemplating grabbing his apprentice's parang and beheading him with it. Tonight, Vestara knew, Ahri would take a beating for saving her and Lady Rhea . . . if Abeloth let them live that long.

Behind Xal and Ahri stood . . . *something* tall and vaguely human, with a long cascade of yellow hair that reached nearly to the ground. Her eyes were tiny and deep-sunken, like two stars shining out of a pair of black wells, and she had a large, full-lipped mouth so broad that it reached from ear to ear. Her stubby arms protruded no more than ten centimeters from her shoulders, but in place of fingers, her hands had writhing tentacles so long that they hung down past her knees. The body was as straight as a tree trunk, and as she started downstream to the place where Vestara and Lady Rhea would be coming ashore, her legs did not seem to swing forward so much as ripple.

Vestara went cold and queasy inside as Ahri lowered her and Lady Rhea to shore. She found herself kneeling in the shallows, retching black silty water into the river and shaking so hard that her body ached. Horrible as it was, the thing she had seen standing behind Ahri and Xal had been familiar to her. The long aquiline nose, high cheeks, the well-shaped chin, all were the face of Abeloth. Just this morning, that face had seemed the most beautiful she had ever seen . . . until Lady Rhea had declared it was time to return home, and Abeloth had betrayed her true nature.

"It's just river water," Lady Rhea said, taking Vestara by the arm. "Stand up. You'll feel better."

Vestara allowed herself to be pulled up. Hoping the thing she had seen with Ahri had just been the product of an oxygen-starved mind, or at least that she would be spared seeing it in its true nature again, she looked back up the shore.

And began to tremble again. The thing was still there, as horrible as it was before—and it was coming toward her, its tiny silver eyes burning a hole right through her, its gruesome mouth smiling ear-to-ear, showing a mouthful of sharp teeth.

"Vestara, it's okay," Lady Rhea said, taking her by the shoulders. "You're going to be fine."

"I . . . I know." Vestara nodded, but she continued to look past Lady Rhea. "Lady Rhea, look. Do you see that . . . that *thing* behind Ahri and Xal?"

Lady Rhea looked, then frowned. "You mean *Abeloth*?"

Vestara's strength drained away, and she would have fallen had Lady Rhea not caught her in the Force. "Vestara, what's wrong? You seem exhausted."

Realizing that she was the only one who saw it, Vestara forced a nod. "I am, but I can handle it."

And perhaps she *could*, Vestara told herself; there was no reason to despair. Now that she saw the truth of what Abeloth was, she could defeat it. A Sith could defeat *anything*, if she understood it.

Lady Rhea must have sensed the return of Vestara's resolve, because she smiled and relaxed her grasp.

"That's better." She patted Vestara's shoulders, then turned to face up the shore. "Master Xal, I need a lightsaber and a report. Do we still have a location on Ship?"

The question was an unnecessary one. Even as Lady Rhea was barking it, Ship appeared in the distance, a tiny speck floating over the jungle from the direction of the shuttle clearing. But everyone was too busy with Lady Rhea to see the vessel, inquiring about injuries and offering her spare lightsabers salvaged from the bodies of their fallen companions. So Vestara pretended not to see Ship approaching, and just reached out to him in the Force.

Why? she asked. *Why did you betray us?*

Because I was commanded to, and machines must obey.

Very well, Vestara replied. *I command you to come to me now. I command you to set down and take us away from here, to take us back to Kesh.*

A low crackle began to build as Ship approached, and Vestara thought for a moment that he was actually coming to land. But then, as Lady Rhea and the others spun toward the sound, Ship accelerated, streaking past so low over their heads that Vestara could actually feel the heat from his propulsion units.

Silly child, Ship said to her. *You are strong in the Force—but strong is nothing compared with almighty.*

Lady Rhea began to yell orders, leading the charge back across the river toward the cave ridge. Vestara did not follow, instead remaining on the shore, watching the horrible thing that was Abeloth continue to approach.

You ignored my warnings, Ship reminded her. *And now you are as lost as I am.*

Vestara shook her head. "We are *not* lost." Speaking the words aloud only seemed to make them ring all the more false, but she continued just the same. "Sith never surrender. Sith never despair."

A wave of grim amusement rolled through the Force. *You are a smart girl, Vestara,* Ship said. *Why do you believe anything* you *do can ever get you off this planet?*

Ship dwindled to a dark spot shrinking against the

cave ridge and vanished from the Force, leaving Vestara alone on the shore with Abeloth. A fan of slimy tentacles slid around her shoulder, and she turned to look into the cold stars that were the thing's eyes.

"Come, Vestara," it said. "I'll see you safely across the river."

Chapter Nineteen

LOCATED A MERE KILOMETER FROM THE GALACTIC JUStice Center, the blockhouse across the skylane was hardly "secret." It did not appear on any public list of government addresses, but it was a hundred-story monolith shoved into a long line of elegant stone-and-mirrsteel spires, with permacrete walls and purple cam bubbles that openly hinted at its fortifications. The only concession to style was a smattering of dash-shaped viewports, scattered across its gray face in globe-shaped clusters that were probably meant to suggest a star and its planets.

"GAS is better than *this*," Jaina said. Along with Mirax Horn and a handful of Jedi Masters, she was standing in the lobby of the Palem Graser Office Tower, ostensibly waiting for an appointment with a Neimoidian lobbyist whose name she had selected at random from the building directory. "Why not hang a sign out front that says SECRET PRISON?"

"Daala *wantz* people to know she keepz a secret prison." As Saba spoke, her slit-pupiled eyes remained fixed on the blockhouse across the skylane. "The shenbit showz itz teeth to frighten, not to kill."

"Psychological deterrence," Kyp Durron agreed. He had prepared for their mission by carefully gelstyling his hair and donning a steam-pressed formal robe, but the effect was ruined by a two-day beard stubble starting to show gray. "Daala wants the lobbying industry to know *they* could disappear into someplace like that, if they're working for the wrong people."

"That would certainly explain its location," Cilghal agreed. The Mon Calamari rolled a bulging eye around to look at Jaina. "You are certain this is where Valin and Jysella are now?"

"It's where the new incarceration order said they were being . . ." Jaina nearly said *stored,* but when she saw the flash of pain in the eyes of both Horns, she decided it would be better to avoid any term associated with being frozen in carbonite. ". . . *held.* From what I can tell, Daala seems to be trying to do everything by the book with this Jedi court of hers, so I don't think she would have had the records falsified."

"This one agreez." Saba finally looked away from the blockhouse, then asked Jaina, "You have the writ?"

"Yes." Jaina produced a flimsi-tube from inside her robe and held it out. "Here you go."

"No, keep it." Saba flicked a talon toward the blockhouse. "Your plan, your hunt."

"Okay, thanks . . . I think," Jaina said.

Actually, the plan was more Jag's than hers, but Jaina knew better than to reveal that to the Masters. They all professed to understand Jag's reason for not mentioning that Daala was going to hire a company of Mandalorians, but they were still irritated. In fact, they had barred him from entering the Temple due to possible "conflicts of interest." And while they had not actually *instructed* Jaina to stay away from Jag, they had made it clear that she needed to reexamine where her priorities lay—and to think about whether a marriage to the Imperial Remnant's Head of State was a realistic possibility for a Jedi Knight.

Jaina was, of course, hoping to convince them that it was. And a good outcome today would certainly help her cause. She slipped the writ back into her robe, then turned to Corran and Mirax Horn.

The Horns' anguish was evident in the purple crescents that hung beneath their eyes. Mirax's black hair was uncombed and dirty, and the jaw beneath Corran's tangled beard was clenched so tight he was probably in danger of breaking teeth. *They* were the one weak spot in her plan, Jaina knew. She was asking a lot by expecting them to remain calm and under control while they stood looking at their children frozen in carbonite, but they were both people of extraordinary emotional resources. Corran was a Jedi Master who regularly made decisions that placed dozens of Jedi Knights, including his own children, in harm's way. And Mirax was, quite simply, Booster Terrik's daughter. That fact alone suggested that Daala had no idea of the kind of storm she had brought down on herself when she decided to freeze the Horns' children in carbonite.

It took a moment for the Horns to realize that Jaina was looking at them, but when they did, there was no need to ask if they were ready. Corran nodded curtly, and Mirax said, "Let's move. It's time to serve the Chief some of that mynock stew you promised."

Jaina smiled. "Let's see if we can make her choke on it." She turned to Saba. "With your permission . . ."

"Permission?" Saba thumped her tail against the floor, then pointed toward the exit. "We have no time to waste with jokez, Jedi Solo."

Jaina dipped her head in acknowledgment. "I'll let you know when I'm inside."

As she left the Graser Tower, Jaina was relieved to glimpse the always well-dressed Javis Tyrr and his stocky camoperator on the balcony of the adjacent building. As expected, the sight of the Horns and several Jedi Masters gathering near a secret GAS detention center had drawn enough attention to alert the media.

She just hoped Tyrr wasn't the only reporter who had been tipped.

Jaina used a pedbridge to cross the humming chasm of the skylane, then followed a balcony walk to the center of the blockhouse. Entry was via a long escalator that ascended a gradually narrowing tunnel toward a pair of tunqstoid blast doors. Over the doors hung a simple sign reading: GALACTIC ALLIANCE STORAGE. Underneath, a motto proclaimed: SERVICE, SECURITY, SECRECY.

Everything about the entryway said *fortress*. The two doors were so heavy they had to be mounted on mag-lev guides instead of tracks. The tunnel walls were lined by tall rectangular panels that just had to be the sliding covers of firing ports. Even the treads of the escalator could be folded down to create a steep, steel ramp that would be difficult to ascend under fire.

Nonetheless, Jaina ascended without incident. At the top of the tunnel, the escalator changed to a moving pedwalk, and the blast doors slid open to reveal a small lobby. As the pedwalk carried her across the threshold, she used the Force to tilt an alignment sensor askew so the blast door locks would fail to engage. To her left she saw two separate seating areas, and to her right, a raised security counter. In the back of the lobby, a pair of turbolifts provided access to the rest of the building.

The pedwalk deposited Jaina in front of the security counter, where a pair of Rodian guards stood with their hands concealed and the sensory saucers atop their heads turned outward in wariness. Even without using the Force, Jaina would have known that each had one hand poised over a panic button and the other wrapped around the butt of a blaster pistol. Both were dressed in black paramilitary uniforms with an arcing yellow GALACTIC ALLIANCE STORAGE embroidered over one pocket and a name patch sewn above the other.

Jaina reached out in the Force, letting the Masters know she had made it inside, then stepped over to the guard counter. She looked up at the two Rodians and said nothing. The pair glared down their tapering snouts, their curiosity keeping their attention on her instead of the misaligned doors. If they had noticed the problem with the locks, their faces did not show it.

When Jaina did not speak first, the larger one finally said, "I didn't know we had any *Jedi* clients." He was so plump that his cheeks looked like they had pouches, and the name on his breast read WEEZE. "Vault number and password?"

"I don't have either," Jaina said. "But you already know that."

Weeze looked to his skinnier partner, whose name tag read ROSII. "I *didn't* know that," he said. "Did you?"

Rosii nodded. "Kind of thought so." His voice was more typically Rodian than Weeze's, buzzy and nasal. "I haven't seen any Jedi in here."

Weeze looked back to Jaina. "We can't help you at this door. You'll have to go over to main reception and rent a vault from an account representative."

"I don't *want* a vault," Jaina said. "I came to see Valin and Jysella Horn."

"Horn?" Rosii echoed. His snout wrinkled in an expression of confusion, but the sudden alarm she felt in the Force suggested that both Rodians knew very well why Jaina was looking for the Horns there. "Aren't those two of those Jedi Knights who went barvy?"

"Who suffered a delusional break," Jaina corrected. She kept her gaze fixed on Weeze. "And I will see them *now . . .*" She paused to allow Weeze's rank to rise to the top of his mind, where she could sense it through the Force. *"Sergeant."*

Weeze's sensory saucers snapped forward. "We're all

civilians here, Jedi." The alarm in his Force aura changed
to decisiveness, and Jaina saw his shoulder twitch as he
finally pressed the alarm button. "Galactic Alliance Storage handles property, not pris—"

Jaina used the Force to shove both Rodians away
from the counter—and any heavy weapons they might
have hidden behind it.

"Never lie to a Jedi, Sergeant," Jaina said. As the Rodians raised their blaster pistols, she sent both weapons
flying with a gesture. "That really annoys us."

The Rodians glanced at each other, then Rosii said,
"You're not going to make it past the lobby."

"This one thinkz differently," Saba said, leading Kyp
and the others through the half-opened blast doors.
"This one thinkz *you* will escort us where we need to
go."

As soon as the Rodians' eyes fell on Saba's hulking
form, their sensory saucers drooped against their heads
and their Force auras grew electric with fear.

"Relax," Jaina said. "We have permission."

"Permission?" Weeze turned his head to regard Jaina
out of one eye. "What kind of permission?"

"You haven't shown him the document, Jedi Solo?"
Saba asked, feigning surprise. "Why do you wait?"

Jaina glanced back through the door and—behind
Kyp, Cilghal, and the other Masters—saw Corran and
Mirax Horn ascending the escalator with a sizable mob
of newsbeings with holocams shouting questions at
them. Javis Tyrr, of course, was in the lead, his fashionable tabard badly wrinkled where he had been grabbed
and—no doubt—shoved away. A puffy cheek and darkening bruise suggested that it had been done with relish,
and Jaina began to have doubts about Master Horn's
ability to control himself once they reached Valin and
Jysella.

Jaina turned back to Saba and dipped her head in

mock apology. "I'm sorry, Master Sebatyne. It took a few minutes to confirm that this is the correct place."

Confident that the Rodians would not try anything foolish with so many Masters in the room, Jaina released them from the wall, then withdrew the writ tube from inside her robe. By then, the Horns were entering the lobby, with Javis Tyrr and another half a dozen news teams pushing through the doors behind him.

Jaina waited while Kyp and Cilghal used the Force to subtly arrange the crowd. Once she was sure that all the holocams would have a clear view of the security counter, she stepped forward and presented the tube, turning it so the Justice Center seal was in plain sight.

"Sergeant Weeze," she said, "this is a legal writ granting us visitation rights for Valin and Jysella Horn, who, as you can see by the accompanying incarceration order, are being held at a secret Galactic Alliance Security detention center located at this address."

Weeze made no move to accept the tube, staring at it as though Jaina were trying to hand him an armed thermal detonator.

"I . . . I don't know what you're talking about," the Rodian said. "This is just a storage facil—"

The Rodian's denial came to an abrupt end as the sizzle of deactivating access shields sounded from the turbolifts at the back of the lobby. Sharp voices began to shout contradictory orders to "get down" and "don't move." Everyone turned toward the sounds—just in time to see a GAS assault squad charging into the lobby in full armor, stun grenades in hand and repeating blasters ready to shoulder.

Of course, the news teams immediately activated their cam lights, and only a few quick Force nudges from Jaina and her fellow Jedi sent the flurry of bolts that followed into the ceiling instead of into the crowd of journalists. The beings carrying the larger holocams merely dropped to a knee and continued filming as the rest of the confused assault squad poured out of the turbolifts and took up positions at the far end of the lobby.

The firing quickly died away as the assault squad realized they were being filmed instead of attacked, but by then the news teams had a full four or five seconds of GAS confusion for the evening broadcast. Things were going even better than Jaina had hoped—and they quickly improved when the familiar square-shouldered figure of the assault squad commander stepped out of the turbolift.

"Bloah!" Jaina started toward the lift. "If it isn't *Captain Atar*!"

She called the name out especially loudly, to be sure that Javis Tyrr and every other newsbeing caught it on their audio. If the plan kept going *this* well, she might even risk revealing that this whole trap had been Jag's idea. That probably wouldn't do much to buy him—or *her*—any slack with her parents, but it just might make the Masters view their situation a little more sympathetically.

Atar quickly motioned his troopers to lower their weapons, then came three meters forward and stood scowling out from beneath his bushy mustache. Jaina was glad to see that both he and his team were in full GAS uniform.

Jaina stopped half a pace away, then—once she felt the cam lights warming her flanks—said, "Captain Atar, I wish I could say what a pleasure it is to see you again." She held out the writ tube. "Perhaps *you* would be good enough to accept this. Your subordinates seem to be rather confused about who they're working for."

This drew a round of snickers from the reporters, and Atar's attitude grew wary and bitter. He had been ambushed inside his own nest, and he knew it. He accepted the tube without comment, then removed the writ and read it in silence.

When he came to the authorizing signature, his eyes grew wide and his face turned red. He lowered the flimsi and studied Jaina with a raised brow.

"You want to visit Valin and Jysella Horn?"

"That's right," Jaina said.

"But they're frozen," he said, "in carbonite."

"We're aware of that," Cilghal said, stepping to Jaina's side. "That order gives me the right to inspect their frigidation pods and make certain everything is in good order."

"And affirms the right of Valin and Jysella Horn to receive visitors while being held in detention," Kyp added, motioning Corran and Mirax forward. "Just like any other prisoner."

"As you can see"—Jaina glanced back, addressing the cams directly—"we've taken pains to acquire all the necessary permissions."

Atar nodded. "So you have." He rerolled the flimsi carefully, no doubt trying to buy himself time to think, and returned it to the tube. "I'm sure the facility director will be happy to make an appointment—"

"No, Captain." Jaina stepped closer to Atar, craning her neck to look up at him—and using the Force to nudge him back. "That order gives us *immediate* access."

"So we can be sure that GAS is maintaining the pods properly, and as a matter of routine," Cilghal added, also starting forward. "If you think we are going to give you a chance to make repairs and forge maintenance records, you are quite mistaken."

Jaina nudged him back another step, but Atar centered himself in front of the turbolifts. "I'm sorry." He motioned the rest of his squad to their feet. "But I don't have the authority to grant you entry to this facility."

Saba slipped forward to stand snout-to-nose with him. "Look again, Captain. You have no authority to *stop* us."

The Barabel snatched the tube from his hand, then poked him in the chest with it. Atar's eyes bulged with rage, but before he could respond, Javis Tyrr shoved forward to push a microphone into his face.

"Captain Atar," the reporter demanded, "is it your position that Galactic Alliance Security is not bound by Judicial Center writs?"

"No, of course not." Atar had barely spoken before the rest of the press began to shout questions, and his face reddened as he realized how his meaning was being misconstrued. He raised his hands for silence, and when that didn't work he shouted, "I mean, the security services are *absolutely* bound by the law, just like anyone else in the Galactic Alliance."

"This one is glad to hear that," Saba said. She handed the tube back to Jaina, then started toward the turbolifts. "We will start our search in the sublevelz and work up."

Atar's red face suddenly grew pale, and he rushed after her. "There's no need to search, Master Sebatyne. I'll escort you myself."

Saba stopped at the entrance to the turbolift and turned. "How nice, Captain." She turned to the cams, which were already pressing in close behind her, then asked, "What are the cell numberz?"

Atar shook his head. "I'm sorry, Master Sebatyne. We'll be going to—"

"The infirmary, perhapz?" Saba stooped down to peer at the turbolift control panel. "Is this it? Level four ninety-eight?"

She extended a talon toward the number pad, but Atar's hand shot out to enter a different level instead.

Saba studied the number, then turned to the captain, her face scales flattened in the Barabel equivalent of a frown.

"Four seventy?" She turned and added the level designation for the benefit of her companions and the reporters. "The *executive officez*?"

Atar dropped his gaze, and Jaina *knew*. GAS was treating the Horn siblings like some sort of prize, putting them on display—just as Jabba the Hutt had put her own father on display four decades earlier. And she could feel by the rising tide of fury in the Force that the Masters realized it, too.

An instant later Atar tried to cover. "We, uh, need to pick up some visitor passes."

Saba fixed him with a cold reptilian glare. "This one doubtz that very much."

She stepped into the turbolift and vanished up the tube.

Atar cursed under his breath, then turned to a young Bothan with a lieutenant's patch on her collar. "The Horns and the Jedi can follow, Rasher. No one else."

The lieutenant—the name above her pocket read KE'E, RASHER—came to attention. "Yes, sir."

"Set the turbolift level yourself," he said. "And check them for weapons first."

Again the lieutenant saluted, but by this time Atar was already going after Saba. Cilghal immediately moved forward to the turbolift and entered the level number herself.

"Hold on, Master," Ke'e said, moving to block her way. "You heard the captain. I need to check you for weapons."

"I assure you, that's not necessary." Cilghal waved a finger, and the lieutenant slid out of her way. "I didn't bring any."

She stepped into the turbolift and rose out of sight,

leaving the Bothan sputtering in anger. Jaina glanced back and saw Kyp standing behind the reporters with the Horns, waiting to bring them forward. She caught Corran Horn's eye, then raised a questioning brow and tipped her head toward the turbolift. This next part was going to be harder on him and Mirax than anyone had expected, and the decision to put them through it in the middle of a media frenzy was not hers to make.

Corran acknowledged her question by turning to his wife, whose impish face was already creased in outrage and grief. She answered with a curt, narrow-eyed nod that told Jaina all she needed to know about the Horns' state of mind. They knew how much this was going to hurt, and they were willing to bear it and stick to the plan.

Jaina turned back to find Ke'e pointing her subordinates toward the turbolifts, growling at them to stop standing around and secure the lobby. Jaina stepped forward to take possession of the entrances. The troopers immediately trained their weapons on her and began shouting orders for her to stand down.

Jaina calmly turned to Javis Tyrr, using the Force to make herself heard above the GAS troopers. "Don't you want to go up and see what Daala is trying to hide?"

Tyrr's narrow eyes lit with something akin to greed, but quickly turned fearful as they swung toward Lieutenant Ke'e.

"Stay where you are, Tyrr," the Bothan ordered. "The news media isn't permitted to—"

"What are you going to do, Lieutenant?" Jaina demanded. "Blast them on a live holofeed?"

With that, she turned and used the Force to slide a couple of troopers out of Tyrr's path. He continued to hesitate—but only until the rest of the cam teams began to push forward. Tyrr and his stocky assistant began to fling elbows and shout that the invitation had been extended to *them*, and reporters began to vanish up the turbolifts.

Lieutenant Ke'e waved her subordinates off, then pushed her way over to stand muzzle-to-nose with Jaina. "You are going to regret that, Jedi. We have a long reach."

"Lieutenant Ke'e, I have been threatened by assassin droids, Yuuzhan Vong Warmasters, and Sith Lords." Jaina watched as Kyp and the Horns followed the last of the reporters into the turbolift, then added, "*Them,* I worried about."

With that, Jaina turned her back on the Bothan and entered the turbolift. She rose three levels to the executive offices, then stepped out into an expansive lobby area with a vaulted ceiling and high stone walls. The spacious sitting area featured three nerf-hide couches arranged before a long, built-in aquarium filled with exotic water species from Pavo Prime.

But the aquarium was not the focal point. Hanging two meters above the tank were a pair of black slabs, each about two meters tall and perhaps a meter and a half wide. Along the bottom blinked a row of control lights, but otherwise they resembled a black, glossy bas-relief sculpture of Valin and Jysella Horn. In the bright illumination of so many lights, it was possible to see every detail of the young Jedi Knights' faces—the eyes bulging in terror, the nostrils flaring with panic, the mouths frozen in mid-scream.

Directly below the carbonite pods stood the Horns, their necks craned back and their mouths hanging agape as they looked up at their frozen children. Jaina's stomach instantly went cold and heavy as she struggled with her own feelings—the guilt of being the one who had suggested using the Horns so cynically, the outrage of discovering the extent of the indignity being visited

on their children . . . who were, after all, her fellow Jedi
Knights.

The reporters must have been as shocked as Jaina
and the other Jedi, for they maintained a respectful distance behind the couches. The only sound from them
was the faint hum of their equipment and a few whispered cam instructions. For a moment, Jaina thought
the GAS officers were going to disappoint her and allow
the confrontation to end on that sad note, with the
Horns watching while Cilghal inspected the carbonite
pods to make sure Valin and Jysella were being properly
cared for in custody.

Then a long, spine-chilling wail rose from somewhere inside Mirax, and she turned to bury her head in
Corran's robes. He clutched her to his chest, his eyes
growing wet and furious as he stared up at the carbonite slabs. The reporters began to shout questions,
though they probably knew better than to expect answers, and a hulking Yaka in a GAS colonel's uniform
came tramping out of the corner office. Escorted by half
a dozen armed guards and twice as many scowling cap-
tains, he was almost certainly the facility commander.

The Yaka marched into the seating area without so
much as looking at the reporters and went straight to
Saba. Even taller and broader than she was, he had a
face that was less brutish only by virtue of being covered in flesh rather than scales.

"Are you the Jedi responsible for this intrusion,
Shorttail?" he demanded.

It was an exceptionally insulting way to address a
Barabel. In other circumstances, it would probably have
resulted in the Yaka having one of his massive arms
slashed off at the elbow, so it could be used to beat him
about the head. But ferocious as Saba was, she was also
a Jedi Master, and that meant that she knew better than

to let herself be baited into making a foolish attack on live HoloNet.

She merely regarded the Yaka for a moment, then rasped, "Who askz?"

"Colonel Retk," the Yaka answered.

The shadow of a smile flitted across his face, and Jaina knew that Retk was doing exactly what she had suspected: trying to turn a public relations disaster into a victory by provoking a rash attack from a Jedi Master. Despite their brutish appearance, Yakas were among the most intelligent and cunning beings in the galaxy— an attribute of the cyborg brains with which most were implanted at a young age.

"Colonel *Wruq* Retk," the Yaka continued, extending his hand toward Saba. "Commander of this facility."

"Ah." Instead of shaking Retk's extended hand, Saba slapped the writ tube into it. "Then you wish to see—"

Before Saba could say *this,* Mirax Horn pushed between her and Retk.

"If you're the commander of this toxiden," she said, tipping her head back to look him in the face, "then you must be the son-of-a-schutta who decided to use my children as decorations."

"Please, it's not meant to insult them." A twinkle of amusement came to Retk's eye, and he turned to face the cams. "I just wanted to put them where I could see to their maintenance *personally.*"

"The *kriff* you did."

Mirax's hand came up so fast that even Jaina did not see it. Retk's teeth simply clacked shut, then his head snapped back and he toppled onto the couch behind him. Like everyone else in the room, his bodyguards were so stunned that they did not react instantly, and that gave Jaina and the other Jedi the half second they needed to reach out in the Force and push the guards' blaster barrels down toward the floor.

Finally, the troopers shook off their confusion and stepped forward, reaching for Mirax with their free hands and ordering her to surrender. Of course Saba, Cilghal, Kyp, and Corran reacted even more quickly, placing themselves between them and Mirax.

Jaina noticed a hawk-nosed GAS captain eyeing the writ tube, which now lay on the couch next to the unconscious Yaka. She began to have visions of her plan backfiring severely. Without the document itself, there was every chance that the judge who had issued it would deny having done so, and then Daala would have an opening to present the visit as just one more example of Jedi high-handedness.

Taking advantage of the confusion around him, the hawk-nosed captain reached over to retrieve the tube—and nearly fell as Jaina extended a hand and used the Force to jerk it away. The captain looked up in astonishment, then merely spread his hands and shrugged, obviously no more concerned about subverting the law than any common street thief.

By the time Jaina had the writ tube safely back in her grasp, the situation had resolved itself into a standoff. Another GAS captain was demanding that Mirax surrender to face charges for assaulting a security officer. Meanwhile, Corran and the other Masters were standing in a silent guard around her. Mirax's small form was too well hidden to see her expression, but her Force aura suggested that she was glad she had knocked the big Yaka unconscious.

Jaina groaned inwardly. The plan had been to generate some public sympathy by putting a human face on the Jedi Knights whom Daala had frozen in carbonite. But now the lead story on the evening news was going to be about yet another standoff between the Jedi and

GAS, this time in GAS's own detention facility. And Jaina had only herself to blame. She had known she would be asking a lot for the Horns to keep their heads when they saw their children in carbonite.

As the thought worked its way through Jaina's mind, she saw again Mirax's small figure craning her neck to look up at the Yaka, and she knew how to save the situation. Leaving Saba and the others to keep the GAS guards at bay, she turned toward the busily humming cams and sought out Javis Tyrr's tall, tawny-haired figure.

At first, he was too intent on describing the confrontation in front of him to pay Jaina any attention. But when she used the Force to tug his microphone in her direction, he finally took the hint and turned to face her.

"Jedi Solo, would you care to comment—"

"Not *now*." Jaina made a cutting motion with her fingers and waited until Tyrr had turned off his equipment, then said, "I've got a proposition for you, sleemo."

Tyrr frowned, but he was too much of a newsman to object to the term—especially when it fit so well. "I'm listening."

Jaina pulled the cap off the writ tube. "I'll give you a shot of the writ."

"Big deal. I can get a copy as soon as we leave here." Tyrr tried to avoid sounding eager, but Jaina could feel his excitement in the Force. "So I'm not killing—"

Jaina leaned in close. "I just want you to ask one question." She glanced around at the other reporters, knowing most of them were too ethical—and too wise—to allow the subject of a story to dictate the questions. "It's a question somebody else is bound to think of anyway."

Tyrr pretended to weigh this, then said, "Let's hear it."

When Jaina told him, he actually smiled. "That's *good*," he said. "I shouldn't even make you pay . . . but a deal's a deal."

He nodded to his camoperator, who waited until Jaina had extracted the writ and unfurled it to turn on her cam. Of course, the rest of the news teams quickly noticed what was happening and swung around, trying to get their own shots—taking their cams off the confrontation between the Masters and the GAS guards.

"Okay, that's enough!" Tyrr hissed. "Put it away."

That wasn't part of the deal, so Jaina merely lowered the writ until Tyrr and his camoperator had turned back toward the confrontation. Then, once their attention was otherwise occupied, she raised the document so everyone else could get their own shots, too. A chorus of snickers and surprised gasps arose as the other news teams noticed the signature on the writ, but by then Tyrr was sticking his microphone in the face of the blond captain leading the demands for Mirax's surrender.

"Tell me, Captain Xanda, does GAS really intend to charge a bereaved mother with assault? A distraught, *fifty-kilogram* mother who resorted to *slapping* . . ."

As Tyrr asked this, his camoperator panned over to the circle of Masters. After a gentle Force nudge from Jaina, they obliged by stepping apart, giving the cam a clear shot of Mirax's small form.

Tyrr paused for dramatic effect while the cam swung toward the hulking form laid out on the couch, then continued, ". . . a Yaka colonel *three* times her size— *after* she discovered he has been hanging her children on the wall . . ." Again he paused, this time while the cam swung up to linger on the carbonite pods containing Valin and Jysella Horn. ". . . as *office decorations*?"

"*No.*" This answer came not from the blond captain, but from the direction of the turbolifts. "GAS certainly will *not* be filing any charges against Mirax Horn. Her grief is entirely understandable—and her actions are completely forgivable."

Along with everyone else in the chamber, Jaina turned toward the all-too-familiar voice and saw Admiral Daala striding into the room. Following close on her heels were Wynn Dorvan, her security detail, and the pair of very nervous-looking Rodian guards from the lobby.

"What we *cannot* forgive is yet another example of Jedi imperiousness," Daala continued, marching to the edge of the seating area. "Now Jedi Masters are *forcing* their way into legitimate GAS detention centers!"

The cams swung toward Daala, lighting her up like a Jabori spirit singer on stage, and Jaina's heart began to pound with excitement. There had certainly been a lot of surprises and a few ups and downs, but suddenly it looked as though her plan was going to exceed all expectations.

Daala basked in the cam glow for a moment, then put on a stern frown. "Is there no *limit* to their arrogance?"

"Actually, Chief Daala, there *is*," Jaina said. She glanced over at Saba and received an encouraging nod, then held up the writ. "As you can see, we have permission from the proper judicial authorities."

Daala appeared unabashed. "So I have been told." She kept her attention fixed on the cams. "But we have all heard about Jedi mind tricks. This is yet more proof of their disregard for the law."

"If you have heard of our mind trickz," Saba said, stepping forward, "then perhapz you have also heard that they work only on the weak-minded?"

Daala turned to smirk at Saba. "I doubt this will come as a surprise to the Jedi, Master Sebatyne, but there *are* a few weak-minded judges serving in the Galactic Alliance."

"There *are*?" Saba did a credible job of feigning surprise, thumping her tail against the floor and turning to Jaina. "This one *is* outraged!"

A chorus of laughter rolled through the chamber, then Daala's assistant, Wynn Dorvan, whispered something in her ear. Her expression paled, and she turned back toward the cams, obviously preparing to start backpedaling. Unfortunately for her, the only being more ruthless than a politician with an agenda was a reporter on the trail of a good story. Before she could speak, Javis Tyrr stepped forward holding a datapad with an image of the writ that Jaina had allowed him to shoot.

"Chief Daala, the signature on this writ happens to be that of the judge overseeing your special Jedi court," he said. "Isn't it true that *you* are the one who appointed Arabelle Lorteli to this post?"

Daala's eyes narrowed. "As a matter of fact, it *is*, and I have complete confidence in her abilities." She turned her gaze, angry and withering, on the Yaka colonel lying unconscious on the couch across from her. "While I am obviously very concerned with the Jedi and their propensity to disregard the laws of this great Alliance, I am *equally* concerned with the abuse of power by our own institutions. The reason I am here today is because I have just been informed of Colonel Retk's tasteless display of the Horn siblings. Rest assured that all parties responsible will be punished. The Galactic Alliance will not tolerate the abuse of power—by *anyone*."

"So you support the right of the Jedi to visit Jedi Knights being held in secret detention centers?" a Falleen reporter asked. "Even if such detention centers are themselves illegal?"

"*Absolutely.* This facility is neither secret nor illegal, but we are all subject to the law." Daala's gaze slid toward Jaina—and sent a cold shiver of danger sense down her spine. "And I hope we'll *all* remember that in the hours and days to come."

Chapter Twenty

THE TINGLE THAT KEPT RUNNING DOWN LEIA'S SPINE couldn't be Jedi danger sense—not with a FloatVan full of ysalamiri right beside her. She and her assistants had already secured thirty potted olbios inside the long cargo vehicle, each tree supporting at least two of the Force-displacing reptiles. So she had to be standing inside a Force void nearly as large as the loading dock itself. Yet she could not shake the feeling that something was wrong, that she simply was not *seeing* some threat to the Jedi patients they were about to move.

Leia looked into the gloom beyond the two-story exit. The opening was covered by a state-of-the-art mirrfield, which allowed her to see *out* without letting anyone see *in*. The labyrinthine depths beneath Fellowship Plaza were among the busiest freight routes on Coruscant, traversed at all hours by a constant flow of cargo vehicles, and beyond the field lay an erratic blur of traffic. Even on good days, traffic was slow, congested, and dangerous, with accidents common and deaths frequent. Today was about average, with hoversleds as long as three hundred meters lurching down the skylane in a stop-and-go river of running lights.

Han came to stand with her on the FloatVan's midbody loading ramp. Three Jedi Knights were already lying in their stasis bunks inside the van, but his attention was not on them. Instead he was looking out into the traffic, the same as Leia was.

"Yeah, I see it, too," he said. "Those boombuggies don't belong down here. And they sure the kark don't have any business parking on the Krabbis."

Leia looked again and realized that Han's instincts were, as usual, dead-on. The Krabbis Inn was one of the grungy under-plaza hostel towers that provided convenient tourist accommodations at cut-rate prices. Resting in the parking area atop its roof were a pair of ruggedly sleek Aratech BeamStreaks. Used by Coruscant Enforcement Services as pursuit speeders, the BeamStreaks were as pricey as they were perilous, vehicles actually advertised as so fast that to crash one was to die in one.

Leia frowned. Obviously, a BeamStreak was the last vehicle a tourist staying at the Krabbis Inn was likely to rent. But anyone hoping to use the hostel to spy on activities inside the loading dock would be frustrated by the mirrfield's reflective exterior—unless they had one of the new PsiCor "wallscope" surveillance packages being developed for military intelligence. It seemed unthinkable that Daala would put such a top-secret espionage asset in the hands of a domestic security squad watching *Jedi*. But lately, the unthinkable had been happening a *lot*. Just a year earlier, who would have believed that a pair of Jedi Knights would be hanging in carbonite inside a government building? Or that a Galactic Alliance Chief of State would view the Jedi Order as a threat to the same society it had served so faithfully since its very inception?

"Some days, I really miss running the government myself," Leia groused. "Who do you think they are? GAS?"

Han thought about it for a moment, then shook his head. "Can't be." He hitched a thumb toward the rear of the loading dock, where R2-D2 and C-3PO stood at a main computer access portal, then added, "Not if Shortcircuit's comm intercepts are right. Daala is worried about Jaina busting Valin and Jysella out of her secret prison, so she's called everyone back to stand watch around the place."

"Jaina *does* have a gift for making people nervous," Leia said, feeling a flush of pride. "She takes after her father that way."

Han's expression darkened and, without responding, he turned back toward the mirrfield. He was still furious with Jaina for keeping Jag's secret, and he was even more upset with Jag for not telling them about the Mandalorians in the first place. Truthfully, Leia was still angry, too. The difference was, Leia actually felt some sympathy for her daughter—perhaps because she herself had once been torn between her loyalty to the Rebellion and her love for a man who did not always share her loyalties. Fortunately Han was the kind of man who always put friends first, so his own loyalties had gradually grown close enough to Leia's for them to make a life together.

But that wasn't going to happen with Jag. The core of his being was built around honor and duty, and his duty now lay with the Imperial Remnant. To ask him to turn his back on *that* would be to ask him to stop being Jagged Fel. So if he and Jaina were going to make a life together, it would have to be *her* loyalties that grew closer to Jag's—and *that* possibility, Leia suspected, was what really frightened Han: that Jaina might choose Jagged Fel and the Imperial Remnant over her parents and the Jedi.

Leia took Han's hand and gave it a reassuring squeeze. "Whatever Jaina does, you know she's going to be okay."

Han continued to look out toward the Krabbis's blinking red sign. " 'Course she is—it's *them* I'm worried about." He pointed at the BeamStreaks parked on the hostel's roof. "A GAS squad would know better than to bring those things down here. Gotta be someone from offworld."

Leia's stomach sank. "The Mandos already?"

"That's my guess," Han nodded. "Probably an advance team. If Daala wants to send commandos in after the crazies—er, patients—they'd try for some reconnaissance. I know *I* would."

"*That's* going to complicate things," Leia said. The whole reason they were sneaking the patients out of the Temple was to put them out of Daala's reach on Shedu Maad. "But we can't wait. Things are only going to grow more difficult."

"No kidding," Han said. "But even if it *is* a recon team, I don't see them causing us a problem."

"I'd like to be sure about that," Leia said.

She glanced toward the back of the docks, where Tekli, Raynar, and half a dozen other Jedi Knights were escorting Bazel Warv's hulking green bulk toward the FloatVan. Because of the Ramoan's near-fatal reaction to being tranquilized the last time, Tekli had switched to Force hypnosis and a gentler benzodi-class drug to put him into a state of anxiety-free obedience. So far, it seemed to be working; he had lumbered all the way down from the Asylum Block without complaining about his chains.

Still, no one seemed to be taking any chances with the powerful Ramoan. The group was flanked on one side by Jaden Korr and on the other by a dark-haired Jedi Knight who was as strong of spirit as he was in the Force, a cheerful young man by the name of Avinoam Arelis. Both were pulling hoverdollies bearing potted olbio trees and ysalamiri. The last thing anyone wanted was Bazel using the Force to counteract his drugs.

Leia caught Tekli's eye, then called, "If you have

everything under control, Han and I need to check on something outside."

The little Chadra-Fan nodded and waved them on, calling, "Feel free. Barv is doing very well."

"*So far,*" Han muttered under his breath. "I still don't see why we couldn't have put him in stasis in his cell like the others."

"Two words." Leia took his hand and started for a small hatch in the wall next to the vehicle exit. "*The door.*"

"We could have knocked out a wall," Han said. "I'm pretty good with a cutting torch."

Leia smiled. "*Coward.*"

"It's called *experience,* dear," Han said. They reached the door, and he palmed the slap-pad next to it. "You can only punch a rancor's nose so many times before you realize there's got to be a better way."

The door slid open, and Han waved Leia out onto a durasteel pedestrian balcony. This far down, the air was damp and foul. A constant stream of cargo vehicles was floating past in the transit lanes, located both a few meters above and a few meters below the portal level where they were standing. Across from their balcony, the silver BeamStreaks sat gleaming in the artificial light of the Krabbis Inn's rooftop lot. Both were parked so they had an unobstructed path straight out the gate.

Leia moved to the edge of the balcony, where a cramped set of stairs climbed into the aphotic murk of the gargantuan superstructure that supported Fellowship Plaza's sunny expanse. After a few steps, she finally felt her connection with the Force return. Han followed her, peering over the railing, his eyes tracing the staircase's zigzagging descent into the abyssal depths of Coruscant's undercity.

"Okay, I give up," he said. "Why are we out here taking in the Huttbelch air? We've got a schedule to keep."

"Bear with me—this won't take long." Leia opened herself to the Force and immediately felt the cold prickle of someone watching her. "You were right about those BeamStreaks. *Someone's* using the Krabbis as an observation post."

"And that's a problem *why*?" Han turned his back to the hostel to prevent any possibility of eavesdropping by way of lip-reading or parabolic microphone. "All they're going to see is a FloatVan leaving a loading dock."

Leia turned to face Han's side, putting her shoulder between her own mouth and any eavesdroppers in the Krabbis. "Unless they've got one of those PsiCor wallscopes Senator Trebek told the Masters about."

"How would they get one of those?" Han demanded. "Even Fleet Command hasn't seen one yet."

Leia stepped back so she could see Han's face, then looked him in the eye and waited. After a moment, he shook his head.

"No way," he said. "That's real off-the-budget stuff. Her own Justice Center would charge her with treason if she put it in the hands of a bunch of Mandos—or even a GAS squad. No way Daala is going to risk that."

"You don't think so?" Leia asked. "Then why would a reconnaissance team set up across from a mirrfield? It doesn't make sense, unless they have a way to see through it. They could even see through the van walls when it pulls out."

Han let out a disgusted groan. "Sometimes I hate it when you start getting logical." He snuck a peek across the skylane at the BeamStreaks, then turned back toward the wall and shook his head in resignation. "But we've got to know for sure. No sense getting all worked up if it's just a couple of dirtscratchers with a big budget and a pair of macrobinoculars."

"No argument here," Leia said. "Any ideas?"

Han thought for a moment, then took her hand. "As a matter of fact, yeah."

He led her back toward the loading dock. She felt a sudden severing as she entered the ysalamiri's Force void, but instead of thumbing the security pad next to the door, Han opened the safety gate at the end of the balcony. Still holding her hand, he led the way out onto the narrow catwalk that serviced the approach lights and guidance sensors arrayed around the edge of the entrance portal. As they passed in front of the mirrfield, their reflections appeared beside them, their hair standing on end with static discharge, their images wavering and slightly blurred.

Keeping one eye on their reflections and the other on his footing, Han led them to within a few meters of the catwalk's midpoint, then suddenly stopped and cursed under his breath. A faint shadow had suddenly begun to limn one side of their reflections, and the image of the Krabbis's blinking red sign had grown a couple of shades paler.

"What do you think?" Han asked. "Look like we're standing in a photonic spray to you?"

"It's a definite possibility." Leia pulled the lightsaber off her belt and pointed the blade emitter over their heads. "But it always pays to be sure."

She thumbed the activation switch, and the blade sizzled to life, bright and blinding in the under-plaza gloom. But instead of a blazing reflection, all the mirrfield showed was a transparent crevice. Through it, she could see Bazel Warv slowly lumbering up the Float-Van's ramp, his beady eyes watching her and Han from beneath his deeply furrowed green brow. Deciding the last thing she needed to do at the moment was give the huge Ramoan a reason to panic, she quickly deactivated her lightsaber and turned to Han.

"Okay, I'm sure," she said. "Whoever they are, they know what's going on in there."

Han nodded. "*Something* is interfering with the reflective overlay, that's for sure. But if it's any consolation, unless PsiCor got the flash-damping fixed, the poor ruk who was looking through their scope just now is going to need a new set of retinas."

"Remind me to send him a box of bomb-bons," Leia said. She raced back toward the balcony. "Come on. We need to get our patients out of there *now*, before Daala realizes Jaina is a diversion."

"Right behind you," Han said, pounding along at her heels. "The first thing we need to do is take out those BeamStreaks."

"And every other speeder on that rooftop," Leia agreed. "They're going to want to follow us, and they won't hesitate to steal something."

Leia reached the balcony and continued toward the stairs at the other end, but Han stopped long enough to place his thumb over the security pad next to the door. She heard the door slide open, then Han calling to the Jedi Knights inside.

"Jaden, Avinoam, we need backup! Everyone else, get that crate fired up and out of here. We've got peepers across the way."

By the time he had finished, Leia was bounding up the stairs toward the pedbridge three levels above. She was in contact with the Force again, and she could feel waves of ire and pain rolling toward them from the Krabbis hostel. It was impossible to tell from their presences whether they were Mandalorians, but there seemed to be about half a dozen of them, all relatively calm and focused on the task at hand.

When Han started to pound up the stairs behind her, Leia paused long enough to look down and give him a situation report. "I feel about six to eight of them, one in pain."

"The one that got blinded," Han surmised. He was taking the stairs two at a time, coming fast—even for a man who wasn't in his seventies. "Are they on the move?"

"Hard to . . ." Leia let her reply trail off as a cold chill of danger sense blossomed between her shoulder blades, then yelled, "Take cover!"

She threw herself flat against the stairs, at the same time glancing down to make sure Han was doing the same.

Leia found him already back down on the balcony, swinging around behind the staircase with his old DL-44 blaster pistol in hand. A trio of loud *krumph*s sounded from the Krabbis as a series of charges blew out three of the inn's top-story viewports, then a flurry of colored bolts began to ring and ping off the durasteel around her, filling the air with the acrid stench of molten metal.

"What the blazes?" Han yelled. "They're *firing* at us!"

"That's what Mandalorians *do,* dear," Leia called. "Cover me!"

"*Cover* you?" Han immediately began to fire across the hoverlane, dribbling bolts back through the deluge pouring out of the Krabbis's freshly shattered viewports. "Are you crazy?"

"I married *you,* didn't I?"

Leia ignited her lightsaber, then sprang up and began to ascend the stairs two and three at a time. She hung her arm over the safety rail and wielded her weapon in one hand, her wrist swiveling and pivoting as her blade windmilled back and forth, deflecting bolts.

Leia had barely reached the top of the stairs when

she sensed a new danger and looked across the skylane to see the coil-wrapped barrel of a magrifle protruding through one of the shattered viewports. She made a slapping motion with her free hand, and the weapon came free of the gloved hands holding it, then went flying along the face of the building. In the next heartbeat she used the Force to grab hold of one of the empty hands, then jerked a figure in red Mandalorian armor out through the viewport and sent him tumbling down through the skylane into the dark chasm beyond.

Leia reached the pedbridge and started across the traffic-filled abyss toward the Krabbis. She was now several stories above its rooftop parking lot. The durasteel decking and side panels of the pedbridge were shielding her, presenting the snipers with a nearly impossible firing angle. For the first half a dozen steps, she could scarcely bring herself to believe that they had really opened fire. Though gloomy, the freight lanes beneath Fellowship Plaza were hardly the undercity. A firefight directly outside the Jedi Temple was going to draw instant attention from a lot more than the usual law enforcement agencies.

By the tenth step, Leia realized why opening fire was the perfect strategy for the Mandalorians. Now that they had been discovered, the PsiCor wallscope was a real problem. If they let it fall into Jedi hands, it would be a huge embarrassment for Daala. She would be forced to admit that she had shared top-secret technology with the Mandalorians—to use against the *Jedi*. The firefight gave the Mandos the chance to secure the wallscope. Even more important, the fight *was* drawing a lot of attention, and that would make it harder to sneak their patients out of the Temple without some nosy reporter or security team getting in their way.

Leia had to finish this, and she had to finish it fast. She pulled her comlink out and, still running, opened a channel to Tekli.

"How close are you?"

"Not very," Tekli reported. "The firefight has upset Barv. He won't go into the FloatVan."

Leia exhaled in anger, then checked her chrono. "All right. We've probably got five minutes before the enforcement services start showing. If you don't have him aboard in three, leave without him."

"Princess Leia, I don't know if that's—"

"Just do it," Leia ordered. "Better to leave one patient in the Temple than all four."

A lucky blaster bolt squeezed between the bridge's decking and a side panel. It zinged past mere centimeters from Leia's knees, then ricocheted off the other side panel and burned a painful graze across her shoulder blades. *Kriffing Mandalorians.* She clicked off the comlink without awaiting a reply, then reached the end of the bridge and turned to start down the stairs toward the Krabbis. On the rooftop below, a pair of armored figures were just emerging from a turbolift into the parking area. One of them, a sturdy-looking blond woman with rugged features, was helmetless and watery-eyed. In her hands was a large crate, which Leia assumed to be the PsiCor wallscope surveillance kit.

The other, a tall masculine figure in blue armor, was using one hand to lead the blonde by the arm and the other to hold a BlasTech R-20 scatterblaster. With an instinct worthy of a Jedi, he raised the scatterblaster the instant he cleared the door and sent a couple of quick volleys howling toward the top of the stairs. Unable to deflect so many tiny bolts at once, Leia dropped behind the bridge's side panels and, cringing as the fiery hail ricocheted off the durasteel, reached for her hold-out blaster.

By the time she had pulled the little weapon from its hidden holster, the two Mandalorians were halfway to the closest BeamStreak and partially obscured by the staircase. She took the shot anyway, then saw her bolt burn through the crate in the blonde's hands.

Showing no indication of even feeling the hit, the woman disappeared behind the staircase with the crate still clutched in her hands. Leia rose, intending to Force-spring down to the rooftop—then heard the cracking *whoosh*es of igniting jetpacks. She spun toward the side panel in time to see five armored streaks come flying out of the Krabbis's shattered viewports.

Had these Mandalorians been attempting to flee, Leia would certainly have let them go and followed the crate. Had they been coming after *her,* she would have been happy to send them tumbling away with a series of Force shoves, so they could take their chances bouncing through the freighter traffic below. But all five were going for *Han,* and they were pouring so much blasterfire toward him and Jaden and Avinoam—who had come out to join him—that, in places, the balcony was red and starting to melt.

Leia extended her hand toward the leading Mandalorian and sent him streaking downward with a violent Force shove. He shot through the traffic lane below in a streak of white flame, causing several booming crashes as startled freighter pilots slammed their vehicles into one another and the surrounding buildings. A couple of heartbeats later a distant blossom of orange erupted in the darkest depths.

The whine of a repulsorlift engine sounded from the Krabbis's rooftop. Leia did not need to look to confirm what she already knew: the blond woman and her escort were fleeing. The entire jetpack assault had been a diversion to help them escape with the PsiCor wallscope, and the Mandalorians were too disciplined—too *cold*—to waste a fellow commando's sacrifice by risking the mission just to save a couple of lives.

Leia raced back toward the balcony, where the last

four Mandalorians were locked in hand-to-hand combat with Han and the two Jedi. Jaden and Avinoam were laying slash after slash across their foes' armor and doing no more than melting shallow furrows into the impenetrable *beskar'gam*. Yet every time the Mandalorians tried to bring their own weapons to bear, they found themselves on the verge of losing either their balance or an arm. Clearly, the two young Jedi were going easy on their attackers, trying to convince them to surrender before it became necessary to kill them.

And that would have been fine with Leia, except that these were *Mandalorians,* not your average run-of-the-processing-plant pirates. They prided themselves on being ruthless, treacherous, and efficient. The entire time Jaden and Avinoam were making nice trying to capture *their* attackers, they had failed to notice Han fighting for his life against the other two. Leia cringed, and Han ducked a line of blaster bolts, took a pistol butt across the spine, then came up cussing and punching, landing a vicious foreknuckle jab in an attacker's throat armor.

Still only halfway back across the bridge, Leia reached out in the Force toward the same commando. As his head rocked back, she gave it a powerful tug and sent him somersaulting over the safety rail. The Mando's jetpack ignited almost instantly, but that merely sent him into a second-long spiral, which ended in a crimson plume as he crashed through the bed of a passing hoversled.

The second attacker swept Han's feet from beneath him and sent him crashing down on his back. The Mandalorian swung the emitter nozzle of his blaster rifle toward Han's head, at the same time lowering his helmet toward Han's face. In response, Han sneered and spat an ounce of phlegm across the commando's eye plates.

Shaking her head at Han's defiance in the face of death—and loving him for it—Leia reached out in the

Force and jerked the blaster rifle aside, though not quickly enough to tell whether the red spray that erupted beneath the muzzle was Han's blood or the balcony's molten durasteel. The Mandalorian's helmet turned toward the barrel in momentary puzzlement; then he grabbed the weapon with both hands and swung it back toward Han's head.

But Han was already swinging his hips around and driving his knee into the back of the Mandalorian's leg. A series of white blaster flashes stitched up the wall beside them, and Leia raced along, close to the pedbridge side panel, trying to gauge the distance to the balcony and whether she had any chance of Force-jumping that far.

She was spared the necessity when a huge jade form came flying out of the mirrfield, a long chain flying from each of its four limbs. The figure landed on the balcony with a crash, and everyone, including Han's attacker, spun around to find Bazel Warv's immense head glaring down at them.

The two Mandalorians fighting Jaden and Avinoam took full advantage of the distraction, leaping over the safety railing backward, then disappearing on pillars of jetpack flame. The one standing over Han was not so lucky. One of Bazel's long arms lashed out and caught the fellow by his ankles.

Bazel smashed the Mandalorian against the wall repeatedly, until the blaster rifle finally flew free, then he closed one hand around the fellow's chest and began to squeeze. At first the Mandalorian remained silent inside his armor, no doubt confident that even a Ramoan's great strength could not crush *beskar* steel.

Then Bazel pushed past Han, still carrying the Mandalorian and leaving the Force void created by the ysalamiri. Jaden and Avinoam went after him, their lightsabers deactivated but in hand, yelling orders for him to stop. Bazel ignored them. Chains dragging on the balcony deck, he continued toward the staircase.

Leia briefly lost sight of him as she neared the end of the pedbridge, but she heard a tremendous clatter of chains, and she could tell by the way Han's jaw dropped—and the shock that Jaden and Avinoam radiated into the Force—that something strange had just happened. She reached the stairs and descended three stories in as many steps, Force-jumping from one landing to the next.

When Leia reached the last landing, she found herself staring at something she did not quite understand. Bazel was standing on the balcony below. His chains were heaped at his feet, and the Mandalorian was still in his grasp. There was blood seeping from every seam in the man's armor, and the Ramoan's fingers were somehow *inside* the chest plate, having sunk through the *beskar* steel without so much as denting it. Obviously, he was using a Force-power—and one that Leia hadn't even heard of.

Bazel suddenly tipped his head back to look up at Leia. His beady eyes widened with alarm, then he finally seemed to notice Jaden and Avinoam behind him. He shook his massive wrist and sent the Mandalorian crashing to the balcony deck. To Leia's amazement, there was not even a hole where Bazel's fingers had pushed through the armor; the dead man's *beskar'gam* remained perfectly intact.

Leia was still contemplating how such a thing could be possible when Bazel's deep voice rumbled up the stairs. *"Princess Leia?"*

Brow rising at the note of recognition in his voice, Leia nodded. "Yes, Bazel." She started down the stairs, moving slowly and cautiously to avoid alarming him. "Do you recognize—"

Bazel raised one of his massive, stubby-fingered

hands. "Stay there!" He glanced back at Jaden and Avinoam, then quickly added, "They'll get you!"

Leia stopped, then shook her head. "No, Bazel, they're our friends."

It was exactly the wrong thing to say. A glimmer of suspicion returned to Bazel's eyes, and his gaze shifted toward the staircase leading down. Han pointed his blaster pistol at the Ramoan's back, and Jaden and Avinoam flipped their lightsabers around so they could use the hilts like clubs.

None of this was lost on Bazel, of course. He glared up at Leia with unconcealed anger, then snarled, "You're one of *them*!"

He stepped toward the staircase, moving toward the *down* flight beneath Leia. Han glanced up, silently asking if he should open fire—with stun bolts, Leia assumed—while Jaden and Avinoam gathered themselves to spring.

But Leia was spared the necessity of giving the order when Raynar Thul called out from the far end of the balcony.

"*Of course* she is, Barv!"

Raynar started up the balcony toward Leia and the others, his unblinking eyes fixed on the stairwell below her. As he moved, the FloatVan's dome-shaped nose began to emerge through the mirrfield.

"We're *all* with them," Raynar said. "You know that."

There were no heavy steps from the stairs below, and Bazel's deep voice rumbled, "I *do*."

Raynar stopped and gestured at the FloatVan, which had now emerged far enough that its mid-body door was visible, hanging open above the balcony railing. Bazel's empty stasis bed could just be seen, too, lying beneath a pair of olbio trees secured to the walls with cushstraps.

"And you *also* know that you need to board the FloatVan," Raynar continued.

"*No!*"

A single heavy step rang off the stairs, and Leia almost nodded to Han.

Then Bazel suddenly stopped and asked, "Why?"

Raynar smiled, or tried to. The stiffness caused by his burn scars made his expression a little cruel and forced, and it sent a chill down Leia's spine.

"Are you willing to leave Yaqeel alone with *us*?" Raynar asked. "When you don't even know who *we* are?"

A low, sad croak sounded from the stairs below, and for a moment Leia thought Bazel might actually abandon his best friend. She waited in silence, not even daring to search his Force aura for some sense of his thoughts, while the Ramoan contemplated his options.

But Raynar had given Bazel a choice that was no choice at all. To flee now was to abandon Yaqeel to the mysterious evil that ran rampant through the Jedi Order. And whether it was the benzodi in his system, making him more vulnerable to Raynar's suggestion, or his own steadfast loyalty, Bazel simply could not abandon his friends.

When Leia did not hear another heavy footstep descending the stairs, she motioned Han and the others to stand aside.

Once they had obeyed, she called down, "Bazel, the choice is yours—but you need to make it now. We're taking Yaqeel and the others away. They won't be harmed, I promise you—"

"As long as you go along." Raynar also stepped aside, giving Bazel a clear path to the FloatVan. "If not . . ."

Raynar let the threat hang. Bazel let out a long, anguished croak, then pounded across the balcony and hopped into the FloatVan, his tremendous weight actually causing it to list momentarily to one side. Tekli, Tesar, and the others quickly surrounded him and, through a combination of firm threats and gentle promises, began to cajole him toward his stasis bed.

As the FloatVan closed its door, Leia descended the stairs. Seeing that Han was already standing—to her relief, seemingly in one piece—at Raynar's side, she went over to join them.

"That was incredible, Raynar," she said. "Thank you."

A hint of red actually came to Raynar's cheeks. "It was nothing, Princess."

"*Hardly,*" Leia replied. "Maybe you should consider helping Tekli on Shedu Maad."

Raynar looked back toward the Temple, then shook his head. "I don't think I'm ready to leave yet."

"You sure?" Han pressed. "It looked to me like you kind of have a knack for dealing with cra—" He cringed as Leia stomped on his foot, but quickly finished, "er, mental illness."

"Anyone can manipulate our crazies, Captain Solo. You just need to work in *their* reality." He watched as the FloatVan glided out into the traffic chasm and began to drop toward the hoverlane below, then turned to Leia and tried to grin. "And to remember that in their reality, you *are* evil."

As earlier, there was something in the way his mouth failed to turn up at the corners that made his smile feel hard and enigmatic.

Leia forced herself to respond with a warmer grin. "I'll try to keep that in mind." She turned to Han, then said, "We'd better advance our timetable. By now, Daala knows we're moving, and the less time we give her to stop us, the better."

"Right. I'll get the droids and Amelia and then get us launched." He leaned forward and kissed her on the cheek, then added, "See you at Alpha Point."

Leia kissed him back. She started for the door, then turned to Jaden and Avinoam. "I know this isn't really your mess—"

"We'll cover it," Jaden assured her. "As far as GAS or anyone else is concerned, you and Captain Solo were already gone when the firefight broke out."

"Thanks," Leia said. "But don't try telling them we were transporting the Temple jewels or something. Daala is going to know exactly who was in that Float-Van, so just refer inquiries to the Masters. Clear?"

"Just one question," Jaden said. His gaze dropped to the Mandalorian Bazel had killed. "What do we tell them about *him*?"

Leia turned to look at the dead man. The last thing the Jedi needed was some GAS investigator reporting that now crazy Jedi could reach through *beskar* steel—or suggesting that *any* Jedi could do such a thing. Daala was already frightened enough of them.

"Just say you don't know," Leia said. "See if you can plant the suggestion that something went wrong with his armor."

Jaden nodded. "That should work."

"On *GAS*," Avinoam finished. He seemed unable to take his eyes off the Mandalorian. "But, well, what *really* happened to him?"

"That's a good question," Leia said, studying the dead man's unblemished armor. Bazel's fingers inside, the blood flowing out, but not a dent on the steel. So far, all of the new abilities that the delusional Jedi had exhibited had been duplications of something Jacen had learned to do on his five-year sojourn. But she had never heard of him being able to reach through *metal*.

She shook her head, then said to Avinoam, "I've never seen any Force abilities like it—I haven't even *heard* of one."

"*We* have," Raynar said. As Leia turned to face him, he lifted his gaze from the dead man. "I mean, the *Killiks* have. When they created the Maw, they could use the Force to change the state of matter."

Leia frowned. Because their species absorbed the memories of any being who became Joined to one of their nests, the Killik sense of history was—to put it mildly—rather muddled.

"Was it the *Killiks* who could do that?" she asked Raynar. "Or their Celestial masters?"

Again, Raynar gave her one of his enigmatic smiles. "I suppose that depends on whose reality you are in," he said. "But the important thing is this: now Bazel can do it."

Chapter Twenty-one

FROM THE DEPTHS OF THE GROTTO CAME THE SOUND OF water, a single drop, *blep*ping into a pool. A week later, another *blep*. Then a month passed before three drops fell in as many seconds . . . or perhaps it was years. Without his body, Luke had no pulse, no living rhythm by which to measure the passing of seconds or days or centuries. He just *was*—an eternal, pure presence standing outside the cave mouth, allowing the mountain's acrid breath to waft out over him.

She was in there, the same familiar presence that had reached out from the Font of Power. Luke could feel her in the damp gloom ahead, calling him inside like a lover in need of a visit. But she was hungry and desperate, all appetite and insistence, and he worried that to answer her call was to be devoured by it.

"You have no need to fear anything inside," said Seek Ryontarr, the onetime Jedi who was acting as his guide. The Gotal stepped down into the overgrown gully with Luke and went to stand beside one of the shadowy columns that supported the grotto entrance, then extended a hand into the sweltering darkness beyond. "Go and have a dip."

Luke shook his head. "I don't like what I feel in there."

Ryontarr's Givin companion, Feryl, descended into the gully and went to stand before the opposite column.

"That is because you fear what is in your own heart," he rasped. "It is difficult to face the truth about oneself." The Givin's skull-like head turned to look into the darkness. "There are not many who have the courage to go inside."

"But Jacen did," Luke surmised.

"That does not mean *you* must," Ryontarr said. "Once a truth is learned, it cannot be unlearned."

Luke furrowed his brow. "If you're trying to *challenge* me into going inside, it won't work."

Ryontarr smiled, his broad mouth just showing the tips of his sharp teeth. "Well, then I guess we can leave," he said. "Where would you like to go next?"

It was a bluff, and Luke knew it. But as Han was fond of telling him, the best time to bluff was when you knew the other guy couldn't call. And Luke *couldn't* call, not if he wanted to find out what had become of Jacen.

That didn't mean he had to walk in there blind, though.

Luke shifted his gaze to Feryl's spectral face. "What I *feel* coming from there is desire—raw, aching yearning." He put on a wry smile. "And I've reached the age where intense feelings of that kind are *always* a lot more welcome than frightening."

Feryl cocked his head in bewilderment and looked to Ryontarr, whose own amused scowl suggested that Gotals, at least, shared that particular aspect of human aging.

Ryontarr dropped his eyes in thought and appeared content to contemplate Luke's reply for as long as it held his interest. Of course, there was no way to tell how long that might be, since every moment felt like an eternity and eternity seemed only a moment. But during the long march from the Font of Power, Luke had noticed that his escorts were beginning to move at a slower, more deliberate pace, as though they were savoring every step in this strange jungle world and were determined to make sure that Luke did, too.

Whenever Luke had inquired how much time was passing for his body, he had received the same assurances: that the Force would sustain his body while he was away, and that he would know if it needed something. Pressing the matter only made things worse. They merely suggested that if he was worried about his body, he should return to it and check on its condition. They also noted that if Luke made such a journey, it would prolong the Skywalkers' stay by several days—but that was of no concern, they reassured him, because time was, after all, an illusion.

In the end, Luke had realized that he had little choice but to continue until his suspicions and sense of danger grew too strong to ignore, or he had learned what he had come to learn. The more time he spent with Ryontarr and Feryl, the more convinced he grew that the key to Jacen's fall lay somewhere beyond shadows—and it was certainly worth taking a few risks to discover it.

Finally, Ryontarr looked back to Luke. "Perhaps you do not fear what you feel, as you say. Perhaps you fear the *cause* of what you feel."

"I'm not *that* old," Luke said. "The cause of this feeling is that I'm a human male. And I stopped being afraid of natural yearnings when I was still a teenage moisture farmer back on Tatooine."

"Of course," Ryontarr acknowledged. "But you are also a human male who lost his wife not so long ago."

Luke frowned. "You think I'm afraid it's *Mara* I feel in there?"

"*Are* you?" Ryontarr demanded.

"Of course not."

Luke started to add that if he thought he *could* see Mara again, he'd be inside the grotto in an instant. But when he turned his attention to the hunger coming from the cave, to the raw, selfish craving that was trying to pull him in, he had to wonder. The Mara he knew would never *demand* like that, would never be so selfish and desperate. But the Mara he knew was also dead—whatever that really meant. And it was at least within the realm of possibility that what he felt reaching for him now was some lingering, primitive part of her, some childish instinct that knew only desire, that understood only what *she* needed, while caring nothing for the wants of others.

But if that was all that remained of his beloved Mara, would he truly want to see it? He looked back to Ryontarr, who seemed to be awaiting Luke's decision with the patience of a tree.

"*Is* that Mara in there?" Luke demanded. He was starting to wonder if this place was some kind of spiritual limbo, where the presences of the dead were torn down so they could be returned to the Force. "Is that what you're telling me?"

Ryontarr spread his hands. "We aren't telling you *anything*," he said. "We can help you find the truth, but we can't tell you what it is because we don't know."

That much, Luke felt certain, was true. Leaving aside the question of whether he was here because he was actually dead—or dying—he could see no logical reason that the Mind Walkers would have a knowledge of the afterlife more accurate than any of the galaxy's myriad religions.

After a few seconds—or a few hours—Feryl asked, "There's only one way to find out, isn't there?"

Ryontarr nodded. "Go inside and see. You'll be glad you did."

Luke continued to stand three paces from the grotto. "As glad as I would have been, say, had I drunk from the Font of Power?"

"*That* was a test," Ryontarr said. The Gotal tipped his horns toward the darkness. "*This* is an offer."

"Of what?" Luke demanded.

"Of what you came for," Feryl answered. "Bathe in this pool, and you'll have the answers you seek."

Luke raised a brow. "About Jacen?" he asked. "Or about Mara?"

"About whatever you seek," Ryontarr replied. "This is the Pool of Knowledge, where you will see all that has passed and all that is to come."

"That's a bit much for one mind to comprehend, don't you think?" Luke was beginning to see their trap—and how it would have been an irresistible temptation for a troubled young Jedi Knight on a galactic search for wisdom. "Did you bring Jacen here, too?"

"Jacen did not need to be *brought*," Ryontarr said. "But he was here, yes."

"Have a look," Feryl urged. "You don't have to get in, but maybe you will learn what you need to know about Mara."

"And Jacen." Ryontarr extended his hand into the darkness, then added, "We all know you really have no choice, Master Skywalker. And *you* are the one who is always asking about time."

At that moment, Luke knew he was walking into a trap. Until now, the two Mind Walkers had done everything they could to keep him from worrying about time, to reassure him that there was no reason to be concerned about it. Yet here they were now, using time to pressure him into a dangerous decision.

Clearly, they did not expect him to resist the temptation they were offering, which suggested that Jacen had not resisted. And that, of course, meant that Luke had no choice except to enter.

Luke shrugged. "Okay, you win," he said. "Let's go."

He was hardly surprised when his two escorts motioned him through the entrance, while they themselves remained standing by the pillars. As he stepped past them, he saw that the grotto was small, and the interior was not as dark as it had seemed from outside. A soft, silvery light was rising from the mirror-like sheen of a pool in the center. Tiny crevices lined the walls, seeping wisps of yellow fume and filling the cave with a stench of brimstone. So foul was the air that, even had he needed to, Luke would not have drawn breath inside.

The desperate longing continued to pull at him, drawing him closer to the pool. He went to the edge and saw that it lay not in a shallow bowl as he had expected, but in a deep, sheer-sided basin with an edge carved in a grotesque, serpentine braid. Through an exertion of will, he stopped half a pace from the water—he *assumed* it was water—and stared down at his own reflection.

What Luke saw was not so much a man as the specter of one, with eyes of blue burning out of sockets as deep as wells. His flesh was yellow and haggard, so drawn and flaky that it resembled cracked leather. His lips had withered to a pair of white worms so cracked and bloody that they barely covered his teeth. The pool was not dark, he reasoned, so perhaps he was not really looking at a reflection. He raised a hand, and the specter raised one, too.

"Is that . . ." Luke turned toward the exit, where Ryontarr stood leaning against a shadowy pillar. "Is that *me*?"

"It is the truth, as you are now," Ryontarr replied. "A man worn to nothing by duty and sacrifice, a dying husk animated by the Force and willpower alone."

"What about Mara?" Luke turned back to the pool. Instead of himself, he saw the honey-haired phantom from the Font of Power, the tiny eyes burning with desire, the broad mouth showing needle-teeth from ear to ear. "Is that her?"

"If you can't tell *now*," Feryl said, "then there is only one way to be sure."

A stubby arm broke the surface of the pool and reached for Luke, the tentacle-fingers waving so close before his eyes that he could see the tiny slit-membranes in the bottom of their suction-cup tips. The hungry presence grew more familiar, somehow a *part* of Luke, and he wanted nothing more in that instant than to step forward into the pool and know the truth of her identity, to know whether *this* was where the afterlife began and the spirits of the dead began their journey back to the Force.

Luke wanted to know what had happened to Jacen and what had made him fall, and he wanted to know what would become of his son, whether Ben would make a good Grand Master and how long he had to prepare for that terrible burden. More than anything, Luke wanted to know whether he had succeeded in his own life, whether the spark he had struck in founding the new Jedi Order would endure and flourish, growing into the bright golden light that he had envisioned, the beacon that would always be there to guide the galaxy safely through the dark times.

And the hungry presence could give him all that knowledge and more. All Luke had to do was clasp the tentacle-hand before him and let it draw him into the warm silver waters with it, let it drown him in the liquid oblivion of absolute, infinite knowledge.

But what Luke *already* knew was this: the choice that Jacen had made here was his undoing. The future was not the province of the living, and no human mind could know all things and remain sane. Luke knew he was still Ben's father and the founder of the Jedi Order, and he knew he was still needed by both. He knew that Mara was gone, that if the thing craving him now had ever been part of her, it had certainly not been the best part . . . that if this was all that remained of her, he would not be doing anyone a service by trying to hold on to it.

Luke backed away from the pool.

Luke.

The voice sounded cold and half-familiar inside Luke's mind, the last whisper of a lost love. The hand slid back into the pool, the tentacle-fingers beckoning him to follow.

Come back.

Luke shook his head and turned away. "I can't."

He found Ryontarr and Feryl in front of him, blocking the exit. The Gotal's flat-nosed face was scowling, and the Givin was shaking his bony head in disappointment.

"Master Skywalker, you don't strike me as the kind to leave without the answers you came for," Ryontarr said. "I don't believe you have seen what Jacen saw yet."

"I've seen enough." Luke started forward, already calling to mind the haggard image of himself that he had seen reflected in the pool's surface. "I'm returning to my body."

"*Before* you have seen what your nephew saw?" Feryl asked.

"If doing so means bathing in your pool, yes." Luke reached the doorway and stopped half a pace from the pair. "I'm only willing to follow him so far. I won't go over the brink with him."

Ryontarr lifted his bushy brows, and Feryl tipped his bony head in disappointment.

"Going over the brink is hardly necessary, Master Skywalker," Ryontarr said. "Jacen didn't bathe in the pool, either."

Luke frowned. "He *didn't*?"

"Didn't even consider it," Feryl reported. "He said

no mortal mind could know everything, and the last thing he wanted was to become a Celestial."

Before Luke could ask what they knew about the Celestials, Ryontarr added, "But Jacen wasn't afraid to stay at the pool until he had seen what he came to see." The Gotal tipped his horns toward the water behind Luke. "Have another look."

Luke shook his head. "I'm done with your delaying tactics," he said. "I don't know what you're trying to accomplish, but I *do* know you're trying to keep me here."

Even without the shiver of guilt that rippled through the Force, Luke would have known by their furtive glances that he had struck at the heart of the matter. Determined not to yield the advantage when he had it, he said, "Tell me what you expect to happen. And don't claim you're just trying to help me. I didn't believe that in the habitat, and I won't believe it now."

Ryontarr looked to Feryl.

The Givin rasped, "What is there to lose?"

Ryontarr nodded. "What indeed?" He pointed toward the pool. "Perhaps she is hiding it from you. Perhaps she doesn't want you to suffer the way Jacen did."

"She?" Luke slowly turned to face the pool again. He did not see the thing that had reached for him earlier, only the silvery mirror of the water's surface. "Who is this *she*? The phantasm I keep glimpsing?"

"The lady in the mists is no phantasm," Feryl replied. "She's as real as you or I."

"Look for a throne," Ryontarr advised. "It's the Throne of Balance, upon which sits the course of the future."

Luke hesitated, suspecting yet another delaying strategy. But what they were implying about Jacen, that he had been both more courageous than Luke and more wise, was too compelling to ignore. It was Luke's duty to investigate what had happened to his nephew, whether it had led to his fall, and that meant that he simply had to do as Ryontarr suggested.

Luke peered into the water, looking for anything that resembled a throne, and soon he saw it, a simple white throne in a brightly lit chamber. There was no one in it, but it was surrounded by a hundred beings regal enough to belong in the seat. They were of all species, Bothans and Hutts, Ishi Tib and Mon Calamari, even Wookiees and Trandoshans—and they all had the easy bearing of old friends.

But what caught Luke's eye, what drew him closer to the pool's edge, was the tall, redheaded woman at the center of the crowd. She had Tenel Ka's thin arcing brows and full-lipped mouth, but her nose was her grandmother's, small and not too long, with just a hint of a button at the end.

Allana.

Luke did not say the name aloud—he felt guilty for even thinking it—but there could be no doubt. He was looking at a vision of Jacen's daughter, perhaps thirty years in the future. And she was preparing to take a throne, surrounded not by the usual treachery and intrigue so common to Hapan politics, but by friends from all across the galaxy, in a time of unprecedented comradery and trust.

"I don't understand," Luke said, turning to Ryontarr. "Why would Jacen be troubled by a vision of his daughter assuming her throne?"

"Because that's not what he saw." It was the Givin, Feryl, who rasped this answer. "*He* saw a dark man in dark armor, sitting on a golden throne and surrounded by acolytes in dark robes."

Luke went cold inside. "A dark man?" he asked, thinking of the visions of the dark man he had experienced as Jacen was rising to become a Sith Lord. "Himself?"

Ryontarr scowled over at Luke. "I doubt a vision of his *own* future would have sent him fleeing back to the galaxy," he said. "It had to be someone *else's* face your nephew saw."

A terrible thought occurred to Luke, as painful as a vibrodagger to the gut and just as frightening. *"Me?"*

Ryontarr shrugged. "Who can say?"

"We didn't see the face behind the mask," Feryl added. "But *Jacen* did, and he turned as pale as my exoskeleton."

"Then what?" Luke demanded. "Did he return to the Font of Power? Did he change his mind and bathe in the Pool of Knowledge?"

The two Mind Walkers looked to each other and shook their heads in disgust, as though Luke's obtuseness were a great disappointment. Then Ryontarr said, "He left."

"He left the Pool?" Luke asked, still struggling to see what had pushed his nephew toward the dark side. "Or do you mean Jacen returned to his body?"

"He left the *Maw,*" Ryontarr explained. "He said that he had to finish his training."

"He *said* he had to change what he had seen in the pool," Feryl added. "He *said* it was probably going to kill him."

Chapter Twenty-two

THE ALERT STROBING, BEN COULD TAKE. AND THE CHIRPing and wailing of the alarms, he had already silenced with a few well-placed blaster bolts. But the acrid smoke rising out of the equipment cabinets—that he could not stop. No matter how poorly the control room's air exchangers worked, no matter how badly the fumes stung his eyes or burned his throat, he did not dare tamper with such alien technology. There was no telling what he might blow up: himself, the entire habitat . . . even the Maw itself.

And there were some things a good Jedi just did not risk.

Deciding he had made every preparation possible, Ben turned back to the entry hatch. He made one last inspection of his spot-welds, then nodded in satisfaction and shut off the energy feed to his plasma torch. No one would be sneaking through that door when he wasn't watching.

Tossing the welding mask and gloves aside as he walked, Ben descended to the front of the trilevel control room. There, bathed in the flickering purple light from the writhing radiance beyond the viewport, his emaciated father lay strapped to a hovergurney from the *Shadow*'s medbay. Both arms had fresh IV catheters in them, one delivering hydration and the other nutrients, but Ben did not know how much longer the fluid drips could keep his father alive. Both of the guides had died more than a week ago, the Givin because Ben had no idea how to insert an intravenous catheter through an exoskeleton, the other one because the *Shadow* simply did not carry the saline-free drips necessary to avoid poisoning a Gotal.

Several meters away sat Rhondi Tremaine, looking human again with fairly clean yellow hair and cheeks that were only slightly hollow. A pair of stun cuffs from the *Shadow*'s security stores connected her wrists to a metal floor beam that Ben had exposed for the purpose. Her brows were arched in fear, and her eyes were rimmed in red from weeping.

"Ben, *please*," she said. "What are you doing?"

Ben did not answer because he wasn't sure yet. His father's orders had been clear: under no circumstances was Ben to go beyond shadows. If something went wrong, he was to report back to the Masters and make sure the Jedi knew about the dark power hiding in the Maw.

But that had been *before* Ben had started to go barvy.

He knew the symptoms of paranoid delusional disorder, and he realized he was suffering from most of them: the unshakable belief that his life and his father's were in danger, the all-consuming fear that haunted his every thought, the reasons he could always find to dismiss any fact that did not support his own convictions. And yet the Mind Walkers *were* trying to kill him. While he might doubt his own sanity, *that* Ben did not doubt at all.

No one had attacked him directly, of course. The Mind Walkers were too clever for that. Instead, they had depleted the *Shadow*'s medbay to the point that he could no longer treat even a simple infection. They had consumed so much nutripaste that Ben had been reduced to foraging old dehydros from other vessels in the hangar. And the *Shadow*'s recycling system had lost so much water to the people who drank and left that it was having trouble purifying itself.

"Ben," Rhondi said. "You can't leave Rolund in that little room to die. That's just . . . sick."

Though Ben did not say so, he thought Rhondi was probably right. It was certainly not normal to leave a man welded inside a sleeping cabin. It wasn't normal to trap the door with a thermite tamper guard, either.

But it *was* necessary, should Ben decide to go through with his plan. And he was beginning to realize he probably had no choice. As bad as it was that both of Master Horn's children had lost their minds, to have Ben *Skywalker* return to Coruscant alone, delusional, and paranoid would be a catastrophe for the Jedi Order matched only by *Luke* Skywalker's death. And it could easily get worse. In Ben's demented state, he might fail to report what he and his father had found in the Maw . . . or he might not be believed.

Rhondi seemed to take Ben's silence as a statement of intention. "Don't do this," she pleaded. "If Rolund starves in there, he'll be lost until his presence disperses into the Force. At least bring him in here, where he can see the meditation chamber and find his way back beyond shadows."

Ben frowned and asked, "Didn't I explain this to you earlier?"

Despite the cynical edge, Ben's question was sincere. He had been under a lot of stress lately, trying everything he could think of to bring his father back to his body, and it just seemed possible that he had forgotten to execute this critical part of his plan.

Instead of replying, Rhondi started to cry. Ben decided he needed to phrase his question a little more gently. He reached out with the Force and turned her head toward him.

"*Did* I explain this to you?" he asked.

Rhondi nodded and began to cry harder. Her tears made him feel a little hollow and guilty about what he was doing to her and to her brother . . . but she *was* one of the people trying to kill him.

"And do you remember what I said?" Ben demanded. There was no sense risking any miscommunication. "Tell me."

"You said that if *you* die beyond shadows, *Rolund* dies in that cabin," Rhondi croaked.

"That's right," Ben said, and he realized that he had finally made his decision. Rhondi was trying to trick him, to remove the threat to her brother so that she would be free to kill Ben. "And *am* I going to die while we're beyond shadows?"

Rhondi shook her head. "Not if I can help it."

"Good," Ben said. He climbed onto a hovergurney adjacent to his father's and quickly strapped his legs in place. "Then we have nothing to worry about."

Ben set the drip on his IV bags, then lay down on the gurney and used the Force to secure the straps over his chest.

"Rolund has enough food and water to last a month," Ben said, reassuring himself as much as Rhondi. "He'll be fine."

Rhondi appeared less than convinced, but she merely looked away and did not bother to argue. "Are you ready?"

Ben nodded. "More than," he said. "What do I do?"

"Just turn toward the light," Rhondi told him. "Listen to my voice and breathe. We'll go together."

Ben turned toward the purple light.

"There is no life," Rhondi began.

More than familiar with the techniques of Force meditation, Ben inhaled as she spoke, then, during the silent pause that followed, exhaled into the purple light writhing beyond the viewport.

"There is only the Force."

Ben exhaled again, and felt himself drifting toward the light.

"Picture the number *one* in your mind," Rhondi said. "That is the first level of ascension. *There is no life . . .*"

Again, Ben exhaled into the light.

"There is only the Force."

Ben exhaled again.

"Now you see the number *two,*" Rhondi said. "There is no time . . ."

Ben exhaled once more.

A few minutes later—or it might have been a few hours—they reached the number 7, and Ben felt himself slip free. He had a thousand questions about what was happening to him, about how long they had been gone and what would become of his abandoned body. But when Rhondi appeared next to him, looking more refreshed and beautiful than she ever had before, he had only one question on his mind.

"How do we find my father?"

Rhondi extended her hand. "Take my hand," she said. "Think of your father and walk with me into the light."

Ben did as she instructed, and together they walked into the crackling purple radiance beyond the viewport. At once, he was filled with an eternal, boundless bliss beyond anything he had ever experienced. He became one with the Force, melted into it and was filled with a calm joy as vast as the galaxy itself. How long he and Rhondi hung there together, Ben would never know. It was less than an eyeblink, as long as eternity.

Then a voice said, *Come.*

And suddenly Ben was looking out on a narrow mountain lake with a surface as still as black glass. From one shore rose a face of sheer granite, sloping up toward a domed summit lit in the lazuline light of a blue sun. Along the other shore lay a boulder-strewn meadow filled with hummocks of knee-high moss and rivulets of purling water. Directly ahead, his father stood next to Ryontarr and the Givin, looking toward a half-hidden female form floating in the silver mists that concealed the far end of the lake.

Ben released Rhondi's hand and started forward, no longer consumed by the same sense of urgency that had been troubling him back on the station. True, his father had grown perilously weak over the last couple of weeks. And true, his own life was also in peril, since the Mind Walkers were trying to kill *him*. But Ben had left such mundane concerns behind with his body. He had swum in the incomprehensible infinity of the universe, drunk of the pure joy of eternal existence, and now he understood.

Life and death *were* the same, because moments did not vanish, could not be consumed like air or water or nutripaste. They existed at once and forever, spread across the entire continuity of being, the same way atoms were scattered across the vastness of the universe. Just as atoms gathered together in clumps of energy, which living beings perceived as matter, moments gathered in packets of minutes and hours, which mortal creatures perceived as time passing.

But those packets were no more the essence of time than sunlight was the essence of a star, or heat the essence of fire. They were simply the perceptions through which the minds of finite beings experienced infinity, the sensations through which their bodies detected the existence of themselves and everything around them.

Ben reached the lake and halted at his father's side, opposite Ryontarr and the Givin. The female form was no more than fifty paces distant, close enough for Ben to see that she was not quite human, with a cascade of saffron hair that seemed to hang down to the water, and a pair of tiny bright eyes set in sockets so deep they looked like wells.

When his father did not immediately seem to notice him, Ben said, "Whoa, Dad . . . that was some trip."

Luke snorted in amusement, then turned to Ben with a wry smile. "You weren't supposed to find that out."

Ben nodded, and suddenly felt like he had made the wrong decision. If time and life were illusions, what did it matter if he went mad? What did it matter if his father died and Ben never reported to the Masters? Both had *already* happened, or they never would. In the end, all he had done was disobey an order.

Ben dropped his gaze. "Sorry about that," he said. "It wouldn't have been a good idea for me to go back to Coruscant—not with things the way they are, thanks to Daala."

Luke frowned. "Because?"

"Think about where we are, Dad," Ben said, forcing himself to meet his father's gaze. "Or at least where our bodies are, and what everyone who's gone barvy has in common."

Luke nodded. "Shelter." He cocked his head and studied Ben for a moment. "Where you . . . ?"

"I think *so*." Ben glanced over at Rhondi, then lowered his voice. "Dad, nobody ever actually attacked me. But I have this feeling—this *really* strong feeling—that they're trying to kill us."

Luke gave him a smile. "Ben, it's not paranoid if it's true." He tipped his head toward his two escorts. "These two have been leading me into one trap after another since we left the station."

Ben felt his eyes widen, then he frowned over at Ryontarr and the Givin. "And you're still here? Why?"

Luke shrugged, then looked back toward the woman in the mist. "I still have a few questions."

"Your questions can wait." It wasn't Ben who said

this, but Rhondi. She reached forward from behind Ben and took his arm. "Get your father. I kept my side of the bargain; now we need to go."

"*Bargain?*" Ryontarr leaned out to glare past the Skywalkers, while the Givin slipped around behind Rhondi. "Why would you do *that*?"

The clear hostility in the Gotal's voice brought to mind the urgency Ben had felt back in the station.

"That's right, Dad." He took his father's arm and started to pull. "You're pretty close to dying. We've got to go."

Luke gently pulled his arm free. "In a minute, Ben." He turned to Ryontarr, then added, "I've known for a while that you're trying to stall me. What I haven't been able to figure out is *why*."

"And you expect me to tell you?" the Gotal asked. "Because we were both Jedi . . . once?"

"That would be the courteous thing," Luke confirmed. "But the reason you're going to tell me is because I'm leaving if you don't."

Ryontarr shot Rhondi a withering scowl, then nodded and reluctantly pointed a taloned finger toward the woman in the mist. "Because she desires it."

Luke turned back toward the lake. "The lady in the mist?"

As his father asked this, Ben looked toward the woman and instantly felt a chill of danger sense. Hers was the same needy presence that he had sensed on the way into the Maw . . . and the grasping touch from which he had retreated as a two-year-old.

Ben took his father's arm again. "Dad, I *really* think it's time to go. I'm pretty sure she's what was reaching for me when I was at Shelter."

"That wouldn't surprise me," Luke said, not allowing Ben to pull him away. He turned to Ryontarr. "We'll leave as soon as we know what she wants with us."

"I have no idea," Ryontarr said, spreading his hands. "Perhaps you should walk out and ask her."

Rhondi said, "Ben, that's not a good . . ." but she let her sentence trail away as the Givin stepped close behind her. Ben tried again to pull his father away from the lake, but Luke seemed almost Force-rooted in place.

"I need to figure this out. This lady . . . I think she knows what corrupted Jacen, maybe even what's been driving our Jedi Knights mad." Luke stepped into the shallow water close to shore. "I won't be long, Ben. You go on back."

"I'm not going *anywhere* without you." Ben looked back at Rhondi, then added, "And you're not going anywhere without me—and a better *guide* than Ryontarr."

Rhondi shook her head in dismay, but she stepped forward and grasped his wrist. "Take your father's arm."

Ben followed her into the water and did as she instructed. When his father did not object, she began to lead them forward, sticking close to the meadow. To Ben's surprise—and unease—the boulders and hummocks along the shore cast reflections not of themselves, but of Wookiees, Barabels, humans, Chadra-Fan, and a few species Ben did not even recognize. These reflections, however, did not seem to lie directly *on* the surface. Instead, they appeared about a dozen centimeters below, just where the water grew too dark to see any deeper.

"This is the Lake of Apparitions," Ryontarr said, following behind Ben. "Perhaps you see why."

"Yeah," Ben said. Actually, he would have been just as happy not knowing the name—but he was pretty certain the Gotal realized that. "Thanks for the hint."

"My pleasure," Ryontarr said. "And this end, we call the Mirror of Remembrance."

"Catchy names," Ben said. "I'll make a note of them for the guidebook."

As they waded forward, they did not make any sloshing sounds, or even disturb the surface of the lake. And why should they have? They were there only in spirit and not in body, and Force presences did not normally impact the physical world . . . assuming this *was* a physical world.

It sure seemed like one. The water was no more than calf-deep, but it was dark, and he could not see his feet. After only a few steps, he stepped on a submerged stone and stumbled, and Rhondi quickly ordered, "Step only where I step. The lake is generally shallow, but there are places where it drops off."

"Into the Depths of Eternity," the Givin rasped from the end of the line. "If you sink into that, even we cannot pull you back."

"Great." Ben gently pushed his father ahead, directly behind Rhondi, then slipped into line himself and reached forward to continue holding his father's arm. "Hear that, Dad?"

"Got it, son." Luke sounded more amused than concerned. "Thanks for being sure."

"No problem," Ben replied. "At your age, the hearing starts to go."

As Ben spoke, he looked down to make certain that he was following exactly in his father's steps—then gasped aloud at the face he saw staring up at him. He had only seen that face when he was too young to remember it, but he *had* viewed plenty of holos of it, and there was no mistaking those ice-blue eyes and that tousled, sandy-brown hair.

Anakin Solo.

At the sound of Ben's gasp, his father stopped and turned to look, then also gasped. *"Anakin?"*

Anakin's image floated up, as if emerging from the

reflection of a boulder on shore. His lips were just breaking the surface of the lake, and his icy-blue eyes swung in Luke's direction.

"Uncle . . . Luke?" Anakin's voice was gurgling and uncertain, like a Mon Calamari's. "Is that really you?"

Luke nodded, and his Force aura grew cold and heavy with the guilt that he still felt, a decade and a half later, about sending Anakin on the mission that had ended his life.

"Yes, Anakin. It's . . ."

Luke's voice cracked, and he seemed too shocked to continue. Ben could understand why—he hadn't even *known* Anakin, and he felt stunned, confused, happy, sorry . . . and suspicious. Everything that the Mind Walkers did was for the purpose of keeping him and his father beyond shadows until they died. It seemed utterly impossible that they were actually speaking to Anakin Solo—almost as impossible as it was to leave their bodies to journey through the Maw as pure Force presences.

Deciding that whatever was happening, it would be best to buy his father some time to recover, Ben said, "Hello, Anakin. It's an honor to, uh, meet you."

Anakin's gaze shifted to Ben. "Ben?" he asked. "Has it been that long?"

Ben nodded. "I'm afraid so. I'm the same age now that you were . . ." He paused, wondering whether it was wise to remind an apparition of its death, then decided that it would be an insult to be anything less than honest. "When you died."

To Ben's relief, Anakin did not seem at all surprised. He merely smiled, then said, "Try not to follow my lead, okay?"

Ben chuckled despite himself, then said, "I'm doing my best."

"Good." Anakin's expression grew serious. "Be

much more careful than I was, Ben. Learn from my mistakes."

"I *have*—not from your mistakes, I mean, but from your example." Ben glanced over and, seeing that his father looked like he had recovered his composure, he added, "You're a legend, Anakin. Your sacrifice saved the Jedi. There hasn't been another Jedi Knight as strong as you since."

Anakin scowled, then looked back to Luke. "You must be going soft on them."

Luke smiled, but shook his head. "Not at all. Ben is right." He squatted down so that he could be closer to Anakin's face. "I have high hopes for Ben, but there hasn't been a Jedi Knight like you again. Losing you was as great a loss to the Order as it was to your family."

Anakin's eyes grew worried. "It *shouldn't* have been. The Order can't wait for a great Jedi Knight to lead it. That's what everyone thought *I* was, and when I died, too much died with me." He turned to Ben. "Don't make the mistake I did, don't let anyone push you into that. Every Jedi Knight has to be his own light, because the light shouldn't go out when one Jedi dies."

Ben nodded. "Okay, Anakin," he said. "I think I actually get it."

"Because wise words are always easy to understand," Luke said. "I'll take your advice to heart, Anakin. But I want you to know that what you did on *Baanu Raas* saved the entire Order. Thank you for that."

"I wasn't alone." Anakin's eyes closed. It appeared for a moment that he was going to sink back beneath the water, then he asked, "What about Tahiri? Is she well?"

Luke's lips tightened, and Ben knew that his father was afraid of answering—that if he began to speak, the whole terrible truth would stream forth, what Jacen had done to her, what Jacen had become—what Jaina had been forced to do to stop him.

"She *will* be, Anakin," Ben said. "I promise you that."

If Anakin had sensed anything in Luke's hesitation, he did not show it. He merely nodded.

"Good. Tell her that I still love her." His head tipped back, and he said, "Now go. You don't have much time."

Anakin's face sank as quickly as it had come to the surface, leaving Ben and his father to stand there in the cold water, wondering what they had just seen, whether it had been real or a phantasm . . . and whether the difference mattered.

Finally, Ben asked, "Was that . . . was that a Force ghost?"

Luke thought for a moment, then simply shrugged. "I have no idea, Ben." He turned back toward the woman in the mist and motioned for Rhondi to continue. "But whatever it was, it was *him*."

Rhondi started forward again, and, despite Anakin's warning, Ben knew better than to try to convince his father to turn back. Whoever—*whatever*—that woman in the mist was, she was a part of what was threatening his Order, the Order that Anakin had died to protect, and Luke Skywalker was not going to turn back until she told him what she knew.

They continued onward for more than Ben had thought the distance to the woman *was*—another hundred paces at least. Then his father lurched forward, his front leg suddenly dropping to the thigh in the dark water.

"Dad!" Ben grabbed him by the arm and was nearly pulled in after him, then he caught them both in the Force and lifted them back onto the path that Rhondi had chosen for them. "Are you all right?"

Instead of answering, his father merely looked into the water. For one terrible instant, Ben feared that he hadn't been quick enough, that some part of his father's essence had already vanished into the Depths of Eternity.

Then Ben saw what his father was looking at.

When Ben had spotted Anakin's face below the surface, he had felt astonished, confused, even frightened. This time, he just *hurt*.

"*Mom?*" he gasped.

His mother's green eyes snapped open. She floated to the surface, looking neither happy nor confused, but worried. Frightened. Maybe even angry.

Her gaze snapped from Ben to Luke and back again. "You two shouldn't be *here*," she said. "What's the matter with you?"

Ben couldn't answer. He had a lump in his throat the size of his fist, and the words just wouldn't come. But to his astonishment, his father merely smiled and dropped back into a squat.

"Hello, Mara," he said. "It's good to see you."

Her expression softened. "You, too, Skywalker," she said. "But I'm serious. You can't be—"

"We're *fine*," Luke assured her.

"Not if you're here, you're not." Her mouth tightened with a sudden wave of horror. "You're not—"

"We're alive, Mara, on a mission." Luke glanced around the lake, then added, "One of the strangest ones I've ever had, but we're still working it. Can you tell me what this place is, exactly?"

"*I* told you," the Givin rasped from behind Ben. "The Lake of Apparitions."

"Not what he meant, bonehead," Ben said, his irritation jolting him out of his shock. "Hi, Mom. Uh . . . long time no see."

The wisecrack finally brought back the radiant smile

that Ben had been aching to see again for nearly three years now. "Ben! You've grown . . . and more than just taller."

Ben nodded and squatted next to his father. "In a lot of ways."

He longed to lean down and kiss his mother's watery cheek, or at least to reach out and touch it. But she was only a reflection, and he did not dare risk it, fearing that he might shatter the moment, or send her sinking back beneath the surface.

Instead he asked, "Mom, what can you tell us about this place? It's pretty weird."

"You're talking to a dead woman, Ben. Of course it's weird." She looked away for a moment, thinking, then shook her head. "I don't know what I can tell you. It's different for everyone, I imagine."

"And for you?" his father asked.

"For me, it's a place of reflection," she said. "To consider what I've done."

Luke's brows rose, alarmed, but also in pain. "Mara, are you suffering?"

"I've done some things that cause me anguish, yes," she said.

Luke shook his head. "But you didn't know better," he said. "Palpatine tricked you."

Mara gave Luke a sad smile and looked as though she would have liked to touch him as much as Ben would have liked to touch her.

"I made my peace with Palpatine a long time ago. You know that." She turned to Ben. "But I didn't serve him my whole life, and that has been both my blessing and my curse."

Ben frowned. "Mom, I don't understand."

"Jacen," she said simply. "I didn't go after him as a Jedi, Ben. I went after him as a hunter . . . a killer."

Ben felt like he had been stabbed in the heart. "But he was a Sith Lord!"

"Not when I went after him," she said. "And you know that wasn't why I did it."

Ben sank onto his haunches. Had his father not grabbed him by the arm, he would have fallen into the water. Because he *did* know. His mother had gone after Jacen because of what Jacen was doing to *him*, because Ben had been too ashamed to share the truth with his father, and he had asked his mother to keep his secret.

"Mom, I'm so sorry," he said. "It's all—"

"It *isn't*, Ben, and I'm not telling you this because I need your sorrow." She smiled up at him. "I'm a bit beyond that now, don't you think?"

Ben forced himself to return her smile. "Yeah, I guess."

"I want you to learn from what I did, Ben. It's not the result that counts, but the action." Her eyes grew hard and angry, then she said, "Jacen's goals were noble; he acted for the good of the galaxy. But his acts were horrific, and nothing can change that. Even if he *did* bring peace to the galaxy, the stain remains, and it will darken him for eternity. Do you understand that?"

The lump had returned to Ben's throat, so large and hard now that he could only barely croak a simple "Yes."

"It's not about the legacy you leave, it's about the life you live," she continued. "Remember that, *live* by that."

"I'll remember, Mom. I promise."

"Good." His mother's hand rose and touched the surface of the water, a prisoner trying to reach through the wall of a transparisteel cell. "*That's* what I need from you, Ben. If you do that, I *will* be at peace. That's my promise."

She started to sink. "Now go."

"Mara," Luke said. "Wait."

"You don't have time." She stopped sinking, and only her lips remained at the surface. "Forget her."

Luke glanced toward the woman in the mist, but said, "That's not what I wanted to—"

"Luke, I know," Mara said. "But she's one of the old ones. Leave her alone . . . trust me."

Luke shook his head. "I can't," he said. "Not yet."

"Then there's nothing I can do," she said. "I love you, Luke. But if you have to do this, may the Force be with you."

With that, she closed her eyes and sank beneath the surface.

Luke remained crouching over her reflection, eyes closed and chin dropped, for an hour. Or perhaps it was only a few seconds. Ben had no idea. The important thing was that neither Ryontarr nor the Givin was inclined to interrupt, and Ben did not dare.

Rhondi was not so patient. After a time, she pulled Luke to his feet, then turned back toward the near end of the lake.

"No." Luke pulled free and turned back toward the mists. "I need to keep going forward."

Before Ben could object, Rhondi was shaking her own head. "I know who Mara Jade was, and who she was to *you*. If she doesn't want you walking into the Mists of Forgetfulness, then it's time to turn back."

Luke's brow rose at the name she had given to the mists, but he did not turn away. "You're probably right." Without turning to face Ben, he said, "Son, you go on back. If I don't join you—well, *soon*—take the *Shadow* and—"

"Dad, the *Mists of Forgetfulness*!" Ben interrupted. "What part of that *doesn't* scream, *Mom's right—get the blazes out of here*?"

His father's Force aura did not even crack a ripple of amusement. "Ben, this isn't a debate."

"You're kriffing right it isn't," Ben said. "If you're crazy enough to keep going, you're too crazy to give *me* orders. And *I'm* not crazy enough yet to follow them. I'm going with you."

His father dropped his head, either weighing Ben's words or gathering his resolve, then said, "Fine. Come on."

Rhondi shot Ben an angry glare, then took Luke's arm and started to lead the way toward the mists again. As they walked, the gallery of reflections continued to peer up from beneath the water, and Ben began to think about his father's weakened body back on the *Shadow,* wondering how much time they really had left—if they had *any.*

"Hey, Dad?"

"I'm not turning back."

"I know," Ben said. "But no more stops, okay? At your age, you probably know a lot of dead people. If we stop to talk to *all* of them, we're going to be down there with them."

Luke chuckled. "Okay, Ben. Not *all* of them."

They had traveled perhaps another two hundred paces when Ben looked up and realized that the mists seemed as far away as ever. Half convinced they were not actually moving, he took his eyes off his father's heels just long enough to glance back over his shoulder—then crashed headlong into his father's back.

"Stang! Sorry, Dad," Ben said. "But I don't think we're ever going to get there. Those mists are just pulling . . ."

Ben let his sentence trail off as he turned forward and saw that his father was staring down into the water again. *Kriff,* he muttered. He didn't *want* to see anyone else; after his mother's warning, stopping to talk to anyone else was going to feel like a betrayal. What he really needed to do was get his father moving again, so they could turn around and go back, like she had told them to do.

Steeling himself to be rude—or at least quick—Ben slipped forward . . . and felt his veins run cold. Peering up from the lake was a gaunt, familiar face with brown hair, a thin Solo nose, and the yellow eyes of a Sith Lord.

Recalling that neither his mother nor Anakin had responded until their names were spoken aloud, he bit back the urge to utter his former Master's name. The last thing Ben wanted was to speak to Darth Caedus right now. There was a time when he might have wanted to speak to *Jacen*—but even that urge had been purged from him in the Kathol Rift, under the tutelage of his Aing-Tii instructor, Tadar'Ro.

Not so with Ben's father, though. Luke squatted down, then deliberately said, "Jacen."

Immediately the yellow eyes darkened to brown, and the reflection grew a little less gaunt and haunted as it rose through the water. When it reached the surface, the eyes, as sad now as they had just been hard, looked from Luke to Ben.

"I won't ask your forgiveness," Jacen said.

"Good." Luke's voice was not unkind, merely firm. "Because I don't think I could give it."

A half-smile crept across Jacen's lips. "Honest to the end, Uncle Luke. That's one of the things I always appreciated about you." His gaze shifted back to Ben. "I want you to know—all the anger and the hate, I didn't bring it with me. Tell Jaina that I forgive her."

Ben's temper immediately began to blow. "*You* forgive *her*?" he spat. "Do you have any idea what you put *her* through? You pompous, self-righteous—"

"*Ben!*" Luke barked. "*That* isn't the reason I let you

come along. Remember what you just promised your mother."

The rebuke was more of a nudge than a slap—a gentle, deliberate reminder that left no doubt in Ben's mind that his father had been expecting this meeting from the moment they encountered Anakin Solo's apparition. *This* was the reason his father had insisted that they keep going. Ben just didn't happen to think it was a good idea. Whatever Jacen—or Caedus—said to them was sure to be a lie—or, at best, a half-truth. But Ben kept quiet. He did not doubt that his father *did* have a plan, and if Ben allowed his own outrage and disgust to drive Jacen away prematurely, he would just be interfering with it.

So he nodded and said, "You're right, Dad." He turned to Jacen. "I hope you'll forgive me."

The sneer that came to Jacen's mouth left no doubt about how likely *that* was. "Don't you think we're past that sort of nonsense, Ben? I did what I did, and you have every right to feel as you do. All I ask is that you show me the courtesy of being honest about it."

Ben's chest tightened. "Fine," he said. "Honestly, I think you're the same kriffing sleemo you were when you were alive, and I'm glad you're dead."

Jacen flashed one of those crooked Solo grins. "Better," he said. "I hope you remember what to do with that anger."

"Ben has developed a few alternative techniques for that," Luke said evenly. "But since we're all being honest here, would you answer a question for me?"

Jacen kept his gaze fixed on Ben. "Why not?" he asked. "You *did* come a long way to ask it."

Farther than you know, thought Ben.

Luke merely smiled in gratitude. "I appreciate that."

Ben thought his father was going to ask about the woman in the mist, or her relationship to the mental illness plaguing the Order's Jedi Knights. He thought his father might possibly ask about whether she had somehow been responsible for corrupting Jacen himself, or even whether Darth Caedus had something to do with the problems currently troubling the Order.

Instead, Luke asked, "When you visited the Pool of Knowledge, who did you see sitting on the Throne of Balance?"

The yellow flash that briefly colored Jacen's eyes betrayed his surprise. But his expression remained calm, becoming almost beatific. Ben realized this was a question Jacen *wanted* to answer, one that he had never expected to be asked.

Instead of replying, however, Jacen cocked a brow. "First, would you mind telling me who *you* saw?"

"Not at all," Luke replied. "Allana, surrounded by a retinue of species from all across the galaxy. She looked quite happy."

A smile of relief—or perhaps it was triumph—came to Jacen's face. "Then it doesn't matter *who* I saw," he said. "But it wasn't you . . . if, by chance, *that's* what you were thinking."

Their conversation was, of course, entirely lost on Ben. He had no more idea what the Throne of Balance was than he did the Pool of Knowledge. And to tell the truth, it all sounded like the kind of mind-boggling stuff that could lead a guy down a dark path before he realized he had stepped into a shadow.

But the relief in his father's Force aura, Ben *did* understand—and he understood the gratitude, as well. And he was thankful to Jacen for those two things, even if nothing else.

Luke gave Jacen a wry smile, then inclined his head and said, "It wasn't, but thanks."

Had Ben not been so attuned to Luke's Force aura, he would not have noticed that his father had just done something that he had believed his father never did. Luke Skywalker had lied.

Jacen returned Luke's wry smile. "I didn't think so."

He closed his eyes and began to sink beneath the surface, and, suddenly, Ben realized he couldn't let his cousin go like that—not if he wanted to keep the promise he had made to his mother.

"Jacen, wait," he said.

Jacen opened his eyes and stopped sinking.

"I, uh, I just wanted you to know," Ben said. "Jacen, I forgive you."

Jacen returned to the surface so he could speak. "That's good, Ben. It's one burden you won't have to carry through life. Go with the Force."

"Thanks." Ben was so surprised by the sincerity in Jacen's voice that he almost didn't know what to say. "You, too, I guess."

Jacen snorted in amusement. "Ben, I *am* with the Force." He paused, as though waiting for Ben to say something else, then finally asked, "Isn't there a question *you* wanted to ask me?"

"Well, yeah." Ben glanced nervously toward the woman in the mist. While he wasn't sure that his father would believe anything Jacen told them about the mysterious figure, the question seemed worth asking. "But I didn't want it to seem like I was trying to buy an answer."

Jacen shook his head. "Ben, didn't I just tell you to be honest with me?" He turned toward the Mists of Forgetfulness. "I wish I could help you, but I have no idea who that is."

Ben's heart sank. He half suspected Jacen was lying to him, but he saw no use in entertaining such bitter feelings. Either he had forgiven Jacen or he hadn't, and it would be better for *him* if he had. At least he *thought* that was what his mother had been telling him.

"No problem, Jacen," Ben said. "Have a peaceful . . . whatever."

"*Damnation,*" Jacen supplied. He turned toward the Mists of Forgetfulness, then added, "But Ben, if you really need to know who she is, the lake doesn't stretch forever. Just keep walking—you have all the time in the universe."

Ben scowled, certain now that Jacen was toying with him. "Thanks, Jacen." He glanced toward his stubborn father. "That was bound to be a *big* help."

Jacen gave him a cruel smirk. "Just choose and act, Ben." He sank beneath the water again, his eyes turning a bright, burning white. "Choose and act."

"Good advice," Ben said. He watched until his cousin had sunk back beneath the water and closed his eyes again, then turned to his father. "Dad, I've just made a command decision. If Jacen tells us we have all the time in the universe—"

"We're in trouble, I know." Luke turned away from the mists, then waved Rhondi and their guides back toward the near end of the lake. "Let's go home."

"But what about the lady in the mists?" the Givin asked, moving to block their way. "You can't leave before you know who she—"

"I know one thing." Luke brought his hand up, planting his palm in the center of the Givin's chest and using a Force-enhanced strike to send him flying out of their path. "It's time to get back to the *Shadow*."

Chapter Twenty-three

STRAPPED INTO THE COPILOT'S SEAT OF THE *MILLENNIUM Falcon* in full vac suit and battle harness, Han's granddaughter looked exactly like what she was: an eight-year-old girl at play. Her small boots barely reached past the edge of the seat, her helmeted head fell five centimeters short of the headrest, and her gray eyes were as big and round as casino chips. But she was also a child princess on her first real mission, an heiress in training for one of the toughest jobs in the galaxy—and that was the thing that tore at Han's heart.

He and Leia had talked it over with Tenel Ka, and the Queen Mother had made it clear that any Hapan Chume'da needed to learn the ways of the galaxy early and well. But it just seemed so blasted unfair. How was Allana supposed to have a childhood? When did she get to be *just* a little girl? Thinking back on the three children he had given to the galaxy already—the two sons he had lost and the daughter he still *might*—Han knew the biggest mistake he had made lay in letting them grow up too fast, in letting their destinies start pulling them away while they were still too young to vote.

And now here he was, under Tenel Ka's orders to do it all again. He wasn't sure if he had the strength to see it through—but he *did* know that he loved Allana too much to give it anything short of his best.

A *ready* tweedle sounded from the engineering

socket at the rear of the flight deck, and then C-3PO announced, "Artoo reports that all hatches are sealed and all ship systems are functioning at optimal efficiency."

"*Optimal?*" Han asked, twisting around to look back at the two droids. "Did we board the wrong YT?"

C-3PO's golden head tipped to one side. "I highly doubt that, Captain Solo. There are only a handful of these antiques still in service, and the odds of another one accidentally occupying the *Falcon*'s berth are—"

"Don't tell me. Just have Artoo do a double check." Han glanced over at Allana and winked. "Optimal *everything* just isn't the *Falcon*."

Artoo trilled a few notes, then C-3PO said, "It seems there's a perfectly good explanation. Before putting her plan into action, Mistress Jaina spent thirty-two hours fine-tuning the ship's systems."

Han knew it was her way of trying to make amends for keeping Jag's secret—which only made his stomach churn that much harder. "Was *Jag* with her?"

A negative chirp came from R2-D2.

"Well, that's something. At least we don't have to check for those fancy eavesdropping bugs of his." Han turned forward again, then glanced over at Allana. "You ready for the checklist?"

Allana nodded enthusiastically. But she did not direct her attention to the datapad in her lap.

"Grandpa, why are you still so mad at Jaina? She's trying really hard to show you how sorry she is."

Han sighed. "I know, sweetie. And I guess I'm not really mad *at* her. It's more like I'm mad *for* her."

"Because she's in such a hard spot about Jag?"

"That's . . ." Han paused, realizing he wasn't being honest with Allana because he wasn't being honest with *himself.* "Maybe. I think it's more because she still doesn't know the kind of spot she's in."

"And being mad at her will change that?"

"Probably not," Han admitted.

Allana furrowed her brow, and her crash helmet slid down so far that the rim almost covered her eyes. "Then why are you *doing* it, Grandpa?"

Han frowned. "You're a lot like your grandmother, you know that?"

Allana smiled. "Really?"

Han let his chin drop in defeat. "Yeah, really," he said. "Okay, if I *promise* to stop being mad at Jaina, can we get this bucket launched? Your grandmother is waiting on us, you know, and it's a long way to Shedu Maad."

"Especially with all those crazies on her ship." Allana winced, then added, "Don't tell Barv I said that, okay?"

"Your secret's safe with me," Han said.

Allana nodded. "I know." She picked up her datapad. "Ready to check off."

"Finally." Han turned his attention back to the control panel, then started down the list that was as much a part of him as Allana herself. "Repulsorlift drives ready to engage?"

"Check."

"Ion drives on standby?"

"Check."

"Nav computer spooled up?"

"Check."

And so they continued, until they had exhausted the list and Han knew the ship was ready to launch. But he didn't stop there, because there was still something that Allana needed to learn about crazy capers, and it was his job to teach her.

"Barabels in the gun turrets?" Han asked.

Allana studied her datapad for a moment, then frowned. "Grandpa, that's not on the list."

"It's not?" Han lifted his brow in mock surprise. "You sure?"

Allana shook her head and looked up, then saw his expression and realized he was putting her on. "Yeah, I'm *sure*."

Han smiled. "But we still need them, right?"

Allana nodded, then thought for a moment and reached out to touch the intercom button on her seat. "Dordi, Zal—are you in the turrets?"

The confirmations came so quick that the Barabels were almost transmitting over each other. "Dordi on the back . . ."

"And Zal in the belly."

The report ended in a fit of hysterical sissing that left Allana frowning at the speaker. "Did I say something funny?"

"Nope. They're just Barabels," Han told her.

During the war against the Yuuzhan Vong, Dordi and Zal had been adolescent pilots in Saba Sebatyne's all-Jedi Wild Knights squadron. Now that they had finally reached adulthood, there was talk of them starting a nest with Saba's son, Tesar.

Han thought of a Temple overrun by dozens of voracious Barabel younglings, then smiled and added, "*Nobody* really gets Barabels."

Allana's eyes lit with comprehension. "So, it's like after we saved Kessel, when you and Lando sat down with all that Gizer—"

"Yeah, it's kind of like that," Han said, not wanting to know how much of *that* conversation she had overheard. "What about Wilyem?"

Allana depressed her intercom button again. "Wilyem, are you—"

"Yessss," the Barabel's raspy voice answered. "Wilyem in the tail."

Another fit of sissing erupted over the intercom speakers.

This time, Allana merely shook her head and asked, "Grandpa, are you sure we need them?"

Han feigned disappointment. "What's the first thing you do on a job?"

Allana smiled confidently. "Find the tracking beacons!"

"*That* comes later," Han said, shaking his head. "It's the first rule of *escape*." He tapped the control panel. "I mean before we even board the ship."

"Oh, yeah," Allana said. "Make sure you have the right crew for the job."

"And what kind of job are we pulling?"

"A crazy one." Allana's eyes brightened with pride. "And that's why you wanted Barabels."

"Exactly," Han said. "When you need crazy—"

"—call a Barabel," Allana finished. "Got it."

"You're a quick learner, kid." Though Han meant it sincerely, his pride carried with it a note of sorrow. She would *need* to learn fast, because everything that fate had demanded of his own growing children would also be demanded of her . . . and perhaps more. He turned away so Allana wouldn't see him choking down the lump in his throat, then checked a gauge. Then he grinned at her and said, "Okay. Maybe you'd better let your grandmother and Saba know we're ready to get out of here."

"Okay."

Allana started to reach for her helmet microphone set, then quickly dropped her hand, even before Han could remind her that they were under comm silence. She closed her eyes, reached for Leia in the Force, and smiled as she felt her grandmother's touch.

"We'd better go," she said. "Grandma feels like she's in a hurry."

"What about Saba?" Han asked. "Did she feel like she was in position with those StealthXs?"

"I . . . *think* so," Allana said, twisting her lips in confusion. "She just feels kind of hungry."

"Close enough." Han commed the flight-control officer to let them know that the *Longshot*—the false transponder code under which the *Falcon* had been berthed at the spaceport—was ready to depart, then said, "Buckle up your crazy-cap."

Allana rolled her eyes. "With you around, who needs a cap?"

Once the dome had retracted, he lifted the *Falcon* out of her berth, then tipped the nose up and pushed the throttles forward. With the inertial compensator not yet engaged, the acceleration pinned him back in his seat, and they shot through the opening into a bank of gray Coruscant smog. Allana squealed in delight while C-3PO sputtered in electronic surprise.

"Captain Solo, perhaps you should check your instruments," he said. "You're still accelerating, and we're already traveling in excess of the legal velocity at this altitude."

"I know, Goldenrod," Han said. "We've got to make this look good."

A moment later they emerged from the haze into the bustling expanse of Coruscant's contrail-laced troposphere. Han activated the inertial compensator and pushed the throttles to the stops, climbing for space at maximum repulsorlift power. R2-D2 tweedled a report.

"Oh my," C-3PO said. "Now you've drawn the attention of Galactic City Air Traffic Control. Artoo says they're querying our transponder."

"That's why we're called the bait, Threepio," Allana explained to the droid. "We want them to chase *us* instead of Grandma." She turned to Han. "Right?"

"Pretty close," Han said. "But we're actually pulling a Toydarian double-reverse spinner."

Allana scowled as though Han had just pulled a spinner on her. "A toy *what*?"

"Toydarian double-reverse spinner," Han explained, taking his eyes off the darkening sky just long enough to glance over at her. "Look, Daala's pretty smart, right?"

Allana nodded. "Give the other guy credit," she said, quoting one of Han's favorite high-stakes credos. "If he's good enough to be in the game, he's good enough to take your credits."

"Exactly," Han said. "So, we gotta think Daala knows that *we* know she'll be watching when we try to sneak our barvies off Coruscant."

Allana looked down, using her fingers to keep track of Han's points, then finally nodded. "Everyone knows. Got it."

"Good. So we're going to show her a little respect."

Allana raised her brow. "We're going to *bow* to her?"

"Not *that* kind of respect," Han said, shaking his head. "We're going to let her know that we think she's pretty smart."

Allana's eyes widened, and she asked, "And you think that will make her careless?"

"A little bit," Han confirmed. "Everybody likes to feel smart, so when you show them you think they *are* smart, they tend to take you at your word."

"And taking our word is the same as taking our bait?"

"In this situation, yeah," Han said. "When Daala sees us making a straight-up speed break, she'll think we decided there's no use trying to trick her. And then do you know what she'll do?"

"Send everything she has to catch us?"

Han nodded. "That's right," he said. "And *that's*

when your grandmother will slip away in the *Gizer Gut*."

"*After* I Force-touch her again." Allana frowned, then added, "There's only one thing wrong with your plan, Grandpa."

Han gave her a patient smile. "And what's that, sweetheart?"

"You're trying to flatter Chief Daala," Allana said. "And Mom says a *smart* woman *never* believes it when someone flatters her."

Han felt his smile melt away. "Well, *this* isn't really flattery," he said, putting more confidence into his voice than he felt. "It's more like just not treating her like she's dumb."

Allana's brows dropped into a V. "You're bluffing."

"What? No way." Han looked forward again, then sighed. "Okay, what's my tell?"

"Your voice rose," Allana said proudly. "Plus, well, I have the Force."

Han rolled his eyes. "That blasted Force—it's been getting me in trouble with women since I met your grandmother," he said. "Anyway, don't worry. I'm ninety percent sure this is going to work."

"And when you're flying with Captain Solo, those are very good odds indeed," C-3PO offered from the communications station. "Even adjusting for his usual exaggeration, that gives us a sixty-seven percent chance of success."

Before Han could turn to bark at the droid, Allana said, "Oh, I'm not worried, Grandpa—as long as we have a backup plan."

Han thought he might have been developing some Force sensitivity himself, because even though he was still looking out at the stars popping into view as they departed the atmosphere, he could feel her staring at him.

"We *do* have a backup plan," Allana said. "Right?"

He switched to the ion drives, then, as the *Falcon* kicked over to the more powerful engines, pulled the throttles back and said, "Sure we do."

"Good." Allana was silent for a moment, then asked, "What is it?"

Han shrugged. "Hard to say. Your grandmother is in charge of backup plans."

Before Allana could press the matter further, the no-nonsense voice of an orbital control officer sounded over the flight deck speaker. "Light freighter *Longshot,* you've just broken every procedure in the manual for departing Coruscant. Please proceed to impound station Trill Aurek Papa for inspection."

"Oh my—*those* orders are certainly going to interfere with our duties," C-3PO said. "Perhaps if I apologize—"

"Don't even think about it, Codejob." Han smiled and winked at Allana, then added, "This game is just getting started."

He activated the tactical display and winced—as he always did—at the dense field of yellow FIXED FACILITY designators that immediately popped into view. There were so many stations, platforms, and habitats floating around Coruscant's satellite shell that piloting a starship through the orbital layers was only slightly less nerve-racking than navigating a speeder across the Big Snarl at the height of Crash Hour.

An instant later vessel transponder codes began to appear between the facility designators, all in "friendly blue" since the *Falcon* was not involved in an armed conflict with anyone. Without a control ship to coordinate and pass along a constant stream of situation reports, R2-D2 could only access the data from the *Falcon*'s own sensor arrays, which made the tactical picture necessarily incomplete. But the display already showed dozens of civilian codes scrambling to clear the area, and Han spotted a new *Nargi*-class pursuit frigate moving to cut off the *Falcon*'s escape route.

A new voice, this one sharper and more insistent, came over the comm speakers. "Light freighter *Longshot,* this is the Galactic Alliance pursuit frigate *Fast Death.* Respond immediately, or we *will* take measures to ensure that you do."

Han ignored the challenge and continued to climb. A massive KDY orbital defense platform flashed past to port as the *Falcon* entered the planet's satellite shell. Han studied the display until he found a huge wheel station orbiting nearby, then swung onto a course that put the facility between him and the *Fast Death.*

The voice returned. "*Longshot,* your evasive action has been noted. We are now declaring you a *suspect vessel in flight.* If you continue on this course, we *will* apprehend you forcibly."

"Then stop talking about it and *do* something," Han groused.

The *Fast Death* vanished from the display as the huge wheel station drifted into a direct line between the *Falcon* and the frigate. Han queried the designator code. To his delight, the station was listed as Pharm-Com Orbital Processing Plant One. Pharmaceutical production facilities were usually several kilometers across, more than large enough for his purposes. All he had to do was hide behind the station until the *Fast Death* came around one side looking for him, then he'd blow ions out the other.

Unfortunately, the *Fast Death*'s skipper had a better idea. As the processing plant began to swell in the *Falcon*'s forward canopy—a huge durasteel web of white rings held together by dozens of glittering yellow spokes—R2-D2 let out a series of contact tweedles. Han turned his attention back to the tactical display.

Swarming past the station's rim were a dozen XJ5 ChaseX starfighters. And they were probably all equipped with the latest in ship-disabling System Burner ion torpedoes.

"Blast and double blast!" Han growled. "He's not falling for it."

"Uh-oh," Allana said. "Does that mean I should ask Grandma for the backup plan?"

Han shook his head. "Not yet, sweetie. We still have a few tricks up our sleeves."

Han rolled the *Falcon* into a wingover, and suddenly it was not the wheel station swelling in front of them, but the hazy yellow disk of Coruscant's day side.

"That's trick number one," Han said. "Now, why don't you pick out a new transponder name for us?"

"Any name I want?"

"As long as it's on the list," Han said.

"Affirmative, Grandpa." Allana began to scroll through the possibilities, her little boots kicking the air in excitement, then she announced, "Got it!"

"Go ahead and send it to Artoo," Han said, swinging toward the gleaming canister of a luxury habitat complex. "And tell him to switch over in three, two . . ."

The habitat's apparent size swelled up so quickly that even Han thought he might crash into it. The facility's automated shielding system began to broadcast an emergency message, warning him to decelerate or change course. He did neither. When they were close enough to see startled faces staring out the viewports, he pushed the yoke down and dived underneath the habitat.

An instant later Han pulled back up on the other side of the station and finished the count. ". . . one."

R2-D2 gave an acknowledging tweedle. By then, the planet itself was coming up so fast that Han had no time to check the display to see the *Falcon*'s new name.

He rolled the upper hull toward the ChaseXs and began to flee toward the far side of the planet.

When Han did check the tactical display, his heart fell. The ChaseXs were still hot on his tail, and closing quick. But the *Fast Death* remained on station, hanging back with no apparent concern about keeping the *Falcon* in tractor beam range.

"Bloah!" He slammed a palm against the yoke. "They've got another one."

"Another what?" Allana's voice was small and frightened.

Han immediately regretted his outburst, and explained in a gentler voice, "Another frigate, kiddo. That's why the *Fast Death* isn't following us."

"*Now* is it time to ask Grandma about the backup plan?"

Han had to bite back an irritated reply. "Not yet, sweetie. Grandpa just needs to raise the stakes, that's all."

Allana's eyes grew curious, but before she could ask Han to explain, a scratchy new voice came over the cockpit speaker. "You're not fooling anyone, *Star Princess*. We know who you are."

Han grimaced and glanced over at Allana. "You picked *Star Princess*?"

"You said to pick any name I wanted," she reminded him. "And *Star Princess* is pretty."

"I think it's a very wise choice, Mistress Allana," C-3PO said. "Statistical analysis shows that the planetary patrols are thirty-four percent less likely to open fire on vessels with endearing names."

Allana shot Han a triumphant smile, but before she could gloat, the scratchy voice began to threaten them from the comm speaker again.

"This is your last warning, *Star Princess* . . . or whatever you want to call yourself—Captain Solo."

R2-D2 gave a warning whistle, and the *Falcon*'s lock alarms suddenly shrieked to life.

"Heave to," the voice ordered, "or that tub won't have a working circuit left."

"The savage!" C-3PO gasped. "I don't think we have any choice, Captain Solo. If you don't do as he orders, Artoo and I will be—"

"Not happening in *this* lifetime, Threepio." Han glanced over at Allana. "Do you think you can still find Saba in the Force, or should I have Wilyem—"

"I'm the copilot!" Allana informed him. "I can find her."

"Then do it." Han turned his attention back to the tactical display. The second frigate had shown up dead ahead—and the ChaseXs were driving them right toward it. "And tell Saba sooner is better."

Allana frowned. "I can't *tell* her anything, Grandpa. The Force isn't a comlink." She closed her eyes and began to concentrate. "After living with Grandma so long, you really should know that by now."

Han smiled. "You'd think." He activated his intercom microphone, then said, "Dordi, Zal, time to bluff. Bring up your guns and targeting computers."

"Can we shoot?" Zal asked—or maybe it was Dordi—Han couldn't tell.

"No, you can't shoot!" Han snapped. "What are you, crazy? I've got Amelia on board!"

"So *she* getz to do all the shooting?" Dordi—or maybe it was Zal—asked.

"*Nobody* gets to shoot," Han retorted. "Well, except Wilyem. But not until I say so . . . and you *can't* hit anything. Clear?"

"Of course I can hit something," Wilyem rasped back. "I'm a *Jedi*."

A chorus of sissing broke over the intercom speaker.

Before Han could snap at the Barabels to get serious,

the voice of a very irritated task force commander came over the flight deck speaker.

"*Quick End* command to the *Star Princess*—or whatever you're calling yourself at the moment. Have you lost your *kriffing* mind, Solo?"

Scowling at the foul language, Han looked over and motioned Allana to cover her ears.

"This isn't funny anymore, Captain," the commander continued. "My sensor officers tell me you're powering up your laser cannons. And we keep getting lock alarms. If I hear that your missile bays . . ."

The commander's threat was drowned out by the startled cries of a dozen ChaseX pilots—a mixture of cursing and status declarations. "Lock, lock!" "Someone's on my six!"

"What the blazes?" cried a starfighter pilot. "We've got . . . break, break, break! Stealths!"

In the instant of silence that followed, Han activated his intercom again. "When you're ready, Wilyem," he said calmly. "And *don't*—"

"—hit anything. This one—"

The Barabel's reassurance was cut off as the task force commander's furious voice came over the flight deck speakers again.

"Captain Solo, please tell me that those Jedi StealthXs did *not* just target Bolt Squadron."

Han checked the tactical display and saw that the StealthX gambit had done its job. The *Fast Death* was finally moving off station, accelerating past the Pharm-Com wheel station to provide cover for its starfighter squadron. At last, the time had come to stop pushing. Han opened his own comm channel.

"*StealthXs?*" He looked over at Allana and winked. Then he signaled her to reach for Leia in the Force by pinching his eyes shut and miming the ignition of a lightsaber. "*What* StealthXs, Commander? The only starfighters around here are your—"

The flight deck lock alarms suddenly began to wail again. Then the *Falcon* bucked sharply as a much-weakened proton torpedo—the one Wilyem had just dumped out the aft loading bay—detonated a couple of kilometers off their stern. Holding the yoke with one hand and scratching his comm microphone with the other, Han immediately put the *Falcon* on a corkscrewing course for the *Quick End*. Trailing out of the modified escape pod bay in the *Falcon*'s aft, he knew, would be long tails of flame and atmosphere. To sensors and naked eyes alike, the trail would look like the *Falcon* had suffered a catastrophic hull breach.

"Solo!" the commander bellowed. "What the blazes just happened?"

"You tell *me*!" Han shot back. He opened the emergency channel, then continued, "One of your clowns just put a proton torpedo into our stern! This is the *Millennium Falcon* declaring out-of-control emergency!"

Declaring a false emergency was, of course, just the sort of thing no good spacecraft pilot ever did. At every rescue station on this side of the planet, crews would be scrambling and tractor ships cold-firing their ion engines. But as far as Han was concerned, getting Bazel and the other barvy Jedi Knights safely off Coruscant *was* an emergency—and Daala had left them no other choice.

Even so, the task force commander clearly remained suspicious—even as the *Falcon* continued to corkscrew toward him. The double-nosed needle of the *Quick End*'s sleek blue hull was already the size of a finger in the forward canopy, and still the vessel showed no sign of moving.

Han looked over and found Allana's gray eyes nearly

bugged out of their sockets. Her mouth was hanging open and, though she was trying not to show her fear, he could tell by her pale cheeks that she thought they were probably going to crash.

And what if they did? Han would never be able to forgive himself. But his job now was to stay on course . . . and help her learn. He closed the comm channel for a moment, then spoke to her in his best no-big-deal voice.

"That's a pretty tough guy, huh?"

Allana nodded. "Is he going to let us ram him?"

"I don't know," Han said. "What do you think?"

She thought for a moment, then shrugged. "Who can tell?"

"Yeah, we're going to have to find out who he is, aren't we?"

Allana studied the spinning shape outside the view-port for a moment longer, watching in silence as it grew to the length of a Wookiee's arm, then finally tore her gaze away and looked over.

"We *are*?" she asked.

"You bet," Han said, giving her a dip of the head that was more confident than he felt. "A guy like that, you don't want to bluff twice."

Han opened the emergency channel again, then began to scream into the microphone. "*Quick End,* clear us a lane! We're out of control! I say again, clear, clear, clear!"

By now the frigate was as long as a Wookiee was tall, its ends vanishing from sight each time they spun below the *Falcon*'s control console. But the commander sounded as cool as a wampa when he replied.

"Solo, this smacks of a trick," he said. "If you think—"

"*Trick?*" Han yelled. "You think I'd pull something *this* crazy with Amelia on board?"

"Your *daughter's* on board?" The commander paused for a moment. Like most of the galaxy, he had no idea of Allana's true identity, believing Allana to be *Amelia,* the Solos' adopted daughter. "Surely, you don't expect me to—"

Allana opened her mouth and, taking a cue as well as her grandmother, let out a bloodcurdling scream. "*Daddy!* We're doomed!"

"I'm glad *you* said it, Mistress Amelia!" C-3PO added. "Captain Solo always trips my—"

"Oh, blast!" the commander cursed, speaking over C-3PO. "Hold on, we're moving."

The frigate was, indeed, drifting out of their path— and not a moment too soon. The *Falcon* passed less than a hundred meters behind the vessel, so close that the wash from its big Slayn & Korpil ion drives sent the transport flipping away from the planet in a true out-of-control spin.

Allana let out another scream, this one even more convincing than the last, and C-3PO began to preach their doom again. Han merely clenched his teeth. Determined not to let Allana's lessons start becoming *too* memorable, he bit back a string of curses as he fought to bring the vessel back under control.

"It's going to take a few minutes to catch you on your present trajectory," the commander announced. "But you're going to be fine, I promise. We're already preparing to deploy our rescue skiffs."

"Uh, thanks . . ."

Han brought the yoke to center and began to ease the vector plates into a neutral position, then glanced over to find Allana settled back into her seat, looking over at him with a big grin on her face. He mouthed the word, *Grandma?* She gave him two big thumbs-up, and Han began to bring the *Falcon* out of her corkscrewing spin.

"We appreciate the help," Han commed. "But it looks like our damage-control team is bringing things under control."

"Your *damage-control* . . . ?"

The commander trailed off, leaving his question to hang.

Han waited a moment for him to continue, then shrugged at his comm unit and began to adjust his jump calculations for the rendezvous with Leia.

A few seconds later, the nav computer beeped its readiness, and the commander said, "Before you go, Captain Solo, I'd like to ask you a question."

"Sure," Han said. He swung the *Falcon* around to the proper bearing and began to accelerate toward jump speed. "Ask away."

"You don't have any of the Jedi patients aboard, do you?"

"With *Amelia* aboard?" Han retorted. "You must think I'm crazy."

"In all honesty, Captain Solo," the commander said, "the thought *has* crossed my mind."

"I'll bet." Han grinned. "But in all honesty, they're not aboard. I'm just taking my daughter for a little joyride."

"She must be quite the thrill seeker," the commander replied. "I trust she's had her fill of excitement for the day?"

Han glanced over at Allana, who gave an emphatic nod. "I think so," he reported. "Listen, I've got to go, but do you mind if I ask *you* a question first?"

"Feel free to *ask*."

Han glanced over at Allana and winked. "Who *are* you?"

The commander considered the question so long that Han was beginning to think he was stalling, still searching for some way to turn the situation around.

Then, finally, he asked, "Why do you want to know?"

"No big deal," Han said. "I just want to know where to send the thank-you note."

The commander was not amused. "Why don't you wait and give it to me in person?" he replied coldly. "We'll be meeting again soon, Captain Solo. Of *that,* I'm quite certain."

The comm speaker fell silent, leaving Han with the impression that he had just added another entry to his long list of enemies. It was kind of a good feeling, knowing that he was still young enough to make them. He shrugged, then looked over at Allana.

"How's your grandmother doing?" he asked.

"She's on her way," Allana reported. "Time to head for Shedu Maad."

Han smiled, then glanced back at R2-D2. "Are those jump coordinates ready?"

The droid answered with an affirmative whistle.

"Good," Han said. He turned back to Allana, then nodded at the controls. "You do the honors, kid."

Allana's eyes grew big, and she leaned forward to push the lever forward. This time, the hyperdrive worked perfectly, and stars stretched into lines.

Chapter Twenty-four

AHRI RAAS WOULD HAVE TO DIE, AND IT WAS GOING TO break Vestara's heart to kill him.

He had been lying next to her all morning, in their usual place on the river beach, and not once had he looked in her direction. Considering what she *wasn't* wearing—and how hard he had been trying since yesterday to behave naturally—his attitude told her everything she needed to know. Yuvar Xal was going to make a move against Lady Rhea—and it would be soon.

The battle was going to be a terrible waste, of course. Only fifteen members of the *Eternal Crusader*'s crew remained alive, and even a short power struggle would reduce that number by half. There wouldn't even be enough survivors to *need* a leader. But the planet's jungle of being-eating plants had devoured Lady Rhea's stature as surely as it had the expedition itself. Xal was finally within reach of deposing her, and when Sith saw a weakness, they pounced. They were like fangflowers that way, always thirsting for a kill.

"Ves, did you ever figure it out?" Ahri asked. His voice sounded a bit muffled and distant, as though he were looking in the opposite direction. "Why Ship picked you, I mean?"

"I don't know." Vestara's connection with Ship was the one factor working against Xal, because there were a handful of survivors who still hoped to escape Abeloth's planet—and to do that, they needed to complete their mission and recover Ship. "Because of my girlish beauty, I suppose."

Ahri chuckled. It sounded forced.

Vestara slid her hand toward the weapons belt lying atop her folded clothes. She would use the parang, she decided, because it was relatively silent. Moreover, unlike the shikkar, its use did not signify any disrespect or loathing.

"Seriously, Ves," Ahri said. "Do you think there's any way you can get Ship back under control?"

"Sure," Vestara lied. "If you can find Ship, I can command him."

Vestara knew why Ahri was pressing. If he could get her to admit that she could not command Ship any better than anyone else, then Lady Rhea's last leg of support would be broken. Over the last few weeks, the *Eternal Crusader*'s entire crew had slowly been drawn down to the surface through a handful of Ship sightings that required effort to pursue. Two of those searches had resulted in the destruction of shuttles, and the second disaster had left the *Crusader* in orbit with only one pilot—and only one shuttle.

That same night, Abeloth had despaired of ever capturing Ship and declared the time had come to flee the planet. Lady Rhea had immediately ordered the last pilot to come and retrieve the search party. Unfortunately, the shuttle had put down on the stony crust of an old lava pit. The boarding ramp had barely descended before the ground collapsed. The pilot managed to leap free, but the vessel itself dropped a thousand meters into a well of magma. And now there were no more shuttles.

After a time, Ahri spoke again. "Okay, show me."

"*Show* you?"

Vestara knew at once that she had seriously underestimated her friend's treachery—and overestimated her own ability to read Force auras. She pulled her parang from its sheath and rolled toward Ahri . . . and found him propped casually on an elbow, looking in the other direction. Slowly, he lifted a beautifully shaped arm, so deeply tanned by blue sunlight that it had turned nearly sapphire, and pointed up the river valley.

"Isn't *that* Ship?" he asked.

Vestara had to sit upright before she could see what he was pointing at, and even then she almost brought her parang around before she realized how wrong she had been. Ahri wasn't trying to set her up for his own kill. He was pointing at a distant winged-ball silhouette coming in low over the river, moving so fast that it swelled from the size of a thumbnail to the size of a fist in the blink of an eye.

"Well?" he asked.

Ahri twisted back toward Vestara and caught her holding the parang. His eyes grew instantly wide and frightened, and he was on his feet so quickly she feared he would have to be killed just to prevent him from crying out in surprise and inadvertently touching off the bloodbath.

"*Sheesta,* Ves!" He stumbled back a couple of steps, his eyes going to his own clothes, and his weapons belt floated into his hand. "Were you just going to *kill* me?"

"No, of course not," Vestara said. She summoned her own belt and returned the parang to its sheath. "I thought I saw a snake vine, that's all. Ever since that siphon reed almost drowned me and Lady Rhea, I haven't trusted Abeloth to keep us safe."

Ahri glanced around the sandy beach. There were no plants of any kind within ten meters.

"Uh, right," he said. He stepped back, then summoned his clothes and dressed. "I think we'd better get back to Abeloth and Master Xal. If *you* didn't call Ship, maybe they—"

"*They* didn't, either," Vestara said. "I promise you that."

She pulled on her own clothes, then started back toward the others, weaving her way around the big drendek lizards that were resting on the beach, taking the sun on their huge green wings. Ahri accompanied her, being careful not to expose his back by leading and not to threaten by following, all the while staying a full three paces away so he would have time to react to an attack. Vestara hoped his caution was more a statement of anger than fear; once his anger subsided, they could probably remain close until the actual killing started. But if Ahri was keeping his distance out of fear, their friendship was over; Vestara was too well trained to allow herself to be alone with any Sith who feared her.

By the time they came into view of Abeloth's customary boulder-top perch, the rest of the crew had already assembled. Baad Walusari and the other two Keshiri officers stood a little apart with Lady Rhea. Everyone else—including Yuvar Xal—stood at the base of Abeloth's boulder. They were all looking upriver toward Ship, their eyes wide with shock and hope.

In Xal's sharp-featured face, Vestara was alarmed to also see resolve. As frustrating as Ship's sudden appearance had to be for him at the moment, he was clearly more determined than ever to move against Lady Rhea. Realizing she had only one hope of preventing the attack, Vestara stopped and turned toward the river.

Ship was almost on them, a red-veined sphere ten meters in diameter, his delicate-looking wings tipped almost vertical as he slowed for landing. Vestara called to him in the Force, *Ship, come to me.*

Ship seemed amused. *Have we not had this discussion before?*

This is different, Vestara insisted. *Even if you obey Abeloth, you serve the Sith. Come to me and save us . . . or go to Xal and destroy us all.*

Ship slowed, but did not veer toward her, and Vestara felt the weight of a dozen gazes on her back. Wary of a preemptive strike, she pivoted on one foot to keep Xal and Ahri in sight. She found Abeloth's gruesome face turned in her direction, the wide mouth straight and grim, the silver eyes shining up from the depths of their sockets like tiny cold stars.

Vestara shivered and looked away. The effort to forestall the coming fight, even to *survive* it, hardly seemed worthwhile. Whether the victor was Lady Rhea or Xal, the entire crew was doomed. They were Abeloth's playthings, pets held for her amusement for as long as she could keep them alive, no more capable of surviving on this planet without her than a Keshiri canakal bird could survive outside its cage. Vestara, Ahri, even Xal and Lady Rhea—everyone was going to die here, and whether they were devoured by carnivorous plants or impaled on one another's blades hardly made a difference.

Vestara knew all this, knew that at best her struggles would buy her only a few extra days of suffering and despair. But she refused to surrender. She intended to continue fighting through her last breath and beyond, to drag any enemy she could into the grave behind her, if only for pride . . . because the only choice that remained to Vestara Khai was *how* she died, and she intended to do it well.

Ship had slowed to a crawl now, more or less hovering over the center of the crimson river, caught, perhaps, between obedience and flight. Vestara extended a hand, grabbing for Ship in the Force, and ordered, *Come. Now.*

And Ship did.

In the flash of a thought, he was there before her, suddenly looming so large that Vestara thought he meant to run her down. Still, she stood her ground and forced herself not to flinch, so she would not die a coward.

But Ship could no more kill a Sith than he could disobey a powerful will. He stopped a meter away and hovered before her. His eye-shaped viewport was turned not toward Vestara, but toward Abeloth.

Deciding she had nothing to lose, Vestara ordered, *Open.*

Again, Ship seemed amused. *As you command.*

A horizontal split opened in his side, and he extruded a short boarding ramp. Obviously, this was all far too good to be true. It could only be another of Abeloth's traps, all the more cruel because it promised deliverance from a certain and painful death.

The rest of the survivors were clearly as shocked as Vestara, though perhaps not as suspicious. For what seemed a hundred heartbeats, they stood staring at the lowered ramp, their mouths agape as though they had never before seen one and could not comprehend the salvation it promised.

Lady Rhea, as usual, was the quickest to recover. She turned to Vestara with a stern expression. "It's about time, Vestara. I was beginning to wonder if Master Xal might be right to doubt your special relationship with Ship."

She waved Xal's supporters toward the ramp and started forward herself. "Let's not stand on ceremony," Lady Rhea said, now addressing Xal's followers. "You may board ahead of me."

Lady Rhea's would-be attackers did not need to be invited twice to realign themselves with her. They scrambled forward at just shy of a sprint, followed closely by Baad Walusari and the other two Keshiri officers who had remained loyal to Lady Rhea all along. Only Xal and Ahri remained behind, the Master openly glaring at Vestara over his change of fortune, the apprentice looking as though he was expecting the most severe beating of his life.

Lady Rhea gave Master Xal a smirk that promised a private, painful death, then turned to Abeloth. "You'll have to board now, Abeloth." Though her words suggested she was issuing a command, her tone was that of a request. "It's only the short ride to *Eternal Crusader* that will be crowded, I promise."

Abeloth responded with a smile so gruesome that Vestara knew it would have drawn a shudder of revulsion from both Xal and Ahri, had they been able to see its true nature—as she herself did.

"I'll be happy to join you aboard the *Eternal Crusader*," Abeloth said, "as soon as we have captured Luke Skywalker and his son, Ben."

The Force churned with astonishment and confusion.

"Luke Skywalker?" Lady Rhea asked.

Abeloth nodded. "And Ben." She turned toward Xal, then said, "Isn't that who you *said* the expedition was originally meant to pursue, Lord Xal?"

Xal's face paled, for laying false claim to the title of Lord was a death sentence. "I never said I was a Lord." He shot a nervous glance in Lady Rhea's direction, no doubt checking to see whether she intended to seize on Abeloth's mistake to eliminate a rival, then said, "I'm *not* a Lord."

"But you *will* be," Abeloth said, stepping to his side. "When you return to Kesh with Luke and Ben Skywalker in chains."

"Our mission would have been to *kill* the Skywalkers, not imprison them," Lady Rhea pointed out. "But that assignment was superseded by the order to recover Ship."

Abeloth's eyes blazed white with fury. "And now you *have* recovered Ship, have you not?"

Visibly shaken by Abeloth's anger, Lady Rhea merely nodded.

"Good. Then you have succeeded in your mission." Abeloth's eyes shrank back to silver stars. "And now Ship can help you with this new task. Imagine how pleased your Circle of Lords will be when you return with both Ship *and* the Skywalkers."

"Assuming *you'll* be there to help us control them," Lady Rhea replied. "Otherwise, I fear the Circle of Lords will be anything *but* pleased to have a pair of Jedi brought to the last bastion of the Sith Empire."

"*Of course* I'll be with you," Abeloth replied soothingly. "Do you think I want to be marooned in this hell forever?"

A triumphant glow came to Lady Rhea's Force aura, and Vestara realized her Master still had no idea she was being tricked. But why should she? Vestara had tried a hundred times to warn Lady Rhea about Abeloth's true nature, always to no avail. Finally, Vestara had been forced to accept that no one else could see their companion for what she truly was.

Abeloth was no castaway, no mere woman marooned here for thirty years. She was much more—a manifestation of an ancient power so dark and hideous it was beyond human comprehension. Against such a being, how could Lady Rhea resist being a thrall? How could *anyone*? The only reason Vestara was still alive, she felt certain, was that it amused Abeloth to watch her struggling to remain sane.

Abeloth shifted her gaze to Vestara and sent a sensation like cold fire rushing through her veins, then draped her tentacles over Xal's shoulder.

"We will talk, Lord Xal." Motioning for Ahri to follow, Abeloth turned Xal away and started toward the other side of Ship. When she seemed to sense Lady Rhea's rising tide of fury, she paused, looked back over her shoulder, and asked, "And what is it they will call *you* when you sit in the Circle, Lady Rhea? *Lady Rhea,* High Lord of the Sith?"

Lady Rhea's fury melted away like ice in the river, and she dipped her head and smiled broadly. "That would be the correct title, yes," she said. "*If* I am chosen."

Abeloth's eyes twinkled in reassurance. "You *shall* be, High Lady Rhea. Have no doubt."

With that, Abeloth turned away again and led Xal around Ship. Vestara waited until they were out of sight, then caught her Master's eye and tipped her head in the opposite direction. When Lady Rhea nodded, Vestara started to walk and began to Force-whisper, directing her words to her Master's ears alone.

"You *do* know that Abeloth is setting another trap for us, right?"

"I wouldn't say a trap, exactly," Lady Rhea replied. Though her words were barely a whisper, they nevertheless resounded clearly in Vestara's head. "Abeloth is just recruiting Xal to be her spy, to be certain I don't revert to our original orders and content myself with only capturing Ship. She wants to arrive at Kesh with an impressive gift: Skywalker slaves."

Vestara shook her head vehemently. "We're not *going* to Kesh," she said. "At least, Abeloth isn't. Haven't you noticed? She's done everything in her power to keep us *trapped* here."

"Because she hadn't lured the Skywalkers into position yet," Lady Rhea insisted. "Now that she has a proper gift—"

Vestara spun on her Master, drawing her parang with one hand and swinging her other arm up so fast that Lady Rhea was still speaking when Vestara's open palm reddened her cheek.

"*No!*" Vestara spat. "*Think*. How many shuttles have we lost?"

Lady Rhea's green eyes flamed with rage. "That's something no apprentice lives to do twice."

Lady Rhea's hand dropped toward her lightsaber, but Vestara was prepared and had her parang pressed to Lady Rhea's wrist the instant her fingers touched her lightsaber.

"Give me two minutes before you do that," she said. "Please, Master. Just answer three questions, then you can kill me however you like. How many shuttles have we lost?"

"Very well." Lady Rhea opened her fingers, but left her hand hanging next to her lightsaber. "All of them."

"And how many crewmembers are still aboard the *Crusader*?"

Lady Rhea's eyes grew cold—and when they were cold, they were calculating. "None."

"Last question." Vestara pulled her parang away from Lady Rhea's wrist. "If you were in your right mind, would you *ever* make such foolish mistakes?"

The flames returned to Lady Rhea's eyes, but along with her fury, Vestara also saw a flicker of recognition. Slowly, Vestara stepped back and sheathed her parang, then knelt before her Master and dropped her head.

When her head was still on her shoulders several seconds later, Vestara was not terribly surprised. Her Master was many things, but wasteful was not one of them. Still, Vestara remained kneeling, playing the penitent apprentice until Lady Rhea herself decided the charade had run its course.

"You may as well stand, Vestara," she said. "We both know I'm not going to kill a talented apprentice over a few inviolable rules."

Vestara rose. "Thank you, milady."

"But if you *ever* do that again, it will be the last

time," Lady Rhea warned. "I will *not* be told that I make mistakes. Is that clear?"

"I apologize," Vestara said, biting her cheek to keep from smiling in relief. "It will *never* happen again."

"Good." Lady Rhea turned back toward Ship, which continued to sit waiting. "Am I correct in assuming that you had nothing to do with Ship's change of heart?"

"Absolutely," Vestara said. "Ship has toyed with me, but he remains completely under Abeloth's control."

"Which means we remain trapped on this death planet." Lady Rhea grew thoughtful. "*Unless* . . ." She paused, then turned to Vestara. "You already have this figured out, don't you?"

Vestara grinned, not even caring that the scar at the corner of her mouth would make her smile appear lop-sided.

"I believe so," she said. "If Ship can take all of us in one trip, the Skywalkers must be very near. And they had to come in *something*. Once Ship takes us to them—"

"Absolutely." Lady Rhea paused as Abeloth and Xal emerged from behind Ship, then turned away and spoke in a Force whisper so low that Vestara was not sure she heard it even inside her own mind. "We kill the Sky-walkers and . . ."

". . . we steal *their* vessel," Vestara finished with a wry smile. "How hard can it be?"

Chapter Twenty-five

THAT AWFUL SMELL, BEN REALIZED, WAS PROBABLY HIM. It reminded him of sour nerf milk, with a hint of ash and mildew. His tongue lay in his mouth like a raw sausage—swollen, numb, and cold—and he felt generally sore and weak, with a muddled, throbbing head that made him feel like he had died and just didn't realize it yet.

Which, Ben suddenly remembered, was a distinct possibility.

He opened his eyes and found himself staring up into the familiar red strobing of alarm lights in Sinkhole Station's smoky control room. He glanced over and saw that his IV drip bags had drained themselves flat, which meant he had been Mind Walking for at least a day—and probably much longer, assuming his symptoms were due to dehydration.

"Mra . . . dhe muck!" he croaked. He swallowed, then tried again. "Now I see why these head cases would rather die than return to their bodies."

When no reply came, Ben looked over and found his father still lying motionless on his gurney, his gaze vacant and fixed on the ceiling.

"Dad?"

Nothing moved but his father's mouth, which opened barely far enough to emit a hoarse whisper. "Uh . . . yeah."

"You okay?"

The eyes closed in what was probably as close to a nod as Luke could manage. "I will be," he rasped. "Just need to . . . get blood to my muscles again."

"Yeah, well, good luck with that."

Ben used the Force to undo the straps across his own chest, then tried to sit up . . . and dropped back to his gurney in a heap.

"It's always like this," a familiar voice said behind Ben. "Give yourselves a minute."

Recalling his reluctant Mind Walker guide, Ben craned his neck around and looked toward the far side of the chamber. Rhondi Tremaine was still sitting where he had left her before going beyond shadows, slumped against an equipment cabinet with her legs splayed out beside her. The stun cuffs he had slapped on her before leaving were still on her wrists, securing her to the floor beam he had exposed. With sunken eyes, hollow cheeks, and a brow furrowed in pain, she looked just as bad as Ben felt. The sight of how little care he had taken for her comfort made Ben wince at his behavior. He had deliberately not offered to set an IV drip for her, believing that if she were in danger of dying, she would be more eager to make their trip a quick one, so she could be certain of returning to free her brother.

"How are you feeling?" he asked. "Better than you look, I hope."

"*That's* nice." Her gaze shifted to Luke. "If you want grandchildren someday, you need to have a conversation with your son about how to talk to the ladies."

"Ben, be nice to the lady," Luke ordered. "And get her out of those stun cuffs."

"Sure." Ben tried again to sit up, and this time he succeeded. "As soon as I take care of *you*."

He freed himself from the IV catheters and the gurney straps, then did the same for his father and retrieved three packs of hydrade from his supply bag. When his father proved too weak to push the suck-nozzle through the punch hole, Ben did it for him.

"Dad, that trip . . . it was pretty dark," Ben said, holding the tube into his father's mouth. "Worse than a triple hit of yarrock, even."

Ben could tell by the way his father's eyes widened that he had used a really bad analogy.

"Uh, not that I'd *know*," he said. "Just assuming, really."

Luke stopped sipping long enough to say, "You'd *better* be."

"No worries," Ben said. "I get plenty of weirdness just being your son."

When Ben fell silent for a moment, his father reached up and took the sip-pack. "Keep talking."

Ben looked away, unsure how to broach the subject of what they had experienced together at the Lake of Apparitions. Actually, he was not even sure they had seen the same things.

Finally, he just asked it. "All the stuff that happened while we were Mind Walking . . . was that *real*?"

"Talking to Anakin and your mother, you mean?"

Ben nodded and began to feel a little more certain of the experience. "And to Jacen."

"Was that real?" Luke repeated. He let out a choked half laugh. "Maybe you'd rather ask me something else, like what's the ultimate origin of the Force."

"We'll save the easy stuff for later," Ben replied. "Seriously, this whole experience is making me barvy. I need to figure it out now."

His father closed his eyes and let out a long breath, then said, "You're the detective, Ben. You can figure this out for yourself—in fact, I think you have to."

Ben sighed. Sometimes he really hated having a Jedi Master for a father. Everything was a lesson.

"Okay," he said. "Let's start with the fact that we both saw the same people at the Lake of Apparitions."

"We *all* saw the same people," Rhondi added. She jerked her stun cuffs against the beam to which Ben had secured them. "How about a little consideration here?"

Seeing that his father was strong enough to hold his own sip-pack, Ben grabbed another and started toward Rhondi. "If we all saw the same thing, that means we really experienced *something*. We just can't be sure *what,* since we were . . ."

"*Outside* our bodies," Luke clarified.

"Because our bodies don't exist beyond shadows," Rhondi said. "Only our true presences."

"Yeah, you keep saying that," Ben said. He squatted next to Rhondi. "But your word isn't evidence. I still don't know whether I had the experience of *really* talking to Mom, or if I just saw what someone in that . . . *place* wanted me to see."

"Then you must agree that the place is real," Rhondi observed, "if you believe someone in it can make you see *anything*."

Ben nodded, the blood in his veins suddenly running slow and cold. "It's real. I felt something there that I recognized from before . . ." He turned to his father. "From when I was at Shelter. It's what drove me away from the Force."

"You're sure?" Luke asked.

Again, Ben nodded. "It's as real as we are," he said. "And I'm pretty sure it's behind the paranoid delusions that Jedi Knights my age keep having."

"It's a good theory," Luke said. "But how is it spreading, for example?"

"The same way *that's* happening." Ben waved through the viewport at all the bodies floating in the meditation vault beyond the control room. "The same way I felt it at Shelter. Through the Force."

"Your Jedi Knights aren't sick," Rhondi said. "They are only being called home."

Ben glanced back to her and realized that he had not yet released her stun cuffs, but he decided it might be better to wait until they had finished the conversation. He prepared a sip-pack for her, then held the tube to her lips and returned his attention to his father.

"You might call *that* evidence, too," Ben said. "Qwallo Mode didn't show up here by accident."

Luke sat up and reached for a second sip-pack. "I'm not arguing against you there, Ben," he said. "I'm just trying to think things through. For instance, why aren't Kam and Tionne having trouble? Or any of the *adult* Jedi Knights who spent time guarding Shelter?"

Ben could only shake his head. "I don't know," he said. "If I'm not affected—or infected—it has to be because I withdrew from the Force. Maybe trained adult Jedi have too many defenses. Or maybe there's something smart behind this. If the Masters Solusar *had* felt that place reaching out—"

"Right," Luke said. "The young ones would have been moved. But why *now*? It's been nearly a decade and a half since there were any students at Shelter."

That answer, Ben did not have to think about at all. It was all around him, in the strobing alarm light and the smoking circuits—in the *timing* of when things started to go wrong in the control room.

"Centerpoint Station was destroyed—*that's* what changed." He looked back to Rhondi. "That's when these alarms started going off, and it's when Rhondi and her brother started to feel compelled to return—along with a lot of Daala's other spies."

"Daala's *spies*?" Luke turned to Rhondi.

"Long story," she said. "Ben's right. When you destroyed Centerpoint Station, everything changed."

"It's like we opened a hatch or something," Ben said.

"And suddenly, whatever we felt in Shelter started leaking out—maybe *reaching* out—beyond the Maw."

Ben knew by the sudden paling of his father's face that he had made a convincing argument.

"Wonderful," Luke said. "Any idea *what,* exactly, is getting out?"

Ben could only shake his head. "And I'm still trying to figure out the Lake of Apparitions," he said. "I'm convinced that it's real. But . . ."

He let the sentence trail off, unable to ask the question.

"But you don't know whether that was really your mother you saw," Luke finished. "It's a hard question to answer—maybe one that we *can't* answer."

Ben turned to Rhondi and raised a questioning brow.

She jerked her stun cuffs against the beam and raised her own brow. He thumbed the release pad, and the cuffs came undone.

Rhondi's jaw fell. "They weren't even *locked*?"

"In case I didn't make it back," Ben said. "I'm not that cruel. Now, what can you tell me about my mother?"

Rhondi rubbed her chafed wrists. "We all return to the Force when we depart our bodies," she said. "Afterward, those who are strong in the Force sometimes show themselves in the Lake of Apparitions. Whether it's where they abide or is only a portal through which they can look, I don't know . . . but I believe those we see are real."

"What about Mind Walkers whose bodies die while they're beyond shadows?" Ben asked. "Do they go to the Lake of Apparitions, too?"

"Not at first," Rhondi said. "At first, they stay beyond shadows with us. But after a time, they seem to lose their way, and then sometimes we see them in the Lake of Apparitions."

"How long do they stay there?" Luke asked. "Could you see your grandparents, for instance, or even your ancestors?"

Rhondi shook her head. "Eventually, they no longer show themselves." She took a long sip of her hydrade, then shook her head. "I'm sorry, but I don't know why."

Ben scowled at her claim, but before he could think of a way to test it, the muffled *karrummph* of a detonating magmine reverberated through the control room floor. Rhondi's eyes went wide with horror, and she turned toward Ben.

"You *promised*!"

"Promised what?" Luke asked.

"That I'd let her brother go if she helped us," Ben explained. He turned to Rhondi. "He's probably okay. That door charge was placed to direct the blast—"

"*Probably?*" Rhondi staggered to her feet and started up toward the exit at the back of the trilevel room. "You murglak!"

"Rhondi, hold on!" Ben stepped to where he could see the mine he had placed on the hatch. "It's welded, remember? And don't forget the door charge!"

"*Welded?*" Luke echoed, intercepting Ben. "*Door charge?* Ben, what the blazes have you been doing while I was gone?"

"I'll explain in a minute," Ben said, continuing to look toward the exit. Rhondi had reached the hatch and was beginning to pound it with the heel of her hand. "Right now, I'd better get to that charge before she—"

Ben was interrupted by a stunned cry as a red circle of blazing heat burned through the back of Rhondi's skull. Her body, lifeless before the scream died, crumpled to the floor. Behind her, the bright column of a scarlet lightsaber began to cut a smoking furrow through the thick metal of the hatch.

A wave of danger sense rolled up Ben's spine. He turned to find his father already standing beside the gurney, his lightsaber in hand and his attention fixed on the entry hatch. Ben could see by how low he held his hand, and by the fatigue in his eyes, that his father was still weak. But he could also feel his father drawing on the Force, pulling it into himself to enliven atrophied muscles and restore dead synapses.

"Ben," his father asked, "who the black empty void is *that*?"

Chapter Twenty-six

THE TIPS OF FOUR SCARLET LIGHTSABERS WERE CHASING one another around the perimeter of the hatch, so bright that Ben could look at them only through the blast-tinting of his helmet's faceplate. The blades were cutting through the thick alien metal as though it were plasteel, and Ben could feel dark presences—a lot of dark presences—standing in the corridor outside.

His father was down in the front of the control room, trying to cut a meter-wide escape hole into the viewport. The metal was only a fraction the thickness of the hatch, but his lightsaber was cutting much more slowly than the blades of the mysterious intruders. It seemed strange that thin transparent material should be so much tougher than a heavy metal hatch, but that was certainly the way it looked.

"Dad, you're cutting really slow," Ben said, speaking into his helmet microphone. After Rhondi's death, the first thing both Skywalkers had done was put on their vac suits with the idea of fleeing back to the *Shadow* as swiftly as possible. "Could your power cell be low?"

Luke's reply came over the helmet receiver, calm and patient. "Son, I'm a Jedi Master. Do you really think I'd forget to check my own lightsaber's power-cell levels?"

"Just asking. Strange things happen around here." Ben checked the hatch again and saw that the four scarlet blades were almost to the corners. "Such as . . .

they're cutting through that hatch about twice as fast as you're cutting through the viewport."

"That *is* interesting." Luke sounded less nervous about this news than intrigued by it. "And you're *sure* you have no idea who they are?"

"Dad, I told you no. But they *had* to hear Rhondi pounding on that hatch." Ben wasn't worried about electronic eavesdropping; even if the intruders had a receiver set to the correct channel, the Skywalkers' communications were encrypted using the latest Jedi technology. "And they still pushed a lightsaber through it at *head height*. Does that sound like Mind Walker style to you?"

"Not really." Luke deactivated his lightsaber and stepped away from the circle he had been cutting, leaving about ten centimeters at the top still attached. "But they didn't manifest out of the void. They're a part of this somehow."

"Yeah, but we really don't have time to stop to talk . . ."

Ben let the sentence trail off as his father raised a hand and used the Force to push the smoking circle of semi-attached viewport outward, opening a hole large enough to serve as an escape route. Instead of leading the way through it, Luke started toward the back of the room, angling toward the corner opposite Ben's.

"We need to take one alive," Luke said.

"*Alive?*" Ben echoed. "Check your vitals readout. You're barely strong enough to make a run for the *Shadow*—much less take *prisoners*."

"True—and feeling better every second." Luke pointed at the hatch. "Ben, we need to find out who those people are—and who sent them. That's the key to figuring this place out."

Ben knew there was no point in arguing. His father's voice had assumed that *I'm the Master* tone. Besides, the logic was sound, at least until it came to the part about them making it back to the *Shadow* alive.

"Can we at least be careful about it?" Ben asked. "Right now, all we know about them is that they don't mind killing people, and they have a thing for red lightsabers. Whoever they are, they seem to have all the advantages."

"Not *all* of them," Luke said, slipping behind an equipment cabinet on the opposite side of the room. He was on the upper tier, about five meters past the hatch. "Are you ready with that gas cylinder?"

Ben checked the hand torch he had used to weld himself and Rhondi into the chamber. The feed valve was wide open, and the safety shutoff was disabled.

"Affirmative."

"Then hide your Force presence and wait for my signal," Luke ordered. "We might learn something just by watching them."

Ben slipped into his own hiding place—the foot well of an equipment console, on the upper tier directly across from his father. He quickly drew his Force presence inward, shrinking it down until even he could not sense it, then felt the floor reverberate as the heavy hatch fell into the room.

Two seconds later the door charge detonated, but there were no muffled screams to suggest that anyone had been near the entrance when the fuse activated. Whoever they were, Rhondi's killers had obviously learned their lesson when they opened Rolund's cell and tripped the first mine.

The blast of the door charge was still vibrating through the floor when Ben felt the lighter pounding of running feet. He guessed that maybe seven or eight intruders had entered, but there was no way to be certain. He waited five long breaths for them to pass his hiding place, then peered out toward the hatchway. The metal was still smoking and glowing white. Even so, he could see a pair of vac suit boots on the floor outside the hatchway.

A double comm click sounded inside Ben's helmet. The signal meant his father was preparing to move, but it would be impossible to see the rear guard from his side of the room. He hit a chin toggle inside his helmet, intending to warn his dad about the ambusher, then saw the intruder's boots charging into the control room and realized his father was already moving.

Holding the gas canister in one hand and his lightsaber in the other, Ben rolled from his hiding place. A line of eight intruders was descending toward the diversionary hole in the viewport, all of them in a hurry. Like the Skywalkers, they were wearing full combat-rated vac suits and carrying lightsabers. Some also carried blasters, and most wore equipment belts with two sheaths, one for a slender glass-handled dagger and one for a curved, heavy-bladed parang.

Ben's father was already sliding onto the top of an equipment console, so intent on capturing a prisoner that he did not sense the rear guard coming through the hatch behind him. The intruder's faceplate was raised, revealing a lavender face with fine features and a long nose, slightly more slender than a human's. In her gloved hand, she was holding one of the dark parangs. Instead of leaping into a melee attack as Ben had expected, she stopped and raised the parang.

"Dad!" Ben commed. "Roll, *now*!"

The parang flew, and Luke rolled, disappearing over a row of equipment cabinets just as the weapon spun past centimeters above his helmet. Unable to hear the commed message, the woman grimaced and extended her hand, using the Force to call the weapon back—and presenting her back to Ben as she moved to put the row of equipment cabinets between herself and Luke.

Ben did not give her a chance to catch the parang. He simply Force-leapt across the last three meters between them, pointing his lightsaber at her heart and thumbing the activation switch. To his relief, both his weapon and his body felt fully powered—though, in the latter case, it was impossible to say whether the fuel was the hydrade he had quaffed earlier or his desperation to save his father.

The woman must have had her own danger sense. Even before Ben's blade extended, she was spinning away, still reaching for her parang with one hand, igniting her own lightsaber with her other, and snapping a vicious heel kick at Ben's groin with her near foot.

It was too fancy, too much. Ben merely stepped back and gave her empty hand a Force tug. Instead of returning to her grasp ready to throw again, the parang sliced her hand off at the wrist. The woman cried out, and her heel kick glanced off the canister he was holding.

She attempted a trailing lightsaber slash at Ben's neck. He leaned away, then used the Force to pull her, center mass, onto his own blade.

In the next instant, Ben's entire body was tingling with danger sense, and he was spinning and slashing, his blade weaving a basket of protection as the woman's companions came charging toward him behind a wall of blasterfire.

He retreated toward the hatch, at the same time comming his father. "Hey, Dad, about that prisoner—"

"Go!" Luke came rolling over the bank of equipment cabinets, pouring blasterfire into the intruder he had been attempting to capture, then hit the floor and began to scramble toward the hatchway. "And cover me!"

"Sure thing," Ben said.

As he slipped through the hatch, Ben deliberately slammed the neck of the hand torch on the jamb. The head flew away on a jet of pressurized gas, and a rime of frost formed instantly on the cooling canister. He tossed it back into the control room. It began to fly about in the weightless environment, spewing explosive azetal fumes and bouncing off smoking equipment consoles.

Ben took cover behind the jamb and drew his blaster. He began to fire around the corner, fully opening himself to the Force so he could sense his father's location. He felt a wave of terror as the anonymous enemy realized what would happen when the concentration of azetal grew high enough to ignite, and then his father came flying through the hatchway feetfirst, low to the floor and pouring bolts back into the control room.

Two heartbeats later, the enemy fire trailed off to nothing. Ben grabbed his father's ankle and sprinted down the corridor, dragging him along while he continued to cover the hatchway behind them. As Ben moved, he had to be careful to keep one foot on the floor so that he would continue to be affected by the station's primitive form of artificial gravity.

Twenty steps later they were at the other end of the corridor, and no one was following. Ben stopped and released the ankle.

"That was some shooting!" Ben cried. "Did you get them *all*?"

Luke shook his head. "Just three. The others were Force-leaping through that bolt-hole I cut." He righted himself, then extended a hand toward the far end of the corridor and used the Force to lift the fallen hatch back into its place. "Whoever those guys are, they're no idiots. They know what's going to happen when the azetal gas gets dense enough."

Chapter Twenty-seven

VESTARA'S ORDERS WERE SIMPLE: SHE WAS TO WAIT IN hiding at the bowl-shaped junction chamber that connected the station's central sphere to its cylindrical wing. If the Skywalkers entered this area alive, she would arm the grenades she had been given and toss them into the chamber. With a little luck, she would be able to pull her hatch closed before the Skywalkers sent the grenades flying back into her corridor. With a lot of luck, there would be enough left of the pair to present to Lord Vol when they returned to Kesh without Ship.

But, as with any Sith plan, there were layers of treachery and intrigue to consider, and so Vestara had a second assignment. After leaving the air lock through which Ship had inserted them onto the station, the first thing Lady Rhea had done was to free the surviving members of her crew from Abeloth's thrall—just as Vestara had freed *her*.

The second thing Lady Rhea had done was to change the team's mission from capturing the Skywalkers to killing them. That had been the strike force's original purpose, and that was what Lady Rhea ordered them to do. Even had she not still been their commander, it would have taken little effort to win the small group over. Returning Ship to Kesh was clearly beyond their capabilities, but Lady Rhea felt confident that the death of the Skywalkers and the news of Abeloth's strange power would be enough to win the Circle's forgiveness. And even if she was wrong, the entire crew had agreed—returning to Abeloth and her strange planet was out of the question.

To the surprise of everyone except Lady Rhea, even Yuvar Xal had readily embraced this plan. In fact, he had proclaimed that *all* of the survivors would be bathed in glory when the Circle learned of Abeloth's power. His enthusiasm had aroused suspicions, of course—due in large part to the fact that earlier, when the crew had stopped at the *Eternal Crusader* to retrieve vac suits and weapons, Ship had allowed only Xal and Ahri to board the frigate.

So, along with Baad Walusari, Vestara had been assigned to keep watch over Xal and Ahri. If the pair attempted to depart their assigned station, they were to be murdered. If they attempted to capture the Skywalkers themselves, they were to be murdered. If they attempted to contact Ship, or even *looked* like they were thinking about disobeying Lady Rhea, they were to be murdered.

In short, neither Lady Rhea nor anyone else expected Xal and Ahri to survive the mission. Of course, Vestara hoped Ahri would prove them wrong, which was one of the reasons she had been happy to accept the assignment. If anyone was going to give him the benefit of the doubt, it would be her. She might even be able to give him a second chance, if no one was looking.

Ahri's voice came over her helmet speaker. "Hey, Ves?"

"Yes?"

"Something's been troubling me about this whole Skywalker mission," he said. *"Why?"*

Vestara grimaced, immediately suspicious of his motivations. "Ahri, don't." She peered through the crack of her open hatch, looking across the chamber toward the partially open hatch where Ahri was hiding. "Lady Rhea gave us our orders."

"Yeah, and *those* orders make sense," Ahri returned. His helmet appeared in the sliver of open space behind his hatch, the faceplate raised so she could see one pale eye. "What I don't get is why does *Abeloth* want the Skywalkers?"

"I really haven't thought about it," Vestara lied. The fact of the matter was that she and Lady Rhea had thought about the problem plenty, and still they couldn't see why Abeloth would risk losing all her Sith pets in exchange for just two Jedi. There was only one reason that made even a little sense—and Vestara was loath to believe it. "Maybe Abeloth thinks they're stronger than we are and can survive longer?"

"Yeah, *right*," Ahri scoffed. "Two Jedi are stronger than fifteen Sith. That—"

His voice was overridden by a burst of connection static. For an instant Vestara hoped it was Xal, ordering them to be quiet. Because maybe then, Ahri's questions wouldn't be what she feared they were: the opening gambit in some backstabbing ploy of Xal's.

But when the static cleared, it was Lady Rhea's voice that Vestara heard. "Coming your way," she commed. "Be care—"

The transmission was interrupted by an eruption of blast static, and the deck jumped so hard that Vestara thought the station was about to come apart.

"—are *very* good," Lady Rhea finished.

"Acknowledged," Vestara said. "And thank you—"

Xal's sharp voice cut her off, ordering, "Silence! You have your orders!"

Vestara acknowledged the reprimand with a comm click. Xal's tone—and her own intuition—told her that Lady Rhea had been entirely right about the Master's

treachery. She took a pair of special grenades off her
equipment harness and removed the safety locks, then
crouched at the hatch, peering through the crack she
had left open and waiting for the Skywalkers to show.
She did not need to comm Baad Walusari to know the
grenades in his hands would be identical to hers; Lady
Rhea had made clear to them both that they were not to
take any chances, that they were to use the special
grenades first if they sensed even the slightest whiff of
betrayal from Xal.

A few breaths later a hatch about a third of the way
around the circle opened. A pair of dark figures came
shooting into the chamber, using the Force to pull themselves up toward the strange membrane air lock at the
top of the chamber. Their helmet faceplates were closed,
so it was impossible to be *certain* these were Luke and
Ben Skywalker, whose faces she had seen so many times
in training briefings. But the two were wearing the same
formfitting Jedi vac suits she had seen in those briefings,
and in their hands they held lightsabers as well as
blasters.

"*Fools,*" Xal hissed over the comm.

Vestara had to agree. They were moving fast, which
was always wise when traversing a potential ambush
site. But Force-users had so many other tools available
that there was no excuse for the kind of risks they
were taking—except maybe arrogance. Perhaps the
Skywalkers were just so accustomed to having the sole
advantage of the Force that they no longer bothered
with the most basic of tactical precautions. If *these*
were the best the Jedi had to offer, the Jedi deserved
what would befall them when the Tribe began its
expansion.

The Skywalkers were about two-thirds of the way to
the membrane—far enough so they would not see the

hatches swinging open behind them—when Xal gave his command.

"Now!"

Vestara opened her hatch and sent the two special grenades she had selected sailing up toward the Skywalkers. As she started to pull the hatch shut to protect herself, she saw Baad Walusari's grenades reverse course and go flying back into his hiding place. Time seemed to slow. In the next nanosecond she caught Ahri looking in her direction. Her own grenades reversed course and came sailing into her corridor with her, and the last thing she saw—just before her hatch closed— was Ahri tossing *his* grenades up toward the Skywalkers.

Vestara dropped to her haunches, her stomach sinking and going hollow as she watched the special grenades—the ones with no detonators—bounce harmlessly down the corridor. Foreseeing that Xal would attempt to kill Vestara and Baad with their own grenades, Lady Rhea had provided them each with a harmless pair to throw first. Now, with evidence of her Master's wisdom rolling down the floor behind her, Vestara found herself filled with both rage and disappointment. It wasn't Ahri's betrayal that disheartened her. They were on opposite sides of a conflict, so *that* was to be expected—even respected. It was the *stupidity* she found sickening. Did he really believe Abeloth intended to accompany Xal back to Kesh with Ship and the Skywalkers as prizes? Or was he just so much of a coward that he would rather die on Abeloth's planet than betray his Master and strike a deal with Lady Rhea?

The thin bang of a pair of stun grenades sounded from the chamber outside, and Vestara knew the time had come to put Ahri out of his weakness. She pulled two more grenades from her equipment harness—both frag models, both fully lethal. Then she went back to the hatch and pushed it open a crack.

There was only one Skywalker in sight, floating overhead, up near the strange membrane. For a moment, Vestara thought Xal and Ahri had muddled not only their double cross but the ambush itself. Steeling herself to report the escape of one Skywalker, she removed the safety locks on the two fragmentation grenades and waited as Xal and Ahri emerged from their hiding places, already opening the shock shackles with which they intended to restrain their captive.

But instead of going toward the prisoner-to-be together, Xal broke off and started in Vestara's direction. She began to fear that he had sensed her survival—then she noticed that his gaze was fixed on the wall just above her hatch. The stun grenades had sent one of the Skywalkers drifting toward her, she realized.

Deciding that she had earned the right to a little selfish indulgence, Vestara used the Force to pull the shikkar from her equipment belt. Valued on Kesh as an art piece as much as a weapon, the thin glass dagger was designed to break off inside the target's body, killing him with as much anguish as possible. She sent it flying straight into Xal's abdomen.

The attack took Xal completely by surprise, the blade sinking a full ten centimeters into his solar plexus before it reached the hilt guards and stopped. Again using the Force, she snapped off the handle, leaving the glass blade buried inside his body.

Had Xal shown his apprentice the courtesy of dying in silence, Vestara might have been able to save her friend Ahri. But the Master bellowed his surprise and anguish like the coward he was. And that drew Ahri's attention away from the unconscious Skywalker he was preparing to restrain.

In the next second a lightsaber sizzled to life, and Ahri came apart along the length of his spine.

Vestara suffered only a heartbeat of surprise before she realized that the Skywalkers had completely escaped the stun grenade attack. Even then, she was a heartbeat slower than Baad Walusari, whose long arm was shooting out from behind his hatch, a pair of armed fragmentation grenades grasped in one hand.

The Skywalker beside Ahri was already extending his free hand in Walusari's direction. As soon as the Keshiri's hand opened, the grenades flew *back* into the corridor and vanished from sight. Half a gasp later the hatch slammed shut on Walusari's arm, folding the limb in a direction no arm was meant to bend.

It was already too late for Vestara to learn from Walusari's mistake. Though she managed to avoid releasing her grenades, a dark-gloved hand clamped down on her wrist and jerked her from her hiding place. A second hand snatched the grenades from her hand and tossed them back into the corridor behind her. Then the hatch scraped past her and closed, leaving her to stare up into an open faceplate, where she found the pale blue eyes of Luke Skywalker.

He quickly slid her faceplate open so he could look into her eyes, then grasped her free hand with his.

"You should know," he said in Basic, "that Jedi can resist stun grenades."

"Fool!" she replied in Keshiri.

Even with both hands trapped, Vestara was far from helpless. Using the Force, she drew her parang from its sheath and brought the blade slashing up toward Luke's face.

Skywalker reacted with incredible swiftness, throwing his head back and to one side. But even a Jedi Grand Master was no match for the speed of the dark side. The blade took him across the cheek and nose, opening a deep cut that sprayed Vestara's face with hot blood that burned like acid.

Skywalker released her hand. She glimpsed four large, black-gloved knuckles flying through her open faceplate, and when they landed, everything went dark.

Chapter Twenty-eight

LUKE WAS ALMOST THERE . . . AS LONG AS *THERE* WAS THE next section of equipment-littered corridor, the next panel of self-lighting wall, the next doorway they passed, the next "whatever" his son chose for him. He was sustaining himself only through the strength of the Force. It was pouring into him from all sides, filling him with a blazing furnace of pain, devouring him even as it empowered him, burning him alive even as it saved him.

Luke would have liked to think he had never been quite this tired, to believe he would never again find himself in circumstances quite this desperate. But the truth was, he had been here many times before—in the wampa cave on Hoth, during the Battle of Mindor, on the approach to Qoribu in the Gyuel system in the Unknown Regions. And Luke had no doubt that he would be here many times again. In the years and the decades to come, there would be a hundred occasions when he thought he was dying and a dozen times when others believed he already had. Yet for Ben's sake, and for myriad reasons that seemed far less important right now, he had to keep going.

"Come on, Dad!" Ben's voice came over the helmet speaker. They had fled the ambush in the junction chamber just half a minute earlier, and now they were fleeing through the depressurized part of the station.

"We're almost back to that detention center with the Killik carapaces!"

Luke didn't have the energy—or the heart—to tell Ben that the steady stream of encouragement was more irritating than helpful. He knew Ben was alarmed to see the blood from his slashed cheek pooling at the bottom of his faceplate, but the wound wasn't as serious as it looked. He had been careful not to let the girl cut too deeply, and it was a small enough price to pay for his prisoner.

Ben had insisted on being the one who pulled her along, and Luke was just as glad. Even though she was floating, it took effort to keep her from drifting away as the deck slowly rotated under her, and Luke needed to keep his concentration focused on all that Force energy he was pulling into himself.

Another section of wall illuminated, this time in a rich yellow, and the corridor behind them fell dark. If Luke remembered correctly, as they advanced toward the end of the passage—about three hundred meters distant—the panel color would deepen to green. That was where they would find the entrance to their hangar, and then it should be a simple matter to board the *Shadow* and depart with their prisoner.

They passed the door to the detention center, and Luke's entire body began to prickle with danger sense. Ben clearly felt it, too, because he suddenly gave their prisoner a hefty Force shove. She went sailing down the corridor ahead of them, her vac-suited body seeming to spin on its long axis as the station rotated around her.

Luke swung around, blaster and lightsaber already in hand. At the other end of the corridor, about two hundred meters distant, the air lock membrane was stretching toward them as someone pushed through. He reached out in the Force and felt half a dozen dangerous presences waiting behind the first.

"Can't those guys take a hint?" Ben asked. "We must've killed *half* of them already."

"They just keep coming, don't they?" Luke agreed. "We have *got* to find out who they are."

"We'll ask the girl . . . later," Ben said, "once we're aboard the *Shadow*."

The first figure pulled free of the membrane. Another began to push through, and Luke sensed danger. He threw himself to the floor, just as the first, faceplate still covered in goo, began to pour blasterfire blindly down the corridor.

Luke felt his son grab his arm. They both started to drift down the corridor backward, Ben using the Force to pull them toward the hangar entrance as the girl continued to float along ahead of them. Luke drew his blaster pistol and began to return the intruders' fire. At that range, even a Jedi was doing well to hit the wall— but he wasn't aiming for the wall. After a dozen shots, a bolt finally found the membrane.

A sudden pang of surprise and pain reverberated through the Force as Luke's shot struck someone still waiting to leave the junction chamber. Then a column of white vapor began to stream through the burn hole, spilling into the corridor in an ever-expanding plume. Finally, the membrane split, hurling half a dozen vac-suited figures down the corridor in a decompression blast.

Luke and Ben continued to pour blasterfire into the tumbling mass, hitting two intruders before anyone started to bring themselves under control. A third figure perished when he hit a round-bellied transport cart and ruptured his vac suit. A fourth died when he brushed a detention-center barrier field and vaporized the shoulder of his vac suit.

But when the intruders finally brought themselves under control and ignited their lightsabers, that still left three coming down the corridor, batting bolts back at the Skywalkers as quickly as they were fired. By then, Ben had pulled them well into the green section, and Luke knew they were within steps of the hangar entrance.

Luke holstered his blaster, then snapped his light-saber off its hook . . . and felt a sudden blossom of danger tickling the back of his skull. Ducking was not really possible while floating, so he settled for dodging instead, Force-rolling himself into Ben and knocking them *both* into the wall.

"Dad!" Ben cried. "What the . . ."

The protest died away as an ammonia breather's air tank went tumbling past. Luke twisted around to look in the direction from which it had come and saw his prisoner, still bound but conscious, standing about fifteen paces down the corridor. She appeared wobbly, with her hands still bound together in front of her, but her faceplate was turned toward a little round-bellied cart that was just rising off the deck where it had lain for the last few centuries—if not millennia.

"Okay, time to dump the girl," Ben said, turning his blaster toward their ex-prisoner. "Even restrained, she's nothing but trouble."

"No!"

Luke knocked Ben's hand down, then grabbed the cart out of the girl's Force grasp and sent it tumbling across the corridor—just slowly enough to make sure she had time to dodge out of the way.

"Are you crazy?" Ben demanded. "That's the *second* time she's tried to kill you."

"Just scare her off," Luke ordered. He hated to let the girl go—he was aching to know why the four ambushers in the junction chamber had seemed as eager to kill one another as him and Ben. But she would serve his purposes almost as well by simply rejoining her friends. "I've got plans for her."

"Plans?" Ben fired a couple of bolts to keep the girl running, then said, "Okay, if you say so."

"I do." Luke looked back up the corridor. The other three intruders had closed to within seventy paces and seemed content to engage with lightsabers, which—if they knew anything about Luke's condition—was probably a sound tactic. "How close are we to the hangar?"

Ben pointed to a dark alcove about three paces away. "Really close," he said. "There's the . . ."

Ben stopped speaking, and the intruders drew another ten paces nearer while Luke waited to hear the end of the sentence.

Finally, Luke snapped, *"Ben!* Stop daydreaming."

"Sorry," Ben said, shaking his helmet. "But I, uh, I know who they are."

"Good." Pushing Ben ahead of him, Luke retreated toward the alcove. *"Now* might be a good time to share, son."

"Okay, but you're not going to believe it," Ben said. "They're Sith."

"Sith?" They reached the alcove and stepped inside. A green illumination panel activated, revealing a small cubicle about two meters on a side. "They can't be, Ben. There were at least a dozen of them—"

"And Sith come in *twos* . . . I know." Ben pushed a lever on the wall, and a panel slid down to separate them from the corridor. "But Ship is here. I felt it looking for us."

"Ship?" Luke asked, deactivating his lightsaber. *"The* Ship?"

"Yeah," Ben said, also deactivating his weapon. "The Sith meditation sphere. That Ship."

The floor sank beneath them, lowering the Skywalkers to the hangar level. As tempted as he was to ask Ben if he was sure, Luke knew better. Ship and his son had developed an all-too-cozy relationship when Ben was still Jacen's unwitting Sith apprentice, and there was no way that Ben would ever forget what Ship felt like in the Force.

A panel slid open beside them, allowing the blue-tinted light of the cluttered hangar to spill into the lift. Luke pointed in the general direction of the *Jade Shadow*.

"Go prep the *Shadow*," he said. "I'll hold them in the lift until we're ready for launch."

Ben made no move to leave. "Dad—"

"Do it *now*, Ben," Luke ordered. "If Ship is working with them, it will be moving to block the hangar exit."

A sigh came over Luke's helmet speaker, then Ben stepped off the lift. "Okay," he said, "but I'm not leaving without you."

"If it comes to that, you *better*," Luke said. "One of us needs to report this. If the Sith are involved with this place—"

"Yeah—I get it," Ben said. "This could be the whole thakitillo."

Luke frowned inside his helmet. "The *whole thaki-tillo*?"

"You know, the big secret," Ben explained. "The reason Jacen went dark, the reason the Shelter Jedi are going barvy . . . the reason the freakin' Sith *keep coming back*."

"You're right." Luke tipped his helmet in agreement. "This just might be the whole thakitillo."

As Luke spoke, the panel slid shut, and he felt the floor rising back toward the access level. He sent Ben a reassuring Force nudge, then drew his blaster and stepped close to the exit, hiding in the Force so that the enemy—the *Sith*—would not sense him coming. There was still a lot that Luke did not understand about their sudden appearance here—a lot that did not feel quite *on*—but there was enough that *did* seem right to convince him that Ben might be on target. The intruders were resourceful, well trained in the Force, utterly ruthless, and deadly even to their own. Whether or not he had ever encountered this particular strain before, they *were* Sith—and that was all that mattered.

The exit panel opened. Luke found himself standing faceplate-to-faceplate with four surprised enemies. Two were small and female, and two were large and male. He put a trio of blaster bolts through the largest male's chest and ignited his lightsaber in the faceplate of the other male, then retreated to the rear of the lift and used the Force to depress the activation lever.

Luke had expected the female survivors to be so shocked by his attack that they would leap for cover and take a moment to regroup before coming after him. He should have known better. These were Sith, and they reacted with all the killing instinct that implied. Even before the exit panel had begun to drop back into place, they were diving into the lift with him, each going to a different corner so they could attack from two different directions.

Luke fired at their former prisoner—he could tell it was the same girl by the furious eyes burning behind her faceplate—then saw the bolt come flying back when she activated the lightsaber in her hands. The invisible hand of the Force slammed him into the lift's rear wall, and the older woman stepped into view, striking for his midsection.

Luke barely brought his lightsaber around to block. In the next instant, he sensed a new danger as the thin glass dagger on her equipment belt left its sheath and came sailing for his ribs. He twisted aside in time to avoid taking the attack directly, but the blade was sharp enough to gouge even the flexible armor of a combat vac suit before it snapped.

By then, the girl was on him again, thrusting low

with her lightsaber. He blocked by countering, slipping a Force-enhanced thrust kick under her attack and sending her sailing away. Still, she did her best to drive the strike home, dragging the tip of her blade across his chest to open a smoking gash that immediately began to vent a thin line of vapor.

But the slash that actually *wounded* Luke, that cut through his suit clear down to the flesh, he did not see—did not even *feel*. He simply sensed the older Sith dancing in, opposite the girl, taking advantage of his divided attention to bring her scarlet blade sweeping toward his throat. He dropped to a knee, driving his own blade up at her midsection, then cursed as she twisted away with nothing but a smoking furrow across the belly of her vac suit.

And that was when Luke noticed the blood boiling up in front of his faceplate. He glanced down and saw a long flap of suit fluttering in the light of his helmet lamp, already venting blood, air, and sweat. What had opened this second, larger gash, he had no idea.

Knowing his enemies would be pressing their advantage already, Luke rolled into a forward somersault. He came up on the opposite side of the lift, spinning and firing, using the Force to lift himself toward the ceiling, his lightsaber tracing a helix of protection around his body. Combat vac suits were designed to isolate and self-seal, but only to a degree. Already Luke could feel the cold of the void seeping in through the gash in his abdomen, and he could tell by the subtle ringing in his ears that his suit was losing pressure.

Luke glimpsed a dark curve tumbling toward him as the two women divided and moved to flank him, and he understood. These Sith wielded the Force like a third limb, using it as naturally as their own hands. While he was focused on their lightsabers, one of them had slipped her black parang out of its sheath and attacked.

Luke stopped spinning and blocked the parang, his lightsaber slicing it in two. The two Sith women leapt in to finish him. He turned his blaster pistol on the girl, driving her back with a flurry of bolts aimed low-then-high-then-low, too fast for her to block. One bolt skimmed off her helmet, then another burned through her boot, leaving her hopping as she vented smoke and vapor.

Then the older woman was on him again, slashing first from one side, then the other with her scarlet blade, driving in close to pummel him from thigh to throat with knee, elbow, and helmet. Luke dropped his blaster pistol to wield his lightsaber with both hands, blocking left and parrying right, kicking at her knees and slamming at her throat with both forearms.

Through their vac suit armor, neither of them was taking much damage—but it would not be long before someone slipped, and when that happened, the end would come quickly. Luke continued to strike and counterstrike, his head starting to spin as his air scrubbers strained to keep pace with his exertions and the atmosphere bleeding from his gashed suit. The Sith woman fought like a shenbit, never letting up, never hesitating, never pausing. It was all Luke could do to stay between her and the wall, and he used the Force to keep her trapped in front of him, using her like a shield to keep the girl from slipping around to attack his flanks.

How long ago the exit panel had opened beside him, Luke had no idea. All he knew was that over his helmet speaker, he heard Ben warning him that the *Jade Shadow* was opening fire on Ship. As the lift filled with bright blue strobing, he glanced toward the wall to keep his faceplate's blast-tinting from being activated by the *Shadow*'s big laser cannons. The Sith instinctively turned *toward* the light to see what was happening.

They realized their mistake the instant their faceplates darkened and leapt into a series of evasive tumbles. But even that tiny slip was too much in such a vicious combat, and Luke was in no condition to be merciful. He followed the older Sith out into the hangar, taking advantage of her momentary blindness to lop off pieces—first a leg, then a sword arm, and finally her helmet.

Expecting the ferocious girl to be on him the instant her faceplate cleared, Luke spun to meet her with a clearing sweep of his blade—and found her a full thirty meters away, floating above a dusty old SoroSuub Star-Tripper that looked like it could have been the prototype for Lando's famous *Lady Luck*. Her partially darkened faceplate was turned toward the lift area, perhaps because she was searching for something she could use to continue her attack from a safe distance.

But she seemed to feel Luke's gaze and realize the odds had turned against her, and she slowly looked back toward him. It was impossible to see inside her faceplate from that distance, but Luke had the sense that she was watching him carefully, either adjusting a previous appraisal of him—or simply awaiting his next attack.

When Luke remained motionless, the girl ignited her lightsaber and raised it in salute. He acknowledged the gesture with a dip of his head. She held the salute for a moment longer, then deactivated her blade and did a backward Force flip, vanishing from sight behind the dusty StarTripper.

Luke turned toward the hangar exit. Seeing no sign of any active vessel except the *Shadow*, he chinned the microphone toggle inside his helmet. "Hey, Ben?"

The *Shadow* instantly swung around and started back into the hangar. *Then* Ben's voice came over the comm channel. "Dad, what's wrong? You don't sound so good."

"I'll survive," Luke said, "if you hurry."

Epilogue

IN THE PALATIAL SUITE CALLED SIMPLY THE PRESIDENTIAL by the hyperattentive staff of the stately Corusca on Fellowship, everything was done on a grandiose scale. Jaina was lounging next to Jag on a hover-sofa that could have seated an entire fighter squadron *with* support staff. Her feet were propped on a table the size of a small landing platform, and she was watching a vidscreen that would have no problem showing life-sized images of a StealthX. Currently, the screen was filled with the wrinkled, Wookiee-sized snout of Perre Needmo, snuffling up and down as his giant gray lips read the news.

". . . remains uncertain who fired on the *Millennium Falcon*," the Chevin was reporting. "Galactic Alliance military spokesbeings categorically deny responsibility. However, the detonation was witnessed by thousands of civilian sensor operators. And several ChaseX fighter craft from the *Nargi*-class pursuit frigate *Fast Death* were in the vicinity at the time. Chief Daala's office has declined to comment."

Jaina muted the sound, then smiled over at Jag. "I'm beginning to see why Dad enjoys this guy so much," she said. "He has a way of getting to the truth despite the cover-ups."

Jag allowed himself a rare smile. "Or at least a version that your father finds palatable." He paused, then asked, "Were there any casualties?"

Jaina shook her head. "Not on our side, at least," she said. "The *Falcon* and the *Gizer Gut* made their rendezvous as scheduled. They ought to be leaving for the Transitory Mists anytime now."

"Good." Jag's expression was one of relief, but his Force aura remained troubled. "Then you've actually heard from your father?"

Jaina shook her head. "No, the message was from Mom." She poked him playfully in the ribs. "But don't worry. Dad will come around."

Jag looked doubtful, but before Jaina could reassure him, the suite's resident valet droid whirred into the room on his repulsorlift.

"Please forgive the intrusion, Head of State Fel," the droid said. "Our staff has just received advance notice about *Javis Tyrr Presents*. There will be a news item concerning you and Jedi Solo, and I assumed you would want to see it."

Jaina closed her eyes and groaned, *"What now?"*

"I'm sorry, Jedi Solo." Taking Jaina's question for a request, the droid used its built-in controls to switch programs. "I'm afraid we weren't given details regarding the content."

An instant later the handsome face of Javis Tyrr—obviously cosmetically enhanced—appeared on the vidwall, three times as large as life.

". . . now for another Javis Tyrr exclusive," he was saying, flashing his too-white teeth.

An image of Jaina and Jag, seated in the backseat of Jag's crumpled limousine, appeared on the vidwall. Jaina immediately had a sinking feeling, and she felt Jag's entire being tense.

"Here's a little clip of what passes between everyone's favorite couple when they have a little alone time," Tyrr continued. "How do we do it? I can't tell you *that,* my friends, but I *can* say you're going to find this little *gem* very interesting."

The image drew in for a close-up of Jaina frowning as she demanded to know what Jag was trying to hide from her.

On the couch in the hotel suite, Jaina turned to face Jag. "I don't know what to say," she began. "I'm so—"

"Hold on," Jag said, turning to the valet droid. "VeeTen, will you please turn that off?"

The vidwall went instantly blank. "Of course, sir."

"Now, please excuse us," Jag said. "And inform the staff that I won't be needing to see any more of Javis Tyrr's reports."

"Very good, sir." The valet droid tipped its body forward in a bow, then added, "If I did something to upset you or Jedi Solo, you have my deepest apologies."

"We'll be fine," Jag said. "Thank you."

As the droid whirred out of the room, Jaina let her chin drop. "Jag, I am so sorry," she said. "Tyrr must have been downloading data from that parasite droid the whole time he was walking down—"

"Jaina, stop." He slipped a finger beneath her chin and coaxed her into raising it. "You didn't put the spy in my limo, and it's going to be okay."

"*Okay?* How can you think *that* is going to be okay?" Jaina pointed at the vidwall. "If you had ever been a Jedi young one at Shelter, I would think you were going barvy, too!"

Jag appeared completely unruffled. "It's not a problem. *We're* going to be okay." He fluttered a dismissive hand toward the vidwall. "*That* is just politics. And I'm not going to let a little thing like politics come between us."

He pulled her closer and kissed her gently, then added, "I'm not going to let *anything* come between us."

Jaina's eyes remained open. "Promise?" she asked.

Jag nodded. "I promise."

"Well, then." Jaina closed her eyes and leaned forward to kiss him. "I promise, too."

LYING UNCONSCIOUS IN THE *SHADOW*'S MEDBAY, LUKE Skywalker looked more dead than alive. He was only half bathed and still stained with blood. But the wounds would heal, Ben knew, and the strength would return after a few good meals. What Ben *wasn't* so sure about was the always hopeful spirit. When he did the math, he realized his father had spent *weeks* beyond shadows. And that didn't seem like an experience *anyone* could recover from quickly—maybe not ever.

Ben had spent only a few days beyond shadows himself, and the brief visit still weighed on him like a sack of rocks on a three-kilometer swim. It wasn't all bad, of course. He had been happy to meet Anakin in the Lake of Apparitions, and deeply grateful for the chance to speak with his mother one last time. And with every fiber of his being, he intended to honor the promises he had made to her.

But as for seeing Jacen . . . how sad it had been to discover him so alone and so lost—not bitter, but completely aware of the monster he had become. Jacen understood the harm he had caused so many, the anguish he had inflicted on the ones who had loved him most. And the thing that really got to Ben—the thing Ben knew would bother him for the rest of his life—was how *accepting* Jacen had been of it all. Jacen had seemed almost *smug* about it, as though all of the suffering he had inflicted on himself and others had been the necessary cost of pursuing some far greater end.

And yet . . . it had been *Jacen* who had finally scared Ben back to his senses, who had finally saved both Skywalkers by convincing them they could go no farther without losing all they had come to save. There was a deeper truth buried in there somewhere, Ben realized, but it would probably remain forever just beyond his grasp.

Ben sensed a stirring in the Force, and he glanced down to find his father's blue eyes studying him intently.

"I wish you wouldn't do that, Dad," Ben said. "It's kind of creepy."

"What?" Luke asked. "Me trying to be available when my son needs guidance?"

"Not that," Ben said. "Always *knowing*."

"Sorry." A familiar Skywalker smile crept across Luke's lips, and Ben's heart immediately felt a thousand kilos lighter. "I can't help it. Sort of comes with the territory."

"Yeah." Ben sighed. After a pause, he asked, "Hey, as long as you're awake, do you mind if I ask you a question?"

"What are we still doing here, hanging out in the Maw, when we're completely out of food and medicine?"

"Naw—I already figured that one out." Ben traced a finger along the cut across his father's nose and cheek. "You put a blood trail on that Sith girl. We're just waiting for her to get her act together and leave Sinkhole Station, so we can follow her."

Again, Luke smiled. "Well, then, it seems you have all the answers."

"Not *all* of them," Ben said, shaking his head. "There's one question that's really been bugging me."

Luke's expression grew serious. "You can *always* ask."

"I know," Ben said. He took a deep breath. "When Jacen asked what you had seen on the Throne of Balance . . ."

"I remember," Luke said. "I told him that I'd seen Allana, surrounded by friends from all species."

"Right . . . ," Ben said. "And then you asked Jacen what *he* had seen."

Luke nodded. "I remember. He told me it wasn't me." His gaze grew distant, and he looked away. "I'm not entirely sure I believe him."

"Because you *know* what he saw?" Ben asked.

"Because I know part of it," Luke replied, continuing to look away. "Just enough to make me wonder."

"Okay," Ben said, "then here's my question: what did Jacen see?"

Luke looked back to Ben. "What Jacen saw on the Throne of Balance doesn't matter—not to you." His smile returned, this time filled with equal parts sadness and hope. "And you know what's really wonderful about that? It *never* will."

Read on for an excerpt from
Star Wars™: Fate of the Jedi: Backlash
by Aaron Allston
Published by Century

THE RAINFOREST AIR WAS SO DENSE, SO MOIST THAT
even roaring through it at speeder-bike velocity didn't
bring Luke Skywalker any physical relief. His speed
just caused the air to move across him faster, like a
greasy scrub-rag wielded by an overzealous nanny-
droid, drenching all the exposed surfaces of his body.

Not that he cared. He couldn't see her, but he could
sense his quarry, not far ahead: the individual whose
home he'd crossed so many light-years to find.

He could sense much more than that. The forest
teemed with life, life that poured its energy into the
Force, too much to catalogue as he roared past. He
could feel ancient trees and new vines, creeping predators and alert prey. He could feel his son, Ben, as the
teenager drew up abreast of him on his own speeder-
bike, eyes shadowed under his helmet but a competi-
tive grin on his lips, and then Ben was a few meters
ahead of him, dodging leftward to avoid hitting a
split-forked tree, the recklessness of youth giving him
a momentary speed advantage over Luke's superior piloting ability.

Then there was more life, *big* life, close ahead, with
malicious intent—

From a thick nest of magenta-flowered underbrush twice the height of a man, just to the right of Luke's path ahead, emerged an arm, striking with great speed and accuracy. It was humanlike, gnarly, gigantic, long enough to reach from the flowers to swat the forward tip of Luke's speeder-bike as he passed.

Disaster takes only a fraction of a second. One instant Luke was racing along, intent on his distant prey and enjoying moments of competition; the next, he was headed straight for a tree whose trunk, four meters across, would bring a sudden stop to his travels and his life.

He came free of the speeder-bike as it rotated beneath him from the giant creature's blow. He was still headed for the tree trunk. He gave himself an adrenaline-boosted shove in the Force and drifted another couple of meters to the left, allowing him to flash past the trunk instead of into it; he could feel its bark rip at the right shoulder of his tunic. A centimeter closer, and the contact would have given him a serious friction burn.

He rolled into a ball and let senses other than sight guide him. A Force shove to the right kept him from smacking into a much thinner tree, one barely sturdy enough to break his spine and any bones that hit it. He needed no Force effort to shoot between the forks of a third tree. Contact with a veil of vines slowed him; they tore beneath the impact of his body but dropped his rate of speed painlessly. He went crashing through a mass of tendrils ending in big-petaled yellow flowers, some of which reflexively snapped at him as he plowed through them.

Then he was bouncing across the ground, a dense layer of decaying leaves and other materials he really didn't want to speculate about.

Finally he rolled to a halt. He stretched out, momentarily stunned but unbroken, and stared up through the trees. He could see a single shaft of sunlight penetrating the forest canopy not far behind him; it illuminated a swirl of pollen from the stand of yellow flowers he'd just crashed through. In the distance, he could hear the roar of Ben's speeder-bike, hear its engine whine as the boy put it in a hard maneuver, trying to get back to Luke.

Closer, there were footsteps. Heavy, ponderous footsteps.

A moment later, their origin, the owner of that huge arm, loomed over Luke. It was a rancor, humanoid and bent.

The rancors of this world had evolved to be smarter than those elsewhere. This one had clearly been trained as a guard and taught to tolerate protective gear. It wore a helmet, a rust-streaked cup of metal large enough to serve as a backwoods bathtub, with leather straps meeting under its chin. Strapped to its left forearm was a thick durasteel round shield that looked ridiculously tiny compared to the creature's enormous proportions but was probably thick enough to stop one or two salvos from a military laser battery.

The creature stared down at Luke. Its mouth opened and it offered a challenging growl.

Luke glared at it. "Do you really want to make me angry right now? I don't recommend it."

It reached for him.

SEVERAL DAYS EARLIER
EMPTY SPACE NEAR KESSEL

It was darkness surrounded by stars—one of them, the unlovely sun of Kessel, closer than the rest, but barely close enough to be a ball of illumination rather than a dot—and then it was occupied, suddenly inhabited by a space yacht of flowing, graceful lines and peeling paint. That was how it would have looked, a vessel dropping out of hyperspace, to those in the arrival zone, had there been any witnesses: nothing there, then something, an instantaneous transition.

In the bridge sat the ancient yacht's sole occupant, a teenage girl wearing a battered combat vac suit. She looked from sensor to sensor, uncertain and slow because of her unfamiliarity with this model of spacecraft. Too, there was something like shock in her eyes.

Finally satisfied that no other ship had dropped out of hyperspace nearby, or was likely to creep up on her in this remote location, she sat back in her pilot's seat and tried to get her thoughts in order.

Her name was Vestara Khai, and she was a Sith of the Lost Tribe. She was a proud Sith, not one to hide under false identities and concealing robes until some decades-long grandiose plan neared completion, and now she had even more reason than usual to swell with pride. Mere hours before, she and her Sith Master, Lady Rhea, had confronted Jedi Grand Master Luke Skywalker. Lady Rhea and Vestara had fought the galaxy's most experienced, most famous Jedi to a standstill. Vestara had even *cut* him, a graze to the cheek and chin that had spattered her with blood— blood she had later tasted, blood she wished she could take a sample of and keep forever as a souvenir.

But then Skywalker had shown why he carried that reputation. A moment's distraction, and suddenly Lady Rhea was in four pieces, each drifting in a separate direction, and Vestara was hopelessly outmatched. She had saluted and fled.

Now, having taken a space yacht that had doubtless been old when her great-great-great-grandsires were newborn, but which, to her everlasting gratitude, held in its still-functioning computer the navigational secrets of the mass of black holes that was the Maw, she was free. And the impossible weight of her reality and her responsibility was settling upon her.

Lady Rhea was dead. Vestara was alone, and her pride at Lady Rhea's accomplishment, at her own near success in the duel with the Jedi, was not enough to wash away the sense of loss.

Then there was the question of what to do next, of where to go. She needed to be able to communicate with her people, to report on the incidents in the Maw. But this creaking, slowly deteriorating SoroSuub StarTracker space yacht did not carry a hypercomm unit. She'd have to put in to some civilized planet to make contact. That meant arriving unseen, or arriving and departing so swiftly that the Jedi could not detect her in time to catch her. It also meant acquiring sufficient credits to fund a secret, no-way-to-trace-it hypercomm message. All of these plans would take time to bring to reality.

Vestara knew, deep in her heart, and within the warning currents of the Force, that Luke Skywalker intended to track her to her homeworld of Kesh. How he planned to do it, she didn't know, but her sense of paranoia, trained at the hands of Lady Rhea, burned within her as though her blood itself were acid. She had to find some way to outwit a Force user several times her age, renowned for his skills.

She needed to go someplace where Force users were relatively commonplace. Otherwise, any use by her of the Force would stand out like a signal beacon to experienced Jedi in the vicinity. There weren't many such places. Coruscant was the logical answer. But if her trail began to lead toward the government seat of the Galactic Alliance, Skywalker could warn the Jedi there and Vestara would face a nearly impossible-to-bypass network of Force users between her and her destination.

The current location of the Jedi school was not known. Hapes was ruled by an ex-Jedi and was rumored to harbor more Force-sensitives, but it was such a security-conscious civilization that Vestara doubted she could accomplish her mission there in secrecy.

Then the answer came to her, so obvious and so perfect that she laughed out loud.

But the destination she'd thought of wouldn't be on a galactic map as old as the one in the antique yacht she commanded. She'd have to go somewhere and get a map update. She nodded, her pride, sense of loss, and paranoia all fading as she focused on her new task.

TRANSITORY MISTS

Jedi Knight Leia Organa Solo sat at the *Millennium Falcon*'s communications console. She frowned, her lips pursed as though she were solving an elaborate mathematical equation, as she read and reread the text message the *Falcon* had just received via hypercomm.

The silence that had settled around her eventually drew her husband, Han Solo, to her side; his boyish, often insensitive persona was in part a fabrication, and he well knew and could sense his wife's moods. The chill and silence of her complete concentration usually meant trouble. He waved a hand between her eyes and the console monitor. "Hey."

She barely reacted to his presence. "Hm."

"New message?"

"From Ben."

"Another letter filled with teenage talk, I assume. Girls, speeders, allowance woes—"

Leia ignored his joking. "Sith," she said.

"And Sith, of course." Han sat in the chair next to hers but did not assume his customary slouch; the news kept his spine rigid. "They found a new Sith Lord?"

"Worse, I think." Finally some animation returned to Leia's voice. "They've found an ancient installation at the Maw and were attacked by a gang of Sith. A whole strike team. With the possibility of more out there."

"I thought Sith ran in packs of two. Vape both of 'em and their menace is ended for all time, at least for a few years, until two more show up." Han tried to keep his voice calm, but the last Sith to bring trouble to the galaxy had been Jacen Solo, his and Leia's eldest son. Though Jacen had been dead for more than two years, the ripples of the evil he had done were still causing damage and heartache throughout the settled galaxy. And both his acts and his death had torn a hole in Han's heart that felt like it would last forever.

"Yeah, well, no. Apparently not anymore. Ben also says—and we're not to let Luke know that he did—that Luke is exhausted. Really exhausted, like he's had the life squeezed out of him. Ben would like us to sort of drift near and lend Luke some support."

"Of course." But then Han grimaced. "Back to the Maw. The only place gloomy enough to make its next-door neighbor, Kessel, seem like a garden spot."

Leia shook her head. "They're tracking a Sith girl who's on the run. So it probably won't be the Maw. It may be a planet full of Sith."

"Ah, good." Han rubbed his hands together as if anticipating a fine meal or a fight. "Well, why not? We can't go back to Coruscant until we're ready to mount a legal defense. Daala's bound to be angry that we stole all the Jedi she wanted to deep-freeze."

Finally Leia smiled and looked at Han. "One good

thing about the Solos and Skywalkers. We never run out of things to do."

CORUSCANT
JEDI TEMPLE

Master Cilghal, Mon Calamari and most proficient medical doctor among the current generation of Jedi, paused before hitting the console button that would erase the message she had just spent some time decrypting. It had been a video transmission from Ben Skywalker, a message carefully rerouted through several hypercomm nodes and carefully staged so as not to mention that it was for Cilghal's tympanic membranes or, in fact, for anyone on Coruscant.

But its main content was meant for the Jedi, and Cilghal repeated it as a one-word summation, making the word sound like a vicious curse: *"Sith."*

The message had to be communicated throughout the Jedi Order. And on review, there was nothing in it that suggested she couldn't preserve the recording, couldn't claim that it had been forwarded to her by a civilian friend of the Skywalkers. Luke Skywalker was not supposed to be in contact with the Jedi Temple, but this recording was manifestly free of any proof that the exiled Grand Master exerted any influence over the Order. She could distribute it.

And she would do so, right now.

DEEP SPACE NEAR KESSEL

Jade Shadow, onetime vehicle of Mara Jade Skywalker, now full-time transport and home to her widower and son, dropped from hyperspace into the empty blackness well outside the Kessel system. It hung suspended there for several minutes, long enough for one of its occupants to gather from the Force a sense of his own life's blood that had been in the vicinity, then it turned on a course toward Kessel and vanished again into hyperspace.

JADE SHADOW
IN ORBIT ABOVE KESSEL

Ben Skywalker shouldered his way through the narrow hatch that gave access to his father's cabin. A redheaded teen of less than average height, he was well muscled in a way that his anonymous black tunic and pants could not conceal.

On the cabin's bed, under a brown blanket, lay Luke Skywalker. Similar in build to his son, he wore the evidence of many more years of hard living, including ancient, faded scars on his face and the exposed portions of his arms. Not obvious was the fact that his right hand, so ordinary in appearance, was a prosthetic.

Luke's eyes were closed but he stirred. "What did you find out?"

"I reached Nien Nunb." Nunb, the Sullustan co-owner and manager of one of Kessel's most prominent mineworks, had been a friend of the Solos and Skywalkers for decades. "That yacht did make landfall. The pilot gave her name as Captain Khai. She somehow scammed a port worker into thinking she'd paid for a complete refueling when she hadn't—"

Luke smiled. "The Force can have a—"

"Yeah, so can a good-looking girl. Anyway, what's interesting is that she got a galactic map update. Nunb looked at the transmission time on that to determine that it was pretty comprehensive. In other words, she didn't concentrate on any one specific area or route. No help there."

"But it suggests that she did need some of the newer information. New hyperspace routes or planetary listings."

"Right."

"And she's gone?"

"Headed out as soon as her yacht was refueled. By the way, its name is *She's a Chancer*."

"Somehow appropriate." Finally Luke did open his eyes, and Ben was once again struck by how tired his father looked, tired to the bone and to the spirit. "I can still feel her path. I'll be up in a minute to lay in a course."

"Right. Don't push yourself." Ben backed out of the cabin and its door slid shut.

SEVERAL DAYS LATER
JADE SHADOW, IN HIGH DATHOMIR ORBIT

Luke stared at the mottled, multicolored world of Dathomir through the forward viewport. He nodded, feeling slightly abashed. Of *course* it was Dathomir.

Ben, seated to Luke's left in the pilot's seat, peered at him. "What is it, Dad?"

"I'm just feeling a little stupid. There's no world better suited to be the home of this new Sith order than Dathomir. I should have realized it long before we were on our final leg here."

"How so?"

"There are a lot of Force-sensitives in the population, most of whom are trained in the so-called witchcraft of Dathomir. There's not a lot of government oversight to detect a growing order within the population. There are lots of individual, secretive tribes." Luke paused to consider. "Jacen was here for a while on his five-year travels. I wonder what he learned and whether it relates to the Maw . . . And there are mentions in ancient records that there was a Sith academy here long, long ago."

Ben nodded. "Well, I'll prep Mom's Headhunter and get down there. I'll be your eyes and ears on the ground."

Luke gave his son a confused look. "I'm not going down with you? I'm feeling much better. Much more rested."

"Yeah, but there's a Jedi school down there. The terms of your exile say that you can't—"

Luke grinned and held up a hand, cutting off his son's words. "You're a little bit behind the times, Ben. Maybe you need your own galactic map updated. More than two years ago, when the Jedi turned against Jacen at Kuat—"

"Yeah, and we set up shop on Endor for a while. What about it?"

"We pulled everyone out of the Dathomir school at the time. Jacen's government shut the school down. The Jedi have yet to reopen it."

Comprehension dawned on Ben's face. "So there's no school, and it's legal for you to visit."

"Yes."

"That's kind of getting by on a technicality, isn't it?"

"All law is technicality, Ben. Get authorization for landing."

DATHOMIR

Half an hour later, Luke had to admit that he was wrong. *Most* of law was technicality. The rest was special cases, and he, apparently, was a special case.

He stood on the parking field of the Dathomiri spaceport. Perhaps "spaceport" was too generous a term. It was a broad, sunny field, grassy in some spots, muddy in others, with thruster scorch marks here and there. Dull gray permacrete domes, most of them clearly prefabricated, dotted the field; the largest was some sort of administrative building, the smaller ones hangars for vehicles no larger than shuttles and starfighters. A tall mesh durasteel fence surrounded the complex, elevated watchtowers dotting its length, and Luke could see the wiring leading to one of the permacrete domes that marked it as electrified. The spaceport facilities offered little shade, so the Skywalkers stood in the darkness cast by *Jade Shadow*, but even without the heat of direct sunlight, the moist, windless air was still as oppressive as a blanket.

Luke poured thoughts of helpfulness and reasonability into the Force, but it was no use. The man before him, nearly two skinny meters of redheaded obstructiveness, would not yield a centimeter.

The man, who had given his name as Tarth "*not* Darth" Vames, again waved his datapad beneath Luke's nose. "It's simple. That vehicle—" His wave indicated *Jade Shadow*. "Neither it nor anything with an enclosed or enclosable interior can be inland under your control or your kid's." He turned his attention to Ben, who stood, arms folded across his chest, beside his father. Ben glared but did not reply.

Luke sighed. "Is any other visitor to Dathomir operating under that restriction?"

"Don't think so, no."

"Then why us?"

Vames thumbed the datapad keyboard so that the message scrolled downward several screens. "Here, right here. An enclosed vehicle, according to these precedents—there's about eight screens of legal precedents—can be interpreted as a mobile school, especially if *you're* in it, especially if its presence constitutes a continuation of a school that's been here in the past."

"This is harassment." Ben's words were quiet, but loud enough for Vames to hear.

The tall man glowered at Ben. "Of course it's not harassment. The order came specifically from Chief of State Daala's office. Public officials at that level don't harass."

Ben rolled his eyes. "Whatever."

"Ben." Luke added a chiding tone to his voice. "No point in arguing. Vames, are you also prohibited from answering a few questions?"

"Always happy to help. So long as it's within latitudes permitted by the regulations."

"Within the last couple of days, have you seen any sign of a dilapidated yacht called *She's a Chancer*?" Luke knew the yacht had to be here; he had run his blood trail to ground on Dathomir, and the girl had not departed this world. But anything this man could add to his meager store of knowledge might help.

Vames entered the ship name in his datapad, then shook his head. "No vehicle under that name made legal landfall."

"Ah."

"Dilapidated, you say? A yacht?"

"That's right."

Vames keyed in some more information. "Last night, shortly after dusk, local time, a vehicle with the operational characteristics of a SoroSuub yacht made a sudden descent from orbit, overflew the spaceport here, and headed north. There was some comm chatter from the pilot about engines on runaway, that she couldn't cut them or bring her repulsors online for landing."

Ben frowned at that. "Last night? And you didn't send out a rescue party?"

"Of course we did. As per regulation. Couldn't find the crash site. No further communication from the vehicle. We still have searchers up there. But no luck."

"Actually, that *is* helpful." Luke turned to his son. "Ben, no enclosed vehicles."

"Yeah?"

"Rent us a couple of speeder-bikes, would you?"

Ben grinned. "Yes, sir."